W9-BQS-731

To Jill!

FLIGHT INTO DANGER

Enjoy Your Flight!

by

E. K. Barber

E. K. Barber

PublishAmerica
Baltimore

© 2004 by E.K. Barber.
All rights reserved. No part of this book may be reproduced, stored in a retrieval system or transmitted in any form or by any means without the prior written permission of the publishers, except by a reviewer who may quote brief passages in a review to be printed in a newspaper, magazine or journal.

Second printing

ISBN: 1-4137-0972-9
PUBLISHED BY PUBLISHAMERICA, LLLP
www.publishamerica.com
Baltimore

Printed in the United States of America

To Ken
You have to be in love to write about love.

Acknowledgements

Thanks to the readers who will recognize in the following pages their suggestions: Kim, Carol, Maureen, Marlane, Judy, Erin, Hazel, Michelle, JoAnne, Eric, John, and Terri.

Initial edits were completed by Ms. Barb Estervig and Ms. Kristen Beach

CHAPTER 1

"When once you have tasted flight, you will forever walk the earth with your eyes turned skyward, for there you have been and there you will always long to return." ~Leonardo da Vinci~

Takeoffs are optional. Landings are mandatory. Captain Skyler Madison stared at the little sticker someone had placed near the altimeter.

"Bill, will you check the hydraulic pressure?" she asked her copilot as her eyes traveled over the gauges and instruments. Something didn't feel right. She was sitting in the cockpit of a Boeing 767, and when her instincts told her to keep her personal radar keen and focused, she never questioned them. She'd been in a cockpit since her father took her up in his Cessna 182 when she was a child and he always instructed her to fly five minutes ahead of her plane.

"Everything looks okay, Skye. All instruments and readings are normal." Her copilot, Bill McGee, felt nothing out of the ordinary but sat on the alert. He never questioned her instincts either.

"Take it off autopilot. I'm going to fly it myself for a few minutes." Maybe with her hands on the yoke she could identify the source of her intuitive concern. Feeling the control transfer to her, she couldn't contain the smile that spread across her face. This was her kind of flying. Not just sitting watching instruments, but having the aircraft in her hands. She did a little maneuvering. The plane seemed to respond well. But there was something…something.

Suddenly the yoke bucked. Her voice immediately took on a serious note of command. "Bill, take your side. Let me fly but stand by in case I need extra muscle."

Bill put his hands on the yoke in front of him. Skye was the captain and had the fundamental responsibility for flying the plane, but he would stand ready. She worked the rudders and moved the yoke from side to side, backward and forward. Everything was within normal parameters. Everything but her gut.

"It feels like the hydraulics," she said absently.

Bill frowned but said nothing. Scanning all the relevant avionics he could see there was absolutely nothing pointing to any problem with the hydraulic system. If she were right, he thought, they would need to take this bird down straight and fast. There would be some maneuverability if the hydraulics went out, but not much. It was nearly impossible to make a soft landing without them.

Skye reached up for the intercom and toggled the switch, keeping one hand steady on the yoke.

"Yes, Captain?" asked Connie, her head flight attendant.

"Heads up. I'm going to ask the passengers to buckle in."

"Yes, Captain." On the ground they were good friends, but when Skye was in the cockpit she was in complete control and worthy of efficient, unquestioning responses from her flight team. "I'll prepare the rest of the crew."

Skye waited a few moments, then flipped the switch to the cabin. "Good morning, ladies and gentlemen. This is your captain speaking. I'm going to ask you to retake your seats and secure your seat belts." Her tones were honey coated and calm, a voice that always inspired both confidence and intense curiosity among the passengers. "We're approximately 45 minutes from Dulles and there are a few clouds between us and the airport. We may experience some turbulence, so please stay seated and buckled in for the duration of our flight. If you need to get up for any reason, just hit your call button to signal for a flight attendant and someone will be glad to assist you."

She repeated her message in perfect Spanish, then clicked off and settled in. They had received the weather reports earlier and were approaching some heavy clouds. She should be able to fly around them, but wanted her passengers safe and in their seats just in case…in case what she felt in her gut was trouble.

For the next five minutes her plane flew true and blue. The tiny, random vibrations were still there, she was sure of it, but nothing too cranky. Having the sensitive hands of a surgeon, she could feel an undifferentiated tug, some reluctance from her big bird to do her bidding. Sensing the nearly undetectable resistance in her fingers and palms, she never relaxed, never lowered her concentration.

Suddenly, the yoke jumped again, then began to fight her violently. Skye's grip had been tight on the yoke, or its vicious jerk to the left might have dislocated some fingers. The plane lurched in response. It was like an invisible hand had grabbed control of her craft and decided to take it down but she'd reacted immediately and with tremendous strength. She needed all of it to keep the plane steady.

Bill looked over at her, the radio to the control tower already in his hand, waiting for her explicit order. He didn't have to wait long. Skye knew every step of the protocol and was as decisive as a commanding general.

"I'm declaring an air emergency. Contact the tower and request immediate landing instructions. We're coming in…direct and crippled." Her voice was calm, her demeanor perfectly controlled.

Bill communicated with the tower, then talked with Connie on the intercom. "The captain has just declared an air emergency. Landing protocol…level 2." That meant a possible hard landing, but not crash protocol…yet.

He talked with the Dulles Air Route Traffic Control to obtain instructions as well as routine wind and weather reports, then looked over at Skye. She was battling the plane but seemed to be winning.

"Thunderstorms up ahead. Solid between us and the airport."

"How's the weather at National or BWI?"

"Worse. National has fog, BWI is deteriorating."

"Okay, then Dulles it is. I think there may be one cable left. I can still negotiate a little, but the strain on it has got to be immense." She saw a lightning bolt and dark clouds ahead of them. "I think I can fly a little to the left, maybe climb 1500 feet."

She no sooner finished her statement when the final cable broke and she was holding a virtually dead yoke. Some manual control was always possible, but it was like maneuvering a bus without power steering in three feet of thick mud with only a few inch radius in the steering wheel.

"Okay, forget that plan." Skye's arms and back were already aching from the effort to keep the plane steady and she would need to exert even more strength to move it in any direction. Bill had a hand on his own yoke, but she needed him for communication and working the instruments. She decided to use what control they had remaining to keep the aircraft at altitude.

"We can't go over it, she won't let me climb that much. And we certainly don't want to give up altitude to go under it. Get on the intercom. Apologize to our passengers, but we're going to have to go through it."

While Bill did her bidding, Skye flew straight into the dark, swirling clouds. They were immediately swallowed up in the thick, gloomy, disorienting storm. Ignoring the frequent flash of lightning and the churning sky, she kept her eyes trained on the altimeter and altitude indicator. What was happening out there was no longer relevant and most certainly out of her control. She had to concentrate on her craft and everything both it and she were designed to do.

"We're cleared for runway two-seven left. We're 28 minutes out," Bill reported.

Skye nodded, already feeling the strain in her back and legs. 28 minutes out. Could she hold on another 28 minutes? Well hell, she thought, since there wasn't any other alternative there was only one answer to that question. Rolling her shoulders, she shifted her position to give her more leverage, then settled in for the duration.

"Let's make our load lighter and less dangerous. Jettison the fuel," she ordered, following standard emergency procedure.

Bill released all the remaining fuel in their tanks save the small amount they still needed to get to Dulles.

"That commits us to Dulles...no other airport options," shouted Bill lending Skye a hand. Lightning flashed all around them lighting up the cockpit and bathing them in an eerie blue light while the deafening thunder made communication difficult.

"At least it can't get any worse," Skye shouted back through clenched teeth, sweating with the effort to keep the plane steady. The plane still bounced wildly in the unstable air. Suddenly, a gigantic bolt of lightning streaked across the sky and hit the fuselage. Sparks shot out of several of the instruments. As the thunder rocketed through the cockpit, smoke started to collect in the air reducing their visibility and stinging their eyes and throats.

"Extinguisher on ready," Skye shouted, coughing. "Priority."

Bill reached over and took the extinguisher, leaving Skye to wrestle with the yoke alone. The added stress tore at her already fatigued arms. When there were no sustained flames, Skye nodded in satisfaction.

"Good. No fire. Stand down. Clear the air, then hands back on the yoke." When the air was vented and once again clean enough to see her instruments, she glanced over at the transponder.

"Oh hell." She wanted to say more and purge her frustration more effectively, but was very conscious that all her words were being recorded and would become part of a permanent record.

He saw it too. No radios. No transponder signal. She could land the plane with no radios, so that wasn't a problem. They already had clearance and a designated runway. The airport knew about her emergency and they would be ready. The problem was they were flying into Washington D.C. airspace. Any plane coming in without radio contact, regardless of status, would be fired upon and brought down by military jets. No exceptions. She glanced at Bill.

"Time?" asked Skye, assessing, thinking.

"21 minutes."

"Plenty of time for the military to scramble their aircraft and shoot," she said. "We have to contact the tower, keep constant communication."

Another violent bolt of lightning lit up the sky, but didn't come near the fuselage. The unstable air created terrific turbulence however, adding to the pull on the yoke. Skye's muscles screamed in protest and waves of agony rolled up her back, but she drowned the pain in determination and continued to work the tactical alternatives.

"Data link?"

Bill looked over at the direct link to the airline company. "Red light. It's down, too."

"Get your cell phone."

"My cell phone?" he asked while reaching back into his jacket pocket for the phone.

"Yeah…I want to call Nicola's and order two pizzas. I'm hungry and I know they deliver anywhere in 30 minutes…guaranteed."

"Jeez, Skye. This is going on the flight data recorder."

"I know…just more incentive to get this bird down safely. I wouldn't want CNN to run those words in an endless loop as my last, greatest gift to their viewing public."

"The phone won't work out here."

"I know, but it should at about 12-15 minutes from the airport. I figure they won't shoot us down before that."

"Can't get any worse, huh?" Bill gave her a satirical look and did as she commanded.

They were losing altitude fast. At 19 minutes out, the stall warning beeper sounded. Skye and Bill put their combined muscle into tilting the nose up as far as the dead controls would let them. The beeper stopped, then started again. They both ignored it. That was the least of their problems for the moment. There was always some tolerance built into the warning mechanisms anyway. They hoped there'd be enough. Right now they had to get in touch with the tower.

The air was more stable as they came out of the heavy clouds and the flight smoothed out. "The good news is that as we lose altitude, we clear some of the really rough turbulence," said Skye through gritted teeth. Her shoulders joined the chorus of agony adding to the intensity of her discomfort but she zoned it out.

"Do you know the number of the tower?" asked Bill, turning on the phone.

"I do." As she recited it from memory, he punched it in.

"I wouldn't have known the number," said Bill, impressed but not surprised at his captain's depth of knowledge.

"And that's why I'm in the left seat." She glanced over at him with a smirk. He had a great deal to learn from her. He nodded and winked.

"17 minutes."

"Start trying the tower," Skye commanded. Bill acknowledged and punched the call button.

The plane fought her efforts to manage the rate of their descent. She only had the slightest bit of direct control and she was finessing it all she could.

"Nothing yet," Bill said, listening to the phone and reading the instruments simultaneously. "8000 feet. You're coming in fine."

"Try again," she gasped when they were at 6000 feet. Her throat was dry, her breathing labored with the effort it took to hold on to their attitude as well as their altitude.

Bill punched the call button on the cell phone at the same time the plane was rocked by another huge wave of turbulence. The phone shot out of Bill's sweaty hands and landed under the oxygen tank. Leaning over he tried to reach it, but couldn't.

"Skye, I have to leave my seat," he said disgusted with himself.

"I'll hold it. Be careful. Go." Skye shifted knowing she would have the entire weight of the plane in her hands as soon as he left his seat.

Bill got up and lurched over to the tank. The plane tilted slightly to the right and the phone skittered across the cockpit floor. Clinging to the arm of his seat with one hand, he stretched out and went after it. Just as he began to inch it back with his fingertips, a fully armed Air Force F-15 attack jet appeared to the left of the cockpit window. Then another one to the right.

"Bill, we've got company. I imagine they're trying to hail us so I think they'll give us a few minutes to respond." Bill heard the note of urgency in her voice. "Get that phone now!"

He snagged the phone as it started sliding away from him again and took a few bruises with the effort. Struggling to maintain his balance, he managed to get back into his seat. The phone looked okay. They'd caught a break. Not much of one, but it could make the difference. Even though the passengers were probably all armed with cell phones, there wasn't enough time now to secure one of them and get back to the cockpit.

He punched call again. Then again. He looked at the F15 outside his window and noticed it was backing away, but only a few hundred feet. It was preparing to fire.

"It's ringing," he was shouting now, so much adrenalin pumping through his system he'd lost all volume control. "Hello? Hello? This is International Airlines Flight 127 from London. I repeat. This is IA Flight 127 from London. Hand this phone to the air traffic control supervisor. Now!" Bill listened for a few seconds.

"They want all the codes, Skye." He put the phone to her ear.

"This is Captain Skyler Madison, IA Flight 127 from London. We're 11 minutes out and have an altitude of 5000 feet." Skye gave the air traffic control supervisor all the number and name codes in the pre-authorized sequence. It had to be perfect so the tower would know they were not under duress or in a hijack situation. After Skye, Bill identified himself and recited all the copilot codes. He kept his eyes on the fighter jets the whole time. Nothing happened. They were still there, menacing, deadly. Bill held his breath.

"Come on. Come on."

Finally, at 8 minutes out, the fighters waggled their wings and disappeared into the clouds. Bill blew out a breath. One problem solved. Not that they were out of the woods. He looked at the instruments. Not by a long shot. He placed the phone between his chin and shoulder and relieved Skye by adding all of his strength to their combined efforts on the aircraft's steering mechanisms.

Skye was still monitoring the avionic readouts and assessing all the sounds in the cockpit. She could hear the stress on the skin of the plane, even through the din of warning bells, thunder, and her own roaring heartbeat. They were in the wrong attitude. It was something she felt more than observed. Something she knew.

"Throttle back, Bill. We have to slow down." Again Bill did precisely what she commanded, no questions, just quick action.

"Just a bit. Yes, that's it." She could hear his unasked question in her head. "Too much structural stress. I can hear the right wing groaning. There. That's better."

"Turn to a heading of two-seven-zero and begin your descent to 2600," said Bill.

"I wish it were that easy," muttered Skye. But she managed to get more out of her arm and back muscles and her precious, valiant bird responded to her touch.

"You're clear to land on two-seven. Emergency vehicles standing by." Bill looked over at his captain, who spared a glance at him. "The Tower says good luck." Bill let the phone fall into his lap. They were on their own.

Skye was going to have to do this completely by visual approach. No gyros, no glide slope, no localizer. The old fashioned way. Eyes only, by hand, feel, intuition, and instinct. Captain Skyler Madison was made for this moment. It was precisely the kind of flying she loved. She was one with the airplane. The runway and the REIL lights loomed on the horizon.

"Lower the landing gear," she ordered.

"They're hydraulic."

"Yes, but there's a backup on a separate line. If that line is still intact, we'll have wheels."

"And if it isn't?"

"We slide farther and make sparks. Didn't you ever watch *Airplane!*?"

"Several times."

"Then you know that either way, we're on the ground. You're going to have to move the throttles and control the speed. I'll take the rudders and the yoke." Skye shifted slightly, positioning her feet and arms to make maximum use of leverage.

"Green light on the landing gear. If we can believe the light, we will have rubber on the runway."

They had done everything they could. It was now just a matter of using their combined strength to keep the plane in its glide path while losing all the remaining altitude. Skye was unable to control the devilish grin that spread over her face. She was ready to bring the plane into its corridor and let gravity have its way with her.

They were both silent as the plane descended. Skye had worked with Bill for over three years and he was one of the best copilots she knew. He would be a captain soon, she thought, and she would miss the opportunity to fly with him. They didn't always fly together, but when they did, it was like dancing with a familiar partner. She led, he followed. Smoothly, automatically, and with a great deal of trust and mutual respect.

When they were 100 yards from the end of the runway and just under 50 feet above it, they felt the last bit of control fall away. The wings lost their lift and the plane fell like a stone. Fortunately the wheels were down and locked and took the stress of the abrupt fall. Both Bill and Skye were jarred, but they didn't let go of the yoke. They were kissing concrete and hurtling down the deserted runway.

Skye worked the emergency brakes and maneuvered the controls with all of her remaining strength. They rode the plane to the far end of the runway where it came to a slow, screeching stop. What drama. A perfect Hollywood moment!

Skye blew out a breath and slowly released her grip. Her fingers were nearly fixed in a permanent fist. She painfully straightened them out, then flexed until she could move them without sparks of pain running up her wrists. Neither she nor Bill spoke. They didn't need to. They could hear the emergency vehicles pulling up, but they gave themselves a minute to catch their breath and savor the moment. Slowly, deliberately Skye reached up and turned off all the switches, then the engines.

"Welcome to D.C.," she sighed finally.

Bill glanced at the clock. "Hey, we're a few minutes early."

"That's the bonus of coming in with an air emergency." She looked at him and grinned. He grinned back. Alive and well and on terra firma. What a rush!

Skye got out of her seat and stretched some of the stiffness out of her muscles. The landing was as physically demanding as it was mentally challenging. "That was a hell of a ride, Bill."

Bill got up too still grinning at his captain. She was a master of the understatement. "Nicely done. 250 souls safe, not to mention a very grateful crew." He held out his hand and she shook it, gingerly. They both winced, shook out the cramps, then laughed.

Skye smoothed out the wrinkles in her skirt. Bill helped her on with her jacket and she grabbed her hat. It wouldn't do to look disheveled, even though she fought a 450,000-pound behemoth for nearly an hour. She slid a battered old compass out of the side pocket of her seat and led the way to the cockpit door. Before she went out, she patted her hair and put on her captain's hat. She tilted it a bit off regulation, deciding she needed a roguish look for this occasion, and stepped out onto a wide, metal platform.

The platform was attached to the International Airlines Simulation Unit, the most sophisticated model currently being used in the industry. Skye looked down from the platform and grinned. All the people assembled in the large hangar applauded wildly. She heard the whistles of the mechanics and the hoots from the computer geeks. Her fellow pilots had been watching on the monitors and against all odds, they had bet on one of their own. They were applauding the loudest. She looked at all of their grinning faces for a few seconds, then took an imperial bow.

Skyler Madison, legendary pilot and youngest person to rise to captain's rank had done it one more time. Woman against machine and their simulated computer-generated scenarios...and woman had won. She'd brought the virtual bird safely back to its nest.

Skye had faced everything the engineers, technicians, corporate strategists, and computer programmers could think of and once again she landed the plane in a simulator so authentic, it was considered the equivalent of actual cockpit time. She'd never lost one. Her record was still perfect.

She then stepped aside, and with a flourish of one throbbing arm she presented for review to the assembled masses, her copilot. Bill stepped out and took his bow. Then he took Skye's hand and like two stars in a major Broadway production, they bowed together. As the applause continued, Bill moved to the side and clapped loudly for his captain.

"Damn, what a sight," said Stan, one of the senior pilots. Skye was absolutely stunning. Tall, nearly six feet, and slender, with beautifully expressive chocolate-colored eyes, she looked more like a model than a skilled commercial pilot. While in the cockpit, she wore her thick wheat-colored hair severely pulled back into an elaborate twist at the nape of her neck. She thought it made her look competent and professional. To the appreciative eyes that gazed at her now, it made her look like a picture of the ancient goddess of love. Not even the trim uniform and hat did much to conceal the magnificent face and body. For many, it magnified the appeal. Her gorgeous features, accessorized with that cocky grin and confident angle of the head, dazzled the eye and would star in more than one hot and heavy dream that night.

Laughing, Skye skipped gracefully down the steps into the waiting crowd of onlookers. There would be an immediate debriefing on what they observed with Skye and Bill as the headliners. The usual assessment team from corporate headquarters would facilitate the meeting.

"Meet you in there," said Skye to Bill, looking back at the huge simulator and all the attached wires and cables. Bill nodded, wanting to make a few phone calls before the meeting.

"I sure could use a drink," Skye said aloud. Connie came up beside her, literally grinning from ear to ear. "Here you are, Captain. Your usual." She handed Skye a large Diet Pepsi with lots of ice.

"Thanks, Connie," she said as she gave her friend a smile. Skye gratefully sipped the cold drink while she watched Connie turn on, warm up, and launch.

"You really did great in there, Skye. That was some simulation. They all thought they had you this time. Those engineers' and computer techs' eyes were all popping when you took it out of autopilot. They couldn't believe it. And then when you were fighting the plane...well...I think Johnny Blight had an orgasm watching your hands on the yoke and your body all tense like that. They didn't think you were going to have the stamina to fight for 45 minutes. I knew that wasn't going to be a problem. I've seen you at the gym. You could've wrestled that plane to London and back." Connie kept chattering as they walked toward the hallway leading to the offices and conference rooms. "When you jettisoned your fuel, I about choked. The computer geeks couldn't resist telling everyone out here what they had planned for you. When you took the landing options down to Dulles or nowhere, they launched into a premature celebration. Had to take it all back, though. It was so radical. I don't think they were playing fair. Honestly, a thunderstorm, hydraulic malfunction, lightning strike, no radios. Like that would ever happen."

"At least they left me Bill. They could have declared he had a heart attack."

"Now that you mention it, I'm surprised they didn't have him tank. They were this close to declaring a victory." Connie held up her hand with her thumb and forefinger nearly touching.

"Oh yeah? How?"

"They had their hand on that button that causes a spontaneous break up when the vibration gets too intense, but that was when you told Bill to throttle back and slow the plane down. That was sheer genius. If you had maintained air speed at that attitude, the wing would have fallen off. They had to take their fingers off the button as soon as you corrected. It was such a bitchin', radical, gilt-edged, over-the-top, head-of-the-class, corking, first-class moment." She shivered with undiluted pleasure as she took Skye's empty glass. "Every one of those techs and execs thought you were going down."

Connie didn't need any acknowledgement when she was on a roll and just continued with her account. "None of the pilots broke rank, though. They were all in your corner. Except for that awful Morrison Connally. He's a creep. None of the flight attendants want to work with him...he keeps calling us stewardesses and wants us to sit on his lap. Anyway, he was sucking up to the corporate people. Like they can't see through all that phony baloney. Telling them what *he* would do. Gads, we all would have been killed. Three times over, no less. If he would have been the pilot, I would have been singing with the angels, never getting a chance to wear that spectacular green dress I bought when we went shopping in London last week. Needless to say he did more annoying than impressing, so I think he may just have been put on the retirement list. One can only hope." The only thing that stopped Connie was the end of the day or the end of the room. They had reached the corridor leading to the conference rooms.

"I'll see you tomorrow," she said, giving Skye a quick hug.

"You have a date tonight?"

"Yeah. With Alabama."

"The whole state?"

Connie giggled. "Haven't tried that yet. No, his name is Alabama."

"Have a sister named Virginia?"

"No, but a brother named Dakota."

"North or south?"

"Didn't say. Anyway, have a good meeting." Skye watched Connie bounce toward the exit. No one could figure out how they had become good friends, but Skye knew. Connie was her inner child. She said and did all the things Skye couldn't and didn't.

Skye walked down the corridor and finally gave in to the pain. She rubbed her sore neck with her aching fingers as she went toward the conference room and her waiting audience.

John Allwardt and a group of pilots came up behind her and walked with her down the short hallway. "Hey Skye, how about going out for a drink after the debriefing?"

"Sorry, John. I'm planning on a long hot shower, a cool glass of wine, and at least 12 hours in bed." She continued to rub some of the cramps out of her arms and shoulders. She didn't want to show any weakness in front of the techs, but she was now among friends.

"Hey, that works for me," said John with a wide grin.

"That wasn't an invitation." Her lips turned up, taking some of the sting out of her rejection. He was a very nice man, but Skye didn't date other pilots. Too messy. Who would take the controls if they flew together?

Undaunted, John pointed to her hands kneading the back of her neck and asked, "do you want me to do that for you?"

"John," she patted his cheek and gave him a heart-stopping smile. "Give it up. You aren't my type." He continued to stare at her as she entered the debriefing room.

"So what *is* her type?" he asked the group of men beside him.

"Not tall," said Jake who was over six four.

"Not Irish," said Ian McDonald.

"Not distinguished and mature," said Kyle, the oldest of them.

Ian snorted. "You mean middle aged and twice divorced?"

"That either."

"What she's looking for in a man is one of the great mysteries of the universe," said Frank. He was happily married and out of the pool entirely.

"Shall we join the party?" asked Bill coming up behind them. As they went into the room where Skye was waiting to report, they tried to pump him for information on how to get Skye's attention.

"Well, I know she's dating the son of a Duke. The guy is as rich as a Lord. Actually, he *is* a Lord."

"So rich and royal seems to work," said John.

"I've seen him. Add young and handsome."

"So exactly what does he have that I haven't got?" persisted John with a wicked grin.

"Money, good looks, and a date for Friday night," teased Bill. The guys were laughing when they entered the room. They all thought the world of Skye, both as a woman and as a captain. Even though many were also a bit in love with her, they thought of her more as a friend and sister pilot.

The Vice President of Operations was in the room as was the Chief Pilot, the safety team, and the new Quality Control Engineer. The Chief Pilot was beaming. One of their own beat the odds and won the day. When everyone was seated, he began the meeting with his standard cliché.

"Everything in the International Airlines corporate manual…policies, protocols, procedures, warnings, instructions, everything…can be summed up to read, 'Captain, it's your baby.' There's no substitute for the human brain. No alternative for the pilot's intuition. No proxy for the captain's heart. Well done, Skyler."

Skye nodded and smiled. For the next hour they went over the simulation in detail…every alternative, every decision, every instrument, and every step.

"I think that should do it. I want written reports emailed to me by the 15th," said the Chief Pilot. "Let's get Skyler and Bill on their way. They must be exhausted." Everyone looked at the two of them, still animated and grinning. Other than the fact that they had taken off their jackets and rolled up their sleeves, they hadn't really changed at all since they walked off the simulator. Pilots could go on for hours discussing any piece of the plane or any part of the flight. It was like jet fuel to them.

"One more thing before you all leave," smiled the V.P. as she slid a disk into the computer and projected on a large screen the series of steps Skye had taken in successfully landing the plane. "In the future, you and every other pilot flying today will be able to locate this new procedure under the file entitled," she dramatically clicked an icon in the center of the screen. "The

Madison Protocol." The room immediately started buzzing. This was big and they were all delighted for her. Skye beamed and basked in the warm flood of pleasure running through her. It was like having a star in a constellation named after you.

"No offense Skye, but I hope I never need to initiate it," said Kyle with feeling. His arms ached just thinking about it.

John stood up and smiled at the other pilots. "Yeah, well, I thought the Madison Protocol had only two steps. Ask her out, get shot down." They all laughed at what they thought was the ultimate wit.

"Oh, very funny, John," said Skye. Nothing anyone could say was going to spoil her mood. "But remember what they say, a good simulator check ride is like successful surgery on a cadaver. You still have to have it in the field." She reached over and squeezed his arm, then poked his stomach. "A few more hours in the gym and a few less prepackaged sweet rolls would be a good start."

The pilots all liked that one, too. The laughter got louder, with a few whoops thrown in. The V.P. just looked at all of them like they were children in a playground. She wasn't a pilot. She didn't get it.

Skye turned down their invitations to celebrate further and walked out of the hanger into a bright sunny day. She should have been tired but she was still pumped from the simulation and the debriefing. Executing a little dance, she threw her flight bag over her shoulder. She loved to fly. She loved to win. She loved to fly and win. Even if the sun hadn't been shining, her day would have been full of light.

She blew out of the building and took a deep breath of air filled with the powerful smell of jet fuel. Ah, perfume, she thought. Longing for a hot shower, she stretched again knowing she had to make a few stops before she could go home. She looked at her flight bag. She needed to pass on some important cargo from the secret compartment located in its false bottom.

As soon as she got to her car in the employee parking lot, she took out her cell phone to call her younger sister. Sloane Madison answered on the first ring.

"Hey parental unit, how were the friendly skies?"

"That's the other airline, sponge head."

"Yeah, Yeah. Whatever. You in D.C.?"

"Just landed…for the second time."

"Sweet! They put the finger on you for another fake and shake? Did you put it together and beat the competish?"

"Sure did. It was a pretty exciting ride. I'll tell you all about it later."

"Excellent. You going to blow on down to the castle?"

"Not yet. I've a few stops to make and I want to check my apartment."

"Okay. I'll be at the book farm digging through the dust in the quantum physics section. There's a new page-turner on Stephen Hawking I want to check out."

Skye grinned. Only her sister would think a biography of the world's foremost contemporary genius was a fascinating read. "I'm sure you won't have any trouble finding it on the shelves. I should be home by 7 or so."

"We'll keep the light on for you."

"Thanks, hon."

"Roger, dodger birdwoman. Over and out."

Skye smiled broadly. She really did love the little monster. Sloane was a tested, certified, card-carrying genius with an IQ of 235 on the standard tests, although none of them really accurately measured the limits of her intellect. She was also a guileless goofball.

Skye dialed a seven-digit number followed by a four-digit code, then another seven-digit number. She waited patiently as the phone clicked and whirred and clicked some more.

"Yes?"

"I'm at the airport."

"Are you coming in?"

"I'll be there soon."

"See you then."

It was a secure line, still, no names, no location, no information. She loved this covert stuff. It gave her the little hit of adrenalin she would need to stay alert for her commute into the city. That and the fact that she'd scored some really superior goods.

CHAPTER 2

Forty-five minutes later, Captain Skyler Madison faded and Special Agent Skyler Madison took form as she skillfully maneuvered her classic Mustang convertible into her assigned spot under the Justice building. She presented her ID to the guards and placed her thumb on the press pad outside the elevators. Security was tight and she had to go through three more checkpoints, including a weapons scan. She'd left her small .40-caliber Glock in the locked glove compartment of her car so she wouldn't have to carry all the permits with her. Since nearly every other person in the building was carrying a gun and they were all on her side, she felt hers would be redundant anyway.

Skye took the elevator to the top floor and stepped into a lobby of one of the least institutional-looking offices in government service. Director Jim Stryker liked the look of highly polished oak panels. His office and those of his staff seemed more like the headquarters of an established law firm than the powerful bureau it was. This was the Department of Justice, Intelligence Division and Special Agent Skyler Madison was checking in to report.

"Skye!" smiled Pearl Shepler, Jim's executive assistant, as she rose to buzz Skye into the inner office. "How was the flight?"

"It was smooth and swift."

Jim, Pearl, Jim's senior staff, and Skye's team of special agents were all privy to her "day job." It wasn't easy to juggle her flying schedule with her assignments for the department, but Skye wasn't looking for easy. She was possessed by two passions…flying and justice. Her life, to her way of thinking, was just about as perfect as a life could be.

It was Jim Stryker's idea to recruit people in all walks of life and train them in covert operations. Several of his agents, like Skye, had established professional careers before joining the team. Some were doctors and lawyers, others were police officers and social workers. It made coordination of assignments more difficult, but it also made his agents nearly invisible. That was his advantage and he had built a highly successful record of arrests and seizures. Some were not public record. None were attributed directly to his department. They worked behind the scenes, gathering intelligence that would later be turned over to local or federal law enforcement agencies. Several cases, like the one Skye was currently working, had international cooperation.

Skye walked through the glass door and handed Pearl the shortbread cookies from a small shop near Victoria Station in London. They were her favorite.

"You declare these?" she asked with delight written all over her face.

"Yeah. Almost had to share them with the guy in Customs."

"Then we would have issued a warrant for his arrest. No one gets these cookies but me." Pearl eyes crinkled with mischief as she discreetly closed out and locked her computer. Not even Skye was allowed to see all that was part of Pearl's every day work. Rising, she led Skye to the beautifully carved double doors in the rear of the inner office.

"Director," Pearl stated formally as she knocked once and opened the door to Jim's office. "Special Agent Madison is here."

It always amazed Skye how fast Pearl would switch from sweet and ingenuous Granny to efficient and stylish Executive Assistant to the Director. She played many parts and did every one very well. Now she was all business waiting her director to indicate Skye's welcome and her dismissal with a nod.

The smiling man made an imposing picture sitting behind a huge oak desk that Pearl had polished into a high gloss. Mementoes of his years in the field decorated the office. Photographs, weapons, citations, medals, a chunk of concrete from the Berlin wall. Bits and pieces of history. His history. As they always did when she entered this room, Skye's eyes went to the picture on the wall of Jim and her father. They had trained together and worked for Justice in the same cell until her father's death fourteen years before. Now Jim was the father figure in her life and because he was also a very fine man, she loved him dearly.

Jim stood. Since the doors were closed and they were alone, he indulged himself and gave her a big bear hug. She savored the feel of being wrapped in the arms of the strong, capable man who had been a father to her for nearly half her life. He smelled of spicy aftershave and peppermint...of home and security.

She returned his hug and gave him a big smacking kiss on the cheek. Then reaching into her pocket, she pulled out the box of peppermint candies she bought on impulse at the duty free shop.

"What's this, role reversal?" he asked smiling as he led her over to the soft leather coach. He had always pulled out a peppermint for her when he visited their home, or when she would come into the office with her father.

"I saw them when I went in to get your Scotch and I couldn't resist."

"Well, that's a relief. I thought maybe you were substituting candy for my usual."

There was a soft knock on the door.

"Come in."

Pearl entered placed a tray with two glasses of ice and one Diet Pepsi on the coffee table in front of them.

"Are those cookie crumbs I see on the front of your suit, Pearl?" teased Jim with a wide smile.

"Hmmm. What sharp powers of observation you have, sir," she said as she brushed the offending crumbs off her normally impeccable gray suit. "You might want to consider a career in intelligence." She turned to Skye. "Will you need me to do any transcribing before I leave today?"

Pearl had top-level clearance and was privy to everything by virtue of her work in transcribing, filing, faxing and translating even the most sensitive documents. The intelligence world spun on the axis of long term, loyal administrative staff.

"No. My report is actually rather short. I typed it up while I was in London." She handed a disk to Pearl.

"Special Agent Madison, you know how I feel about that. You bring your work for me to type and file. If you keep doing your own transcribing, you're going to put me out of a job. Then I'll have to retire and spend my days with Stan. I don't think the marriage would survive that."

"You might as well go on home then, Pearl. I'm not sure how long this is going to take," said Jim smiling.

"Thank you, I will. Sammy is pitching tonight and I don't want to miss an inning. The beltway is already starting to back up."

"Tell Sammy I said 'hi,'" said Skye. "And could you ask Dan to stop in before he goes home?"

"Sure thing. Goodnight."

Skye reached over to her flight bag and pulled out the bottle of Jim's favorite single malt Highland Scotch. Jim opened it, poured a little over the ice, and put the bottle on the table. Skye poured the Diet Pepsi into the other glass and gratefully sipped the cold drink.

"Before you give your report, I understand congratulations are in order. The Madison Protocol. Sounds like a Robert Ludlum novel."

24

Skye raised her eyebrows in surprise, then grinned, "I forget you're omnipotent."

"Only when it comes to my agents. Seriously, it's quite an accomplishment. Makes me proud."

"As my boss, or as my godfather?" Skye felt the rush of warm pleasure run through her.

"Same person." He raised his glass to her and grinned liked a prideful parent. She grinned and toasted him back, the ice tinkling in her glass. "Your father would have been bursting with the news." The look in his expressive eyes was both melancholy and kind. He knew she loved hearing the words. "And more than a little envious. You're just like him. Actually there are times when I talk to you that I swear I see his face superimposed on yours."

Skye's grin broadened as she took a drink and lifted an eyebrow.

"Like right now." It wasn't just her face, the shining brown eyes, the strong features, it was the attitude as well. He had to shake himself to stay in the present. "Now your mother…"

"She never quite understood Dad's and my obsession with the air." Skye's smile faded a little and Jim knew it was a prelude to changing the subject. Skye still deeply grieved for her parents and was uncomfortable talking about them for any length of time. He was right. Skye nodded to her flight bag. "I've got some good stuff in the bag."

Jim settled back, the boss putting the godfather away for the moment. "Okay, Special Agent. Report."

Skye reached into the bag and opened a well concealed inside pocket. She pulled out three disks and a small bag with white powder.

"Wow. You wouldn't want to get caught with that in the airport," said Jim eyeing what was obviously cocaine.

"I know someone in Justice I could call," Skye said with a casual air.

"Tell me about your investigation."

Skye's voice changed, as did her demeanor. She sat straight backed on the edge of the couch and her tone was clipped and practiced.

"The disks contain all the information from Phillip's laptop. The white powder I found in two places in his home. I turned over the bulk of the powder to the British liaison to maintain the chain of evidence. This sample can't be used in prosecution. I just thought you might want some so the lab people could do their magic. If they could pinpoint the region it came from, it would help our investigation of possible sources."

"Good thinking. Do our British liaisons at Scotland Yard think we have enough evidence?"

"No, but we're getting close. It's been over three months of very intense work and we're now in the process of proving what we know…gathering evidence so the Blythes can be prosecuted."

Jim nodded. When his agents were in report mode, he rarely interrupted. Skye's reports were always well organized and concise.

"The last time I was in Phillip's London townhouse I worked with his home computer. I asked him if I could use it to email Sloane and I was able to get into his personal files. They were painfully easy to access. I made copies of everything, but the people in the Tower of Terror tell me they contain nothing of real importance. Not one incriminating thing on them."

The Tower of Terror was what everyone in Justice called the sanctum of the computer geeks. Because no one ever really knew what they were doing in there or how they were doing it, they were both feared and greatly admired. They had their own language; they never seemed to go home; they were in love with their machines, and they were all as pale as ghosts. They were definitely not of this world, yet indispensable to the department. They were a team of geniuses who everyone relied upon heavily in the gathering and interpreting of intelligence.

"We grab it, they nab it," Skye would say. She appreciated them all and the feeling was mutual. They would fall all over themselves to get a report to her as soon as possible. While other agents had requests languishing in in-boxes gathering dust, Skye could count on getting a preliminary report within days. She was counting on it this time. She really wanted to know what was on the latest disks she brought.

"Tell me more about how you acquired these disks. You say they contain information from his laptop?" Jim rarely questioned her methods, but he sometimes worried that her enthusiasm for her mission might push her to do things she really shouldn't do.

"Do you mean did I seduce him, screw his brains out, then while he slept in an exhausted but extremely satisfied stupor did I slip out of his bed and take advantage of the situation to plunder his laptop?"

She laughed at Jim's half-amused, half-horrified look.

"I'm afraid I'm no Mata Hari. I picked his pocket, nipped his key, made a wax impression, and had a duplicate made. I took the key, went to his home in London, and located his laptop on the table in the foyer where he always puts it. I knew the location because I've accompanied him to his home on several occasions…for a drink, or dinner, and always properly chaperoned."

"And where was he all this time?"

"He was waiting for me at the restaurant. I called him several times on my cell phone from his home to tell him I was almost there, then to order for me. It was all I could do to keep from laughing. What a bonehead. I was all apologies and soothing words. It didn't take me long to get the information transferred to the disks. I arrived at the restaurant before my soup got cold."

Jim nodded approvingly and sipped his drink. He loved to hear the details of his protégé's work.

"I was able to get into everything. Email, document files, coded financial records. I really couldn't linger so I only glanced at them."

"How were you able to access everything? You have good computer skills, but certainly not like Sloane."

"No," she said with pride. "Sloane's a genius."

She took another drink, sat back, and crossed her remarkably long and shapely legs. If Jim hadn't been her godfather, he might have swallowed an ice cube. She continued her report.

"However, you're talking about pitting my brain against Phillip's. That's like having an intelligent conversation with an unarmed man. He's very dim. I think it's the result of all the inbreeding among the royals. Eventually that blue blood gets rather thin."

"Don't underestimate him," Jim warned.

"The only danger I'm in is being bored to death," snorted Skye derisively.

"If we're to believe the evidence, he's neck deep in distributing high-grade cocaine to the privileged elite of London," reminded Jim.

"Well, that doesn't take a whole lot of brains. Just a lot of contacts. And that he has. He must have a thousand names in his PDA. Whenever I ask him who someone is, he whips it out, tells me their spouse's name, where they live, where they went to school, and a brief history of their lineage. It can curb your curiosity in a hurry. I'd rather get the information in one big chunk."

Skye paused and a familiar gleam sprang into her intense brown eyes. She grinned her father's grin again and Jim suppressed the surge of envy that sprang into his heart. There were times like these he really missed field work.

"I'm going after that PDA next. I thought I would nip it on our next date and disappear into the ladies room to suck it dry. It has to be filled with evidence of his contacts and we know that translates into customers for the cocaine you have there. Once I have all the information, I can just tuck it back into his pocket. If he misses it while I'm gone, I'll stick it under the seat of his car and help him find it."

"I think I'm going to have to arrange extra hazard pay for you on this assignment. Sounds perilous to me," Jim laughed. He liked the plan and knew she would pull it off without a hitch. He had personally taught her to pick pockets and she was his best pupil.

There was a hearty rap on the door.

"Hi there, Nancy." A tall, good-looking man in his late fifties entered the room, strode over to her, and planted a kiss on her cheek. He grabbed a glass and helped himself to the Scotch. "When are you going to get off that sissy diet drink and get with the program? This goes down so much smoother."

Dan Dickson was the department's Chief of Administration. He always claimed he was a glorified bookkeeper and data drone, but Jim relied upon him heavily. He wasn't involved in the direct operations work, but he made sure the bills were paid, information was processed, and resources were available.

Dan had called Skye "Nancy" since she was a child because she always had her nose in a Nancy Drew book, most of them purchased by Dan and his first wife, Abigail. Of course, that was back when she only knew him as the family lawyer and friend. Now she was an ace detective herself and Dan was her colleague. He, too, had tried to talk her out of joining the department. He hadn't been able to slide into the role of her colleague as easily as Jim. To him, she would always be 14 and worried about the freckles lining her pert little nose.

Skye smiled broadly, took another sip of her sissy drink, and the three of them talked as the late afternoon fell into shadows. Three people with a rich and remarkable history. Jim, Dan, and Skye's father were in the same group of young agents and had trained together, worked together, and played together. They were a trio of fast friends. Dan was an attorney and had decided on administration over fieldwork. Jim always had a flair for decision-making and leadership and that, together with his work in the field, put him in the top spot.

Perry Madison, Skye's father, was the cowboy of the group, always preferring direct action and undercover work. His early exploits were legendary. After he married Skye's mother and had two daughters, he became a bit more conservative, but still chose working in the field over supervisory or administrative duties. He was tall, lean, and had a head full of unruly wheat-colored hair. To look at Skye today was to look into the face of her father. The resemblance was uncanny and not lost on his two closest friends as they sat in this room sharing information, stories, and intrigues with their best friend's daughter.

Skye had never heard the stories about her father's other life until she joined the department. To her he was just dad, a handsome, funny, loving man with a ready laugh and a killer smile. It was interesting for her to hear a story and then try to remember bits and pieces from her own perspective…the times he was away for weeks, or once when he came home with 75 stitches in his leg and a story about a man-eating alligator. She found out later he tore it while jumping out of a window with a file of the names of several KGB agents.

There was nothing Skye liked better than to sit with Jim and Dan and have them reminisce. For Dan and Jim, it was like old times. It truly was like father, like daughter. Now she was the cowboy.

"So, Skye. Can I expect the requisitions and invoices for your expenses on your last month's cycle by this time next week?" asked Dan.

"God, you know I hate all the paperwork. Maybe I can con Barclay into doing it."

"His handwriting is illegible. Last month you almost got forty-two desks instead of forty-two disks and one of my younger staff was quite confused about your need for dancing transvestites in underwear. I figured you'd asked him to requisition advanced translation software."

"Hey…I really needed those transvestites to cover both the ladies and men's rooms in the Underground."

"I know it isn't too exciting, but it has to be done. Us paper drones keep things running so you special agents can go out there and ride the wave without a single bill to swamp you."

Skye laughed and finished off her drink. She wanted to work out before she went home and the facilities in the basement were among the best in the city.

"I'll see you on my return trip early next week. Jim, going to join me downstairs?" asked Skye.

"No. I have a 7 o'clock meeting. You two go on."

"Nope. Not tonight. I've got to bring home dinner. It's my turn to cook. I think Chinese is in order," said Dan rubbing his hands together. "I'm going to stop at Beijing Kitchen."

They all got up and started for the door.

"How is Betsy?" asked Skye. Dan had been married and divorced three times. He was currently dating a tech from the third floor.

"Bitsy."

"Sorry." Sounded like something you would name your dog, Skye thought.

"I know. Ridiculous name for a 28-year-old woman. But she's thinking about going back to Norma when we get married."

And God, they're getting younger and younger.

"Married? Oh Dan, congratulations. How wonderful," she said putting on her pleased smile. She was a special agent, trained to lie and should be able to pull off this little exaggeration with no problem.

Dan smiled back. She was good, he thought. She could almost pull off that performance if he hadn't known Skye her whole life. Bitsy was a fun loving, rather empty-headed woman who would love him for the next five years or so. What more could a man of his age ask for?

Jim glanced at his watch. "Skye, you be careful and we'll see you on your return trip. We're close now. Very close to putting this particular family of vipers away."

Jim watched as Skye passed through the outer office and to the elevator, chatting with Dan, laughing easily, then giving him a peck on the cheek. Jim loved his two sons dearly, but Skye was something special. And he knew he was about to do something that would hurt her. He took a deep breath. At least he was going to keep this one tightly contained. For now no one but he and Alexander Springfield were going to know about the operation. Jim figured Skye would never have to know and that gave him some comfort. He glanced at his watch. Alex would be there in less than an hour. Jim turned back into his office to prepare.

CHAPTER 3

Jim looked at the man sitting across the desk from him. If Skye was his pride and joy, then Alexander Springfield was his prototype of a special agent. He was the best and Jim needed the best on this one. He was a tall man, over 6'4" with a finely muscled, well-toned body. He had penetrating light blue eyes and dark brown, curly hair, worn long but well cut. He came from a family of cops so he was into firearms early and gained marksman status within days of arrival at the training facilities in Colorado.

Alex had an MBA from the University of Chicago and a law degree from the University of Wisconsin, where he played fullback and was an All-American his junior and senior year. Before he joined Jim's elite team at Justice, he was a highly successful corporate attorney and businessman. He was a multi-millionaire before he was 30, making most of his money in real estate investments. This made him ideal for assignments requiring travel or access into the upper echelons of the financial world. Like Skye, his professional career was excellent cover for his clandestine operations.

Alex was also a superb undercover operator. He had done some deep cover covert work for Jim over the years. He was bold, brilliant, and daring. A personal tragedy had turned the young man from engaging in business to pursuing justice, and now, years later, he was as passionate about bringing down the lawbreakers as he had been about building an empire. Jim mentored him along the way and thought he might be well suited to administration. But like Skye, Alex favored hands-on fieldwork.

After a warm greeting, Jim led Alex to the less formal sitting area where he and Skye sat earlier. They discussed sports scores, some local political scandals, and personal information over drinks before getting down to business. Jim always prided himself on the rapport he built with his agents and realized it was something that took time and effort. Finally, after the two were relaxed, he brought up the reason for the meeting.

"I have a special project for you."

Alex merely nodded, an engaging grin spreading across his face.

"Make it a good one. After the last assignment, you owe me. Big time."

Alex had been sent into a large accounting firm to investigate a case of insider trading. All those debits and credits gave him a headache. He considered it very boring work. He wanted to feel his gun in the small of his back and go after some really bad guys. Not accountants, who are about as dangerous as a box of puppies.

Jim laughed. "Consider that last job a holding pattern. How do drugs, danger, and possible mayhem suit you?"

"Just fine." Alex grinned, a glint in his steely blue eyes. "Throw in a beautiful woman and I'm yours to command."

Jim grinned back. Some days, he really loved his job.

"This one beautiful enough for you?" Jim tossed a picture of a stunning blonde on the table in front of Alex. She had long curly hair the color of sand with coffee-colored eyes and a broad, full mouth.

Alex's eyes nearly popped out of his head. "Please tell me you want me to follow her, seduce her, and recruit her to our side."

Jim laughed. "Follow her, yes. Seduce her, and I'll have you marked for torture and death. And she's already on our side. Your job is to confirm that. Here's her dossier." Alex took it, scanned it, and memorized it. He was impressed and it took a great deal to make that kind of impression on him. "I didn't know International Airlines had a female captain. Did you set that up?"

"No, she earned it all on her own." Jim smiled. "And I know for a fact Skyler doesn't like chauvinists who assume someone in the left seat of the cockpit has to be male."

"Hey, Jim. My mom's a cop, remember? I grew up in a house where the women were armed, for God's sake. I rarely make that mistake." He gazed down at the picture, already half in love. "It's just that this woman looks more like a model than a pilot. And she certainly doesn't look like an experienced field agent."

"Exactly. That's the idea behind covert operations."

"When was she recruited?"

"Actually, I believe she was a teenager when she ran her first mission."

"Excuse me?"

"Her parents were Angelina and Perry Madison."

"Oh," he said seriously. He remembered the headlines and horrific pictures of the tragedy. "Go on."

"Perry was one of ours. We never knew which one was the target. Skye called in right after the bombing and asked if she could help us find the people responsible."

"She knew what her father did?"

"She has a near genius IQ. She was always very precocious and even back then had the instincts of an agent. Called us on her father's secure phone. She was a very determined young lady. We managed to use her knowledge of her parents' movements to narrow the field of suspects. Never got anywhere with it, however. It's still something that drives her. She was in the piazza when the bomb went off. She would have been in the car, but she convinced her father to stop at a bakery."

That would explain some of the guarded mystery in her eyes, Alex thought.

"She an only child?"

"No. She has a younger sister, Sloane. She was just a baby when it happened. She's 14 now and she's not just a near genius…she *is* a genius. Her IQ is off the charts. Perry's Aunt Hazel and Skye have done a good job raising her. They make their home in Virginia."

Alex looked down at the dossier. Angelina Madison was the Ambassador to Italy and her husband Perry was, on the surface, an international financier when a bomb destroyed the car they were riding in. After months of intense investigation, it was concluded that it was a case of mistaken identity. No terrorist group or crime syndicate ever took responsibility. Not even the considerable resources of the CIA, the FBI, the State Department, Justice and all other international police agencies could find the people responsible.

"Maybe it really was a case of mistaken identity."

"I guess we'll never know."

What would it be like, he thought as he gazed back down at Skyler Madison's picture, to have seen your parents blown up, then never have the satisfaction of bringing the killers to justice? He was a man who tried to get into the minds of the people he was assigned to cover and understand their motivations. This kind of trauma was a defining event. The incident was still unresolved, a fact that must continue to weigh on Skye's heart, mind, and soul. He was going to find this assignment fascinating, and, as he continued to stare at the picture, stimulating as well. It sure beat the hell out of debits and credits.

"Anything else I should know about her?" Alex's eyes never moved, but in his peripheral vision was a silver frame on a shelf containing a color picture of his assignment, smiling into the camera with Jim's arm wrapped around her.

"It's all in the dossier."

"Words and factual descriptions are, not stories and impressions. Tell me."

Jim nodded in approval. Alex was a man who wanted to hear what was on paper fleshed out. It gave him an edge. Jim settled back and tried to condense a fascinating woman and an interesting background into a few concise descriptions.

"Since she was a girl, Skye has had an interest in flying and the martial arts. Her early heroes were Bruce Lee and Amelia Earhart. Her parents encouraged her to cultivate these interests and found her the best teachers and coaches. She was a black belt in tae kwon do before she was 13. She has become a 6th degree since. Because her mom was with the State department, they moved through Europe a great deal and her work with the martial arts was a solitary, but satisfying way to occupy her time."

"Her fascination with planes was a love affair that began when she was just a child. Her family was constantly at airports and in flight. To her the time on the ground was just filler to be tolerated between her joyful return to the air. Her father taught her to fly before she could reach the pedals and she got her license on her 16th birthday. After her parents' assassination, she spent more and more time flying. For her, both the martial arts and flying were escapes from reality and that meant escape from pain."

"Because she graduated from high school a year early," Jim continued, "she was able to attend Embry Riddle Aeronautical University, one of the finest aviation schools in the United States. She got her commercial license, and her degree in Aeronautical Engineering in three years. She set out to be the youngest captain ever to fly for a major airline. Because of the incredible amount of hours she had in the air as a youth, she reached her goal three years ago."

"When did she start working for you?" Alex detected a slight change in Jim's demeanor. Nothing an untrained eye would see, but Alex was a skilled and accomplished observer. Did it mean that Jim recruited her? Liked what he saw and decided to bring her in?

Jim answered, "She wanted in when she was 15. I talked her out of it, and thought I had successfully steered her into aviation." Another trauma then sent her back to him, but Alex didn't need to know any of that. It was deeply personal and wasn't relevant to the case or to this assignment.

"Several years later, she made another bid to join the department. We talked about how we could successfully weave the assignments into her flying schedule. We've made it work. She started on several small domestic cases and gained experience and a reputation along the way. She's the ice queen. Cool under pressure and ruthlessly controlled. She uses both her uncanny intuition and her incredible brain to take people down in record time. She has an astonishing success rate and a level three clearance."

Did Alex now see love on Jim's face? He was sure it was more than professional pride. This could really complicate things.

"Skye is fluent in French, Italian, Spanish, and Greek and competent in German as a result of her European upbringing. Even though she's a black belt in tae kwon do, she prefers down and dirty hand to hand. She's a bit weak on the rifle range, but she can hit a pig's eye at 50 feet with a bow and arrow. And she makes great French toast. I can't think of much else that's relevant. The dossier can fill in the dates and specifics of her cases, citations, and record."

Did that French toast comment have a special meaning, wondered Alex? French toast usually implied breakfast and that could mean his director spent the night with her. No. He could feel a little knot form in his stomach. He really, really wanted to get that picture out of his mind. Somehow Jim was like his parent and he couldn't even imagine him sexually active, much less intimate with a young, attractive agent like this one. No sex. *No sex*. Besides, wasn't Jim a happily married man? He had thought so. But then that face could tempt a saint. And what he could see of the body. Hell. He could feel his own temperature rise.

He looked back at the picture. She really was easy on the eyes. He was going to particularly enjoy this mission. He smiled. Look out, Jim, you old bastard. If you have a thing for this special agent, I intend to give you a run for your money. Without a twinge of guilt he passed all the information back to his director. He had it memorized, including the shape of those delectable lips.

"Tell me about the assignment."

"Skyler is the Special Agent in Charge of a major operation located in London. We're closing in on the base of operations and hope to locate the center of the source of high-grade cocaine distributed among the most elite members of London society. We believe it's one of their own who is the key distributor and we're working to follow the trail to the ultimate source."

"Makes sense. How come we got involved?"

"The connections are international. We've formed a task force at the request of British Intelligence and Scotland Yard. They'll do all the work relating to arrests and prosecution. We're there for intelligence gathering only. We hope to gain access to the communications systems of the English branch of this international drug distribution system and get information that will assist us in our attempts to break some of these international drug cartels. The sources of these drugs are the same as the sources that supply US dealers. The criminals aren't restricted by national boundaries. Now, neither are we. We've signed international justice agreements with most of the European community to assure mutual cooperation in stopping the flow of drugs. We share resources and records so the suppliers won't have a place to hide."

"We were asked to bring in a team of special agents who are both unknown to local dealers and who would be unlikely to attract attention. We've used Skye to develop a relationship with a man who was identified as the son of the possible hub of the drug operation. Through her, we've gained huge amounts of information, almost too much to process. While successful for the purposes of cutting off distribution, our ultimate goal is to find the site of the central store and dust it, along with all the information we can find. The destruction of the distribution is important but our real target is the data."

"Sounds impressive. And Skye Madison is SAC?" Alex took another quick glance at the rather intimate picture of Skye and Jim on his shelf.

"Yes."

"So why have you called me?"

"We have a problem. As I said, Skye has been fast tracking and we've used her in several very sensitive and involved operations. For the last two years she's been Special Agent in Charge in three major busts. We've cleared out a lot of criminal activity because of her and her teams. It's been a point of frustration for us that over the years some of the sharks have slipped through the net. There are several reasons this could happen. It could have been their keen understanding of timing...when to get out of the current game and move on to the next big market. It could have been luck. Or it could have been someone within the department has jumped...switched sides. Feeding information to the highest level of these cartels. We get the soldiers, even as high as the colonels. We just have never been able to take the general. We started to trace a pattern and an independent high-level task force has been formed to investigate the possibility of a mole in our department. I don't want to believe it. I take pride in the personnel I have selected since taking the helm and in the people who surround this office."

"What's this all have to do with Captain Madison?"

Jim looked pained but determined. "A few months ago, the chief prosecutor for a case Skye wrapped up late last year uncovered correspondence left behind by the key player in an international drug distribution network. It was buried very deep and took extremely sophisticated tech skills to uncover. It was located in deleted and destroyed files left behind by the person we believe ran the illegal operation. The computers and the drug warehouse had been fire bombed, but one of the magicians in the Tower pulled out a few phrases and sentences. Not very useful, but there were several references to Nancy and N.D., specifically related to information he received and used. In one instance, they found a sentence fragment that read, 'we will use N.D. to verify our routes' and another one that said 'use Nancy on this one.'"

Alex frowned, waiting for Jim to make a connection. Jim took a deep breath and made it. "Skye's code name is Nancy Drew."

"Oh Christ." Alex ran his fingers through his thick wavy hair. Damn, and he was looking forward to working with her. Something about the eyes. Now it seemed he was going to have to work to bring her in and put her away. "Have you gotten anything out of the people you've arrested?"

"No. According to them, they are completely innocent. They speak only through their lawyers and have never heard of Nancy Drew."

"It seems too incredible to be a coincidence."

"There's more. In the last few weeks, one of my personal contacts at MI5 has monitored three instances in which reports written by Skye have been communicated to one of the major drug distributors in London."

"How did England's top intelligence gathering agency get involved?"

"This particular dealer engages in the lucrative drug trade to finance international arms deals and my contact's team has been monitoring everything going in and out for months."

"Go on."

"She contacted me with the information that Skye appears to have been sending regular reports to the dealer. They were coded with ciphers that would only be known to elite members of the intelligence community and our top agents."

"Would Madison's team be savvy to the codes?"

"Certainly, as well as anyone here with a level three clearance or above."

"It narrows the field considerably, but there are still a lot of people in that category. Were the reports significant?"

"They could have been very significant had they not been intercepted."

"You say Madison 'appears' to have been sending reports? You aren't sure?"

"Oh I'm sure, all right," Jim said, looking Alex right in the eye and making it clear to Alex there was no doubt. "I'm sure there's no agent working here that would be less likely to jump. I'm sending you in for one reason. Regardless of my personal feelings, I'm going to play this by the book. You're going in to observe, monitor, and report. Once you have cleared her, we can concentrate on finding the real culprit."

"So you think someone is playing with you...wanting you to think she's been compromised."

"Exactly."

"This does have the feel of a set-up. If Special Agent Madison is as good as her dossier indicates, this seems pretty sloppy for her caliber of work. To send reports directly to a dealer without some intermediary steps and blinds is incredibly careless."

"Agreed, but I have to look into it. For me to do nothing would be a serious breach of my responsibility."

"Why would someone want to set her up like this?"

"I don't know. That will be the second level of my investigation. There are many reasons someone may be building the frame. From wanting to take Skye down personally, to wanting her out as Special Agent in Charge of this case, to creating general internal suspicion and strife. I'm not sure if someone is after her, she's a random or convenient cover for the real mole, or she happens to be the SAC of an operation where information is being fed to the people she's investigating. Right now, it doesn't matter. This needs to be cleaned up."

"Are you going to put me on her team?"

"No. That would be too contrived at this point in the investigation. It's not something I would normally do and Skye is far too savvy to believe any cover story. I want you to shadow her and she needs to be unaware of your surveillance. I think this has to be covert to be credible to the special task force. When the next correspondence comes through to the dealer, I want you to have Skye in your sights to prove it couldn't have been her. I want her to be sipping a cup of tea or jogging in Hyde Park when the communication is posted. In addition, I want you to be sure there are no clandestine meets or personal contacts with the other side. It appears as though they have someone from Justice in their pocket. I have to eliminate Skye before we can proceed to the next phase. When you find there is no basis for further investigation of her personally, you'll present your report, I'll file it, and we'll move on to finding the dirty agent."

Alex nodded, wondering if Jim may be thinking with his dick instead of his head.

"How can you be so sure she hasn't gone over if the evidence supports it?"

"Let's just say I'm sure."

"There's the lure of the money."

"She's a wealthy enough young woman."

"The power?"

"She flies a Boeing 767. In her hands is one of the greatest tests of power a human can have. To win the battle over gravity. I don't think she could be seduced by more power."

"Love? Could she have turned for love?"

Jim snorted as he remembered Skye's description of Phillip.

"No, I don't think so. You'll have to trust me on that one."

"Okay, but if I turn up evidence that implicates her and proves that she's dirty, you'll file that report as well?" It wasn't that he didn't trust Jim, but sometimes humans didn't see what they didn't want to see.

"Son, if you turn up such evidence I'll file it as my last official duty for this department. If I could possibly be that wrong about someone, I don't belong behind that desk."

"Okay. We'll let the evidence speak for itself."

"Agreed," said Jim.

"What about the members of her team? I'm assuming they all know about her code name and could be using it to divert suspicion. They would also have access to current files and could have passed her reports on in her name."

"Yes. I think any one of them would have the skill to carry off both the betrayal and the building of a trail to Skye, but I just don't see them doing it."

"Someone apparently is."

"All right, I concede that point. It could be someone here, perhaps in the Tower. There's also a possibility the leaks are coming from various agencies we've worked with in the past or are currently working with on this case. For that reason, no one in this office will be privy to your mission but you and me. The members of the task force have been briefed and they've agreed to let me handle this."

"Tell me about her team." They both knew this would also be a briefing of possible suspects.

"These are the people in the field." He handed Alex another file. "There are six of them. Special Agents Linda Hauser and Maxwell Feller are undercover. They trained with Skye in Colorado and have worked with her on a number of cases."

"Including the one in which the Nancy Drew reference was found?"

"Yes. Linda is a Rhodes Scholar, accomplished in the martial arts, and a superb role player. She would have made an excellent actress if she were inclined to the stage. I have seen her play every part from a L.A. hooker to a college cheerleader. None better. She did a grieving widow once that could have won her an Oscar. Max is a real handful, but Skye really seems to like him. Brash, sarcastic, loud, but also a genius in the field. People underestimate his brain because of his nonstop mouth, but he's extremely intelligent. He used to be very volatile, but Skye has managed to smooth out some of his rough edges."

"Barclay Kimkoski is a computer genius Skye plucked out of the Tower to work the onsite computers and do some preliminary analysis with her captured data. He's worked with her for years but this is his first field assignment. As far as I know his social development stopped with the influx of personal computers, but Skye has managed to get him to integrate fairly well with the team. On the surface, he worships her."

"He has the tech skills to carry out the task of burying the original data and planting the documents."

"True."

"Do you know if it was he who found the original reference?"

"No, but I'll get that information for you." Jim took notes, then went on. "Lucas Kim is the electronics expert. He's in charge of all the surveillance equipment. There is no one better at what he does. If Barclay is a little vague around people, Lucas is unconscious. But if it has moving parts, Lucas can fix it, break it down, seduce it, and make it purr. Maureen Herman is a brilliant international attorney Skye relies on her to make sure all laws are carefully followed. Harvard grad and a real straight arrow. I will tell you, because you're going to read it in her dossier, she had a significant drug problem when she worked with an influential law firm in Alexandria. It was quite a plunge in prestige for her when the firm let her go and she came to work in our legal department, but she has blossomed and has become a first class field consultant. And finally, Judy Oxford has been with the department for almost three decades and takes care of all the administrative details and tactical coordination with local officials. She is a gem who has known Skye since she was a little girl. I think she had quite a thing for Perry back in the old days before he met Angelina. Of course every one of the young female admins around here did back then. I don't think even Pearl was immune. Dan Dickson and I would stand next to him just to catch all the women who bounced off. After her divorce she wanted out of Washington, so Skye pounced on the opportunity to use her skills on field assignments. What she used to do in the office, she now does in the field, increasing the efficiency of operations tremendously."

"Impressive, but nothing immediately suspicious."

"They are all top-notch people with impeccable records. Together they've been an incredible team and their work has been unimpeachable. The cases they have put together result in huge international busts and there are no loopholes or loose ends."

"So the only way anyone could escape the net they cast is to be forewarned and disappear?"

"Yes. And that is precisely what appears to have happened with the last case."

"Same team?"

"Yes, although Barclay was not an exclusive member. He did a lot of her work from the Tower. She always requested him. Strictly speaking, I should be taking her off the case and allowing the internal investigation to proceed without her at the helm of this critical international operation."

Alex considered the situation and said thoughtfully, "but if it isn't her, then someone is setting her up. And the reason could be precisely to get her off this case. That could be an even bigger problem and potentially very dangerous to her. Someone has made her or someone has turned on her. If she's as good as you say, it's most probably the latter. Either way, it's distracting you and if you react by pulling her out, it's diverting time and attention away from the central case. If they're trying to create a rift in the department or hamper the effectiveness of the current operation with an internal investigation, you'd be playing right into their hands by replacing her. And if much more time passes and you haven't done that, they may try to take her out more directly."

"Exactly." Jim got up and stared out the window at the Capitol. His troubled face set in a contemplative mask. "First things first. Do your investigation, file your report. Then we will determine our next step. She's smart and she's someone who can take care of herself, but if she needs a shield we will discuss a security plan. Follow her Alex, and watch her back."

"That will be one of the biggest pleasures of my life." Alex said as he conjured up the memory of that face, those eyes, that hair, that neck. Suddenly he stopped the mental inventory. This could be someone who had gone bad and if that was the case, he would bring her down.

"Now let's discuss the details," said Jim, getting down to business.

Early the next evening, Skye picked up Connie on the way to the airport. Half of her brain listened sympathetically to Connie's chatter about her dreadful date, while the other half went over the details of her assignment. When they walked through the terminal, Connie engaged Skye in her favorite game…spying men and rating them according to strict criterion, known only to Connie herself.

"Wow, there he is…the one I saw in the gift shop while you were getting the manifest…he's a definite 10…look over my shoulder…five o'clock," said Connie while she and Skye waited at the snack shop for their turn to buy an overpriced, watered-down soft drink.

"Connie, for God's sake, I'm not going to meet the man of my dreams in an airport. It just doesn't happen that way. Rating every man is something you should have given up when you stopped being a mall rat at 16," said Skye, chuckling over her friend's enthusiasm.

"But Skye…this one really looks like a God and his travel bag is a Gucci. The woman at the gift shop practically drooled all over my LifeSavers when he came in for a *Wall Street Journal.* She had to pop her eyes back into her head before she could make change. Oh man, oh man. You two would make the most gorgeous babies."

"Connie, I just…oh…all right." Sometimes it was easier to humor her than to fight her. Connie was the kind of person who bubbled you to death until you gave in under the sheer need for self-preservation. Rolling her eyes, Skye took a peek over her manifest in the age-old method of clandestine observation used by women for centuries to assess a man without the man knowing. She was just a bit better at it than most since she was a trained and seasoned agent for the Justice Department.

"My, oh my," she whispered appreciatively and Connie all but hooted in triumph. "You're right. That travel bag is a Gucci and top of the line, too. It's a beauty."

Connie blew air out of the back of her throat, half dismayed, half amused. "God, Skye, get a life!"

Skye smiled good-naturedly. It seemed like they had this conversation every time they walked together through an airport. "That's Captain to you until we leave the airport, and for your information, I have a life. I fly jets, I read books on jets, and I watch "Top Gun" every weekend."

"Well, Captain, at least that flick has the yummy Tom Cruise in it."

"It does? Hmmm. I'll have to watch it again. I must have missed that."

"That's because you probably fast forward through all the naked kissing parts right to the ball-busting flying parts."

"One male body is pretty much like every other male body…but the planes. Now that's something to watch in action," said Skye.

"Yeah…like you've seen a bunch of male bodies. Good grief, Skye. I'm beginning to wonder about your hormones. What are you made of anyway? Steel?"

"Yup. They insist on it in flight school." Skye squirreled another peek at her quarry. She wouldn't have admitted it to Connie. To encourage her would be to court insanity, but from the quick glance she stole she had to admit that Connie was right on this one. He was an eye full.

"Look, if he's on our flight, just signal me and I'll arrange to fly into some turbulence when you walk the aisles. Maybe if it's rough enough, you can accidentally tumble into his lap," said Skye.

"Yeah…right. If you flew into turbulence, he would probably turn green and ralph all over me." She lost sight of the perfect 10 and swiveled her head as a tall black-haired man swept by to look at the monitor. "Besides, he's a little pale for my tastes." Connie had skin the color of rich mahogany.

"Wow…there's another one. He's only an 8, but that puts him in my league. See you on board, Captain. I think I'll follow him around until he catches me."

"See you on board, Connie," Skye laughed out loud as Connie walked up to Mr. 8 and asked if she could help him find his flight.

Alex continued walking down the concourse with the *Wall Street Journal* under his arm, never suspecting that Skye had an image of him neatly filed away in her memory.

CHAPTER 4

"So, you going out with that knight of the round table again when you're in London?" Bill asked Skye when they had reached altitude and switched on the automatic pilot.

"Yes I am. We have several functions scheduled."

"God, Skye. Listen to yourself," said Bill, shaking his head. "You schedule appointments instead of have dates. Honestly, sometimes I fret over whether you're ever going to find anyone."

"Stop fretting. I'm not looking for a serious relationship right now."

"You've said that ever since I've known you. Loosen up. Don't be so rigid. It turns men off. You're already about the most intimidating package under the sun. Soften your smile and your attitude. Be natural, artless, unstructured."

"Oh yeah. I'd try that and I would explode into thousands of little body parts. I'm not made that way," said Skye.

"Can't you be spontaneous?"

"You mean like decide on the spur of the moment to fly this bird to Paris because I feel like a baguette?"

"No, I mean in your personal life. When a guy asks you out, I bet you say 'Pick me up at eighteen hundred' instead of something a bit more friendly like '6ish,'" said Bill.

"You're so not funny."

"But am I right? Huh? Huh?"

She remembered the last time she was in London and she and Phillip were determining the best time to meet for tea. "When shall I bring the car around to fetch you?" he had asked in that very proper way of his. "How about eighteen hundred?" she had said and actually had to translate it for Phillip. Bill was right again. She looked over at him, gloating and pretending to read the altimeter. The guy was really aggravating.

They landed in London right on schedule. Skye felt the rush of anticipation every time she walked through the terminal, anxious to start work again on her other job.

"Have a great time at the museums, Bill. See you in a couple of days," said Skye as he walked toward the terminal exit.

"Oh my gosh…there he is. In person!" explained Connie.

"Who?" Skye looked around.

"The stud muffin with the title. He's so gorgeous. And rich. And titled. I see his picture in the tabloids nearly every week. He's much, much yummier in person. A 10 plus, because of all the property he owns."

She kept up the running commentary as they moved out of the Customs area and into the terminal, telling Skye about the photographs she saw of the estate he grew up on and would some day inherit. Connie described it and many of the fascinating tidbits she knew about the Blythes. Skye smiled. Maybe she should forget dating Phillip to find out his secrets. Maybe she should just ask Connie.

Skye was surprised to see him. Phillip never met her flights and it was unusual to see him here mingling with the mass of humanity one sees at an airport. All the classes in one crowded spot. It would make him queasy. He was a snob of the first order and never really liked being around people who were not polished, well bred, and upper class. He was standing there regally aristocratic in his expensive suit, holding flowers, roses of course, and smiling benignly. He didn't approach her. He would expect her to come to him and, because he was her assignment, she did. And, because she knew it would annoy him, not that he would ever show it, she decided she would introduce him to Connie. In his mind, Connie was a subordinate and should be kept in her place…far, far away.

And Phillip was thinking just that. As Skye walked over to him, she gave him her most dazzling smile. It was blinding. In her uniform, with her cap pulled down over her forehead, and her hair severely tamed, she was the picture of both beauty and control. Perfect, Phillip thought. Now if he could only wean her of her fondness for people beneath her. She was walking with a stewardess, for God's sake. Neither her social equal, nor her professional one. Colonial attitudes. Well, if she could fly a plane, she could most certainly learn the rules of comportment. And he was willing to be her teacher. He considered Skyler Madison to be one of the luckiest women alive. Feeling like Professor Henry Higgins in *Pygmalion,* he decided he was going to transform this ravishing creature into a Lady.

"Phillip!" exclaimed Skye putting just the right tone of delight in her voice. She was a consummate role player. There was no Academy Award on her mantle, but at times like these she felt she had earned one. "How nice of you to meet me here."

"Skyler," acknowledged Phillip, making a mental note to remind her it was *Sir* Phillip in public. He stood aloof and nodded his greeting. There was never to be any public displays of emotion or affection. Her first lesson in becoming a Lady. "It's a pleasure to see you."

Connie felt the chill and almost shivered. She couldn't imagine anything colder. Suddenly, in a complete reversal of opinion, she lowered Phillip's ranking to a 7 minus and hoped fervently that Skye wasn't gone on this guy. He may be just about the handsomest man she'd ever seen, but how could you get by the exterior shield of ice to enjoy it? And money wasn't everything. And country castles? Phewy. You'd probably need a map to find a bathroom in that big estate of his anyway. No. This wasn't the person to melt the heart of her friend. She had much higher hopes for Skye.

"Phillip, this is Connie Monroe. She's the head flight attendant and my friend. Connie, this is Lord Phillip Blythe."

Connie wasn't sure what she should say. "How's it shaking, Lord?" would have been her preference, but she was positive that wasn't it.

"How do you do, Lord Blythe," she said with proper respect in her voice. Hey, her mom taught her manners. Besides, she'd served enough snobs in first class to know their sense of entitlement and how to play to it. "It's a pleasure to meet you."

Phillip moved his gaze over to her for the briefest glance and nodded slightly. He didn't offer her his hand. He didn't acknowledge her again. She was invisible. He focused his attention on Skye.

"I came to offer you a ride. Your man at the front counter told me that I should meet you here. I was going to send Franklin, but I thought this might be a nicer surprise." He was going to knock her off her feet. It was part of his plan to turn up the heat on their relationship.

Skye ruthlessly suppressed her inclination to shove his flowers up his tight ass. His dismissal of her friend was cold and cruel. But she wasn't going to invest any more emotion than was necessary on this man. The fact that he was delusional enough to think she was in love with him worked in her favor. She would make it up to Connie later. Her smile broadened and she put on an expression of undiluted pleasure.

46

"Phillip. You have truly made my day."

Connie's puzzlement was evident in her confused look. She'd expected a slice, dice, and burn from Skye. She'd seen her leave men bleeding from the jugular with their balls in their pocket for the smallest slight. Her friend could split concrete with just one look then pound it into dust with her tongue. Oh, well. They would talk later. Skye was obviously acting. She could see it in the contradiction of her signals. They were subtle, but someone who knew her as well as Connie could see them. Skye's face was smiling, but not her eyes. Her words communicated pleasure, but not her posture. Was the guy a dolt? His rating was plummeting. Down to 5 and sliding fast.

"Nice to have met you, Lord Blythe. I'll see you later, Captain. I'm meeting Vince and I think I see him now." There was a gaggle of teenagers in a corner of the terminal surrounding a tall, smiling man with orange hair.

"'Bye. Have a nice time this evening." She smiled at Connie, her eyes apologetic and signaling they would talk later.

Connie smiled back. She already had it figured out. Being the daughter of an ambassador meant Skye had a need to be polite to the Lords and Ladies of another country. Kind of like an Ambassador of Good Will. One couldn't stamp out years of early childhood training. Skye sure wasn't hot for this guy; that was clear as glass. Having a logical explanation put Connie's mind at rest and she walked over to the guy she was meeting. She decided she would not offer to introduce him to Lord Phillip Blythe. Her guy was a lead guitarist for a heavy metal band. The fact that he was as rich as a Lord still didn't put him in Phillip's class. The British and their royalty. Posh.

Without another word, Phillip turned and started toward the exit. Skye fell into step beside him. They were of equal height and Phillip considered that a bit of a flaw. She would just have to wear flat shoes when they were together in public. Her long shapely legs could support the look, he thought critically.

"Are those for me?" Skye asked, indicating the flowers.

"Indeed they are." He handed them to her as if he was giving her the wealth of nations.

She accepted them in the same spirit. "They're absolutely lovely. Are they from your gardens?"

"Naturally. We have the finest gardens and the most extensive greenhouses in England. We grow our own hybrids. Remove all flaws in the line through rational, careful breeding. Rather like British royalty." He chuckled at his amazingly sharp wit.

Skye joined him with her best phony titter. The flowers were beautiful, but she noticed they had no fragrance. Just like him, she thought. Over-bred and superficial.

"This really is a wonderful surprise. Are we still on for tonight?"

"Still on?" He knew what the barbaric phrase meant. He just didn't want her to use it in his presence anymore.

"Still engaged for the evening," Skye corrected, remaining civil and smiling only by employing a visualization technique…imagining him walking through the terminal in only a thong. A pink one. A teeny weenie florescent pink one. It worked well. It kept an amused look on her face that Phillip took for pleasure of the highest order.

Unaware of his near naked status in Skye's mind, Phillip thought her selection of words was more appropriate and gave her an approving smile. Reward her after her behavior conforms. This was how his trainer maintained the proper decorum of the several dogs in the kennel. Corgies, of course. The Queen's favorite. Should work with this female, as well. He had no idea how close he was to being maimed.

"Actually, that's one reason I'm here. I'm afraid other matters have come up and it's impossible for me to get away for dinner. I thought we could have luncheon before I have to dash off."

"I couldn't think of anything I would like more," said Skye, her voice dripping with sincerity.

This time she meant it. Hot damn! After an insufferable lunch she would be able to ditch him and go to her room for a long shower and a nap. She could work with her team tonight. It was like Christmas in March. The smile she gave him was genuine and dazzling.

Phillip liked the look. Good dentistry. He rewarded her by putting his hand on the small of her back when they reached the automatic doors and led her out to his waiting vintage limousine. His driver, Franklin, bowed slightly, opened the door, and allowed Phillip to give Skye a hand. She gracefully got in the back seat as if she was born to royalty. Phillip heartily approved of her elegance and style. There was nothing wrong with the long, well-defined leg she showed as she moved over to make room for him. It was her manner, vocabulary, and other traits that would need modification.

Alex got into his waiting rental car. He liked what he saw so far. Her picture didn't do her justice. She wasn't just beautiful, she was ravishing. As she walked through the terminal, heads turned. The fact that she didn't seem to notice and if she did, could care less, actually added to her appeal. It wasn't just the looks, it was the attitude. She was confident, self-assured, and in complete control. His reaction to her when he saw her exit from Customs was a physical jolt. The facts in the dossier and the briefing he received from Jim cast her in a very favorable and sympathetic light, but he was determined to be objective and impartial. It was far too early to draw any conclusions…except one. On a purely physical level, she was every man's fantasy.

He kept telling himself he was a machine. He would observe, record, watch, monitor, and scrutinize her every move. And what moves. The tilt of the head, the graceful stride, the full lips parted in a smile. She looked impeccable and her eyes bright even though he knew she'd been flying a plane all night. He wondered what she would look like without the uniform. Whoa. He had to shake that thought. Then he visualized her hands on the throttle of the plane, those long, lean fingers gripping the controls. He turned up the air conditioning full blast and loosened his tie. It was time to change his appearance anyway.

He got himself firmly under control and reflected on his observations so far. First of all, he had to agree that she hadn't turned for love - at least not her love for Phillip. From her very subtle body language and the flash in her eyes when Phillip wasn't looking, Alex would say she was tolerating him only because he was her assigned mark. She was very, very good, but so was his eye for detail.

There had been no unusual activity on her part. No extra movement, no interest in the cargo, no hidden private cell phone, no suspicious conversations with passengers or other people at the terminal. She went right from the plane, straight through Customs, then out the door with that prick Sir Phillip. If she had been passing on information, he didn't see it and he was the best Jim had. She made one call from her personal cell phone, but no other. Alex made a mental note to check her phone records, but he thought he heard her say Sloane and remembered that was the name of her sister.

They were booked into the same hotel. It made things simpler and was his preferred London hotel anyway. He was going to stay close to Skyler Madison. She was an intriguing, dazzling, captivating woman. This assignment was going to be more pleasure than pain, that was for sure. If she was dirty, then at least he had something nice to look at while he collected the information to bring her down. It sure beat gathering data on fat old accountants and their bank accounts.

CHAPTER 5

Skye saw him out of the corner of her eye. She didn't turn her head and she didn't change her expression. Phillip was in the middle of one of his mind-numbing monologues, this time about the cleaning and care of his heirloom jewelry. He probably thought this would impress her because he got to tell her about every exquisite piece. Every single piece. No piece was too small to mention. God, where the hell was their lunch? At least if she was eating, she could pass the time productively. If Skye would have been at all interested in Phillip's blather she would have missed the sighting. As it turned out, she had nothing better to do than subtly scan the room.

There was Mr. 10! Connie's dream man. Hmmm. Now that was a coincidence. He was alone. Hmmm. Now that could be interesting. More interesting than the ruby stickpin that Phillip's great aunt someone or other brought back with her from somewhere or other.

Einstein once said, "Sit next to a beautiful woman for an hour, it seems like a minute. Sit on a red-hot stove for a minute, it seems like an hour. That's relativity." Well, thought Skye as she recalled the quotation, she felt like she had her ass planted on a red-hot stove. The only thing that kept her awake and alert was her inner dialogue. She went through lists, evidence, conversations, the design of her dream house, and the entire plot of every Shakespeare play she had ever attended, read, or saw on public television. Must be all the British accents.

She used to think that if she listened to his drivel, she would learn something useful to the case. The man hadn't said anything relevant in, well, never. It was his files that gave her the only useful tidbits of information they had gleaned from this contact. Still he was her entrée on to the huge family estate. Skye was convinced that they would find the lair there. And when they did, they could schedule a raid, find the drugs, seize the data, arrest this moron, and put her out of her misery. She kept that picture in her mind as a tool for making her smile more genuine. Anything that worked.

She already had all the information from his Palm Pilot on disks secured in her purse. She pulled it out of his breast pocket so artfully that he didn't even blink. Not only a dolt, but one with absolutely no external perception. She'd returned it as he pulled out her chair when she came back from the ladies room. Her relatively long absence must have meant nothing to him. He had himself to keep him company, after all.

She allowed herself just the quickest peek at Mr. 10 when the waiter served their lunch. Now, here was a man she would like to get to know. Very handsome, interesting face, great body. Obviously connected and wealthy or he wouldn't have been allowed in this bastion of high-end snobbery.

She smiled at Phillip, who was ordering dessert wine in his imperious voice. Just one quick punch to the face, she thought. It would only take one. Then she could end this wretchedness and she would be free to go over and introduce herself to Mr. 10. She sighed. Internally, of course. No, she had to exercise restraint. Sometimes her monumental self-control was a pain in the ass and a real killjoy.

A headache was coming on strong right behind her eyes, probably the result of being up for over twenty-four hours, then being bombarded with pretentious drivel. Suddenly she perked up. Her adrenaline gave her a little booster. What had he just said? She knew he would probably repeat it seventeen times before the end of the meal, but it was something important. Damn, she let Mr. 10 distract her for a second. Wrong second. It coincided with the first thing she wanted to hear in weeks.

"What was that, Phillip?" she said in a sweet, fascinated voice. "I was admiring your ring and I must have let my mind wander to its fascinating history."

Phillip beamed. God, the guy was clueless, thought Skye. He fell for that.

"You're forgiven my dear. It was fascinating wasn't it? Anyway, I want to invite you to our country estate at the end of the month. The Duke and Duchess are having a charity gala." He never called them Mom and Dad. It made her shudder…inside, of course. "You said you would be in town, and I would love for you to drive down. You might as well. No one who is anyone will be left in town." He chuckled again at his incredible wit.

Feeling very, very charitable, she chucked, too. Hot bloody damn. This was excellent. Just what she'd been waiting for. Her friends at Scotland Yard weren't sure this was ever going to happen. She was a commoner and that made her, well, common. The very proper Duke and Duchess wouldn't want the lower class to think they could enter the glorified world of the gentry. The hordes of modern day provincial serfs might just stage an uprising and start subdividing the old estates in the country, maybe even thin the blue blood by intermarrying. In Skye's humble colonial opinion, some of this blue blood could use a boost of plebian red. Not that she was willing to make the sacrifice.

Skye's smile was dazzling and her added energy was evident in her enthusiastic response. "Oh, Phillip. My fondest wish. You sure know how to make a woman's dreams come true." She picked up her wine glass to wash down the words. Christ, what she didn't do for her country. Phillip's chest expanded. Not large enough to house his ego yet, but getting closer.

Phillip watched her, pleased with her enthusiasm for his idea. This was part of the plan, he thought. His plan. He wanted her for himself and the Duke and Duchess wanted her for the operation. He knew he was up to the task of seducing this incredible woman, but having the backdrop of a sixteenth century manor house would be his coup de grace. She was his. She was theirs. It was only a matter of time.

"You may, of course, bring an escort. I'll have multiple duties assigned to me, being the heir, so you may wish to have an attendant. Just call my office with the name."

He felt anyone she brought would definitely be found lacking in the direct comparison. Another step to her eventual surrender.

As Phillip watched her eat, he started making a list of the things he would have to modify. The Duke and Duchess wanted Skye to continue to fly. That was the reason they marked her. A captain on a major airline. Well, that would be an incredible asset. When he met Skyler, quite by accident, at the home of a mutual friend, she fascinated him because of her stunning good looks and her, well, equally luscious body. The Duke and Duchess encouraged him to cultivate her and try to turn her. Not that it was a hardship. She was beautiful.

Now, let's see, he thought, back to the list. She would have to do something about all that hair. It looked tolerable right now, but he had seen it when she went horseback riding and it escaped the clip. It was unruly. Phillip hated anything unruly. Then there were her associates. They were gone. She smiled at him as she brought a spoonful of chocolate torte to her lips. Her table manners were above reproach, but her appetite! Far too robust for a woman of quality. Yes, this would be his *Pygmalion*. His *My Fair Lady*. His finest hour. Churchill had World War II and he had Skyler. What heroes England produced! When he was through instructing her she would be fit to meet the Queen. Yes, things were going well. He flashed his ring and told her its fascinating history one more time.

Alex watched them. They were an eye-catching couple with his aristocratic good looks, if you liked that kind of thing, and her regal bearing and dramatic beauty, which everyone in the room with a dick appeared to appreciate. People were staring at them. There was so much speculation flying around the room, he felt like ducking. Why was he so annoyed? Must be the jet lag.

He saw her snag the Palm Pilot. That was neat. Well done, Captain. He found himself wanting to applaud the skill and speed she exercised in nipping it right from under his elevated nose. What hands. He swallowed hard and took another sip of his wine. He just got a flash of those hands running over his body. He was glad she excused herself and disappeared for a while. It gave him time to get himself back under control. When she returned, he leaned back and surreptitiously watched the repeat performance, but in reverse. She was really remarkable. The dunce never felt a thing.

He noticed that Skye didn't say much. Just gazed into the man's supercilious, patronizing eyes…with just enough superficial adoration to puff up his atmospheric ego even more. Once in a while she would react to something he said with a smile or low laugh. Near the end of the meal, he must have said something that set her off, because he noticed a change in her posture. More animated, more interested. Maybe he misread the distaste in her eyes earlier. No. He didn't think so. That was during an unguarded moment. She had her guard up now. A complete façade as far as he could see.

They never touched. Not once. Cold. Impersonal. Aloof. Alex smiled. Made him feel a bit better about the whole thing, actually. He told himself it was because he wanted her to be innocent for Jim's sake. But ever since he saw her picture, an unfamiliar little voice inside him whispered that he wanted her to be clean for his sake, too. For his sake? God. When he heard the voice again as she got up to leave, he told it to shut the hell up. He was going to have to use the hotel gym tonight to work out some of this tension. It had to be the jet lag.

When they left, Phillip placed his hand on the small of her back. He stopped to chat with a number of people at the tables but never introduced her. She was his accessory, an ornament, just another family heirloom in the making. How did she stand it? She was either over the top in love with this asshole…that made him exhale derisively…or the most controlled, polished, professional he'd ever seen. Jim assured him it was the latter. Ah, there. The tiniest flash of annoyance appeared on her face when he stopped yet again and was looking at his acquaintance and not her. Alex smiled. You're very good, Special Agent Madison, but not completely superhuman.

Alex watched as Skye and Phillip parted company at the hotel. She got out of the car, waved adoringly, and smiled brilliantly. Alex almost choked and had to bite down on the laughter when Phillip was out of range and her face instantly changed into a look of complete disgust. She even gave the disappearing car the universal gesture of 'up yours.' Not superhuman, but completely human. Then she made an exaggerated shudder, shook out her tired arms and went into the lobby. He knew she was headed for her room. Her sleep cycle was long overdue. Staying in the background, he watched her cross the lobby.

As Skye got on the elevator she glanced in the mirrors just to the left of the doors. Old habit. Just a little peek to see if anyone was following. She nearly jumped when she caught a quick glimpse of Mr. 10. Getting on the elevator, she turned and pressed the button for her floor, as natural and as spontaneous as a woman without a care. He was gone. Maybe he was so much on her mind that she imagined it. No. She wasn't a woman who imagined such things. Hmmm. Twice, maybe a coincidence. But three times? Thoughtful and watchful, she scanned the lobby again as the doors slid shut, her training and intuition on high alert.

Alex continued to shadow her when she was on the move. And could she move, he thought. When she jogged, he was glad he was in shape enough to keep up. She was in awesome physical condition. Every time he returned from one of her runs, he was winded. He always had to resist the temptation to jog up beside her. He would have loved to run by her side in the early morning air when things were cool and fresh.

Alex had to keep reminding himself that she was an assignment. An assignment for God's sake. A job. A duty. A special operation. A possible liability for the department. It worked pretty well in the abstract, but he could feel it dissolving when he saw her in the flesh. Then she was a living, breathing person. Or rather a medley of people…many different faces, many different roles. She was the controlled, confident agent Skye. The uniformed, polished, pilot Skye. The laughing, good-natured, softer Skye. The serious, professional Skye. The physical, hard body Skye…his personal favorite. It was a fascinating parade and they were all uniquely and genuinely her. She was continually changing. It was why she was a superior agent. He had seen the records of her past cases and there was a reason why she was rising through the ranks so quickly.

When he wasn't watching her, he was thinking about her. Alex would pace his suite when he knew she was in her room sleeping or resting. He would imagine her there, in her bed, in the shower. When he couldn't shake the images, he would pace even more. One morning, he woke up and realized he had dreamed about her. They were having dinner and then they were dancing. He had her in his arms and they were moving to the music…she fit perfectly, her lithe and shapely body pressed to his. He got up, looked down with a mixture of horror and humor and stepped into a cold shower.

He had no idea the precise moment he stopped being a detached observer—rational and objective—but it gave him a jolt when he realized it. God, he was a mess. Who would have thought this would happen at this stage of his career? At this point in his life? He wasn't young or inexperienced. Skye was on her flight back to Dulles and wouldn't be back for four days. Four days for him to get a grip on himself. He looked down at the messages from the various women in his life. When he looked at their names and their numbers, he realized he had one in every port, but none in any part of his heart. Not one of his past lovers could measure up now that Skye had become the standard. He threw the messages into the trash. Alex realized he was becoming obsessed and the worst part of it was he didn't care. He really liked his obsession. Was becoming quite attached to it, actually. And if he was the only one who knew about it, who would ever know, what was the harm? No one had known about his obsession with Miss March 1987 either, and he got over that.

The next day, while he was shaving, he stopped in mid-motion, his face half covered with lather, his razor poised near his cheek. Alex looked at the familiar face until it smiled back at him. He could have sworn he saw a stupid love-struck look on his face. He nearly cut himself when his hand went back into motion. Christ. This was getting bad. He was just going to have to call one of those numbers and get laid. What was the name of that shapely attorney who represented the London broker? Damn. He couldn't even work up a tiny spark of interest. Nothing. Special Agent Springfield you are losing your mind.

Alex didn't want to admit to himself that it wasn't his mind he was losing, but his heart. He never did call any of the numbers or go back to try to uncover the name of the curvaceous attorney. Wasn't even tempted.

Alex reported to Jim every day he was on Skye's tail. All the reports were favorable and perfunctory. Nothing suspicious. Nothing to report other than the fact that Skye was efficiently and effectively doing her job. It helped him recapture his equilibrium to talk to his boss about an operation. He needed to be objective at some level because she still could be dirty. She could dazzle, to be sure. But he knew that it could be a tool for covering a black and jaded heart. Jim was blinded one way or the other and Alex knew that his first allegiance was to his oath and the mission. He didn't want to hurt Jim, but if the evidence revealed deception and corruption, his mentor could and would handle it. Alex knew he could handle it, too. He would have to. Still, there was a stone rolling around in his gut when he thought of her possible duplicity.

Their first break came about ten days into the mission. Jim called while Alex was watching Skye and Connie shopping in Harrods. It was more difficult for him to maintain invisibility in the ladies shoe department, but he proved his highly toned covert skills by managing to blend. Today he was a silver haired gay dress designer looking for just the right pair of beach sandals to compliment his new line of swim wear. He was completely baffled by the selection presented to him by an enthusiastic salesperson and wondered if he finally accepted a mission that had him swimming in water way, way over his head. When his secure phone pinged in his pocket, he grabbed it like a lifeline. It was Jim's voice. The question was direct and to the point.

"Where is she and what is she doing."

"She's right in front of me and she's working her way through her second dozen pair of shoes. If she doesn't make her selection pretty soon, I think you are going to have to accept my resignation."

Jim chuckled. "I take it she is not in a position to be sending messages."

"Not unless there is a covert communication device in a snazzy pair of red ankle boots and Harrods has become a hotbed of criminal activity."

"She's shopping."

"I swear she considers it an aerobic exercise."

"Excellent. File an official report tonight, Alex. She's just cleared the first step."

"Fine, now if I can ask you for some critical advice?"

"Go ahead. We're scrambled."

"What do you think would go better with a blue thong bikini, sandals with sunflowers between the toes, or a high-heeled gold weave?'

"She's driven you crazy already?"

"I think we can consider that a fact."

"Stay in touch."

"Count on it."

As Skye and Connie made their selections, Alex left an ecstatic salesperson in his wake. He had saved himself from making a decision by buying all the alternatives presented to him. His bravery, dedication and mental stability were tested further as his quarry moved into the lingerie department.

One day after an early morning flight back to London, Skye saw Mr. 10 again, just a glimpse. She was jogging through Hyde Park when a strange man came up behind her. He was large and not very fit, so he was winded. This gave her the advantage when he placed his hand on her shoulder. She knew he was there and had expected him to pass. When she felt a hand firmly grip her shoulder, she spun around in a lightening quick pivot, grabbed the stranger's hand, flipped him over and pinned him to the ground with her knee in his back. A constable came running over and as she looked up, she saw Mr.10 retreat into the shadows.

That did it. She was going to take direct action. Mr. 10 was stalking her and she was going to find out why.

"I almost broke cover." Alex was reporting to Jim. He had placed a call right away, considering it important enough for an immediate report. "She may have seen me, but I don't think so. A man came up behind her and made a grab for her."

"Christ, Alex, is she okay?"

"Yeah, she's fine. There's a part of me that's wondering why she needs backup. I almost didn't see it, it happened so fast. One minute the guy had his hand on her shoulder, the next he was on the ground, completely immobilized. A constable was right there and took him in. She may have gotten a glimpse of me when I reacted automatically and started to move forward, but it shouldn't be a problem. There were a lot of people around."

"Do you think he was after her, or was she just a random mark?" asked Jim.

"I think we have to assume this wasn't a random incident. Do you want to check this out, or shall I?"

"I'll do it. I don't want you to break cover, even with the local authorities. I'll get back to you," said Jim.

When Jim called him later that day, Alex was more than a little angry to learn that Skye had not pressed charges. The man claimed to be a tourist from Ohio who was just going to ask her the way to Buckingham Palace when all of a sudden he was on his stomach in the dirt. He showed an ID and was very contrite. When Jim pressed the officer he talked with, they ran a standard check on the ID. It was phony.

"I talked to Skye and she didn't mention it. I couldn't tell her I knew about it," said Jim.

"I think you should tell her about this, Jim. Tell her about me so I can come in closer. You're putting her in jeopardy. We know that for sure now. She's unaware that the dealers over here might know who she is. You might have to consider pulling her in after all." Alex's concern was deep and genuine. He was afraid for her and didn't want to see her in danger.

"I need to give it a few more days. By then she'll have made a third run into London with you on watch. That will provide enough corroboration of her incorruptibility. I'm counting on you to keep her safe. You're now both her shadow and her shield. As for pulling her in, that would have a serious negative impact on the operation. Besides, I would be playing right into the hands of the people responsible for this set-up."

"At what point is Skye more important than the operation?" snapped Alex. He wanted her out of London. It made his blood run cold to think of Skye being attacked again.

"I'll pretend I didn't hear that," Jim said coldly. "Skye is more important to me than my own life." Jim's voice had an edge of forged steel. "I understand your frustration and duly note your concern. It's one we share. I'm counting on you to keep her safe. Now go do your job."

There he was again. She saw him cross the lobby and enter the elevator. Perfect. "Hold, please," she called and slipped on just before the doors slid shut.

This was far closer than Alex ever expected to be. He could smell her subtle but spicy scent. It did very powerful things to his stomach. His physical reaction was unexpected and potent, but nothing in his demeanor revealed his discomfort. Others on the lift weren't nearly as circumspect. All male eyes in the small elevator slid to her, some surreptitiously, some not so subtly. Alex wondered where the slight feeling of annoyance came from. Didn't these guys have anything better to do than ogle a woman in the elevator?

Skye looked at the elevator buttons before she pressed her own floor. She was on the 11th. Buttons 6, 14, 18, 20 and 24 were lit. The penthouse suite was on the 24th floor. She noted his expensively tailored suit, his hand-made Italian shoes and his Rolex watch…Presidential Gold…over $15,000. He was definitely headed for the 24th floor. People got on and off and she never looked back at her quarry. When the elevator reached the 11th floor, she got out and went right to her room.

Alex realized he was holding his breath. Damn. Was that a coincidence or had she deliberately chosen the same elevator? She hadn't looked at him. As a matter of fact, she made a special point not to. Was that a factor? God, she was even more beautiful up close. She was taller than most of the men in the elevator, but that wasn't the only thing that made her so physically compelling. It was that alluring mouth, that wonderful hair a man wanted to bury his fingers into...he stopped abruptly as he was sliding his key card in the lock. Christ...what was he doing? She was his assignment, not someone he was going to ask to the prom. And he was a trained agent, not a schoolboy. But he was alone now, he thought. Alone with those fabulous, fabulous eyes.

As soon as he poured himself a glass of wine he made a call to Jim in Washington. He was put on hold and asked to wait. Jim didn't pick up for nearly 20 minutes. This wasn't unusual and Alex had completed his analysis of a draft for an offer to purchase on some warehouses in Philadelphia by the time he heard Jim's distracted and slightly irritated voice.

"I was just going to call you," Jim said. "I don't know how Skye did it, but I can tell you she definitely made you." Was that a little pride Alex heard mixed in with the information?

Damn it, her presence on the elevator wasn't a coincidence. "How did you find out?" asked Alex.

"She called me a few minutes ago. She requested an in-depth inquiry into your credentials and background and asked that the department go as deep as legally possible. She knew you were going to the 24th floor by how you were dressed. Actually priced your watch within $150. I guess she and the maid just had a breathy conversation about the fabulous looking man in the penthouse suite and she got your name."

"She said fabulous looking?" asked Alex, pleased. Then he realized he had actually been made for the first time in his career. "Shit. She's good. I swear I don't know what tipped her off. Fill me in."

"She said she noticed you at Dulles. Her head flight attendant pointed you out to her. Said she rated you a 10 and thought you two would make beautiful babies."

Alex nearly choked on his wine. "Skye said that?"

"No, her head flight attendant, Connie."

"Connie and I would make beautiful babies?"

"No, you and Skye."

"What's this...some kind of new code?"

"No…I guess it's a Connie thing. Anyway, Skye only got a glance at you, but it was enough. She imprints faster than anyone I know. Just bad luck. We didn't really factor in that Connie would be trying to set Skye up and that she, that would be Connie, ranked you high on her male scale, or something."

"It's a curse," said Alex sarcastically.

"I think this is all losing something in the translation. Anyway, Skye saw you again in the hotel, of course. We hadn't figured she would have ever seen you before, so we didn't think that would be a problem. Apparently she caught a glimpse of you in Hampstead's when she was having lunch with Phillip."

"Damn, she must have incredible peripheral vision. She never looked at me that I could tell. Quite the contrary. She looked completely enthralled with what Phillip was telling her," he said a bit sharper than he had intended.

Jim never missed a thing. He heard the harsh tone in Alex's voice. "You got a problem with how Skye is handling the case?"

"She sometimes looks like she's enjoying her assignment, that's all."

"That's her job. Phillip is a fool, but he does have some brains and intuition. She has to have him believe she's interested in him."

"How far have you directed her to go, Jim? Have you asked her to prostitute herself for the operation?"

It was a question he wanted to ask since he saw her but he never intended to say it out loud. Stupid move, Alex, he thought. You sound like an idiot. He regretted it as soon as he said it, but he found a part of him was anxious to hear Jim's answer.

"You're way, way out of line, Alex," Jim said with barely controlled rage. "I'll forget you asked that monumentally stupid question. What's gotten into you?"

Skye, his mind whispered. Skye has gotten into me. But he didn't say it out loud. Best to not finish making a complete ass out of himself.

"Nothing…sorry…just pissed that she made me, that's all. Actually this is quite serious. Do you think I'm completely compromised here?" asked Alex.

"Skye has an intuition that's phenomenal. Almost a sixth sense. She'll do a search on you on her own. We know what she'll find…all the press you have generated over the years. All the public information on you and your financial success. We've culled a great deal of it out of public circulation, but there will be enough to satisfy her. We'll give her a bit more, but there's really nothing that she'll find the least bit suspicious."

"Well, you certainly can control the information flow from your end. What now?"

"Let me give that some thought. In the meantime, whenever you leave your room, take everything you don't want her to see."

"You mean like my copy of *Sexual Fantasies with Animals*?"

"Yeah, like that. She'll toss your room. When she does, just be sure to give her peace of mind."

"Thanks for the warning. I usually leave a few traps, just to be sure of my privacy. She would have wondered why I wanted to do that. Seriously, all I really have over here that she would find suspicious is this secure phone, the weapons, and some alternative papers in case I need to disappear. I'll be sure I take them with me when I go out."

"Good idea," said Jim. "Don't think you can hide them. She's an ace when it comes to taking apart a room."

"I won't underestimate her again."

"I'm thinking about sending in Drake, and taking you out of it."

"No...don't do that. Give me a few days to see what I can do here," said Alex.

"Okay. Report frequently. I have to get something written up on you to send her by tomorrow."

Alex always thought a good offense was the best defense. A plan was formulating in his mind and he wanted to see how it played out cognitively before he acted on it. The next day, during Skye's sleep cycle, he thought and walked most of the afternoon. By the time he returned to the hotel, he was ready with a plan of action.

When he entered his suite, he knew she'd been there. She was good...very, very good. Almost uncanny. Nothing was the least bit out of place. Everything was precisely where he put it that morning. But he could feel it. She'd touched everything. His room had been thoroughly and expertly searched. What was it? Why was the feeling so strong? Was it the fact that he knew she was going to be here? Was it instinct?

He turned around slowly in the middle of the bedroom. Then he knew. He inhaled little snatches of the air like a wolf sniffing out its prey. That was it. He could barely, just barely smell the lingering scent of her. Had it not been so recently implanted in his mind, he would have missed it. He smiled. And sniffed deeply again. Even though he felt like a fool, what the hell. There was no one else in the suite. Within a few minutes the scent was completely gone. Alex felt a moment of regret, then changed his clothes and prepared for his next move.

His conversations with Jim included Skye's itinerary. According to his notes, she should be at a briefing at Scotland Yard until 6 p.m. so he decided to place himself outside the building in an outdoor café. He followed her there, then waited. He saw her step into the street, laughing and chatting with three men who appeared to be completely captivated by what she was saying. She, on the other hand was covertly scanning the environment while appearing to be engaged in intense conversation. That took talent, he thought, and his respect for her, already high, went up a solid degree.

He looked down at his paper and sipped his tea the exact moment he knew her visual scan would sweep him and his position. She knew he was there and she would know it wasn't a random event. When she began walking toward the hotel, he slowly folded his paper and followed. The game was afoot. Starting right now, he wanted to be seen.

Skye saw him again. They were just fleeting glimpses, but there were too many to be random or coincidence. Her search revealed nothing out of the ordinary. Or rather extraordinary. The man who was following her was Alexander Springfield, a wealthy, successful businessman. As soon as she had surmised he was headed for the penthouse on the 24th floor, she'd pumped one of the maids for his name. The maids were often willing to share information when asked by a friendly, regular guest. They knew everything, from who slept with whom to what people wore beneath their clothes. All she had to do was pretend a womanly interest in the "great looking man she just saw on the elevator," and Charise, her chambermaid, filled her in on everything she knew. Charise included his name, the fact that he liked a full American breakfast, rarely had women in the suite, was a regular, and brought all kinds of sophisticated equipment when he traveled. And also that he was a generous tipper and a very tidy man.

Her Internet search gave her a picture of his career from being a successful corporate attorney to building an empire in real estate through remarkable investing and legendary risk-taking. Jim's report would be sent through later the next day, but he had called to report that the preliminary research revealed nothing sinister. He was definitely someone who took risks, but he appeared to be a straight shooter and an unusual breed of businessperson…an ethical man who believed in being a good corporate citizen. Still…what was on the surface didn't always tell the story. The man she was currently pursuing was the son of a Duke after all, and she strongly believed he, his father, and possibly his mother, were connected to the high-priced illegal drug trade exploding throughout London's elite. Appearances and public information were not always indicators of a person's true character.

Skye didn't turn around once during her walk to the hotel, but she knew he was back there. She could feel it. He didn't have to stay too close. He would know the hotel was her destination from the direction she was headed.

By the time she arrived, she'd come to a decision. She thought a direct approach would be best. It occurred to her that she might just be paranoid, but then, that was an admirable feature in her line of work. Studying the list of hotel events, she lingered just inside the lobby when Alexander Springfield walked through the doors. She timed it perfectly. As he turned to go into the hotel bar to look for her, she was right beside him.

"Excuse me," asked Skye.

He turned and looked into the eyes that had been a part of both his nighttime and daytime fantasies of late. He ignored the current he felt running up and down his spinal cord. It was like she materialized out of his own thoughts. Nothing showed on his face, however, but pleasure.

"Yes?" he said casually, raising an eyebrow and smiling pleasantly.

"Are you by any chance following me?"

"Why, yes...as a matter of fact, I am," Alex answered.

She'd picked this very public place just in case she needed a backup. The one thing she didn't expect was his direct, almost casual manner and his quick admission that he was indeed deliberately following her. She had expected either a frustrated denial or a swift physical attack. This was beyond her experience. It was also fascinating.

"Is there any particular reason why?" asked Skye.

"Actually," he said as he turned and faced her directly. "There is a very particular reason why. First things first. My name is Alexander Springfield."

His whole manner was completely disarming her. She almost said, I know, but held her first reaction in check.

"And..." she prompted.

"And, would you like to join me at the bar for a drink while I attempt to explain myself?"

If for no other reason than plain curiosity, Skye found herself nodding slightly.

"Okay. I have a few minutes before I have to prepare to go out for the evening."

Alex smiled, nodded, and took her elbow to steer her toward a small table in the corner of the room. Her arm was muscular and as hard as the iron she must pump regularly. He liked how it felt under his fingers. He liked it very much.

Skye felt his strong hand on her elbow and resisted an urge to shake it off. This was, after all, a public place and she was in no immediate danger…unless she counted the way her heart was beating more rapidly than it should. Involvement could be very dangerous. Then she gave herself an internal scold. For heaven's sake, this was only a drink, not a proposal of marriage. But he was so good looking, even up close he appeared flawless. He rated a 10 in Connie's scale, and that was almost unheard of. Okay, Mr. 10, she thought. Let's see what else you're made of.

"What would you like?" asked Alex as a young woman came over to the table.

"A cup of tea, please."

"How British. A pot of Earl Grey and a pint of Guinness, please."

Alex turned his sky blue eyes to meet her chocolate brown.

I always did love that particular shade of blue, she thought. Like the color of the sky on a cloudless summer day.

He was thinking about how much he liked Swiss chocolate.

For a few heartbeats, they didn't speak.

"So you were going to tell me why you were following me," she pressed.

"I apologize. I thought I was being subtle, but I'm not very good at clandestine surveillance. Sam Spade, I'm not."

Liar, she thought. If Connie hadn't pointed him out originally, she wouldn't have perceived him…or at least not quite so quickly. He gave off none of the prickly vibes that people will throw when watching you. It was a fluke that she made him so quickly. But she was willing to put away her suspicions until after the full explanation.

"I'll concede that point and accept your apology, if it's sincere," said Skye.

He paused for a moment while the server discreetly placed the tea and Guinness on the table. She watched him while he signed for the tab. He was left-handed. His signature was neat and legible and he signed with tremendous authority. He was used to signing things…probably his law background. Probably took a class in signing things.

He nearly lost his train of thought as she brought her tea to her lips and delicately sipped the steaming hot brew. Just this simple act was performed with such a combination of grace and precision, he found it utterly erotic. Combine the act with the fact that it highlighted her incredible full lips and…*God. Get a grip, Alex. The woman sips her English tea and you're ready to jump her right here on the table.*

His eyes revealed nothing he didn't want her to see, however, so she remained comfortably in the dark.

"Okay, where was I?" asked Alex.

"The sincere, heartfelt apology and the explanation as to why you're stalking me."

"Oh, I'm sincere, and I assure you I'm not stalking you, Ms. Madison."

"Then how do you know my name and why do I see you every time I turn around?"

"The explanation is an easy one. It's no great mystery and there's no malevolent intent. You were the captain on the International Airlines flight scheduled just before mine on British Airways a couple weeks ago. I saw you in the terminal and was intrigued. I simply asked one of the people at the International counter for the name of the captain of Flight 127. I thought I would have to wait to contact you until I returned to the States, so you can imagine my delight when I saw you in the lobby of this hotel. I thought when my schedule freed up, I would like to ask you to have dinner with me. Today, my schedule became clear and I followed you to Scotland Yard and waited. Having trouble with the law?"

She couldn't have been more shocked. Her jaw almost dropped, literally. She decided to ignore the law question and key in on his intent.

"To dinner? You've been following me so that you could ask me out to dinner?" She fully intended to check out his story about his flight to London. If he had a different agenda, these small details could trip him up. She was a stickler for small details. In the meantime...

"Yes, just dinner. And I've hardly been following you around the city. I'm staying at this hotel and today I just conveniently put myself in your path. It's how I do business. I see something that intrigues me and I find a way to make it happen."

His story sounded just improbable enough to be the truth. And it did jive with what she read about him. One of the articles described him as a creative, aggressive, risk-taker. Still...

Alex laughed at the skeptical look on her face. "Have dinner with me. It'll give you an opportunity to get to know me."

"Just dinner?" asked Skye, doubtfully.

"Yes." For now, he thought. "Still suspicious?"

"Well, I can think of many more direct approaches for getting a date than following a woman around London," said Skye.

"And those would be...?"

"Call, leave a message, send an email, oh...I don't know...put your request in a box of Godiva Chocolates."

"If I did any of those things, it would have been too easy for you to say no. I'm a businessperson. When I have something I want to pursue, I like to be engaged personally." He gave her one of his best smiles. He sounded sincere because he was sincere.

"So I am an objective? Like a corporate take over, or something?" Her tone softened...a little.

"More like a potential merger," he said in a friendly, amused tone.

She liked it. She liked him. What the hell, she thought. After all, she had his complete dossier on the way and she'd found nothing odd or suspicious when she tossed his room. Besides, he was a 10. And those eyes. She was used to fast, intuitive decisions. This felt okay. Actually a lot better than okay. She made her decision and smiled.

"I'm busy this evening, and I have a flight out tomorrow. However, if you're still in London when I get back at the end of the week, I think dinner would be fine."

They continued to chat and she began to relax, enjoying the conversation and the feeling of anticipation.

His heart rate continued to climb and he made a mental note to send a box of Godiva Chocolate to her room with the confirmation of their date secured inside.

"This complicates things a bit," said Jim, annoyed that Alex proceeded with a tactical plan without consult. The fact that it was what he trained his agents to do in the field was beside the point.

"Not really. We're having dinner later this week," said Alex.

"I told you to stay close, but I didn't mean it had to be that close."

"I think it works. It gives us a reason to be together. If necessary, I'm perfectly willing to sacrifice my body in the pursuit of information. No cost is too great for my country."

"God damn it...don't tell me these things. Dinner is approved, but hands off. I mean it."

Alex bristled at Jim's possessive and slightly threatening tone. "Oh really? Staking a prior claim, sir?" asked Alex with far more sarcasm than he intended. He could feel the heat rising inside him and it made him far less tactful than would be his usual style.

"Exactly what do you mean by that crack?" responded Jim, irritated by both the tone and the implication.

Alex took a deep breath. Well, he just about ripped it completely, might as well go all the way in.

"I'm sorry sir, but to really do my job, I have to eliminate the possibility that your judgment is clouded by an intimate relationship."

The silence was deafening. Alex knew he crossed a line, but he also knew how to wait for an answer. Finally Jim responded and Alex realized he had spent the time getting himself under control. His tone was barely civil and chilled to the bone.

"Since I can't punch you out over the phone, I think I'll just be flattered instead. I should let you stew about it for a while, but I can't have your mind distracted by that possibility. You're talking about the daughter of my best friend. Skye is my godchild and I think of her as one of my own. Harriet and I've stood in for Angelina and Perry at every important milestone in that girl's life. I've known her since the moment she was born. I know her character. I know what drives her. She's straight. There's no doubt in my mind. I would trust her with my life, and have on more than one occasion. Does that adequately enlighten you as to our relationship, Special Agent?" His voice was firm and frosty.

"Sorry, sir. Really. I was out of line," said Alex, feeling both utterly ridiculous and totally relieved.

"Now, back to this sacrificing your body issue," Jim said, obviously appreciating the apology and getting some of his sense of humor back. "You know it's something we haven't required of our agents in a long time. In Skye's case, we would have had too many volunteers. As a matter of fact, I think restraint is the best course of action here. It'll keep you on your toes. From what I hear from the younger agents, she's responsible for more than one cold shower and sleepless night."

"Sir, I could safely say that she would tempt the Angel Gabriel himself. On the other hand, out of respect for your prowess with firearms, I'll clamp on the restraints."

For now, he thought. In the meantime, he was going to take yet another cold shower.

Later that week, Alex met Skye in the lobby. He took her arm and escorted her to the limousine he had rented for the evening. They could have taken a cab, but the little boy lurking in every grown man wanted to impress the pretty girl. He gave the driver the address and settled back.

Skye was impressed...and fascinated. They chatted over iced champagne and engaged in the normal dating ritual of searching for things in common. They discovered a lot of things to talk about. God, she really needed a night off, and to spend it in the company of a witty, wickedly handsome man, well…all the better. It beat going over reports in her hotel room. She would try to fit that in later.

They had a delicious meal in an exclusive restaurant and exchanged stories of various cities they both had visited over the years. Everything she was hearing coincided exactly with Jim's report and her research. She found herself relaxing and really enjoying herself.

"Skyler isn't a very common name, but one that seems perfect for a captain of an airline. Is it a name the company gave you when you got your wings or did your parents predestine you to seek the sky?" Alex was intrigued by everything about her.

Skye cocked her head and smiled. "I never really thought of a name being part of a person's destiny. So, do you think if my name had been Rose, I would have been preordained to be a florist?"

Alex laughed. "I guess that was a pretty fanciful theory."

"Actually it isn't as serendipitous as it may seem. My father was a pilot and he selected the name. According to what he told a family friend, I was conceived, shall we say, during my mother's initiation into the Mile High Club. So Skye was inspired by his…interests."

"Ah. That certainly explains it. So I guess if he had been an author, your name would be Paige?"

"Something like that. Although flying wasn't his profession, just his hobby. He was an international banker, so if he hadn't preferred the sky to currency exchange, my name might have been…"

"Penny," he interrupted and was rewarded by her easy, contagious laughter. "Although Goldie may have been a better choice."

He reached over and touched one of the blonde curls spilling from the top of her head. It was an oddly intimate gesture and sent a spark of fire right down to the center of her body and back up to her throat.

"Now you really are getting fanciful." She found she liked the combination of the light tone of the conversation and the heavy dose of sexuality underlying it.

Alex liked the feel of her curl, something he had wanted to touch since he was in the backseat of the limo. It took a moment before Alex realized it might be his turn to say something.

"So, what did your mother think of his choice?"

"According to family folklore, she was delighted. Skyler means scholar, so she actually thought a professor in the family would be perfect.

Unfortunately I took the controls of my dad's Cessna before I went to school and that settled my destiny." Sky swallowed and realized her throat had opened up again. "Tell me about your family. Are you from a long line of rich tycoons?"

"No, I'm actually from a long line of cops," responded Alex.

"Cops?" That surprised her.

"My Grandpa was a Chicago cop before he and my Grandma retired to the good life in Sun City, Arizona. My two uncles are cops. One is a state trooper in Illinois, and the other works for the FBI."

"Man, that's really what you call being protected and I bet you never have to worry about a speeding ticket," said Skye.

"That's right. And I get to go to the head of the line when I take out-of-town associates on tour through the Hoover Building."

"Now that's a reason to tap your connections. What about your parents?"

"Mom's a captain of detectives with the Chicago police department and Dad is a District Attorney for Illinois. Mom bags 'em and Dad puts 'em away."

"Sounds like a nice arrangement." She smiled, delighted with the picture he painted of his parents.

"Yeah, makes for interesting dinner conversations. Autopsy reports, chain of evidence, dismemberment."

"Brothers? Sisters?" asked Skye.

"One of each. Tank, that's what we call my little brother, is at the academy and will get his shield this summer. My sister Rita," he paused. His smile faded and his eyes took on a melancholy, somewhat haunted look. Skye's heart clutched and swelled with compassion. She knew what his next words were going to be before he said them. The look of grief and regret was something she recognized. She'd felt the wave of sorrow too often herself not to know just what was in his heart. Instinctively she placed her hand over his.

"She was a cop in New York City. She wanted to get away from all the Springfields haunting the Chicago area. She…she was killed in the line of duty."

Now her heart bled. She hadn't gotten to the personal information in his dossier yet and had no idea. She squeezed his hand with soft understanding and complete empathy.

"God, Alex. I'm so sorry. Was she married?"

He shook himself and a small smile formed on his lips. The sadness didn't leave his eyes, however and he turned his hand to take hers, grateful for the contact. "David, her husband, is still a Detective on the force up there. He's a great guy. It took him years to find his center again, but I think he's going to be okay. His boys kept him from swallowing a bullet after it happened."

"Boys?" God, could it get any worse? "She was a mother, too?"

"Yeah. You'd think that would make it more horrific, harder to accept, but actually that hasn't been the case. They're both so much like my sister that it seems like she's still around," said Alex.

"That's really nice. How old are they?" asked Skye.

"The little beasts are 7 and 10. Of course they both want to be cops. If they stay out of jail, they just might make good ones. They're fearless in the face of superior forces and they're as diabolical as hell."

"You see them a lot?" asked Skye.

"Oh, yes. I'm their source for all things electronic. Gameboy, Nintendo, Playstation. They spend a lot of time with me. It gives David a break and it seems like it gives me a bit of Rita back. They really are terrific kids."

"Sounds like you wouldn't mind having a few of your own."

"Oh, God." Alex chuckled easily, shaking the last shards of pain out of his eyes. "I'm not quite ready for that kind of insanity yet."

"It's surprising you didn't heed the call of law enforcement yourself."

He shuddered. "Christ, no. I got all the wimp genes in my family…and they're pretty powerful. Saved them up over three generations. I want no more excitement in my life than anticipating the direction of the Dow Jones Average and nothing more life threatening than eating oysters at the New Jersey shore." He hated lying to her, but he knew he was good at it. All part of the training, he thought with derision. "Now, shall we do something really life threatening and order dessert? I noticed they have Death by Chocolate on the menu." He really, really wanted to change the subject before he dug himself a deeper hole.

Skye smiled. Somehow the wimp factor didn't really jive, but she found it appealing. And safe. She needed and wanted safe. Skye let her guard down and felt the impact of his considerable charm and charisma. Maybe it was time for a little diversion. It had been a long time since her last relationship and she was hungry. She refused to date other agents and pilots, and passengers were out of the question. That didn't leave a whole lot of men in the dating pool.

Alex was a whole new category of man. He looked to her like a full-course meal, complete with dessert and champagne. Her mouth nearly watered and it had nothing to do with Death by Chocolate. Her eyes flashed passion; her smile turned beguiling, and she took another slow sip of her wine. She sat back, raised an enticing eyebrow, and shot sparks across the table straight to his heart.

They hit their mark and nearly laid him flat. He could tell she switched something on and he didn't think it was his suggestion of dessert. His heart skipped a beat and he actually stopped breathing for a minute while he enjoyed the feeling of being assessed, appraised, and deemed worthy. Of what, he wasn't yet sure. He knew there was going to be hell to pay when she discovered his deception. For now, though, he was going to enjoy the ride. He turned his testosterone up a notch, put more dazzle in his smile and nearly blinded the hostess as he motioned her over to the table to order dessert. This was far from the end of the meal, he thought. He intended to savor the flavor of one Skyler Madison before morning. To hell with the consequences.

Just then his phone vibrated. Taking it out of his jacket pocket, he looked apologetically at Skye. "Would you excuse me for just a second. It's a call I've been expecting. I sure I'm breaking several solid rules of etiquette, but I promise to make it up to you."

Skye laughed easily. "I understand completely." She patted her purse. "I'll take the opportunity to check my own messages."

Nodding, he walked to the lobby and took Jim's call.

"Where is she and what is she doing?"

"She's at Velentias and she is, I believe, just about ready to order dessert."

"She with someone?"

"Yes."

"Someone we can verify has no ties to the cartel?"

"Yes."

"Unimpeachable?"

"In the extreme."

"Well?"

"Me."

There was a very loud silence on the other end of the line, then a cool request to file a report followed by the equivalent of a high-tech, secure dial tone.

"You're welcome," he said putting the phone back in his pocket and smiling. Skye was looking cleaner, then realized she was on her own cell phone. Did she have the capacity to initiate a transmission from her portable unit? He would have to take a look. Maybe tonight while she was sleeping in his hotel room. Feeling like James Bond, he returned to the table.

"Let's walk," she said after he paid the bill and they left the restaurant. She wanted to stretch her legs and extend the tension a bit to increase the sweetness of the final payoff.

"Great idea." Alex took her hand in his. Her fingers were strong, long, and completely captivating. He was done in by the image of them moving over his body. Taking a deep breath and letting it out slowly, Alex decided he better turn down the heat of his desire or he was going to singe her pretty fingers.

Skye sensed his thoughts and because they ran fairly parallel with hers, she relaxed into conversation and enjoyed the balmy evening. They paused to look out over the Thames.

"So, do you own any buildings here in London?"

"Not yet, but that's the reason I'm staying for a few extra days." He stopped and turned her around to look at him. "At least that's one of the reasons."

Alex looked down at her smiling eyes, then lower to her full, alluring lips. They were already parted in anticipation and his desire screamed through his brain and into his nervous system. He concentrated the power to his lips as he lowered his head and lightly touched them to hers. His first taste of heaven. His mouth became more possessive as he gave into his body's need to feed. Her arms came around his waist as she returned his passion.

Their first kiss was an incredible combination of heat and sweet desire. They both gave, they both took, and they both felt...something. It felt like a beginning.

"I've wanted to do that all evening," he whispered moving his lips only a breath away, then recapturing her mouth and gradually deepening the kiss.

Breathless, Skye pulled back, sighing and giving him an appraising look.

"Me too," she smiled and stayed in his embrace. Her voice was teasing and strangely seductive. "But sometimes anticipation is so intense that the reality can fall short."

"Yeah?" He planted a few quick pecks on her lips and smiled broadly. "So did I measure up?"

"Oh, yeah. My reality meter is measuring a reading that's off the charts."

She smiled in a friendly way even while her heart was pounding energetically. Pulling back to give herself a moment to breathe, she was surprised he couldn't hear it or feel it.

Alex may not have been able to hear her heart, but he saw the look of approval in her eyes. Excellent. This was going well. Very well, indeed.

He turned, leaning into her, and placed his hands on either side of her on the low stone wall, effectively trapping her in the circle of his strong arms. "Let's try again. I think you should have more data to work with."

"Most definitely. One can't make generalizations based on such a small sample."

She gladly obliged, her lips smiling easily as they met his in another passionate kiss. When he drew back, she was nearly panting and her knees felt weak. Man, the guy put enough electricity in one kiss to light the city.

"Well, judging by my own well calibrated and automatic reality measuring instrument, I would say we'd better keep walking, right now…or call a cab and get back to my room to finish this interesting exploration of reality vs. expectations."

Skye laughed easily and looked down. "Hmm. Impressive. I see that there is some urgency…"

She never finished the thought or the sentence. Ever alert, she saw movement out of the corner of her eye. Stiffening, she turned her head toward the motion.

Alex detected her shift in mood and body language and turned around rapidly. Skye was impressed with the quickness of his movements, but didn't have time to think about it. They both sprang to attention.

There were four of them. They had malice on their faces, purpose in their movements, and they were not from the London Chamber of Commerce. They were there to do damage and Skye and Alex were obviously the targets.

Skye assessed the situation in an instant and planned her moves spontaneously. She had no way of knowing that Alex was doing the same.

Skye straightened and firmly shoved Alex aside, going immediately into an offensive posture. To be strictly defensive when it was four to one was foolhardy. This wasn't a civilized practice session on mats with rules of engagement. This was a street fight and she actually smiled as she faced the menacing faces of four men.

"Stay back," she said, automatically. Protect the civilian. She stood poised in a magnificent stance, challenge and brashness in her posture. In an instant she went from soft, sexy woman to dominant protector and imposing warrior. While Alex was busy being impressed with her transformation, the first guy got in a hit to his jaw. Skye took him out with two swift jabs—one to the side of his face, and one to the back of his neck.

"*Porca puttana*. I got him," she shouted at Alex. "Back off. *è il mio*. He's mine."

The hit to the jaw turned Alex on to the action. As Skye went after the two coming at them from the right, he protected her flank with a few kicks and punches of his own.

The first guy shook off the chop to the neck and got up behind Skye. His knife was out and he was going for her back as she whirled and knocked it out with a swift side kick. She followed up with a full leg thrust up the inside of his legs into his crotch.

"*Budiulo. Cogglione Lei figlio di buona donna.*"

Even Alex winced at the solid crunching sound her shoe made as it connected. The man should have gone down right away, but somehow he pulled a bit of reserve from his store of meanness. Fueled by pain and fury he grabbed her leg and twisted. She went with the twist, turning her body so he couldn't get a good grip and bringing her other foot up to finish him off with a blow to the face. Blood spurted out of his nose as he went down, but even then he didn't give up. He was full of drugs and thought he was super human. Finally, she reached down and squeezed his jugular until he stopped struggling.

"*Mannaggia, che una minchione.*"

The man coming at her now was a giant. He was at least 6'3" and outweighed her by 150 pounds. Looked like muscle, too. Alex was about to join that battle when he realized he couldn't move in to save Skye from the monster. He had a more immediate danger. The fourth man was circling him with a knife. He couldn't take his eyes off the weapon, and cringed from the sounds of a brutal attack behind him. A great deal of Italian was weaved into the sounds of battle. Flesh on flesh, the crunching sound of bones breaking, grunts, heavy breathing, then silence. Alex timed his move, lunged at his man, twisted his arm until he heard a satisfying snap, then brought his knee up into the screaming face. His man went down and stayed down.

He quickly turned to assess Skye's danger and found her standing over the huge man. She was bent over at the waist, hands on knees, breathing heavy and grinning like a delighted kid looking at a new bike. It was surreal. Skye straightened slowly and turned to him. Christ, he was so in love right now.

"*La prossima volta di scegliere su qualcuno la sua propria misura, cornuto.* Next time pick on someone your own size, bastard," said Skye, blowing out a breath. "Damn, what a bunch of boneheads."

"Well I guess that'll teach them to jump a couple of out-of-town tourists," he said casually.

She raised her eyebrows and smiled broadly. His eyes traveled up and down her body in a quick assessment. Her hair had come out of its clip and was flying in wild curls around her face and shoulders. There was a rip on the knee of one pant leg and she was generally grimy all over. She looked utterly adorable. There didn't seem to be any permanent damage so he let out a long breath and returned her grin.

"I gotta sit down." Alex puffed out the words.

Time to start covering up. He looked at the four men lying on the ground and decided they were going to be down and out until the back-up arrived. They sat side by side on the ledge of a stone fence regaining their balance and letting the adrenalin drain away.

"When I thought we might engage in some heavy breathing tonight, this wasn't what I had in mind," said Alex.

She laughed. "Well, sometimes fun just jumps out and grabs you."

"What do you call that last move you made on that poor chap over by the wall?"

"My version of the Vulcan neck pinch," said Skye.

"Star Trek fan, huh? Well live long and prosper."

"Where did you learn to fight like that?" asked Skye.

"I could ask you the same question. I didn't know that street fighting was part of a pilot's training. Where did you learn it?"

"Very neatly evaded, counselor. I asked you first."

"I told you. I grew up in a house full of cops. Some of it was bound to rub off," said Alex.

"That's a bit weak. Actually, you did a complete Clark Kent on me."

"What?"

"You know...acted all wimpy...didn't go for all that tough cop stuff...wanted to be safely behind a desk...blah...blah...blah. Then, when you were confronted with danger, you whipped off your glasses, metaphorically speaking, flexed your muscles, and came out of the phone booth as Superman."

"I hardly think subduing a few thugs classifies me as Superman." Alex straightened his tie and ran his fingers through his hair. "I can't even see through that thin blouse you're wearing."

"You're doing it again," said Skye.

"What?"

"Changing back into Clark Kent."

"Well, you're no Lois Lane, that's for sure. You actually shoved me aside. The guy in the leather there wouldn't have gotten my face if I hadn't been put off balance by your gallant little gesture. Next time we're attacked, would you stand aside, put your hands over your face, wait for me to single handedly wipe out the bad guys, then stand ready to sigh expansively and give me, the hero, his well deserved kiss?" She laughed at that picture of herself. He looked beautiful in the light of the street lamp. Skye felt a tug of desire shoot through her. Must be the after effect of hand-to-hand combat, she thought. Still…why not indulge herself?

"Ohhhh…you brave, brave man…" she leaned over, fluttered her eyelashes and kissed his bleeding lip. "How can I thank you?"

She tasted his blood and her eyes lost some of their humorous gleam.

She stared.

He stared back.

She started to pull away, but as she looked into his blue eyes, still dark and dangerous from his reaction to the attack, something about them compelled her to stop. Then slowly, cautiously, she put her lips to his as his arms went around her and pulled her gently to him.

His split lip stung like hell just moments before, but now his lips where hot and tingling with pleasure and passion. He completely ignored the shot of pain and deepened the kiss. His arms tightened their hold and she leaned into him, putting the same kind of intensity into her kiss as she did into her fight for life. God, she was hot.

Just a delayed reaction to danger, she thought, as her arms went around his neck and her fingers entwined in his thick, wavy hair. She actually felt herself sigh and her mouth opened to the onslaught of a new and different kind of personal attack. Their lips were locked in combat now. Their tongues explored and discovered mutual surrender. Waves of pleasure tore through her. The soft moan that escaped her throat fanned his excitement and for just a moment everything around them faded. It was just the two of them now.

Alex couldn't get enough of her. All the time he spent watching her, dreaming of her, thinking of her, and now she was in his arms—warm, willing, and so very real. Moving his hands under her blouse and feeling warm, soft flesh, his control dissolved under the onslaught of need and passion.

His hands became bolder and as if they had a mind of their own, began to explore her curves. Her moan ended in a sharp intake of breath. She jerked and he forced himself to pull back. He opened his eyes and looked into hers. It was the flash of pain he saw that brought him back to his senses, fast and hard.

"Damn…sorry…sorry, Skye…I didn't…" he began hoarsely, then frowned fiercely. "Are you hurt? Christ. Where'd he get you?"

Skye didn't answer right away. Her head was spinning and her pulse was pounding so vigorously in her throat, she couldn't locate her voice. She shook her head. More to clear it from the reaction her body had to his caresses than to shake off the pain. Pain. Yes. There'd been some pain when his hands had connected with a bruise.

Alex looked down as Skye began to lift her blouse.

"Hold the thought while I check out the flesh, Clark," she said as she gingerly pressed her fingers on a big, ugly bruise forming on the lower section of her rib cage. Alex's eyes narrowed and his heart clutched in his chest. "Damn. I think my guy got a shot or two by me. Pretty superficial for such a big bozo, though."

The reality of her position as an agent hit Alex like a blow from a linebacker. Up to now, the danger of her job was hypothetical and ambiguous. Now it was very real to him. The bruise on her flesh, he realized, could have been much worse. He looked at the four men who had intended to do her bodily harm, maybe even leave her dead. Dead, damn it. Not just bruised. He knew she probably could have taken them all on tonight, but it was that 'probably' that caused cold sweat to form on his skin. He stared at her, his eyes taking on the color of ice.

"What?" asked Skye when she looked back at him.

He had to force from his mind an image of her being pounded by four assailants and vowed he would stay close, very close, from now on.

"Nothing," answered Alex.

She lowered her shirt and touched his cheek. "It's just a bruise." She could see the concern in his eyes. "No big deal. I earned my black belt when I was 13. I won a silver at the world championship when I was 14. I've been bruised, battered, and thrown so many times that black and blue are my two favorite colors."

When he continued to stare, she felt a compelling, almost tender need to reassure him. Where did that come from?

"There are plenty of non-bruised areas of my body you could explore," she said with an inviting smile.

Alex took her hand and kissed her palm. It sent shivers all the way down to her toes.

"Yeah, well the worst of this little encounter is that my reality measuring instrument couldn't stand up under the stress. It ducked out of sight after the first hit." Alex looked down with a rueful look on his face. "It's trying to make a comeback, though."

Skye let out a delighted snort of laughter. He joined her laughter until they were giggling like a couple of idiots. Definitely a reaction to the adrenalin rush that flowed through them moments before. It wasn't that funny.

They wound up in another passionate embrace, this time Alex's hands stayed buried in her hair. His instrument decided it definitely wanted in again. Down boy, he thought. All that pent up energy had to go somewhere, but they had business to attend to first. He reluctantly pulled away and smiled down at her. They looked over to the men on the sidewalk. One was beginning to stir. She read his thoughts, stood up, and looked around.

"Right now we have to get this mess cleaned up."

"Was that the guy who put the bruise on you?"

"Yeah, son-of-a-bitch outweighs me by a ton and a half…kind of reminds me of Bluto." She gave a short ironic laugh and was about to go over and put him back to sleep. "Bluto never won a fight either."

Alex beat her to it, walking almost causally over to where the guy was sitting shaking his head and trying to stop the ringing in his ears. It looked like Alex was going to help Bluto to his feet and Skye was about to tell him to step back when he planted his fist into Bluto's stomach and raised his knee into his face at the same time. The big man went down hard and didn't stir.

"Feel better, Popeye?" she said rolling her eyes. She was impressed but didn't want to show it.

"Much," answered Alex. "I don't think he'll be much good for questioning for a few days. We'll let the police worry about that." Alex was amused at how hard they both were trying not to act like agents. He was at an advantage there. Making a pretense of going for his cell phone he said, "I'll call this in." He knew she would have her own team take charge of this, but he didn't want her to know he knew. "Do they have a 911 thing over here? I forget."

She put a hand on his before he completed his call. "Here, let me. I know someone in the London Constabulary. We can get people here faster." And get some answers faster, she thought.

"Good," he said. "I'm anxious to get on with our date."

"They must have been after money," she said. Skye dialed and asked for Captain Bargis. "I think maybe it was your Rolex and those $2,000 shoes," she said as the phone rang at a special office at Scotland Yard.

"Hello, Lillian?" asked Skye. "This is Skyler Madison. I've had a bit of a problem on one of your side streets."

They only had to wait ten minutes but they used their time efficiently.

Working together they searched the pockets of their assailants. They were clean. They did find a gun and another knife, but that wasn't unusual. The suspects were just starting to come around when the police arrived. The first uniform on the scene, who looked duly impressed, was given a brief report.

"Hey...sure looks like the two of you came together on this one."

"Came together," Skye whispered, a giggle bubbling up in her throat again.

"Actually officer, we were interrupted before that could happen," said Alex.

At the confused look on the officer's face, Skye shrieked with laughter and Alex joined in until they had to hold themselves up. When Captain Bargis arrived they had managed to get under control so only a few brief chuckles and one or two snickers escaped them. They made quite an impression on the officers on the scene who just shook their heads and chalked up their behavior to the fact they were Americans, appeared to be in love, and were probably drunk. Powerful combination: lunatic American culture, sex, and wine. Add to that the adrenaline rush and, well, more than one of the officers smiled broadly.

CHAPTER 6

"Come up for an aspirin or two?" Alex flexed some of the aches out of his muscles, touched his swollen lip and pressed the button for the elevator. He definitely wasn't ready for the night to end.

"Now that's a real turn on. You make it hard to resist, but," Skye stretched and winced. "I think I need more than a few aspirin."

He knew he could do better. Smiling his most winning smile, he touched her cheek with his long, warm fingers.

"How about a drink, some aspirin, and a full body massage?" asked Alex.

"Now you're talking," answered Skye. "Let's go."

He wiggled his eyebrows at her as he took her hand and pulled her onto the elevator.

"Great. I sure could use that massage."

"Careful, or you'll need more than an aspirin to take care of the pain." But she laughed when he kept her hand in his as they walked down the hall.

Skye waited until he unlocked the door to the penthouse suite then removed her hand. She liked it, but it seemed far too possessive and intimate for the more casual air she was trying to project. Her room was spacious enough, but this was like a small palace. Not wanting Alex to know she'd been in these rooms before, she looked around appreciatively.

"Wow. It seems the world of commerce really pays off. This is beautiful."

He looked around. It was such a part of his life now, he took it for granted.

"Yeah, well…it serves when I have to travel away from my mansion in the States or my villa in Italy."

"You have a mansion in the states?"

"No, actually a townhouse in Alexandria, Virginia."

"Same thing. And the villa?"

"Okay, it's an apartment in Rome, and I don't get there very often. Want to go?" he asked casually from the bathroom where he secured a bottle of aspirin and doled them out like tiny hors d'oeuvres. Although his tone was deliberately light, he thought he would love to travel the world with her someday.

His future traveling companion knocked down the tablets and sipped some water. Her ribs were beginning to stiffen up. Alex saw it on her face as he pointed her toward the sofa facing a magnificent marble fireplace. He pushed a button and a fire flared on the hearth. Sighing with pleasure, she sat down and started to relax. He went to fetch them some wine and when he looked over at her he smiled at the picture she made. Her head was resting back on the soft fawn-colored cushion, her long, elegant neck exposed. She finished taking the pins out of her hair and let it fall down around her face and shoulders. It gave him a jolt to see her there, all casual and rumpled and relaxed. So unlike her usual sleek, well-groomed appearance. So that was what lurked underneath, he thought. He liked it. No, he more than liked it. He wanted it.

"I'd be glad to take you," he continued with the thought and he meant it. "That was Italian I heard in the alley, wasn't it?"

"Yes, it was. When I get really worked up, the words sort of pop out."

"I didn't recognize some of them."

"Don't ask me to translate. We don't know each other well enough."

Yet, he thought. "So, when would you like to go?"

"Maybe I would some day. I'm half Italian." She gratefully took the glass of wine he offered.

"Which half?" he said smiling.

She raised her eyebrows and winked. "The hot half."

"Get your calendar. I don't think we should wait."

"Actually, I would have mixed feelings about going. I haven't been back to Italy since my parents were killed there."

He said nothing as he sat down beside her and sipped his own wine.

"How were they killed?" he asked, pretending not to know.

"It…ah…was a car bomb." She never talked of it and usually gave cryptic answers to that question. Somehow, in the cool atmosphere of pre-dawn, sitting in front of a fire, surrounded by soft leather and hard man, she felt comfortable enough to be straight.

"Bombed?" He acted like he was just now beginning to put the names together. He was actually very good at this, although it was giving him a twinge of guilt right now. "Of course. Madison. I take it your parents were the Ambassador and her husband?"

"Yes. Angelina and Perry Madison."

Alex saw a flash of pain before she managed to veil it. "Again, I'm so sorry. Did they ever catch the people responsible?" His arm went around her in an automatic gesture of both sympathy and intimacy. She didn't move away so he went a little further and gently pulled her closer.

"No, no, they never did. Officially, they ruled it as a case of mistaken identity. It was a long time ago." She shook herself free of the pain. "Anyway, I think I would like to go back there someday. *Lo ha il caldo italiano sangue.*"

"Translation?" Alex held her and unconsciously stroked the side of her neck with his fingertips.

"I have the hot Italian blood."

Her response to him was automatic. Her body was seeking warmth and her soul was seeking comfort. Nothing felt more natural to her than to put her head on his shoulder.

"Would you like to tell me more about it, or would you like to drop it? I'm never sure if it helps or hurts to remember."

"I think it depends on the individual. I would prefer to drop it."

"All right. Then tell me about what it was like to be the daughter of a diplomat."

As they sipped and talked, she found it easier than she usually did to tell him about the young girl who traveled around a lot. As she talked, Alex watched her face. He refilled her glass and decided she wasn't going anywhere that night. He repositioned himself and gently put his arms around her. She didn't protest, and put her head on his shoulder again. Just like it knew it belonged there. He took her glass from her as her voice started to fade.

"I should go," she said without much conviction.

"Stay," he whispered, lightly kissing the top of her head. "The sun will be up soon."

"Okay," she sighed and cuddled up closer to his side. "So who gets the massage?" she asked suppressing a yawn.

He smiled down at her. "Maybe later." As she looked up at him, he saw the tough independent woman mingled with the grief-stricken little girl. He felt completely undone by the poignant combination. Taking her face in his hands, he gently kissed the little girl. When she responded he increased the pressure of his embrace and thoroughly kissed the woman.

"Alex, I…"

"No pressure, sweetheart," said Alex. "I think you've had quite enough physical exertion for one evening. Let's heal these aches and pains before we take the route to the bedroom."

"Thanks, Alex," said Skye. "That was the absolutely perfect thing to say." She sighed again and let herself slide into sleep, feeling safe, protected. It felt very, very good.

As she slept, Alex let his guard down and looked at her with longing and tenderness that would have seized her heart had she been awake. When her hand dropped innocently into his lap, he cursed and gently removed it. I must be nuts, he thought and shifted into a more comfortable position himself. Watching her so long from a distance hadn't prepared him for either her flawless beauty or her incredible heat. He couldn't believe she was actually here with him, curled up in his arms, allowing him the luxury of looking at every inch of her incredible face. He watched the pulse beat steadily in her exquisite neck and wanted to kiss and caress. He decided to stop the torture and forced himself to relax.

He floated awhile before sleep caught up with him. This is nice, he thought as he drifted. Not exactly the steamy night of hot sex he had envisioned, but really, really nice. As he fell asleep himself he didn't have time to wonder about the surge of tenderness he felt for the woman sleeping in his arms.

The sun was up when his eyes flew open. Instant wakefulness was one of his strong suits. Even his mother was annoyed by his ability since childhood to pass from unconscious slumber to total awareness in the blink of an eye. He looked down at Skye's face. She was still wrapped in his arms and sleeping soundly. He gave her a little shake.

"Sweetheart. It's morning. If you get off me, I'll order some coffee."

Her eyes came open but she wasn't someone who could shake off sleep easily. When she realized where she was, she blinked, groaned, stretched and nuzzled back into his chest.

"No, not done…cell phone in purse… call from here." Then she slid her arms around him and faded back into a light slumber.

His mouth twitched as he reached over for her purse, pulled out keys, a comb, lipstick, a silly little gun, and her phone. Looking down at her and determining she was indeed back to sleep, he manipulated all the buttons on her phone, most particularly the latest calls and memorized the numbers. Then he checked it out for any non-standard functions and found it clean. He would include that in his report. The twinge of discomfort he felt had to be balanced with his long-range goal of clearing her. Clearing her? When had the mission changed from uncovering any and all information on her activities to proving she was just as she seemed…a dedicated, talented, driven agent? She stirred and he looked down at the face that had been the star of all of his dreams of late. The minute he saw her picture, he thought.

After getting the number of the hotel, he called the front desk and was connected to a confused concierge. He ordered a full breakfast for two sent up to his rooms, then settled back in to enjoy the sensation of having Skye in his arms. This isn't entirely a bad way to wake up, he thought. He loved the sensation of her against him. Even the tingling of sore muscles could be ignored when weighed against the soft, sweet feel of her wrapped around him, the scent of her hair, the look of her fabulous lips. Now if he could just get the sight of her kicking those men into oblivion out of his mind, it would be a thoroughly, all around memorable moment. Kind of nice and normal.

He shook her again when he heard the soft knock on the door. When she just groaned and snarled, he very intelligently worked his way out from under her and left her curled up on the sofa as he went to open the door. He nearly jumped out of his skin when he saw Jim through the security glass.

He quickly opened the door, walked out into the hall and shut it behind him.

"What the hell went on last night?" Jim demanded.

"Nothing, absolutely nothing." Alex ran his fingers through his hair and smoothed down some of the wrinkles in his shirt.

"What? Being ambushed by four highly trained goons is nothing?"

"Oh, yeah, that," said Alex.

"What the hell did you think I meant?"

"Keep your voice down," said Alex.

"Why? It's past 8:00," said Jim.

"Um…have you checked in with Skye?"

"No…I thought I would hear it from you first, then go talk with her."

"What are you doing here?"

"I'm meeting with Skye and her team this morning. Routine. Then halfway over here, I get a call from Lillian Bargis. Now, let's get out of this hallway, shall we?"

"Um…"

"What the fuck is wrong with you?" fumed Jim.

As the room service cart with two place settings came rolling down the hallway, it finally clicked into place for Jim.

"You aren't alone."

"No, not exactly."

Jim eyes narrowed suspiciously and he speared Alex with a withering look of suppressed rage.

"That better not be Skye in there," he growled.

"Um…"

"God damn it! What's wrong with your vocabulary this morning? Tell me now. Who the fuck is in there?"

Suddenly the door opened.

"Alex, who are you talking to? Jim?" Skye looked utterly confused. Beautiful, disheveled, sexy as hell, but totally perplexed.

"Skye?" responded Jim. Skye turned her now alert eyes to Alex. "Alex?"

The man with the breakfast cart didn't know what was going on, but he had been serving breakfast in this hotel long enough to recognize real trouble when he saw it. One man was sheepish – that would be the lover. One man was going red with fury – that would be the aging husband or enraged papa, then there was the beautiful, but puzzled woman in the middle. Blood letting for sure. He figured he could get a signature later. The only thing left to consider was the need to weigh the tip against his own skin. Bloody hell, he could always do without the bit of luxury the tip would provide. His life was another matter. Making the only decision an intelligent man in his position would make, he turned and almost ran to the elevator.

Skye was the first to recover. "Were you looking for me, Jim? What time is it? I thought we were meeting at 10:00. Did you leave a message? I spent the night here so I must have missed it." She said it with such innocence and in such a reasonable, friendly voice, Jim's fury settled back into a low simmer. When neither man spoke, she tried again.

"Alex, quit looking like you've been caught with your hand in a cookie jar. Jim, calm down. I hate making introductions in the hallways of hotels, but Jim, this is Alex Springfield. He's a man I met a few days ago here in London. Alex, this is my, well, I guess you could say my surrogate father, Jim Stryker." When they didn't shake hands, she just sighed. "Well, this remains as uncomfortable as hell."

"And just how many times have you had to introduce your surrogate father to men in hotel corridors?" Alex leaned against the door jam and played the wealthy tycoon role, even though his nerves were fraying fast around the edges. He had wanted to tell Skye about his position with the Justice department…but he wasn't prepared for her to have it shoved in her face without some preamble and a lot of preliminary groundwork. Obviously Jim was of the same mind, because he nodded at Alex noncommittally.

"10, 15 times. I lose count," said Jim, smirking a little at Alex.

"How did you find me?" Skye said, awake now and more than a little confused.

"I thought we could have some breakfast before our meeting. When I didn't find you in your room, the man at the front desk discretely, very discretely, mentioned I might find you here," said Jim.

Good save, thought Alex, and he nodded back to Jim.

"You're welcome to join us here," said Alex.

"Thanks, Mr. Springfield, but no. I'm sorry you went to so much trouble. I would like to have a private chat with Skyler. You understand," said Jim.

Skye turned to Jim. "All right. Then be a dear and get a table in the lobby restaurant. I'll be down in 20 minutes." She watched as Jim nodded.

"Mr. Springfield."

"Mr. Stryker."

"Well now, that was a bit of fun," said Skye with a humorous gleam in her eye after Jim got back in the elevator and sent a final scowl in Alex's direction. "Kind of makes you forget your business, though, doesn't it?"

"Wasn't exactly how I would have scripted the morning," mumbled Alex sourly. Skye laughed.

"Are you pouting?" she teased.

"I don't pout," said Alex. "I'm just disappointed. And more than a little frustrated."

"Hold that thought."

"I won't get anything done today if I do that. When will I see you again?"

"What's your day like?" They went back into the room. She was all business now as she gathered her purse and shoes. She ran her fingers through her mass of wheat colored-curls. "Damn, I hate this hair in the morning."

"I have some calls to make, a conference at 2:00, but I'll be available for tea at about 4:30." He fingered her curls. He thought they were utterly delightful.

"I'll be tied up until after 6:00."

"How about dinner?"

"Can't. Wait." She just had a brainstorm. Even though her brain was still a little fuzzy from the late night and the shock of seeing Jim at the door, she was formulating a plan. She'd told Phillip on a couple of occasions that she was involved with someone. Not deeply and she was a bit conflicted about the relationship, but it was a convenient lie meant to put a proper barrier between them. Not that she seemed to need it, but you never knew when Phillip might want to make his move. To bring a real live escort to the party tonight would punctuate that position. It was a delicate balance. She didn't want to either encourage or discourage him. A complicated business, but she had the balance of a tight wire performer. She'd intended to go alone, but with such a convenient hunk at hand…how could she pass it up? And if she got a personal rush from the evening…well, consider it her bonus.

"Got a tux?"

"Of course."

"Would you like to escort me to a formal party this evening at the country estate of a friend of mine, Phillip Blythe?"

"The son the of the Duke of Stanhopeshire?" This was great. By escorting her to the function, she would be taking him right into the lair of their quarry. He could watch her by her side, not from a high vantage point through binoculars. Plus, he knew he looked great in a tux.

"Yes, do you know him?"

"Of him."

"Well, would you like to go?"

Alex didn't want to sound too eager. "I would rather have a private dinner right here. Is it an important function?"

"Yes, it is. At least to the charities this party will benefit."

"Then I'd love to be your escort. How about a kiss to sustain me until then," said Alex reaching for her.

"Come to my room about 7:00."

She gave him a quick peck on the cheek and ran off to her breakfast with their mutual boss.

He nodded and took his first full breath since opening the door. God. He rubbed the cheek she'd kissed absentmindedly. Not exactly the kind of kiss he had in mind. All he wanted to do was come clean and join forces with her. He had to somehow convince Jim they should tell Skye everything.

Instead of meeting in the public dining area, Jim and Skye went back to her room. They called room service for breakfast and Jim made himself comfortable. He didn't want Skye to see how shook he was over seeing her and Alex together. Not that they weren't a spectacular couple and for an instant it flashed through his mind what a splendid team they would make. It was just, well, Skye was like a daughter and she was Alex's assignment. He supposed he could like and admire Alex on one level and want to shoot him on another.

"I thought our meeting was at 10:00," said Skye from the bathroom. She was changing into jeans and a t-shirt for her meeting with her team.

"Our formal meeting was. But I wanted to talk with you about last night."

Actually that was a lie. He wanted to talk with Alex first. He never in a million years thought they would be together. He thought he would cover up his frustration with a little bluster…both as her boss and her godfather.

"What the hell were you doing in that man's room? I come here to talk with you. You're not here. Scares me a little because of last night. So on a hunch I ask if Alexander Springfield is registered. He is. I also ascertained from the more chatty members of the staff that he's in the penthouse suite." Jim was glad she was in the bathroom and couldn't see his eyes. "What am I now, a dating service? You have me check someone out and then I find you in his room? What were you doing? More data collection?"

"Hey, I'm entitled to a social life. Not much of one, I admit, but maybe a little one. Who better to have it with than someone you have checked out and reported clean as a whistle?"

For not getting much sleep the night before, she was feeling pretty good and her elevated mood wasn't lost on Jim, who was making all sorts of worried faces. She popped her head out the door of the bathroom, a mascara wand in her hand.

"Besides," she said wickedly, "for months I've been telling Phillip I'm not sure I can commit to a deeper relationship with him, because I'm so conflicted about a man back home. From your report, I think he could fit the bill as this fictitious other man. I've been appropriately vague about him so I could pop someone in if I needed to. I'd like to do that tonight at the estate. I'm afraid if I don't bring someone, Phillip will be all over me and I won't get to look around. It took me months to get an invitation to the Palace Blythe, now I want to make the best use of my time."

"Do you have a feeling Mama and Papa don't want you coming to their house in the woods, Goldilocks?" It was his pet name for her when she was young and had a full head of bright golden curls.

"Well let's just say I think that Baby Bear got this invitation by them before they could censor it. If I can find something tonight, I can crank up the timetable. I'm convinced the lair is at the homestead. We've looked everywhere else. That place is harder to get into than Fort Knox. It isn't somewhere I can just drop in for a casual chat with the mother of my relatively steady beau."

"And to make it absolutely perfect," continued Skye. "This party of the season is going to be catered by Kings Catering Service, among others. Apparently, they have secured the services of the top five caterers in the city. Big, big party." Max and Linda worked for the catering service, so she would have plenty of back up. "We're going to be meeting with them at 10:00 as well. They have to be at work by noon. I'm going to have Linda mess up Alex. Poor man, he'll be forced to either go home and change his tux, or take care of major repairs right there. Either way, I'll be blissfully on my own so I can nose around. Max will be my backup."

Skye finished applying her make-up and let in the room service waiter.

"Just put it over there." She indicated the table by the window and signed. The waiter looked at her bare feet and Jim's jacket and tie over the chair, thanked Skye for her generous tip, and let himself out.

Skye frowned after him. "I think perhaps we should start the day by investigating that man. The vibes he was sending set off all sorts of alarms."

"Skye," laughed Jim. "That was the waiter who delivered breakfast this morning to the penthouse and witnessed that very delightful scene in the hallway. Probably wants to know why a dish like you chose me over that Springfield fellow."

She joined in his laughter. "Oh God! Poor man. Well, then he must not be a very good judge." She leaned over and gave him a big mushy kiss on the cheek.

"That's nice to hear. Um, if I could switch over to the role of your godfather now..."

"None of your business," said Skye sipping her fresh cup of coffee.

"Skye..."

She smiled indulgently. "Okay...so our date tonight may not be strictly business."

That was what I was afraid of, he thought.

When Skye and Jim went to the meeting, he saw that Alex was on the job and keeping them in sight. He was sure Skye did not.

CHAPTER 7

Alex knocked on the door of her suite, smiling at the feel of nervous energy surging through the muscles in his inner thighs. Maybe she was naked in there. No. Best get that thought out of his mind, or he might scare her when she opened the door.

When she did, it was in a cloud of wonderful, exotic scent. She was wearing a wide, inviting smile and a simple long, black dress. Not naked, but this look was strangely even more alluring. The dress completely covered her and gave her an air of sophistication and seduction that neither her uniform nor her casual look the night before had prepared him for. He stepped inside the suite and closed the door behind him, never taking his eyes off the fascinating dimple that formed just to the right of her smile.

Alex realized he was staring like a besotted schoolboy and was just about to say how spectacular she looked when she turned… revealing nothing but a long, graceful exposed back. He couldn't get his breath. The smell of her, the site of that naked back, the images of her in his arms. His brain seized. Nothing was working…well almost nothing. He could feel a surge of lust pushing blood from his brain down below his belt.

"Could you zip me up, please. I'm running a bit late."

Skye knew exactly what she was doing. She'd deliberately selected the exclusive perfume she had formulated just for her in Paris. Her dress was form fitting and the form that it fit was perfect for its sleek straight lines. She'd zippered herself into it several times before tonight, but thought it would be just fine to get a little help, now that someone so capable was at her door. The timing was perfect. It was an impulsive decision, but when she saw the hungry look in his eye turn absolutely ravenous, she knew her impulse had been right on target.

So there, Bill, she thought as she presented her back to Alex. I can be spontaneous sometimes. When she felt his warm, steady fingers work their way slowly up her back, she thought it was more like spontaneous combustion.

By the time he reached the top of her dress, they were both so sufficiently turned on that had she not been on assignment that evening, and had he not known she was on assignment that evening, they would have been tearing at each other and rolling on the floor before she had a chance to turn around. Alex could feel her tremble with pleasure and nearly lost his tenuous hold on reality.

"Thanks," was all she managed to say when she could take a breath. She peeked at him over her shoulder. He looked wonderful…debonair, dashing, and handsome. He was made to wear a tuxedo and this one fit him like a second skin. Obviously hand tailored and expensive. And he kept staring at her with those beautiful blue eyes. It was disconcerting.

Alex smiled and knew that as long as he lived, he would never, ever, forget the smell of her tonight. He put his hand to her cheek. "Is there any way…any way whatsoever, that I can talk you out of going to this party tonight?"

"Why? Aren't you feeling well?" she asked with mock concern. "Was the late night last night too much for you?" Amusement made her eyes sparkle.

She stood there, tempting and completely irresistible. He really should respect the time she spent getting ready and keep his distance…exercise some restraint. Christ. What the hell. He grabbed her around the waist, took her in his arms and kissed the carefully applied lipstick right off her mouth. There was no way she was going to get away from him tonight. Seduction was a game he knew how to play. He fully intended to turn up the heat and activate all the burners. He knew they had to go to this party, but he wanted to give her something to think about all evening. His mouth became more demanding and his hands gave the kiss more punch by roaming all over her back and up her sides to the swell of her breasts.

"You got anything on under there?" he whispered, although he was afraid if she said no, he would completely lose his head.

"Who are you, the underwear police?" She smiled wickedly, planting quick little kisses on Alex's lips. "I think I'll just keep that little bit of intelligence to myself." There. That should give him something to think about all evening, she thought. Between the two of them, they appeared to have a lot to think about all evening.

Skye started to pull away, but for every move she had, he had a counter move. He was a man with seduction on his mind and decided to take inventory of her underwear situation as best he could through the thin fabric.

Just when he was sure she was sufficiently melted, he pulled back. She gave a small moan of disappointment and nearly begged for more. To hell with duty and justice and ...her eyes came open and refocused. What was she thinking? She had work to do. Bloody hell.

She pulled away from him slowly and reluctantly. Trying to get her equilibrium back. "You want some wine, or would you just like some ice for your pants? Both are over there by the bar. I have to go fix my make-up again."

"Complaining?"

"Hell, no. Just grabbing an excuse to leave the room so I can compose myself in private."

Laughing, he went over and poured himself a glass of wine while she went into the bedroom. He took out his handkerchief and wiped the lipstick off his own lips. He stared at the color and thought about how he might preserve the fabric. For sure, he wasn't going to have it laundered. God, he was getting sappy. He was in a really fine mood. Last night's attack, as horrific as it might have been at the time, all but cleared Skye of any suspicion in his mind. He had always known it in his gut, but it felt good to have his mind at rest as well. The attack wasn't random, he was sure of it. And if she was working with the drug cartel, it wouldn't have made any sense to take her out now, just when things were heating up. Someone wanted her...because she was in the way, not because she was playing the game.

He heard her moving around in the bedroom and again his imagination got the better of him. No way he was going to be sleeping alone tonight. Although there wouldn't be much sleeping, he was sure of that. Skye looked like she had a whole lot of endurance and he knew he had a whole lot of need. Thinking that the ice might be a good idea after all, he forced himself to reflect on other things.

They would be going into the den of the enemy tonight. He had to remember that no matter how elegant the surroundings, the people living in it were suspected criminals. When the privileged class went bad, they could be particularly vicious. It was their sense of entitlement. They needed things, so they felt they could use whatever means necessary to secure them. Skye was most certainly playing with fire. He knew she was well trained and very smart, but he intended to stay close. After all, he was going to find out what she wore under that dress tonight and he didn't want a repeat of last night's frustrating interruption.

She came out of the bedroom an absolute vision. She'd swept up her hair in some kind of a clasp. It exposed all of her neck and he was sorely tempted to plant his lips on that really edible spot just behind her ear. Damn, that was distracting. How was he supposed to carry on an intelligent conversation tonight?

"Pardon?"

He hadn't realized he had spoken his thoughts out loud. "I said how am I supposed to have an intelligent conversation tonight? Do you have to wear your hair up like that? It exposes way too much neck, and I can't think of anything clever to say when my mind is imagining what it would be like to run my fingers over it and kiss it right here." He had been walking slowly toward her, talking in a low, hypnotic voice. And like a doe caught in headlights, she let him keep coming. By the time she recognized danger, he was barely touching the back of her neck with his fingertips and running them gently up to the spot his eyes had fixed on when she came into the room.

Even though Skye felt herself quiver and nearly passed out with pleasure, she firmly reigned in her emotions and got herself back in control. She had to remember she was on assignment and Alex was a prop. Window dressing. A cover. Handsome. Sexy. Hot.

Moving quickly to a safe distance, Skye looked at him with both indulgence and exasperation. "I'm not going to fix my makeup again. Hands off until after the party, or at least until everyone is so drunk they won't notice. "

She picked up a box on the table near the window. "I bought these at Harrods last week." She pulled out an elegant pair of strappy high-heels that Alex actually recognized as one of the dozens she had been trying on. "I so seldom go out with someone tall enough to allow me to wear something like these," she said with such undisguised pleasure that Alex laughed as she sat down to put them on.

"Glad to oblige. You know that women in heels like that are every man's fantasy."

"No, I didn't. But I do know that shoes like these are every woman's passion." She stood up and the impact of almost three more inches on her was striking. She stood well over six feet. He was still several inches taller, but she looked liked a fucking Amazon. She would intimidate the hell out of the men in the room. That suited him just fine.

"Phillip will hate these. He's already self-conscious about the fact that I'm a bit taller than him. I was getting tired of wearing flat shoes to these events. Oops. Sorry. Didn't mean to bring up Phillip." She was admiring her shoes from every angle and didn't catch his dour expression. "We're just friends...at least that's my definition and the more distance I can put in our relationship, the better. I think he was just about ready to forget his very proper aristocratic upbringing and make a serious pass at me. But he got himself under control and suggested I cut my hair instead. I'm surprised his ancestors ever procreated." She said it with a delightful mock British accent. Then her expression got comically diabolical. "These shoes will stop him cold."

If they don't, I will. Alex thought. How could she stand in those, much less walk? When she came over to him, she did so with the ease and grace of a circus performer. He helped her on with her coat so he could smell her hair. "So, I take it the reason I'm escorting you tonight is to keep Phillip at bay."

"No...the reason you're escorting me tonight is so I can wear these shoes." She patted him companionably on the cheek and went through the door, leaving her scent in her wake. Women were a mystery, he thought. And he did love a mystery.

He could have been just a little bit jealous, she thought, as she swept out the door in front of him. She hadn't really meant to mention Phillip, but since she did, he could have exhibited some manly antagonism. Oh well. Didn't matter. She was going to do a job.

Skye didn't know that he was a highly skilled agent and that hiding his emotions was part of his training. Phillip wasn't only a criminal, he was an idiot, thought Alex. On the other hand, Alex was relieved the man had not yet made a play for her. Too late now. If Phillip moved in, it would have to be through him. Alex was sure he could take him down without too much trouble. And there was a part of him that wished he would try.

CHAPTER 8

The estate of the seventeenth Duke of Stanhopeshire was magnificent. The limousine Alex had rented for the evening got in line with the others and allowed Skye time to assess the house and grounds. While she appreciated its beauty and grandeur, she was mentally stripping it down and thinking about the logical places to search.

"You know, it isn't too late to chuck those shoes and make a play for the estate instead."

"Excuse me?"

"Well, if Phillip is the heir, it would seem to me that he might just make that play for you if you were at his level and you would be, what, a Duchess or something?" He found royalty pretentious and more than a little pompous.

"Darling, a lot you know about British aristocracy. I'll never, ever be at Phillip's level. He would keep me in town while he would find a suitable blue-blooded wife to have the, let's see, nineteenth Duke. I'm not nearly rich enough for his family to overlook my flaws."

She thought she'd amused him from the delighted expression on his face, not knowing the pleasure came from her endearment. She'd said 'darling.' A sharp, hot feeling shot straight to his gut. Maybe a little lower. He liked it. A lot. It was something he could build on. The fact that Phillip would only have her as a mistress and not a wife was completely moot now anyway.

"Besides, these shoes were made for me alone," Skye went on. "Who needs a palace when you have a pair of shoes like these?" She continued to converse, but Alex could see her comparing the reality of the buildings and grounds with the drawings they had secured and imprinted in her brain. It was fascinating to see her operate on two levels. Too bad he couldn't tell her so. He made a pretense of making several business calls so she could concentrate on her reconnaissance. Some day they could return as a team. Soon, he hoped. He intended to talk to Jim about it as soon as he got back to Washington.

Skye looked at everything. Her mind was like a camera, taking a series of pictures and filing them away to be developed upon reflection. She saw the trucks from Kings Catering bringing in some of the food for the party, followed by trucks from Grather's Liquor and Wine Emporium, Branigan's Rental, Le Fleur Floral shops, R and J security, and The Westchester Orchestra. Other trade vans and vehicles lined the service entrance. She took note of all of the names. Feed her brain enough raw data, and sometimes patterns would emerge. She rarely forced conclusions. They would come. She would wait for them.

Harry Charles Albert Blythe, the seventeenth Duke of Stanhopeshire and his wife, Lady Emily Hawthorne Blythe were in the huge entryway greeting guests and making small talk. They were a handsome couple. He was tall, well built, with hazel eyes and a full head of thick silver hair. She was slim, blonde and had the most beautiful face money could buy. Only her hairdresser and makeup technician knew where the scars were. She was disciplined and worked hard to keep her body from plumping up like many of her friends at the club.

She watched the entrance, anxiously waiting for one guest in particular. They knew that Skyler Madison was to be escorted by an Alexander Springfield. She'd phoned Phillip's secretary earlier and provided his name.

When Lady Emily heard that her son had invited this Madison person to their home...their home! She was livid. She and Henry supported his seduction of this pilot and the use of her in their operation, but that didn't mean she had to have the common, vulgar, colonial bitch on their estate...the place reserved for people of position, wealth, impeccable connections...not ordinary working people. People who serve others simply do not come in the front door of a Duke's palace.

There were many positive reasons for Phillip to bring a captain of an international airline into their operation. Lady Emily was sure the creature must have slept her way to the cockpit...there was a reason they called it a cock pit. One simply had to ride enough cocks. It would not have happened at British Air. Those Colonials never did know their place.

Lady Emily was always able to carry on an inner dialogue with herself while she robotically performed the functions of her station. One only had to automatically recite two or three platitudes to each person, give them an air kiss, and send them off to the buffet table, private rooms, or bar, depending on their addictions. She did not sanction the use of illegal drugs on her estate. Only the buying and selling of them. And she never saw the contradiction. One was socially unacceptable, the other was business and allowed her to buy things. It certainly didn't worry her or trouble her conscience in the least.

She was smiling at the next person in line when she saw an absolutely stunning woman walk into the room on the arm of an astoundingly attractive man. Lady Emily Hawthorne Blythe was used to beautiful people in beautiful clothes, but the sight of the two of them was staggering. Each one would have turned heads in their own right, but put them together. Well. They were definitely stealing the spotlight, *her* spotlight she thought as her smile faded and was replaced with a look of malevolence. It was that slut Skyler Madison, she was sure of it.

The fact that they were standing in *her* home stealing *her* attention added immeasurably to the objections she had with this woman coming here and the bohemian she brought with her. Since nearly everyone had turned to see the spectacular couple, most people didn't see the daggers flying out of her well made-up, nearly wrinkle free eyes.

Sir Henry, whose back was to the door, turned when he caught the look in his wife's eyes. "Put your Lady Emily face back on, my dear," he whispered to her softly. "It wouldn't do to have our guests frightened out of their wits."

Sir Henry and Lady Emily had long ago fallen out of love with each other, if indeed there had ever been any love there to begin with. Once she'd produced the eighteenth heir they hadn't spent another night together. Theirs was now a strictly business arrangement that suited them both just fine. He had his mistresses in London, Bath, and York. She had Juan when she wanted Columbian, and Allen when she was feeling like someone from the colonies. Publicly, however, they were the picture of genteel devotion. They made it work, and it had, very nicely, for over thirty years.

"Lady Fran," she cooed in her smooth cultured voice to the next woman in the receiving line. "How nice of you to come down from the country for our little party." The fact was that the 'little party' had over 600 invited guests and it took twenty-five catering trucks to bring in all the food. Well, it was all in the frame of reference.

By the time the butler formally announced the entrance of Ms. Skyler Imogene Madison and Mr. Alexander Blake Springfield, Lady Emily had her antipathy firmly under control and shook their hands with polish and elegance. With a frozen smile, she greeted them and welcomed them to her home. She nearly got a kink in her neck from looking up at the couple. It made her seethe…but this time only on the inside.

"Thank you for the invitation. You're most gracious." Skye could see through Lady Emily's mask right into the dark thoughts below. She knew full well the invitation had come from Phillip without his mother's knowledge or sanction. He hadn't checked with her first. She supposed that Mama didn't like her little boy playing with the riffraff. Wait until Mama found out her son's new playmate had a badge and a gun and was going to bring her down. It wouldn't be long now and they would have enough evidence to start the ball rolling. The two consummate actresses continued to spar.

"Phillip has told us a great deal about you. He failed to mention, however, your...," she looked Skye up and down, "flair." The way she said it, it sounded like a definite flaw. Her cold, hard eyes emphasized that it was an egregious, unmistakable, unforgivable imperfection. "My husband, the Seventeenth Duke of Stanhopeshire, Sir Henry Harry Charles Albert Blythe."

Skye lowered both her eyes and her head slightly in deference. "Your Grace." She didn't present her hand. She wasn't wearing gloves. He noticed her bare hands and didn't offer his to her. Instead, he simply stared at her chest. Enjoy the party Sir Henry Harry Charles Albert Blythe you pretentious, lecherous prick, she thought; this may be your last one. Outwardly she smiled pleasantly.

"May I present my escort, Alexander Springfield from the United States." Alex knew Skye was teethed on protocol and her upbringing was showing. She was as smooth as silk and her voice was low and refined.

There was one thing that Lady Emily appreciated and that was a handsome man...especially one with an Armani tuxedo and a Rolex watch. She turned to him with genuine interest and said. "Welcome to our home, Mr. Springfield."

She presented him with her gloved hand and he dutifully raised it to his lips. "Your Grace, it's indeed a pleasure."

"Is Sir Phillip inside?" asked Skye. Since he was the person who issued the invitation manners dictated that she greet him as well.

"At the moment I'm not sure where my son is. He has many duties as the host and could be anywhere. He's invited so many of his acquaintances. Once he gets started on a guest list, I'm afraid he just gets a bit carried away. No matter. If you don't see him this evening, I'm sure you can leave your card with Mr. Jenkins, his secretary. You'll find him in the hall." This was a complete breach of both etiquette and decorum. Lady Emily issued the slight in an imperious, frosty tone.

"Please enjoy." Lady Emily turned away from Skye and Alex and aimed her bright smile and extended her hand to the next guest.

Very effectively, Skye and Alex were brushed off and left to their own devices. Skye slid her arm through Alex's and entered the noisy ballroom.

"As I said, I can't believe their class ever procreated."

"So Phillip failed to mention your...flair, did he?" Alex chuckled.

She looked back at Lady Emily, busy with her platitudes and air kisses. "And he failed to mention your little pinched face and that prominent stretched out smile from one too many face lifts, you old cow," said Skye under her breath using the same cultured voice and urbane demeanor. Alex chuckled louder as they made their way into the ballroom.

"My goodness. Could it get any chillier in here?"

Skye giggled. "Maybe we'd better go back and get our coats."

"Tell me again why we're here?"

"To mix, mingle, and be seen by everyone who is anyone."

"Ah, yes. So tell me," Alex said casually as he grabbed two flutes of champagne from a tuxedoed waiter. "Just how many people in the known universe know about the Imogene?"

"I have a feeling one too many."

Everything was absolutely breathtaking. Candles lent both light and atmosphere and were everywhere. The flower arrangements were magnificent. Skye leaned over to smell a rose. No scent. Must be one of Phillip's royal hybrids.

Skye barely made eye contact with the pretty Asian woman moving through the room with a tray. It was Linda. She was nearly unrecognizable. She'd changed her hair and wore altogether different makeup. She didn't walk with her usual self-confidence and looked like she put on 20 pounds. It was all in the grooming and the bit of subtle padding, but the effect was perfect. The lovely Rhodes Scholar was transformed into an Asian immigrant anxious to serve hors d'oeuvres to the pampered gentry. She had just the right combination of awe and subservience.

As Linda moved closer Skye saw the mushrooms on the tray. God, why did it have to be mushrooms? She hated mushrooms and Linda knew it. Skye smiled as she took another sip of champagne and nodded to an acquaintance. Just wait, Linda. Your time will come.

"Something funny?" asked Alex.

It would have been so nice to voice her thoughts and impressions. He would make a great sounding board and she could share the inside joke with him. She could tell him that Linda was an agent and that she was bringing the dreaded mushrooms right for her in such a way that she would probably have to take one of the damn things. Well, he didn't have clearance, and that was that. She would have to lie to him, deceive him, use him.

She shook her head. "Nothing's funny. I was just wondering if I would have to kill you now that you know about my middle name."

"What…you're going to shoot me with that ridiculous little gun you have stashed in your purse?"

Skye's eyes narrowed. "How do you…?"

"I dug through there this morning to get your cell phone, remember? Someone didn't want to move off the sofa."

"God, was that only this morning?" Better to just ignore the gun comment and move on.

Alex watched the crowd with a practiced eye. While many heads turned in Skye's direction, none had a look of someone who wanted to do her harm. Not since Lady Emily, he thought with some amusement. He liked the feel of her arm through his. It gave him a wonderful feeling of possession.

His intuition punched him into alert when he saw the Asian waiter subtly making her way toward Skye. She stopped, moved and served in a perfectly choreographed manner, but Skye was definitely the target. And he was Skye's shield. Alex was about to put himself between her and Skye when it dawned on him who it was. He didn't know Linda personally, but her pictures were included in Skye's dossier. She must have been assigned to watch Skye's back. And, he thought, to get him out of the way so Skye would be free to do some checking around. Anticipating that it might be a tray of mushrooms in his lap, he decided to save his tuxedo and find someone he knew to chat with for a while. He could also do a bit of checking around himself. It would be nice if he could remove the barrier of lies between them and work with her openly. It would be both exciting and entertaining to be a team tonight.

"Darling?" he said and Skye turned to him with anticipation, raising her eyebrows. Strange how quickly she adjusted to exchanging endearments. "I think I see someone over there I know. The man is deadly dull, so I won't take you over. How about we circulate, you find Phillip, impress him with your shoes, and we meet for a dance later?"

Perfect, she thought. He was leaving her alone. Could it be too perfect? She pushed that thought out of her mind, or at least into the back of it.

"Sounds like a plan. Phillip will hear we've arrived and will have a full description of your physical attributes including the size of your underwear by the time we meet up again."

"Yeah, well at least I'm wearing some," said Alex.

"Still curious, huh?"

Linda was almost right beside him when, with a slight shake of Skye's head that Alex pretended not to see, she veered off.

Alex leaned down and gave her a soft kiss on the lips. The sparks were there even though the contact was brief and she had to remind herself again that she was working. "That'll give Phillip something else to hear about," whispered Alex in a low sensual voice.

Skye wasn't accustomed to public displays of affection and was a bit rattled when Alex turned and walked slowly through the crowd toward the billiard room. Linda came up to her with her eyes lowered, but with a telltale smile on her face.

"Well, well. You're playing your cover very nicely," she said softly. "Mushroom?"

"Body punch?" retorted Skye sweetly.

"Sorry, madam. My English not good. Bloody punch on table in other room. Only have delicious mushroom."

With that, Linda moved on, laughing on the inside but never breaking stride. She was very glad she didn't have to bump the waiter's tray of champagne all over Alex. Although she would have liked to have been in on the clean up. She definitely would have volunteered for the trouser detail.

There was the added advantage of being able to stay with the caterer. She would have been fired for the mishap. Linda and Max had joined Kings Catering Service a few months earlier so they would be in a position to mix without being suspicious. Skye figured that the Duke would eventually use them since they were one of the finest in London, and she was right.

Discreetly Skye made her way to the hallway. She'd hoped this was the first of many invitations, but judging from Lady Emily's reaction to her, she'd better see all she could this time around. She may not get another chance.

There were people everywhere. Skye tried to blend in by stopping and chatting from group to group until she reached the door to the office. Standing with her back to the doorknob, she tested it. It was locked. Only a minor inconvenience. She would have to come in from the outside. Fanning herself, as if she was warm, she slowly walked out on to the grounds. She didn't notice the sharp blue eyes of her escort and protector following her every move.

There weren't many people out on the terrace. It was a cool night, and Skye was glad she wore long sleeves. She studied the windows surreptitiously. They had a Series CV72 security alarm system. The good news was it was a Mickey Mouse system that would barely keep out a determined teenager. The bad news was that if there were something of great importance in there, the security system would be better. She decided not to waste her time and possible discovery by breaking into the office.

Taking a stroll around the terrace, she casually looked at each window. The moon was full and lovers where walking by hand in hand, but Skye was all business now. The full moon meant both additional light and additional vulnerability. She could see better, but she could also be seen. She wore the long-sleeved black dress for a reason, and that was to blend more easily into the night if she had to. Judging from the fact that the lovers along the path barely looked up, she was feeling quite invisible and pleased with her plan.

The place was huge. She didn't want to be gone more that 45 minutes at a time. Linda and Max would keep an eye on Alex and would improvise, if necessary. She didn't want to be missed by any one of the Blythes, either. They had a great deal to do as the hosts but they may have other people in the crowd working with them. Turning, she walked down to another terrace that sat lower in the ground. It was fairly isolated and relatively new. The bricks were old, as old as the others, but the feeling of them beneath her feet was different. Spongier. Work had been done here…more recently than the rest of the terrace. With a manor house that was nearly 400 years old in some parts, that may not mean much. Still, it's the little things that add up and she was a master at noticing the little things. It was an interesting detail and like the others in her mind, would stay filed away until she needed it. She memorized its precise location and looked casually to the left and right. With complete nonchalance, she leaned over and placed her nose in the roses at the base of the bank of windows on the side of the building. Again, no scent. Her eyes slid to the window sill. Bingo. Top-of-the line security cameras hidden everywhere. That was good. It meant there was something important to guard. On the other hand, she was probably already on tape. Damn. That was bad.

She started to turn back, when she heard movement behind her.

"Getting a little air?" How did Alex find her out here? "Or did you have plans to meet someone else and dump me?"

He came up out of the shadows where he had been watching her work without looking like she was working. She was very, very good. She appeared for all the world like a woman without a care taking an evening stroll. It was only her alert and probing eyes that gave a clue she had the house under close surveillance.

He had ditched the server's surreptitious scrutiny when she'd returned to the kitchen for more mushrooms. He wasn't sure who else was at the party to watch either him or Skye, but his job was to keep her in sight, and he intended to do it thoroughly…full coverage…from top to bottom.

When her heart settled, she smiled broadly. This was perfect. *Too perfect?* That voice whispered again. She ignored it and decided the best course of action was to play it out as if she really did plan to meet him here. There was no audio with the security tapes, so she acted out the part of an excited lover. It really wasn't much of a stretch.

As he came up to her, she walked into his arms and kissed him passionately, effectively cutting off what he was about to say. The words evaporated from his busy tongue as she moved her hands over his chest and up under the tuxedo jacket.

Alex knew that he was providing cover for her now, but he wasn't beyond taking advantage of the situation. Deciding he was more than willing to sacrifice his body in order to give her a reason for being there, he held on to her and started to work his way down her jaw line, kissing her soft neck, aiming for the place that had been driving him to distraction since he picked her up at the hotel.

Well, that worked, she thought as she reluctantly pulled away. She was sure the embrace looked authentic to anyone watching on the cameras. Looked authentic? Listen to herself. It *was* authentic. That was a bona fide, unadulterated, indisputable hot body clutch. All done in the line of duty, she told herself severely. A perfect cover. Yeah, right. Her body temperature had risen considerably and the cool air felt good against her heated skin. The fact that it was an utterly fabulous experience that made her forget her line of duty…well. That was a bonus. Her heart whispered to her, more like a windfall Skye.

"Hi," said Alex. Not too clever, he thought, but it was the best he could do without any air in his lungs or wit left in his searing brain.

"Hi," answered Skye, in the same state as he.

"I was missing you." His hands casually moved up her back.

"Done with your boring companion?" asked Skye.

"Yup. I think he's already talking someone else into unconsciousness. I don't think he'll notice I'm gone," answered Alex.

She got what she needed out here and knew they should probably return, but she couldn't seem to get her legs to move.

"How about we go in, maybe have a dance or two, and then blow on back to the hotel," said Alex.

"Tired?"

"Far from it. I'm anxious to start the evening together."

His arms were still firmly around her. She didn't seem anxious to pull away, so he just kept holding her. It was nice.

"What have we been doing?" asked Skye.

"I feel this has been one long evening of foreplay so far. What we've been doing is making me frustrated as hell."

Skye laughed. He was so direct. After being around a cold fish like Phillip, Alex was just about as different as two men could be and still be the same species. "Let's go in. I have to find Phillip and at least say hello."

"Give me a minute here," he said, smiling. When she started to close in on his lips again, he deliberately held her at arms length. "No, I mean give me a minute without full frontal contact. I would hate to have to walk behind you the rest of the evening."

Skye laughed heartily. "Perhaps you should take these things into consideration when you get your tuxedoes tailored. Maybe a fuller cut?" she suggested helpfully, but 'accidentally' bumped him so he had to start all over again. His eyes narrowed.

He was, however, a man of iron will. After a few moments of deep breathing, he managed to bring himself under control.

"Must be the full moon," she said as he took her hand and walked slowly back to the ballroom doors.

"Yeah. That's it. It has nothing to do with the unbelievable perfume, that ravishing dress, the thought of you with no underwear. Damn. Maybe we should talk about debits and credits or something," said Alex.

"I guess now is not the time to tell you the name of the perfume is Midnight Seduction," teased Skye. "And it's 11:57."

He just groaned.

"Okay, how about I tell you all the parts of a jet engine and how to dismantle it for routine maintenance."

"That could work."

They were laughing, his arm around her waist, his hand gently riding her hip, when three security guards passed them dressed up as guests. The guard in the screening room had seen Skye and called them to duty. When the man arrived, they relaxed. Looked just like a couple of lovers to them, but they were still required to check it out. It was the location of their meet that alerted them. They were hoping he would go a bit farther and they could see what was under that dress, but it seemed he had more restraint than they would have in the same situation. She was a stunner, all right. The guards were dispatched to make sure the couple kept moving.

Both Skye and Alex spotted them but continued to walk, each pretending they didn't see a thing. Skye was continuing her litany about the component parts of a jet engine and he was just enjoying the sense and sound of her.

Alex could feel the slight stiffening of her muscles under the soft fabric of her dress when she spotted them. He smiled to himself. Ready to do battle, are you darling? Such a sweet thing he was...was what? Not falling in love with. Was he? God. Get a hold of yourself man. He was in the middle of an operation. A pleasant one to be sure, but...but what? What was he doing? What was he feeling? A crush? He wasn't a schoolboy. He didn't get crushes. Okay, then. Infatuation? That sounded so brainless. Well, Alexander, then that leaves love. He looked over at her and smiled as she explained the mechanical details of propulsion at the same time she kept a wary eye on the passing guards. Shit and damnation. Then that leaves love.

He didn't get to finish the thought, as Skye spotted Phillip and waved. Alex frowned. He really was a handsome devil. Phillip thought the same thing about Alex, but was too aristocratic to frown.

"Phillip Blythe, this is Alexander Springfield," said Skye as she introduced the two men. Things were a bit less formal with the younger generation and the men shook hands. Phillip had a warm, firm grip that Alex didn't like.

Phillip felt the same way. In his mind this Alexander Springfield wasn't going to step into his place beside the glorious Skyler. He was glad this was his turf. No upstart colonial was going to be able to stand up under the weight of eighteen generations of royal blood and an estate that dated back to the seventeenth century. To his mind, any woman would be insane to throw away a chance to be a Duchess. And contrary to Skye's assumption, he fully intended to marry her. His ego didn't see any of the obvious pitfalls, and his ego was monumental.

"Mr. Blythe. Skye's told me a great deal about you," said Alex pleasantly, implying he and Skye talked all the time, and had over a period of many years.

What a strange thing for him to say, thought Skye. She'd told him practically nothing. Except maybe that Phillip wouldn't like her shoes. Boy games, she thought.

"Mr. Springfield. I'm at a disadvantage. She has told me nothing about you," Phillip said genteelly, his fabulous lips parted to reveal a friendly, if aloof, smile. "How nice of you to escort Skyler this evening. I'm afraid I have far too many duties as host to be able to attend to her as I should."

He turned his smile to Skye. He knew from years in front of a mirror that his smile was nearly deadly when it came to charming the ladies. He had legions of women who would attest to that. "Skyler, I have a few moments now, and hope that you'll have the first dance with me. The orchestra is about to begin."

Alex wasn't fooled by Skye's false show of friendly welcome. Phillip was deadly handsome, with a finely tuned body, heir to an incredible title, and standing in one of the oldest and largest estates in England. He was a singular catch. But Alex also knew he didn't have a chance to win Skyler's heart.

Well, he was almost sure Phillip didn't have a chance. Skye was investigating him, after all. Her sense of justice wouldn't allow it. Would it? He simply didn't know enough about the female heart.

Alex suddenly felt a hot stab of jealousy. Goddamn self-absorbed prick. He would have preferred to slam his fist into pretty boy's smiling face than shake his well-manicured hand. Well, he could act too, and he decided to turn up the old Springfield charm.

He smiled warmly and tightened his hold on Skye's waist. Take that you fucking asshole. Out loud he said. "I'm feeling generous tonight. I'll go mingle and I won't be back to claim her until your other duties take you away from her again."

Christ. A male pissing contest right here on the terrace, thought Skye. She knew that Alex's possessive grip on her waist was a signal to Phillip. Mine. She caught Phillip's momentary flash of annoyance. So he had feelings under all that polish after all. She was almost too fascinated by it to feel resentment herself. Almost. *Okay boys,* she thought, *enough of the growling. You're making me feel like a bone.*

"I would be delighted to have the first dance with you, Phillip." She moved away from Alex's encircling hold and took Phillip's arm, a move that Alex didn't like a bit and that Phillip thought was long overdue. "How about I meet you later in the ballroom, Alex?"

She smiled back over her shoulder and winked. Yes that was definitely a wink. It kept Alex from grabbing her back to his side. He crossed his arms and watched with a great deal of satisfaction as Skye had to lower her head a bit to engage Phillip in conversation and that he looked down at her shoes more than once. He was too civilized to show distress, but Alex knew it was there. It made him chuckle as he went to the bar to order something stronger than champagne. Being tall made it nearly impossible to buy clothes off the rack, but it sure had its advantages. And besides, he hadn't bought anything off the rack in years. He figured he won that skirmish and ordered a very manly double shot of Scotch.

A battle won was sweet, but the feeling of victory faded as Skye stayed with Phillip for the next few hours. Or, more accurately, Phillip never let her out of his sight and was by her side constantly. Alex frowned as he looked at Phillip's hand move from the small of her back to around her shoulders. Why did she let him do that, he thought irritably.

He knew Skye was doing her job, making assessments and watching for associations. Hoping Phillip or his associates would say something she could use. But enough already. Now the prick was moving his hand up and down her back. The fact that she nonchalantly pulled away from him didn't dampen the seething temper that was rising in his gut. He'd had enough. Shoving himself away from the wall he was leaning against, he was about to start across the room when a hand appeared on his arm.

He hadn't even perceived the woman who was attached to it coming at him. She was a beautiful blonde with exotic green eyes and a broad, seductive smile.

"Hi there." Her eyes were a bit too bright. From alcohol or from something stronger, he wasn't quite sure. If she was stoned, it was just a light buzz. "I saw you standing here alone and I thought I would come over and introduce myself." Actually she'd asked around, found out he was filthy rich, and laid the groundwork for seduction. She needed a new source of income and decided this handsome American was the winner of her double sweepstakes…financial backer and bed partner.

"I'm Samantha Mountbatten Firth." She held out her hand and waited for him to take it in his. This Alex did automatically. Did everyone in this damn country have three names, he thought, slightly resenting the barrier she made between him and his target. Skye was starting to move on, and he wanted to get to her.

Samantha was confident in her ability to bring him around and was undaunted by his apparent lack of interest. "And you're…?"

"Oh, sorry. The name is Alexander Springfield." Hoping that would do it he looked at her again and gave her hand a perfunctory kiss. Even distracted and preoccupied, he was handsome and rich enough to make Samantha's heart leap. She tried again.

"Would you like to join me for a drink so we can get to know each other?" She took his arm companionably.

Why was this woman talking to him? He thought as he saw Skye laugh at something Phillip was saying and frowned.

Samantha followed his glare. Was this man dense? Was he looking at that tall, rather pretty bitch, or was he staring at Phillip? Maybe he was gay. That would explain his total lack of interest.

She thought she would give it another try, leaning into him and pressing her very generous breasts against his arm.

"Do you know that woman talking with Phillip?"

He nodded.

"Far too tall for him. Actually far too tall to be wearing three-inch heels. Probably one of those anorexic fashion models who just want to be noticed."

"Well it's working," he said as another of Phillip's associates rushed up to him, anxious for an introduction to the ravishing beauty on his arm.

Yes, she thought. Definitely gay. His arm didn't even quiver when she brushed up against him.

"Well," she said, looking around for another possible quarry. "If you're ever in the mood for a little side dish, give me a call." She placed one of her cards into his pocket and patted it.

He looked down at her and smiled obediently. She was a lovely creature, but right now she was just in his way.

"I'll remember that." But he had forgotten her by the time he had crossed the room.

He almost got to Skye, when an older woman grabbed his arm. "Alex! How are you?" It was a woman he had been avoiding all evening. If he hadn't been so intent on Skye, he would have seen her coming and been able to escape. As it was, years of indoctrination by his mother forced him to be polite.

"Hannah. How are you?" he said. He knew he would only have to ask her one question, then nod periodically. Hannah Freason was the wife of a business associate. She was probably on the guest list because she was with the International Red Cross. He admired her work, but she had a daughter at MIT, or was it Berkley? Anyway it was Hannah's fondest wish that they meet, marry, and have babies.

Damn it! A man who looked like a woman's dream of a Latin lover was now escorting Skye to the dance floor. Alex was irritated to see he was tall enough for her and that he wanted more than just a dance. It took all of his willpower to refrain from flying across the dance floor and tackling the perverted middle-aged son-of-a-bitch. She was talking to him animatedly and listening to his banter, looking like a relaxed guest and seemed to be enjoying herself immensely.

Then he saw the operation. Well done! The tall, very good looking man in a server's uniform had read something in Skye's movements and was making his way to her. Just as the music stopped, she turned with her arm looped in the arm of her dance partner. The waiter, Alex saw it was Maxwell Feller, offered them the tray carrying the flutes of champagne while Skye kept her hand on the Latin lover's arm. Playing on a man's natural tendency to take charge in this situation, she waited a few beats. Her partner didn't disappoint. He took two flutes, handed her one and kept one for himself. She took the offered glass by the stem, all the time engaging him in conversation. He wouldn't even remember this chain of events, Alex was sure of it. It was all so perfectly timed, choreographed, and executed. Skye now had a full set of complete fingerprints on the perfect medium. She raised her glass and drank the liquid. Always chatting. Always listening. The man was getting more aggressive now, his hands going to her waist, his body invading her personal space. Alex decided to rescue her. She got what she wanted. Now he wanted to get what he wanted.

He left Hannah in mid-sentence, crossed the room, and walked up beside her.

Skye knew he was there; she had felt his eyes on her all evening. It gave her a warm, tingly feeling. Right now, she was trying to disengage herself from a very enthusiastic friend of Phillip's. She'd gleaned a great deal of information. Most of it would be useless, but she would mentally process it when she was alone and separate out that which may be important. Her mind was like a machine, taping conversations, making connections, remembering dates and times. Skye was ready to leave so she could have time to think.

This last man was someone she was sure she knew. It wasn't just his face, that didn't look all that familiar and his name, Juan Michallini, didn't ring any bells. Handsome, close to 60, great dark eyes, nice hair. She took a picture of his face into her mind and the only match was a brief encounter sometime in the recent past...Phillip had probably introduced them at some function. She knew they hadn't talked, because it was his voice that nudged her memory. That voice made her spine tingle. Not in desire, but in recognition. And it wasn't recent. As a matter of fact it was a very long time ago. She would process that later. He said he was a wine merchant. It was strange that he didn't know about some of the California wines. That only reinforced her decision to single him out for special finger printing.

"Well, Skye. Ready for that dance?" Alex asked as she turned to him. From the dark, smoldering look in his eyes, he hadn't been having any fun. She thought she'd better dance with him before he started up with Phillip again. She could see Phillip coming to claim her. "I would love it. It was nice meeting you, Señor Michallini." He took her hand, held it for a moment longer than Alex thought was necessary, then turned to Alex.

"She's a delightful partner. Enjoy your dance and the rest of the evening, señorita." He lightly kissed her fingers and moved away into the crowd. Alex frowned after him.

Under her breath, Skye said, "stay close." She finished most of the champagne and reached out to place it automatically on the nearest waiter's tray. Alex smiled when he pretended not to recognize the deft moves of Max as he placed himself back beside Skye at the precise moment she needed to put down the glass. It wasn't like Max did anything obvious such as hover around her elbow. He had simply timed his rotation perfectly. Alex was sure that the glass would be bagged and ready for the lab within the next few minutes. No eye contact, no obvious signal. When he got into a position to be open with Skye, he wanted to find out what she did to signal Max. It was fascinating.

Phillip hurried over as Alex took her arm. In another deft move, she extended her hand and before he could speak she said to him in honeyed tones, "Phillip. I think we'll leave right after the next dance. Thank you for a lovely evening. You really should get back to the rest of your guests. I've monopolized you enough."

Alex's sentiments exactly.

"You're right, of course." Phillip took her hand and lightly kissed the knuckles, then leaned over and kissed both cheeks. Anything more in public wouldn't have been proper. This was going the very limit. A bit too racy for him, but with that oaf standing there, he felt it was necessary to mark his territory. He then handed Skye's hand over to Alex. "I'll see you soon, Skyler. I'll have Mr. Jenkins give you a call."

The man can't even say goodnight to a beautiful woman properly, Alex thought, realizing that if Phillip would have made the display any less platonic, he might had decked him right there.

"Mr. Springfield." Phillip nodded at Alex barely acknowledging his presence.

"Mr. Blythe." Alex did the same, deliberately ignoring the fact he should have acknowledged Phillip's title and position with a 'sir' in there somewhere. It may have been petty, but it gave Alex a kick all the same.

"No 'thanks for coming'?" Alex said as Phillip walked into a crowd of people gathered around the bar. "And who is Mr. Jenkins?"

"His secretary," answered Skye.

"He has his secretary call you for a date?" snorted Alex derisively.

"Yes."

"Putz."

"That would be Sir Putz."

"And you go for this guy?"

She just smiled enigmatically. They reached the dance floor and Skye moved easily into Alex's arms. He was a bit stiff from the residual annoyance with Phillip.

"Relax," said Skye softly, running her hand over his broad shoulders and letting it rest lightly near the back of his neck. She was amused with herself when she had to fight her hand's desire to continue the journey and run it through his wavy hair.

As the lovely music of a Mozart waltz played, Alex automatically led Skye in circles around the room.

"That's easy for you to say. Every man in the place has been standing in line to touch the magnificent Captain Madison. And all the time Phillip the Splendid, at least in his own mind, had his hands all over you," said Alex, more petulantly than he had intended.

Skye laughed with genuine delight. "Phillip never had, nor has he ever had, his hands all over me." It was a bit insulting to be the object of two men's struggle, her strong female mind insisted. But she was amused by it. And, okay, it was rather cute. Alex looked so...so peevish. Competition was definitely something he was unaccustomed to. And it was endearing. She knew she should stop herself from sliding any further toward a liaison with Alex...or more accurately falling for him. But at the moment she couldn't think of one reason why.

"And you go for this guy?" he asked again.

"I'm going home with you, aren't I?" she asked simply and made him hot all over.

Alex drew her closer and she willingly moved into his space, molding her body to his. He was beginning to relax as some of the annoyance drained out of him. She could feel it. He was a wonderful dancer. His moves were automatic, but fluid and graceful. She placed her cheek against his and they let the music move through them.

"This is nice." Closing her eyes, she sighed as she felt his hands...one on the small of her back, and one gently holding her hand, palm to palm. It was a delicious feeling to be in the hands of a master and she let herself soften in his arms.

"Yes. It is," he agreed, holding her closer still. He'd never danced with someone so close to his height before and it made for a perfect fit. A perfect match.

He smiled over at Phillip when he turned Skye around and their eyes met. Phillip's eyes narrowed with rage and he sent daggers across the room. Alex raised his eyebrows and put more into the smile. Mine now, pal. You lose! He then turned his back on Phillip in a gesture of manly dismissal. Not only did he have the most beautiful woman in the room in his arms, engaged in the age-old socially acceptable method of making love in public, he could rub it in the face of his rival. It just didn't get any better than that.

Skye felt the smile. "What?"

"Nothing."

"Alex?"

"Okay, okay. Phillip looks like he could chew glass. And I'm not a big enough man to be gracious about it."

Men, she thought. "Now Alex. Don't gloat."

"Who's gloating?"

"I do believe you are." She pulled back and smiled into his eyes. She didn't realize the picture she made...the tall, slender beauty smiling into the eyes of her virile, handsome companion, dancing a waltz in a mirrored ballroom full of light. But Alex knew, and it was all he could do to keep himself from putting his mouth over hers and devouring her in one big bite.

"Let me have my fun. I had to fend off matrons with eligible daughters all evening."

"You sound like Cinderella's Prince Charming." As a matter of fact, she thought he was the picture of Prince Charming. With the romantic ballroom setting and Alex dressed in an impeccable black tux, he was the image of every little girl's fairytale and her little girl's heart skipped a beat.

"What?" asked Alex.

"Oh nothing, I don't want to feed that titanic ego of yours," answered Skye.

"Come on, feed me. Remember the sacrifices I made tonight."

"Okay. I just was thinking how much like Prince Charming you look."

"Now where did that come from?" He wasn't sure why he was so delighted by it. It seemed so un-Skye like to give in to the fantasy.

"Too much champagne, I guess," she said.

His smile transformed from friendly to seductive.

"Does that mean I get to kiss the princess?" he asked devilishly, lowering his lips.

The music stopped just then and Skye moved away from him. She placed her hand gently on his chest. "Not here, prince," she said with more than a little regret. There was enough magic in the look he gave her, that it may have been a spell. "What do you say we snag the carriage and get the hell out of here?"

"I'd say you rule, your majesty."

It took some time to work their way through the room. And all the while, Emily watched Phillip on one side of the room and Skye and the American on the other. When was Phillip going to make his move on her, sweep her off her feet, and bring her into their employ? Sometimes Emily was afraid Phillip was a bit on the slow side, both physically and mentally. She still had no doubt he would be able to seduce her. The tall bitch looked as sleazy and easy as hell and their son was handsome and rich enough. Then there was the push of the title and castle. With the number of women they'd had to pay off over the years she knew his equipment was operational. What was he waiting for? Where was Henry? Maybe he could give the boy some advice.

Henry discreetly disappeared several times during the gala. Emily knew he was bouncing on his bed upstairs. That was okay with her. Juan promised to spend the night with her. What a dear. He knew how keyed up she got. It was almost five years ago they met. He wined her, dined her, seduced her, and screwed her silly. Then she casually mentioned their dire straits. They were actually thinking about letting go of some of the servants. Juan looked richer than Midas to her, so she thought she would just let it slip into the conversation.

He suggested that there were many ways to finance her lifestyle. She detested drugs, but found she abhorred a lack of money more. So she listened to his proposition. They had been both bed partners and business partners ever since.

Juan got her all set up. He was their savior. Provided all the consulting and only took a cut of the profits, after expenses or some such thing. Didn't matter. The money was pouring in and she was a happy woman.

When she saw Juan and Skye dancing she did a slow burn. Wasn't it bad enough she had to watch her son courting this...this common person? When she saw the slut dancing with Juan, she almost chewed off the edge of her glass with her teeth. Did he have to look so delighted with her? And those ridiculous shoes she was wearing, put her right at his eye level…those fabulous, irresistible, burning dark eyes. She saw his hands roaming the bitch's back and wanted them on her. This time the stem of her flute snapped. Tossing the pieces on a passing tray, she decided to break them up.

She was almost there when she saw Alex approaching them. Good. She hoped he was going to take the tall sluttish tart away from Juan and away from here. She frowned. It showed how deep her agitation was that she allowed her face to create a worry wrinkle between her eyebrows. She'd just paid a fortune to have the skin around her eyes tucked and smoothed out. Aghast, she remembered herself and raised her eyebrows until the line disappeared. She turned to chat with the wife of one of the lesser Lords while she watched the exchange between her son and the colonial couple. It looked like that common person might have cut out Phillip. She actually felt somewhat relieved with that. After what she witnessed, that woman practically throwing herself at Juan, maybe they had better rethink their strategy of bringing Skyler Madison in.

Lady Emily looked around the room for Juan and saw several of their clients. Juan's plan was so clever, no one would ever know the Blythes were their supplier. The Blythes, along with their socially connected son, would identify likely customers in the clubs and shops around the city. One gets very adept at recognizing the signs of either a potential addict or a current user. Once identified, Juan's people would set the bait, recruit them, and the money would start to flow.

Their clients bought their drugs in exclusive flower shops located in prominent sections of the city, a perfect front for well-heeled people to buy high-grade cocaine. Clients would pay an exorbitant amount of money for a few roses, and they would leave with a box of flowers and a little extra something tucked into the corner. Inside the little packets that usually contained a powder to preserve the freshness of the blooms, they packaged their product. Nose candy. All very civilized and right under the watchful eye of the silly, common constables. Everyone was happy and no one was hurt. These people weren't filthy addicts mugging people in the streets. They were just partial to cocaine for their recreation and could easily afford the habit…what's a few thousand a week to them. Emily felt not a shadow of guilt or concern. She was providing a service, and in return, she could maintain her lifestyle. It was what she was born to…entitled to. Juan was taking her to Paris shopping next week so she hoped they would score big this evening. Since the thought of shopping made her hormones run wild, she decided maybe she would sandwich Allen in before she spent her night with Juan. She went in search of him, leaving the wife of the lesser Lord to wonder if it was something she'd said.

Alex's driver opened the door and they gratefully sank into the rich leather cushions of the back seat.

"My feet are killing me," sighed Skye as she kicked off her shoes and accepted the mineral water he handed her.

"Then why did you wear those shoes?" Women. Still a mystery.

She looked at Alex like he was a moron.

"It wasn't the shoes. It was the feet of all the half-smashed idiots who thought they could dance. I kept getting stepped on."

"Oh. I see." He leaned over and took her feet in his hands and positioned her until they were in his lap. He gently started to massage the ache from them. She made little whimpering noises in her throat. It was all he could do to keep his mind on the task. His hands wanted to move up her legs and explore what there was beneath the dress.

"Did I die and go to heaven?" sighed Skye in a breathy voice that sent shivers right through Alex's spine.

"Close enough," Alex said as he looked at her. "Why don't you lay your head back and close your eyes. We're still an hour from the hotel."

"What a wonderful idea." It would give her time to process her information without the distraction of small talk.

She had her eyes closed, but Alex knew she wasn't asleep. She was replaying the night's impressions and conversations. Making plans. Never once did she turn off the brain. He could see it working and he let her do her job.

"The time has come," he said when the limo parked in front of the hotel.

"What? It's morning and you turn into a pumpkin?" asked Skye, opening her eyes and smiling at him. She stretched and yawned and Alex's willpower took another beating. He had restrained himself as he engaged in Skye watching all the way back. He had on the early business reports from Tokyo and was taking notes for a meeting he had the following week, but mostly he just enjoyed the view inside the limo...Skye with a slight smile on her lips, her eyes closed, her body relaxed. She was a mouth-watering sight.

"No, that was the carriage." Alex got out and turned to offer her his hand. She took it and gracefully exited the back seat.

"Oh yeah."

She smiled and thanked the driver.

"No, the time has come to answer the question that has occupied my thoughts all evening," said Alex as he walked toward the hotel lobby.

"And that is?" She liked the feel of his arm around her as he escorted her up the front steps.

"Are you wearing any underwear beneath that dress?" She stopped cold in front of the door as the doorman opened it, and looked up at him.

"And that occupied your mind all evening?"

She smiled and thanked the doorman as they walked into the lobby.

"All evening."

"My, my. Maybe you should get out more."

"I'm very focused," answered Alex and let his hand slide slightly south of her waist. They walked across the lobby and Alex pushed the button to call the elevator. The doors opened almost immediately.

"Indeed," she said as she stepped into the elevator.

As soon as the doors shut, she put her arms around his neck. "So you thought about what lies beneath this dress all evening...how odd." She gave him a peck on the lips. "How curious." And another. "How strange." Now she was lingering a bit longer. "How single minded." And longer still. "How extraordinary." She molded her body to his and parted her lips to deepen the kiss.

"You have no idea," he said as the elevator doors slid open and he moved her out into the hallway still holding her in his arms. He stopped halfway to her room and pinned her against the wall. His lips came down on hers for another assault. She moaned and it fueled his desire. His kiss went from playful to lustful as his hands moved expertly over her body. "You're so beautiful," he whispered and kissed the side of her neck just under the ear. "Please. Let me..." He didn't finish his sentence as she moved her lips back to his. He could feel her yielding, her heart beating faster, her breath quickening with his own.

They continued kissing and touching as they wound down the hall. When they got to her door, she took out her key and swiped it through the slot, swiftly and expertly. Hands steady, even though she was trembling all over. Pilot's training. Steady hands, no matter what.

The door opened somehow and they were in the room. She leaned against the back of the door to close it and he surrounded her again, putting both hands on either side of her and pressing his body against hers.

"Skye." His mouth greedily, hungrily devouring her lips, her neck, then back to her mouth. "Oh, Christ, you smell so good."

Her scent filled his head and her body's response under his exploring hands left his palms tingling with anticipation. But he pulled back, his eyes reflecting passion, need and longing. Still, they were asking for her consent. Begging for her sign to go ahead. "Skye?" was all he could say.

Her eyes held a welcoming glow. They were bold and dark and filled with the same need he felt running through him like a wave. She smiled a devastatingly sweet smile.

"Would you take my word for it now, if I were to tell you what I have on under here?" She gave him a teasing nip on his lip.

He managed to get his breathing under control. "Of course, I would. But I'd much prefer to uncover the mystery myself." He looked so wonderfully expectant, so boyishly hopeful, so incredibly sexy, he was completely irresistible.

She laughed and started to pull the studs out of his shirt. "Uncover away. But I get to play too. Please tell me I'm not going to discover boxers with Tweetie Birds on them."

"Good God, no. Those are in the laundry." Laughing and totally aroused, he swept her up in his arms as if she was weightless and kissed her brainless as he kicked open the bedroom door. She remembered admiring his strength before her brain emptied and she was lost in another wave of desire.

The sun was coming up and Juan was on his secure phone in his limousine. His real name was Juan Carlos Franscious Laimenteir, a man who had eluded the law for over three decades through his ruthlessness, connections, and ability to become someone new every time the authorities got close. He altered his facial features with delicate plastic surgery and developed a unique style for each character he played. He had assumed the Juan Michallini persona for almost five years now. It was nearly time to move on. His affiliation with the Blythes was extremely profitable and would be difficult to replace, but he was used to jumping into new opportunities and leaving others to take the jail time. It was why he was still alive and on top. That and the fact that he had a pocket full of 'partners' at all levels of law enforcement in nearly every country.

Juan Carlos Franscious Laimenteir, alias Juan Michallini, had been an active part of the drug business nearly his whole life, starting out as a laborer in the cocoa fields of Columbia, then graduating to runner, then dealer, then regional distributor, until today he was one of the top ten players in the world. He was sharing information with one of his more valuable assets on the inside.

"She was a goddess tonight. When she walked in, I have to admit, it gave me a rush. Damn it, she wasn't supposed to be there. I'm afraid our man in the park was about as effective as a puppy, but at least he got away clean."

Juan listened to the angry voice on the other end of the line.

"Yeah, I know. The fucking gang I sent in last night obviously didn't do their job. What did you hear? How the hell did she overpower all four of them?"

He listened to the explanation.

"What?" Juan barked into the phone. "I think he was with her again tonight. Probably some guy she's been banging. When her Ladyship told me her idiot kid invited Skyler Madison to the estate, our central location for Christ's sake, I just about put a kill order out on him, too. If he weren't so connected, I'd have him snuffed…better yet, I'd do it myself. Tell me what you think she knows."

Juan didn't like what he heard.

"What about the communications you've been sending to our York branch? Nothing? No one is investigating? Maybe you need to give it a nudge. All right. Just keep at it…someone is bound to make a connection soon and then she'll be pulled. We have to get her out."

More shouting on the other end.

"Goddamn it! All right, all right. Fine with me. Time to cut the ties and move on anyway. It was a very lucrative run but these fucking aristocrats and their moronic son have become a liability. When we have this batch distributed, we'll activate the usual escape plan. If they go down, so be it. I'll send the next few months' shipments to our Washington warehouse until Toronto is completely set up. That's the safest place. This has been a profitable five years, but every arm has its day. We've survived longer than anyone else in this business because we know when to fold. We should have a few more months to wrap things up, yes?"

Juan listened to the comments from his source…then responded to a question about the security of all the incriminating data there would be in the accumulated computer files. Five years worth of records and contacts for the future were kept on disks and in computers secured with the cocaine.

"They have it very well hidden and protected. They have done a good job with that. They have 600 people at this fucking party and none of them would suspect. Even your superwoman will not be able to locate it. I'm not too concerned. I'll be sure to get everything out by this time next month. I have everything backed up, but I'll still need all the information on the data links to process the transactions. It's a long shot, but if they do discover the room, they'll only need to open the door and the room will flash. Boom. A fucking fire ball. Maybe we'll be lucky and she will go up with it."

His face became impatient as he listened to more questions.

"No, no," he continued. "She looked right into my face. She didn't recognize me, I'm sure of it. It has been so many years. I just wanted to test it. She was there, I was there. She barely acknowledged me the last time. When Phillip introduced us, I thought she might have perceived something. But now I don't think her radar even blipped...as a matter of fact, I'm sure of it. Tonight I held her in my arms. Nothing. She was friendly and open...no suspicion on her face at all. By the way, she has become a beautiful woman and luscious, too. I would love to have tried to seduce her. Too bad her brain is a ticking time bomb."

Juan laughed at his source's reaction.

"So she wouldn't be willing? I've rarely let that stop me when I've wanted to enjoy a woman. You'll keep me informed of all the action. Your people have cost us. And that fucking bitch has been the driver behind it. I'll talk with you soon about the movement of goods back to Washington."

CHAPTER 9

Skye awoke slowly and found herself curled up beside Alex's naked body. She lay very still and smiled wickedly. Gently, she raised the sheet to take a look in the daylight. He was as wonderful as he felt last night. She didn't want to wake him so she just looked. Fabulous musculature, great abs, a few bruises left over from their skirmish a few nights before, a flat, hard stomach. Her eyes went lower and grew wide with surprise and more than a little appreciation. It looked to her like he was primed and ready for...then it dawned on her and her eyes flew up to very amused blue ones. Wide awake blue eyes and very alert.

"Finished taking inventory?" Anticipation mixed with desire made his voice husky. He had been watching her slowly wake up and was trying to control his body's natural reaction to her smooth naked breasts planted on his chest. His body had a mind of its own and its cooperation crumbled as she lifted the sheet like a curious child and her eyes started their descent. It was too cute. By the time she got down to his crotch, his mind joined in the fun, imagining the feel of her hands if they would have replaced her eyes in the exploration.

He lost the tenuous hold he had on his body and willingly surrendered to a blast of lust. His arms tightened their grip.

"If you are, perhaps you would like to join us for a shower," said Alex.

"Us?" asked Skye.

"Me and the mutinous little guy down there. You know if you waste too many of those, it makes a man crazy?"

"Is that a fact?"

"It's a fact."

"And all the research was conducted by men, no doubt?" asked Skye.

"No doubt."

So much for the possible uncomfortable 'morning after' moment. She jumped out of bed, completely naked, and smiled down at him. "Give me a few moments alone in there first and you and your friend can join us."

As he watched her stride across the room, his little friend, not so little anymore, enthusiastically nodded its assent.

After they showered and made slow, soapy, wet love in the hot steamy spray, Alex ordered breakfast while Skye picked up the clothes scattered around the room, smiling as she picked up the sheer black teddy that had been under the dress. It had proved no defense against Alex's aggressive assault.

Since it was her room, she had the advantage of having something to put on. She put on jeans and a t-shirt that made her look youthful and relaxed. Alex was still dressed in the hotel robe, looking adorable with his wet hair glistening in the morning sun. He was unshaven, having absolutely refused to use her pink razor on his face.

"I grew up in a house where the women would nip the razors from our bathrooms when we weren't looking and use them. We could never figure out what they did with them to make them as dull as a plastic shoehorn, but they were useless for shaving manly beards after that. My sister thought if she returned them to exactly the same spot, we would never know. But we knew. We had to resort to hiding them. That's how my mom and sister practiced their detective skills. Never could find a spot they didn't uncover."

It was nice to hear him talk about domestic things. It reminded her there was a really nice, normal person under that polished and urbane exterior. She wondered how many people got to see it. And she liked how he talked about his sister so casually. He must miss her a lot, but that didn't prevent him from remembering her and keeping her alive that way. He had something to teach her about that. She would always answer Sloane's questions about their parents, but she rarely brought them up in conversation. That seemed wrong to her now. It was something to think about, but not now. She had too much on her mind.

Alex had been watching the play of emotions on her face. She was beautiful this morning in her casual look. What a chameleon. It was one of the things that made her an outstanding agent and he found it utterly fascinating.

"I guess I'm reduced to putting my tux back on. I'm glad you resisted the temptation to rip everything off me." He reached for his underwear, black and silk and not a Tweetie Bird in sight, and slipped them on. "Nothing screams 'I got lucky' like riding the elevator in a tux before noon."

As he was reaching for his shirt, he caught her taking inventory again.

"Want another round?" he said, smiling and wiggling his eyebrows at her.

"I can't. I have to go to a meeting, then be at the airport polished, rested, and ready for the flight back to Washington by 6 p.m." She said it so casually. Like women every day went out, got in a cockpit of a 767, and piloted it across the ocean.

"How about we get together over there sometime tomorrow?" asked Alex.

"You flying back?"

"Yeah."

"Business complete?"

"Yup. It seems the negotiations went better than I expected and the merger I was hoping for surpassed all expectations."

"You mean you nailed it," said Skye, grinning.

"You could say that," answered Alex. She laughed easily and came over to help him find the studs that had flown all over the room.

"Ever wonder why they call these studs?" She found another one beneath the chair and handed it to him.

"I think you might say they were appropriately named for the man who wore them last night."

"Excuse me. If you're going to beat your chest and howl at the moon, you can find your own damn studs." She bent over looking under the dresser, giving him a very tantalizing view of her trim, firm butt.

"I'd rather have you." He grabbed her by the waist and gathered her to him. His shirt hung open and he could feel her breasts through the thin fabric of her t-shirt.

She looked up at him, then ran her hands under his shirt, over his ribs and up his back, kissing his chest, his neck, his chin, and finally fastening her mouth on his in an enthusiastic, penetrating kiss.

When they came to their senses again, they were lying naked on the bed with the sheets tangled around them.

Contented, sated and just plain satisfied, Skye sighed against his chest. "Good God, what happened?"

"Darling." He kissed the top of her head, so totally captivated that he couldn't see straight. "I think you found the stud you were looking for."

"Now I've got to rush." But she kissed his chest and went back to using it as a pillow. "When are you getting in to the U.S.?"

"I have a few papers to sign later today before I catch an 8 p.m. flight."

"Not flying International?"

"No, sorry. British Airways. From now on I'll only fly International, and only when I know you're the captain. So, how about a date tomorrow night?"

"I can't. I want to go home. Check in with the family. Hey, why don't you drive down to Virginia with me and meet them?" asked Skye.

"Meet the family? Aren't you rushing things a bit?" He didn't think things were rushed a bit at all. He was delighted she wanted to take him home. And somewhat astounded. "Damn. You spend one night with a woman and she wants you to meet the family," he teased, pulling on the ponytail she wore. A goddamn ponytail. How could she get more adorable?

"Well, I really think you should assess the gene pool before we have our third date."

"Wouldn't going home to meet the family be our third date?" asked Alex.

"No. That would be a test."

"What happens if I pass?"

"You get a third date, of course."

Skye reluctantly got back up out of the bed and started the process of getting ready for the day all over again. Having a love life was wonderful, but sure shot the hell out of your schedule. Now it looked like she'd better cut out lunch and the side trip to Harrods. Hell, she could eat on the plane and she really didn't need another pair of shoes. This feeling of utter satisfaction was well worth the price.

She picked up his jacket from the floor and put it to her face. She could smell him and it did funny things to her stomach. It probably cost him a couple thousand dollars and he had carelessly thrown it across the room when she'd peeled him out of it last night. Nothing gets respect when it stands between you and your passion.

Alex was in the shower again. She could feel him just by thinking about him. She smiled. Then shook herself. She was daydreaming. What the hell? She never stood around daydreaming. She was going to have to enlist some discipline if she was going to get anything done today.

Alex came out of the bathroom and started dressing again.

"Didn't we just go through this process?" he asked as he pulled on his pants. Grinning and shaking the water from his hair he looked expectantly at her. It really curled up when it was wet. He dragged his fingers through it and managed to look even more delectable. "Do you want to tell me now if you're going to seduce me again so I don't have to do this for the third time?"

"Me, seduce you?" asked Skye.

"It was the perfume."

"They guaranteed it in Paris."

"Worked like magic. Someone as ugly as you. Only way to get a man in bed." She threw his jacket at him, laughing with delight.

A card fell out of the pocket and she bent to pick it up. She didn't mean to read it, but the bold lilac print was familiar to her.

"Here," she said as she handed it to him. "You'll want to keep this somewhere safe."

He frowned. What the hell was it, he thought. He didn't remember putting anything into his pocket. He turned the card over a few times trying to jog his memory. There was a bold lilac script embossed on the small card.

Samantha Mountbatten Firth it said, followed by an address and telephone number.

He was still baffled and shot Skye such a look of skepticism and confusion, she laughed uproariously.

"Hmmm. Let me see if I can jog your memory. Blonde, beautiful, petite, green eyes enhanced by obvious contacts, 36D's." She cupped her hands in front of her own generous firm breasts and pulled them away from her body. "Enhanced by Dr. Davis. Hot. Horny."

It finally dawned on him and he grinned wickedly. "Clinging. Phony. Desperate. Obvious."

"Yes, that's her," laughed Skye.

"Yeah, I remember her now. She thought you were an anorexic fashion model who wore those shoes to call attention to yourself." Did every woman notice shoes, he wondered. "I guess I was too intent on grabbing you away from Phillip to pay much attention to her."

Skye placed the card carefully back into his pocket. "Just in case you're very, very desperate."

She could have been a little jealous, he thought with a brief pang of disappointment. The knock on the door prevented any further discussion as their breakfast was delivered. When he turned his back on her to go answer it, she took the card back out and crumpled it up in her fist. So much for tacky, desperate Samantha Mountbatten Firth.

She went out into the living area and nearly laughed out loud when she saw the horrified look of the same room service waiter from the day before. He was looking at Alex, with his shirt still unbuttoned, then her, then back again. Alex gave him an outrageously generous tip and sent him on his way, shaking his head and muttering something unintelligible.

"Something I should know about going on between you two?" Alex asked when the waiter had left.

"No. It's just that..." She couldn't tell him that the waiter had seen her and Jim together the day before. She couldn't believe how much she wanted to tell him everything. Share the real joke. "He was the man who witnessed the scene outside your door yesterday. He's probably wondering why we've suffered no visible signs of violence. He scooted before things got civilized yesterday. It's hard telling what kind of spin he put on the three of us in the hall."

"I sure could use a cup of coffee." He knew that she and Jim had been together in this room yesterday and that the waiter probably saw them here. Cool evasion. Nicely delivered. Logical explanation. No change in tone. She was good. He really had to talk to Jim at the first opportunity. Convince him that he and Skye should be working together. He knew she had a meeting with him as soon as she arrived back in the States. He didn't want to risk running into her at the office, so he would call Jim and set something up for the day after tomorrow.

After breakfast, they parted and went their separate ways. The goodbye kiss at the door turned so hot so quickly that Alex almost didn't make it out. He just couldn't get enough of her.

"How about you call International and tender your resignation and we stay in this room for a week?"

"How about you call your accountant, tell her to sell all your properties and turn over all of your assets to the Department of Revenue," she said sweetly. "Then we can spend the week making love in the park."

"Are you saying we still have to make a living?" asked Alex.

"Something like that. Now go before your idea becomes as irresistible as you."

She slammed the door, but not before she saw the wolfish grin on his face. He turned and threw the jacket over his shoulder. Pleased with himself, his life, and how things were turning out. She thought he was irresistible. He could still smell Midnight Seduction on the collar of his jacket. He chuckled aloud. That certainly was appropriate.

He neatly sidestepped the maid's cart as he whistled his way to the elevator, then completely missed it as it came and went while he was leaning against the wall thinking of soft curves, thick wheat-colored hair, and big, beautiful chocolate-brown eyes. He was in love all right. He saw his reflection in the mirror beside the elevator when he realized he had to push the button again. Yup, that was the look of a man in love. He smiled. His reflection smiled. It was like they were two conspirators. It didn't terrify him nearly as much as he thought it would. As a matter of fact, it didn't terrify him a bit. He was, after all, a courageous secret agent man. No. Something better. A Prince Charming. He whistled some more as he got on the elevator. He rode it to the lobby before he realized he never pushed the button to his floor.

Skye slid into her covert role easily and seamlessly. Calling her team together, she prepared to listen to their reports so she could present a coherent summary to Jim on her return trip to Washington. She studied them, proud of what she had been able to put together. Individually, they were terrific. Together, they were unstoppable.

She took inventory of her personnel as they assembled in the secure office they rented for the duration of the operation. Linda was a trained and effective covert agent, fluent in most of the languages of southeast Asia. Her mother was Vietnamese. She was petite, pretty and tough as they come. Max was a large, handsome rouge. He took nothing seriously except his job. He preferred covert work to any kind of strategic thinking and was experienced and highly intuitive. They were two of the department's best.

Barclay and Lucas were pure techies. Skye plucked them out of obscurity and brought them along with her in the field. Both of them preferred objects that could be plugged in to any human contact.

Judy was an administrative genius and was responsible for putting together the necessary reports and files. Maureen, a specialist in international law, kept them honest and advised them on how to proceed from investigation to prosecution. She would remain with the case through the courts and into the sentencing. Skye handpicked them all for both their talent and their ability to build coalitions.

"Hey Linda, where's the subservient attitude?" Skye smiled broadly at her friend. Linda was back to her cultured, professional look.

"Hey Skye, where are those incredible shoes?"

"Liked them, huh?"

"Stunning. Not that I could pull them off." Linda was barely five two. "I would look like a kid playing dress up in her mom's closet."

"Who's playing dress up in her mom's closet?" asked Max as he entered the room munching on a bagel. He had finally found a bakery in London that served New York style jaw-bending bagels. He was from Brooklyn and looked with distain on the fancy, round bread with a hole that people the world over called a bagel. They were just facsimiles, as far as he was concerned.

"No one. Did you bring enough for everyone?" asked Linda.

"No. I brought you scones. Your dental work has got to work up to these bagels. I swear this guy must import them from Brooklyn." He sat down with a whoosh and threw the bakery bag in Linda's direction. She deftly caught it, even though Max meant it to sail right past her. They had known each other since training and had been sniping at each other since the day they met. "I knew a guy once who played dress up in his wife's closet. He made an excellent agent. Was willing to go either way."

"Let's compare notes before Jim calls so we can make a complete, concise report." Skye was back to business now.

"Here's a list of names of everyone at the party," said Max, handing Skye a printed copy. "I put a check by the ones who would disappear for any length of time. Some may just have been making phone calls or had diarrhea from those lousy clams, but that should give you an idea of the people who may have come to the party to make contact. I color coded them if they disappeared at the same time."

"Nice job," complimented Skye.

"I also watched the Bythes. And while you were probably out getting lucky last night from the looks of it, I spent the time putting it all together. Interesting. Very interesting," said Max, his mouth overflowing with bagel. He had been chewing on the same mouthful for a few minutes and it was almost ready to swallow.

"Yeah. Nice prop you brought to the party, by the way. Is he authentic?" asked Linda.

"I had Jim check him out before I asked him to escort me. Just your typical drop dead gorgeous, millionaire tycoon," responded Skye as she quickly scanned the list. A lot of names she recognized from Phillip's Palm Pilot. She knew that it was a list of users and middle people and would turn it over to the local authorities along with her report.

"Can I have him after you're done?" shouted Judy from the coffee room. She acted as liaison with the Scotland Yard and Interpol and was coordinating all the shared information. She would be transferring all the data to them as soon as they formulated their conclusions.

"You're a better woman than I. He would have distracted the jazz out of me. Man he was hot," said Linda. For some reason this disturbed the hell out of Max. For some reason, Linda knew that and was glad.

"Can't we cut the estrogen plunge and get back to important business? I sure as hell don't want to interrupt your little bonding rituals, but the only thing I found distracting all night was that blonde dish's 36D udders."

"Pig!" snarled Linda.

"Oink, oink."

"Can we get this discussion out of the barnyard? Just give us a brief verbal report," Skye said to Max.

"Sure. The missus…"

"The Duchess."

"Yeah, the missus Duchess, she went upstairs with two different men at two different times. Their names are there," said Max.

"Worth checking them out?" asked Skye.

"Yeah, I think so. One dark guy…probably Columbian…"

"You could just be projecting," interrupted Linda. "It seems you tend to do that when anyone has an ethnic look." She'd yet to forget that Max would forever get a perp mixed up with another when they had any Asian features and out of frustration one day claimed they all looked alike to him. He felt bad about it because he knew it hurt Linda. It was insensitive and he was wrong, so he worked very hard on the differentiation exercises provided by the department. He wasn't going to admit it to her, however.

"This is different China doll. And you have helped me immensely to come to understand that not all Asian women are alike. Some are actually pleasant," said Max.

"One of these days your mouth is going to hang you," Linda said, but she did know about his hard work in trying to be a better, more enlightened human being. She just wasn't ready to tell him about it, yet. Skye ignored them. It was an old argument.

"Anyway, the Duchess must do it standing up, cause not a hair was out of place, but they had post-fuck flush all over 'em," said Max.

"Post-fuck flush?" asked Skye.

"Yeah…kinda like you got right now," said Max.

"You know Max, I'm your direct supervisor." Her frown did nothing to wipe the grin off his face. He could see the sparkling eyes underneath.

"Yeah, I know. You scare me."

"Back to the Duchess," continued Skye, wanting to change the subject.

"Well, from how they were acting, it wasn't a one-night stand. I think they have relationships. But here is the interesting part. Are you ready?" Max always liked an audience. And Skye was glad to give it to him, because what followed a comment like that was usually gold.

"The dark man making time with our hostess was the same guy that was taking inventory of your body while he was dancing with you and whose fingerprints Judy is running right now."

"Good call, Skye!" exclaimed Barclay. He was an administrative computer geek of few words. But when Skye showed such brilliant intuition, he just couldn't contain himself. The words would pop out and he would blush. He was blushing furiously right now.

"There was something about him. His voice," Skye said smiling at Barclay, who went from red to magenta, and suppressed the same nagging feeling she had the night before when the man asked her to dance. Skye was more disturbed by the vibration from this man than she wanted to admit. Even to her team. "Any news on that yet?"

Judy came back in. "It should be in any minute."

"What about Lord Henry?" asked Skye.

"He was porkin' everything in sight. Didn't seem too discriminating and didn't send off any warning bells. I have the list here." Skye smiled broadly at the sight of Samantha Mountbatten Firth's name near the bottom of the list. Now that was desperate.

"I hope you didn't put the word porkin' in your report," said Skye.

"Nah, I wrote 'boppin'...more civilized." Max liked to act the part of a Brooklyn tough guy, but Skye happened to know that in addition to a master's in criminal justice he had an elementary education degree and used to be a fourth grade teacher. He liked to say that he took up undercover work because it was safer. He was really a very good agent. As a man, well, he was a work in progress. He'd been with Skye all of her years with the Justice Department. He'd told her countless times that he considered hitting on her in the early days, but quickly dismissed the thought when she took him down two out of three times on the mat. There was just so much a man's ego could take from a potential lover. They had remained close friends, and only close friends, over the years.

"Okay, so we have two unfaithful, not too discriminating, aristocrats. It seems they're also the head of a very big drug distribution system. We were sent here to prove it. What about Phillip?" asked Skye.

"He mostly spent his time staring in your direction. I think he has a major case on you. Are you going to continue to use it?" asked Max.

"I don't know. It depends on how everything plays out. I'd like to get everything resolved before our next date, but it may not go as quickly as I like."

"Anyway, I made a list of the people he seemed to take an interest in. He asked a lot of people about the guy you were with."

"Good work. I'll collate all the data and take it with me to my meeting with Jim tomorrow. You two got a party tonight?"

"Nope. Our night off," said Linda.

"I hope that we can get this wrapped up soon. I'd hate to have you get so attached to catering that you wouldn't want to come home when the assignment is over," smiled Skye. She understood the frustration and monotony of undercover work. Because she really did understand and was empathetic, Linda was satisfied.

"Oh yeah, like I love serving rich clueless snobs and playing the submissive Asian immigrant," said Linda, shaking her head.

"Yeah, and the size of those little nibblers give me the creeps. I scarf as many as I can while the boss isn't looking. It takes ten of those little sandwich things to make a mouthful," carped Max.

"It depends on the mouth. I find them to be both dainty and delicious," sniffed Linda.

"Ha ha, Linda," answered Max pronouncing her name 'lin-duh' with an emphasis on the 'duh.'

"You two are giving me a headache. Any other impressions you want to share before I take a few dozen aspirin and grab a nap?"

They shook their heads. Then Skye gave them a number of assignments and other leads she gathered from her evening at the estate. They all turned as the fax hummed.

"Here it is," said Judy, waving the fax from Interpol. Then her eyes grew wide. "Wow, Skye. I think you hit the jackpot!"

CHAPTER 10

The day was bright and balmy in Washington D.C. when Alex picked up Skye at her small efficiency apartment on Connecticut Avenue. He was surprised at how much he anticipated this drive to her family home. He felt it took their relationship to a whole new level. Of course, how many levels could there be with a woman you've known only a few weeks and dated only twice. On the other hand, he had read her dossier and had been watching her nearly every minute she'd been in London. He had a meeting scheduled with Jim the next day. He was to submit his brief but positive report in written form, then end the assignment and beg for a new one. He would really like to stay with this operation in some capacity related to security for Skye. He thought Jim would go for it. At the end of an operation, there was usually a need for extra assistance. And if Jim thought there might be another attempt at Skye, he could be on the protection side of it.

Alex was convinced someone wanted her off the case. The person or persons tried a subtle approach first and when that didn't appear to be working they went for her directly. This was all in his report, but he intended to have a face-to-face meeting to reinforce his position. It was how he did business. Especially when he was negotiating for something important.

Skye looked ravishing in a simple blue cotton dress. Her hair, or most of it anyway, was pulled up into a clip. She wore sunglasses, which made her look sexy as hell, but kept her eyes from his view. That was all right, because he already had memorized the shape, color and at least twenty different expressions in the eyes beneath the shades. She seemed relaxed and comfortable around him, like they had known each other for years instead of days. The air between them didn't have that electrical snap today, more of a companionable tension. He liked it. She looked like she did too.

When he drove up in this battered old green two-door Ford pickup truck, she laughed and clapped her hands. He thought it was just about the sweetest reaction his truck ever got. He remembered one of his dates, he thought it was that model from New York, who actually refused to get in it. He had other cars including a Porsche 911 GT2, a classic Corvette convertible, a long, sleek

Royale Magnum Limousine, plus his Custom Harley Screaming Eagle Deuce, but loved this old truck the best. Maybe he drove it to test her. Love me, love my truck.

He did have leather seats installed and a CD player. Otherwise it was mostly rust and dust. She seemed to like it, though, and that put him in a lighthearted mood. She selected a Jimmy Buffett CD and they sang "Cheeseburger in Paradise" as they pulled onto the beltway and headed for Virginia. They discovered they were both wild Buffett fans and Alex was ready to commit right then and there. They chatted amiably all the way to Stafford. When they approached the quiet residential town, Skye turned down the tunes and looked at Alex.

"I um…well, I have to warn you, I think. I know you've faced a back alley full of thugs, but you really shouldn't go into this situation without a bit of orientation," warned Skye.

"Excuse me? I was under the impression we were going to have dinner with your family," Alex asked quizzically.

"We are. But I want you to know that I live with two of the most eccentric people imaginable."

"So shock me some more. I come from a family where morgue reports are perfectly acceptable table conversation," said Alex.

"Yes, well, then maybe you're better prepared than most. My sister is a genius. Chronologically and emotionally she's 14, but she already has advanced degrees in computer science and literature, undergraduate degrees in mathematics, biology and economics and wants to be an astronaut…this week, that is. Aunt Hazel…well…Aunt Hazel is around 80, we think…and she…um…she's not of this planet. She's miles beyond strange and well into the country of odd."

"That's not unusual for someone of around 80."

"I understand that, and at least now her advanced age gives her an excuse for her peculiar behavior. But she was always like this…a constant source of delight. I'm not censuring her, just warning you. Also, Hazel never really learned how to cook. Meals around our house are usually pretty scary and always a mystery. And one other thing. She doesn't deal from the top of the deck," said Skye.

He laughed. "Okay, I get the picture."

"No, I mean literally, she doesn't deal from the top of the deck. Never, ever play cards with her. She can manipulate a deck so everyone at the table has precisely the hand she wants them to have."

He gave a mock shudder. "Okay…one genius sister and one wacky aunt. I get it. I've walked into a situation comedy and you brought me here to monitor my ability to adapt and adjust."

"Exactly the mindset you need. Turn down here."

The street was a lovely residential area with big older homes and mature oaks and maples. The one that Skye indicated was a large white Victorian with a huge front porch. A very unusual combination of plants, flowers, shrubs, and what looked like prairie grass, gave the house a quirky character that somehow worked. He parked his pickup in front, and somehow that worked as well.

A woman barely over five feet tall with bright red hair, orange stretch bell bottoms and a Green Bay Packer t-shirt threw open the door as they reached the top step.

"Skyler!" She wrapped her thin arms around her niece as Skye bent to plant a kiss on Hazel's tanned, wrinkled cheek. "Oh my God…be still my heart! Who the hell is this mouth-watering hunk? He can't be a bone-picking lawyer."

"No, I'm a lawyer of the money-grubbing variety. I would never just go after the bones." He smiled down at the genuinely warm and generous smile Hazel flashed in his direction.

"And a smart ass, too." She nodded her head. "Good. Just what you need. You a criminal lawyer?"

"Nope, corporate. More money and I don't have to deal with the lawbreakers, only the law benders. Safe, secure and just this side of boring."

"Love your truck, son. Had one like it myself, only my baby was red. They're built to last, all right. Just like the commercial says. Used it when I was living in Vegas. It was great for off-road running. Maybe later, you'll let me take a look under the hood."

"Make her promise not to touch anything first," warned Skye.

"Now, cookie, how nice was that?" asked Hazel, giving her niece a playful swat on the butt. Alex wished he could do that and get away with it. Maybe later.

"Hazel, the last time and the only time I let you under the hood of my car, you installed a totally illegal, non-regulation horn," admonished Skye.

"I thought it was a gas! Bought it down at that permanent rummage sale on Van Buren." Hazel looked at Alex to explain. "We got a subdivision down off of hwy 62 that has streets named for all the presidents. Only way you'd remember some of them guys. Who the hell was Van Buren, anyway? And who the hell cares?" She slapped Alex on the back and he just shrugged and grinned. He knew he didn't care. "I got this horn from a guy who has a tattoo of the entire state of Rhode Island on his chest. Road maps, towns, and everything. So I put it in Skye's sissy car and when you press the horn it says 'get out of my fucking way' in a rough scary voice. I can't believe she made me take it out. I sure hope you can help with her sense of humor."

"The first time I used it, I practically put a pedestrian into cardiac arrest!" exclaimed Skye, frowning and laughing at the same time.

"I took it back to the guy and traded it for some of those seat covers that look like a black and white cow. Skye didn't like those either, so I put them in my Bug." Alex smiled at the picture in his mind of a VW with black and white cow seat covers.

His smile could bring sight to a blind woman, Hazel thought. Maybe just the thing to give her niece a little meltdown. Maybe she could help her out a little. "Might be able to get a pair for your truck."

Alex shook his head slightly as the picture of the same seat covers in his truck came into focus. He was saved from responding, however, by waiting a beat too long. Hazel shifted and launched in a different direction.

"So, do you know how copper wire was invented?" Hazel completely changed the subject. Alex was agile in both mind and body, however, and kept up nicely.

"No, but I'm sure you're going to tell me."

"Two lawyers fighting over a penny." Alex laughed with genuine pleasure, capturing Hazel's heart and firmly securing her allegiance. It was actually one he hadn't heard before.

"I'm going to have to remember that one for my dad. He's a lawyer of the 'put the crooks away' variety."

"A D.A., huh?" asked Hazel.

"That's right. So…how can you tell a lawyer is lying?" When Hazel shook her head, her dancing eyes registering both delight and shrewd approval, Alex responded. "Other lawyers look interested."

"How do you stop a lawyer from drowning?" shot back Hazel. Alex had heard that one before.

"Shoot him before he hits the water," he responded. Then it was his turn again. "What do a lawyer and a sperm have in common?"

"Both have about a one in three million chance of becoming a human being," Hazel said quickly, laughing and slapping her hand on her knee. Skye noticed she wore nearly all her rings for the occasion and that her nails were a very beautiful shade of purple.

"How do you get a lawyer down from a tree?" she asked.

"Cut the rope," he responded.

"What's the difference between a lawyer and a hooker?" he asked. Hazel had to concede this one and shook her head. "A hooker will stop trying to screw you once you're dead."

They did the battle of the lawyer jokes while they crossed the porch into the house. Skye stayed out of it and just watched. The man was adapting and adjusting just fine. She knew the minute she saw his old truck, this was going to be a good day. It nudged her closer to the commitment stage of their relationship.

"Sloane is still at the computer lab, and I was just starting dinner," said Hazel. "I hope you like bear meat pizza." She slid one arm through Skye's and one through Alex's and led them through a large foyer to the back of the house. "Keep me company while I grate the mozzarella."

They passed a sunny parlor, a book filled library, and a large family room before entering an impressively appointed kitchen. "Can I get you something to drink?" asked Hazel.

"What kind of wine do you recommend with bear meat?" asked Skye casually as she went to the wine cooler and looked through the well-stocked unit.

"Hmmm…" pondered Alex. "I would say something with a bit of a bite."

"Oh…you kids crack me up. It really isn't going to have bear meat. I got the recipe from Hunter's Quarterly. I got some really fine pork tenderloins to substitute for the bear."

"Oh, in that case, how about that Château l'Angélus 1994?" asked Alex, impressed with Hazel's wine selection.

When Sloane came home from the computer lab, Alex faced another set of critical eyes. Sloane wasn't anything like her sister. There was nothing controlled or reserved about her. She was short, very dark, beautiful, with huge hazel eyes that reflected gold lights. She didn't walk across the room, she bounced.

Sloane was a young woman who formed instantaneous connections with people. Because of her naturally friendly and gregarious nature, she was generous with her good graces, and she was usually nonjudgmental. She took one look at Alex and fell instantly in deep like with him.

"Yeah…Sloane. What a handle. Mom and Dad thought Skyler and Sloane were so chart worthy, but I think it sounds like we belong in a centerfold together. Skyler and Sloane, the Madison sisters." All the time she was chatting, she was unloading her backpack on the coffee table. Advanced level Microbiology, Anatomy and Physiology, *A Brief History of Time* by Stephen Hawking and *Teen People*. "Of course I would have to grow breasts first. Did I tell you, Skye, that Laurie is wearing a bra now? How hot is that? Not that she really needs it yet, but she wore a white t-shirt to the arcade today so all the boys could see through it and get a load of the straps. Super ice."

"Don't despair yet, honey. All your energy goes to your brain right now, so you may have to wait a little while for your body to catch up." She smiled at Sloane and Alex saw all the love one person could pour into another. He liked the look and wanted some of that for himself.

"So, did you know that in the last five years Skye has brought like, maybe, only three other boyfriends here? They were pretty orgasmic, but we never saw them again. Either she killed them on the way back to the city and buried the bodies, or they had really bad moves and she dumped them at the truck stop. Remember that really, really handsome guy with the fake-bake? He was wicked. But I think he was only after Skye's astronomically crusted breasts. Couldn't take his eyes off them all night. Gross check. So I guess he's walking funny through the city these days."

Alex was laughing with such obvious delight that Skye couldn't be too horrified. She had long since stopped trying to modify the behavior of her younger sister.

"Sloane, please," she said in mock disapproval. "I don't want to give Alex the impression that I'm desperate."

"No, we sure wouldn't want that to happen," she gave Alex an exaggerated wink and he returned it. Allies.

"So what's it with you and breasts tonight? Is this something I should worry about?" asked Skye.

"No. Not that it isn't kind of a natural preoccupation for virgins my age. Tonight my fetish is based on the simple fact that we're studying female anatomy in AP class. It's really chinky. You got this nerdy corndog standing in front of the room with last decade's threads on his body cadaver talking about the vagina. Well, I tell you every woman in the room crossed her legs and that's no lie. Of course, statistically speaking, more than half of them have an intimate knowledge of how the whole thing works, anyway."

"You have plenty of time for that," said Skye with mock severity. "I don't want you engaging in any primary research."

"More like primal research, I'd say. Anyway, don't worry, Skye. I'm saving myself for Terry Pickford."

"Who's Terry Pickford?" Skye asked, trying to remember which of the boys hanging around was Terry Pickford. Sloane was a beautiful girl and always had scores of boys around her. She wanted to get a line on this Terry kid.

"Lead guitarist for the Restless Pretzels," said Alex, winning a dazzling smile from his new ally and cementing the partnership.

"Who?" asked Skye.

Sloane and Alex gave each other that, 'she's so not cool look' and Sloane rolled her eyes.

"Clueless. Blonde, so she should try to fight the stereotype. And, not too eclectic in her tastes," said Sloane with a shrug over Skye's hopelessness. "Squaredom."

Of course the fact that Alex knew who Terry Pickford was put Alex in the 'way cool' category and sent her interested appreciation of his obvious attributes into a case of full-blown love. She couldn't wait to get on the phone with her best friend Libby Hanson. She sure hoped Skye wouldn't blow this one.

"I had a chance to see them last summer, but I had a graduate seminar I couldn't miss so I didn't get to go. Major bummer."

Alex made a mental note to send over his signed CD to Sloane in the morning. Terry's signature was on it, he was sure. He knew how to suck up. He had taken his nephews to their concert a few months before or he would have been as clueless as Skye. Sometimes timing was everything.

"You go to summer school?" asked Alex.

"Yeah. I want to finish my masters in biology by August graduation," answered Sloane.

She laughed delightedly at Alex's expression, kind of a combination of pity and admiration.

"Chill. Don't worry about the development of my age-appropriate social skills. I have plenty of friends my own age and find them both interesting and easy to communicate with. Of course, Andy and Bob were driving us girls all to freeksburg when they were discussing for hours why there are no A or B batteries. There are only AA and AAA and C and D. They wanted to know what happened to A and B. They asked me like I know everything. Can't unwrap a mystery when there's nothing inside the box. They think it was a government conspiracy or something. Gruesome. Even went on the Internet. Totally bulbazoid."

Alex smiled at Sloane, completely captivated. But it was a good question. Why weren't there A and B batteries? He didn't think that Andy and Bob were totally bulbazoid.

"So are you staying for dinner?" asked Sloane.

"I am," said Alex.

"Skye warn you?

"She did."

"Sweet. Eye toffee and brave heart, too. You're going to engage in an enormous escapade. The National Geographic version of foods of the universe. Hazel was perusing her hunting magazines this afternoon. Can I assume a wild meat adventure?"

"Bear meat pizza."

"Yum. Gotta go call Libby and check in with gossip central. I have a few choice bulletins. See ya." Sloane snagged her *Teen People* and was off to her room. Skye smiled after her.

"You'll notice that Sloane's vocabulary is a rare combination of teen speak and doctoral quality rhetoric."

"I like it." And he found that he really did like it, and her. She was a special child. And she was Skye's only family. Besides Hazel and he had already won her over by letting her look under his hood. Having to check before he left for any foreign objects was a small price to pay for having Skye's only family on his side.

After a meal that wasn't half bad, Skye and Hazel loaded the dishwasher together. They could hear Sloane quizzing Alex on the law. She was interested in pursuing another degree, but wasn't sure law was in the running.

Hazel chuckled. "Funny how Sloane had absolutely no curiosity about the law profession until tonight. I do believe it's the man and not the pull of jurisprudence that's stimulating this budding interest."

"I think you're right," said Skye.

"He's a traffic-stopping, neck-turning, eye-catching dreamboat. Have you bopped him yet?"

"Hazel!"

"Skyler! It's a perfectly legitimate parental question."

"No it's not."

"Well, excuse me. I never took on parenting until you were almost fully grown. None of the books were all that useful."

"You never read a book on parenting."

"No...I'm talking about *How To Train Your Pet In Less Than A Week.* Anyway, have you bopped him yet?"

Skye sighed and smiled. "As a matter of fact..."

"Oh please, please tell me those shoulders are not just clever padding."

"Nope. That's all man underneath."

"Be still my heart. And what about underneath his…"

Skye held up her hand laughing. "Enough! You've just gotten all the information you're going to get. I think I'm going to go rescue Alex and remind Sloane of her exam in Molecular Biology."

She turned and went toward the family room before she could see the smile and satisfied gleam in her aunt's eagle eye. Skye, she thought, you're completely smitten. And it's about time.

Later when Sloane closed herself up in her room with her books and notes, Skye, Hazel, and Alex decided to have their coffee and what looked like cheesecake topped with jelly beans and avocadoes on the front porch. They chatted companionably about the upcoming football season, the weather, the price of beef in Tokyo, and thoroughly enjoyed the balmy evening.

"I hope you don't mind, Alex," Skye put down her coffee cup and stood up. "But I would like to make a call on a neighbor before we head back to the city. Do you think you're ready to face Hazel alone for a few minutes?"

He smiled broadly. "Absolutely. I think I'll have another piece of that…um…"

"It's a torte, dear," said Hazel beaming with pleasure.

"Yeah…I knew that." Alex turned up the charm a notch and bravely faced another plate of the very interesting dessert. God, he was perfect, Skye thought.

"Are you sure you trust me alone with your man, honey?" questioned Hazel with a wiggle of her hips and a wink.

"Make a move on him and I'll cut off your supply of Swiss Chocolate."

"Consider me properly subdued. The cookies are on the kitchen table. Tell Carl and Jean I said 'hi'."

"Will do."

As soon as Skye walked down the street and disappeared through the neighbor's front door, Hazel cut off the small talk by fixing her clear, concentrated gaze on Alex. He picked up his coffee cup and waited. He knew an approaching interrogation when he saw one and waited patiently for the first salvo. It didn't take long, but he was a bit shocked at her direct approach.

"So, young man, is it too early to ask you your intentions? I know that's usually the father's ultimate question when a gentleman has that look in his eye, but Skyler was put under my care way before I was ready for the responsibility and she didn't come with an instruction manual. I'm playing this by ear, and since you're parallel parking with my niece, I want to know what's on your mind."

"Ah..." said Alex, not quite sure what to say or how to say it.

"I'm a liberated woman, young man. Burned my bra way before my sisters in the feminist movement were born. Mostly cause I didn't need it, but you get the point. I know there can be great sex without any commitment and that you young people don't necessary think that far ahead, but..."

"I want to make the relationship permanent," Alex said, as shocked by the blunt response as Hazel was.

"Well, Jesus, Joseph and Mary...glory be. You didn't have to go that far, young man. But now that you have, I think you're just the ticket." Hazel was as delighted as she could be. She knew they hadn't been seeing each other very long, but sometimes those sudden hot beginnings were good fuel for a long-lasting flame. "Ah, does she know about this? She didn't say anything to me."

"No, actually, you're the first to know. As a matter of fact, the very first. I didn't know myself until I just now said it." He hadn't intended to say it, but now that he had a few seconds to process the statement, he found he liked how it felt. He was a man who used his instincts and quick decisive moves in business and it made him a very wealthy man. Were his instincts in love going to be as fruitful?

"I think you got a chance of getting what you want. She's definitely besotted," said Hazel.

"Besotted?" He could only wish.

"Okay, so once in a while I forget myself and get into the language of my generation. Comes from hanging out with all my sisters in the red hats. Anyway, as I was saying...she's very attracted to you; she's of an age where she should be looking for a commitment and you're as far from being a cop as she can get. A namby pamby lawyer and all around tycoon...kind of like Matlock, I'd say. Only better looking, better dresser, younger and nicer muscle tone. Perfect."

What was that about being as far from a cop as she could get? And why should that make a difference? Alex slowly put down his coffee cup.

"You know I come from a family of cops." He was beginning to feel a wave of unease. Someday she would have to know he was more of a cop than a tycoon these days.

Hazel turned serious. Not a good sign, he thought. Even her voice changed...it softened and became somewhat melancholy.

"I don't imagine she told you…she hasn't really talked about it much at all and most certainly not in the last few years."

Alex felt very uneasy. He thought that once he told Skye about what he was really doing in London and the initial shock wore off, their mutual interest in law enforcement would be a good thing.

"Skye was engaged. His name was Jeffrey, a wonderful man. They grew up together." She nodded to a large yellow house down the street where Skye went just moments before. "His parents still live there. That's where Skye is now. She takes them cookies. Makes sure they have everything they need."

Alex said nothing, so she took a deep breath and continued.

"She had the dress, the invitations were out, they rented an apartment in town. She made arrangements to fly only domestic flights out of Dulles. She flew copilot for United back then. He was a Washington D.C. cop. A good one. A fearless one." Hazel took another small sip of coffee and looked into his eyes. "This is the first time you've heard this, isn't it?" He nodded, remembering her empathy when he told her about his sister and feeling a shock of sympathy for her now.

"Doesn't surprise me. It's no secret, but she never shares pain. Ever. Always keeps it inside." She faded away, then got back on track. "Anyway, two weeks before the wedding we were sitting right here on the porch. Chatting with her bridesmaids over the final preparations when a car drove up and Jeff's captain got out."

Alex's heart skipped a beat. He knew where this was going. There was a stiffness in his chest for the pain she must have suffered that day.

"She knew. She knew the minute she saw his face. The chaplain was with him too, I remember." A tear slid unheeded down Hazel's cheek. "You can't imagine. She just sat there while they told her. He was killed outright. Shot three times in the chest with a Saturday Night Special."

"She closed down that day. Just sat and stared out the window for hours. Sloane and I tried to get her to talk, but she barely responded. Just like when her parents were killed. First her parents died in front of her in that horrible way, then Jeff. Jim Stryker, a family friend, and his wife came immediately and tried to help. They couldn't get through either. I didn't know what to do. We buried him just a week before his wedding. The service was in the church where they would have taken their vows. On the day of her wedding she disappeared for hours. We were so afraid. We thought maybe it had been too much…maybe…well, anyway, Jim found her. She was walking along the lake where they were going on their honeymoon. Something Jim told her, something he did, put some life back into her. At least she made an attempt to go through the motions of living. She started flying for International and now there are long periods of time we don't see much of her. I've been waiting…waiting." She wiped her face, blew her nose, and smiled up at Alex's serious, concerned face. He looked down the street, and she could see in his eyes that he was moved.

None of this had been in her dossier, Alex thought, a cold fist clutching his gut. He felt her pain and knew first hand what it could do to a person and the choices they made.

"One night when we'd consumed a bit too much wine," continued Hazel. "I think it was after one of those bridesmaid's weddings, we talked about her heart. She dated a few times by then and I thought it was safe to bring it up. She told me in words coated with high-grade steel that she would never, ever put her heart in that kind of jeopardy again. She would never even date a cop. Somehow, it seemed she knew a lot of them in her youth. She was always interested in detective work. Always reading Nancy Drew books and having imaginary adventures with her friends."

Well, he thought, little Skyler grew up and her adventures were no longer imaginary.

"So you see how perfect it is that you're a desk jockey? It puts you in the running." Hazel beamed at him.

Just then, Skye came walking back down the street. A small dog from one of the neighbor's yards jumped after her yapping a greeting and she bent down to rub its belly. Alex smiled as she pulled out something from her pocket and handed it to the little white ball of fur. It wriggled with delight and ran back home to devour its treat.

Laughing, she looked up and he captured her gaze in his. It held for a moment. They smiled and didn't break off eye contact until she turned to acknowledge another greeting.

Hazel caught the look and went to refill Alex's cup. "Something in her has been turned back on, Alex, and I'm grateful. I know it has something, maybe everything, to do with you."

Alex didn't let her see the troubled look that came into his eyes. This bit of history complicated things a little. Maybe a great deal. He thought he would have to melt only ice to get through her defenses. Now, when she found out his true passion, he was afraid he would have to melt steel. Well, he thought with determination, that just required him to turn up the heat. He meant it when he told Hazel he wanted the relationship to be permanent. He may not have realized it until just that moment, but he meant it all the same.

Skye joined them and the three of them continued to talk as the sun set.

"I could get used to this," said Alex sincerely.

"Did I hear you're rich?" asked Hazel.

"As a Sultan."

"Great. You can come with me to the Senior Center sometime. I go down there a couple times a week to help with the old people. We play for...um...a dollar a point. Can't hear, can't see...some have lost their memory and can't remember the bid..."

"Hazel, you hustler...you play for a penny a point and no one has collected since 1989. You just want him as a new mark. I already warned him about your card tricks," said Skye.

"Hey, can't blame me for trying to work up a new source of revenue. Social Security isn't keeping up...goddamn politicians."

"Hazel!"

"Skyler!"

"Do you have the time?" asked Skye, pointedly turning to Alex.

"Translation, boy...it's past my bedtime. That's okay dear...I wanted to turn in early. Got a date with Tommy Lee. He's going to make me feel like I'm 65 again." She gave both Skye and Alex a peck on the cheek and went in.

"Tommy Lee?" asked Alex as he snagged Skye's hand and pulled her from the rail of the porch where she was sitting to his lap.

Skye grinned. "She and her group of Red Hat ladies rented *Men in Black* again this afternoon. She thinks Tommy Lee Jones is just the hottest thing in Hollywood."

"And who do you think is hot?"

"I say," as she kissed him passionately and thoroughly, "who needs fantasy? I have Hollywood right here."

"Will you come back to my townhouse and stay with me tonight?" he asked with feeling. He figured the deeper he could get her into the relationship, the more difficult it would be for her to want out if what Hazel said about her aversion to cops was as strong as she had implied. He wanted her in his bed, in his home. He wanted her in his life. He nuzzled the side of her neck. "I'll show you the movies I starred in."

"You have movies?"

"Yup, my mom was obsessed with saving everything for posterity. Of course I would have to censor them until we know each other better. Her posterity had a lot to do with my posterior."

"As good as all that?"

"Better, I'd say. I particularly think the one of me running naked through the sprinklers needs to be saved until you're ready."

"Give me two seconds to turn out the lights and lock the doors."

He ran naked through sprinklers, she thought as she walked through the house and doused the lights. How cute was that? She was already warm and fuzzy inside. She was looking forward to seeing how this pickup-loving, money-grubbing lawyer lived. And where he slept. She went from warm and fuzzy, to hot. Look out Alexander Springfield, you're in my sights.

CHAPTER 11

Skye woke up slowly and stretched. She was in Alex's big bed alone. He had meetings in town and wanted to get an early start. Since she wasn't particularly fond of early starts, he let her sleep in. It felt so good.

Sighing, she looked around the large master suite. All man. Bold colors. Maroon, forest green, and deep, rich wood. She reached over, snagged his pillow and buried her face in it. She could smell him and it made her feel giddy. Giddy? She wasn't sure if she was horrified, mystified, or just plain satisfied. One thing she did know, she sure liked waking up in his bed. And sleeping in his bed. And making love in his bed. She hadn't felt this carefree in…well, years and years anyway. She wondered what it would be like to have breakfast with Alex in this bed.

When she came home with him the night before, she met his housekeeper. An absolutely delightful older woman named Cynthia. She took one look at Skye, then enveloped her in large, generous arms and said she was just about the most beautiful creature she'd ever seen. A bit too thin, but she could take care of that little detail.

What Skye hadn't known, was that Alex had come home from London the night before and told Cynthia he had found 'the one.' When she looked up from her bread dough and asked "Which one?" Alex had smiled broadly, picked up Cynthia, not a task just any man could accomplish, smacked her on the lips and said simply. "*The* one."

Cynthia had known him for ten years and watched the progression of lovely young women pass through this house, mostly through his bedroom, then pass right out again. Some were after his money, some his position, some his power, some his good looks, some all of the above. But from what Cynthia witnessed, painfully few were interested in what was inside. People would be surprised to hear that she thought of him as a solitary man. Not exactly lonely, but alone. Well, I guess the lone wolf found his mate, she thought. And what a worthy and magnificent mate she will be. Strong, self-assured. A bit reserved, but she was sure Alex could take care of that. As much as she was attracted to and fascinated by Skye, her approval of the young woman was based on what she saw on Alex's face when he looked at her. He came alive. His eyes followed Skye around the room with a soft possessive glow in them that Cynthia had never seen before.

This morning, Alex had come down early for his coffee. There was a roguish grin on his face. Ah, youth, and young love. Cynthia was a romantic. Her employer always looked handsome and polished, but today he was positively glowing.

She was just whipping up some pancake batter when the source of the glow walked into the room. She smiled warmly. Yup, thought Cynthia as she looked Skye over, thoroughly satisfied and over the top herself. This was going to work.

Skye smiled back. "I didn't see a manual on the protocol of Cynthia's well-run home. Is this where I can grab a cup of coffee?" Then she looked into the bowl. "And is that pancake batter?"

"Sure is, Ms. Madison. Mr. Springfield thinks of everything. Would you prefer to eat in the dining room?"

"It's Skye, please." Skye nodded to the round table over by the window. It looked so cozy. Perfect for pancakes and conversation. "How about over there? And how about you join me and you can fill me in on all of Alex's secrets."

"Oh now, that wouldn't be very discreet of me, would it?" asked Cynthia, grinning from ear to ear. So, this beauty was more than a face and a body. No airs, no pretense. The last woman who had spent the night here wanted breakfast in bed and was a condescending bitch. Gorgeous, but shallow. She lasted only one night. So Skye will eat in the kitchen with the help and wanted to know his secrets. This was a very good beginning.

"No, but if he fires you," Skye said as the wonderful smell of pancakes filled the room, "I'll take you to my home and worship you as a goddess."

Cynthia laughed out loud and poured two cups of coffee. She'll do. She'll do just fine.

By the time Skye had finished and excused herself to get dressed, she and Cynthia were fast friends. And she knew Alex's favorite color, his favorite meal, his penchant for video games, all about his relationship with his nephews and the subtle fact that if Skye hurt Alex, she would be marked for death. The motherless child in her opened up with information she rarely shared with anyone but her closest friends. Skye liked how Alex lived and who he lived with. And the feeling was mutual.

Alex rode the elevator up to Jim's office feeling wonderful. Skye was in his house and he intended to make a pitch for her to stay there. He would broach that subject when they went out to dinner. She was flying back to London in the morning, so it would be an early evening. He thought they would go to the new Italian restaurant off Dupont Circle, then straight home to bed. Just the thought of it gave him an itch.

He was going to file his final report to Jim, then ask to be assigned to her team. He wanted in. And he wanted to come clean with Skye. If they were going to share a bed, he needed to be completely honest with her. It was going to be hard enough getting her to trust him again. If he could tell her in his own way, she would understand. She was a professional. He would just have to find the right time and place. Maybe while she was naked, her body wrapped around his, he could hold her and tell her gently, easing into it and relying on her contentment to soften her anger. Then he had an image of his own naked body sailing across his bedroom. Better do it in a public place. He laughed. The woman next to him in the elevator looked at him and smiled. Not knowing what was so funny, but being attracted to the sound.

"Something funny, or just feeling good?" she asked.

"Both," said Alex with a broad smile as he exited the elevator. The woman smiled back and sighed.

Alex delivered a clear, concise verbal report to Jim and gave him his conclusions. "I think the incidents pointing to Skye's defection were sequential and increasingly blatant. The deeply buried information using her code name was the original leak…the first attempt at discrediting her and taking her out of the game. That initial move seems much less obvious…much more deeply hidden. It could have been planted back when the communication was supposedly written, or more recently by a clever tech...possibly right in the Tower. I think the person who planted it saw no action. Becoming impatient to get her off the case, someone sent the secure files which created a much more obvious and less concealed connection to Skye with the purpose of starting an internal investigation. Again, the individual saw no action, so decided to go direct and take her out rather than push her out. I think someone desperately wants her off this case. One other thing. The timing of the attack in the alley. It was the evening before her visit to the estate. Her theory that there was something there to uncover probably has a great deal of merit. I'm anxious to hear what she uncovered and look forward to being able to share information. This is the written report on my surveillance clearing her from suspicion." Alex handed the folder to Jim. "Now I want to talk about our next move." He leaned forward. "I want to tell Skye everything and I want to be a part of the operation over there."

Jim studied the man. He had known and liked Alex ever since the earnest and heartbroken young man had entered his office and had asked to be put to work. After the tragic death of his sister, he wanted into the law enforcement community but he wanted to do it his way. A friend in the FBI gave him Jim's name knowing that Alex would fit the new profile Jim was trying to institute of agents having an established identity then slipping in an alternate life behind it. Alex not only fit the profile, he was the prototype for it. He trained like a maniac and was judged the best of his class. Jim would have been hard pressed to choose between Skye and Alex if asked who was his finest agent. It passed through his mind that they would make a great team.

"I had intended to have you move on the margins of Skye's life. Fade in, fade out, your identity unknown and intact. You really fucked up that strategy."

Alex opened his mouth to speak, but Jim's hand went up and stopped the protest.

"I was furious at first. But it really was circumstance and very bad luck that she made you."

"And her amazing talent."

"That too," Jim said. "I guess I have to confess having a special place in my heart for that girl, but I must admit a part of me is proud of her. I have my two best agents out there and the first match play went to her. She tagged you. It wasn't one of our planned tactical contingencies when we were laying out the strategies."

"She's a challenge. Unpredictable and unbelievably intuitive." Alex guessed he was a little proud of her himself. That was kind of a satirical twist. He was proud because for the first time in his career, someone made him. No one had ever come close before. He was deep covert. She was something special and she was home sleeping in his bed. He thought he would keep that bit of information to himself, at least for now. "Anyway, I would like to join the operation," persisted Alex.

"Skye is Special Agent in Charge. She gets to select her own team," said Jim. He could intercede at any time, but he always preferred to give his key people autonomy.

"She's also a target. As my report indicates, they may escalate the personal attack. It seems to be directed right at her. Whether it's because she's Skye Madison or because she's Special Agent in Charge, we haven't determined. I would like to be her shield. You've placed me in that capacity before in the field."

Jim nodded. Then he looked directly into Alex's eyes and Alex knew what was coming. He was prepared for it.

"You have developed a close personal relationship with Skye." Jim believed in being direct.

"I have." So did Alex.

"That was pretty quick."

"It was."

"Was the relationship you developed for the sake of expedience or was it something…more personal?" Jim was having some difficulty with this. He had agents develop relationships before. It was bound to happen, sending people off together for long periods of time. This one developed so spontaneously, he didn't predict it or plan for it. He didn't like surprises when it came to actions in the field.

Alex smiled comfortably, meeting Jim's penetrating gaze.

"I…." The words stopped in his throat. He turned when he heard Skye's voice, a cold dread running through him. Shit.

There was a quick rap on the door and Skye peeked around the corner. She was smiling broadly. "Pearl must be on a coffee break, Jim. I just stopped by to give Dan his damn invoices and thought I would give you a report from the Tower of…oh…sorry, I'll come back…" Her voice trailed off as she noticed someone sitting in Jim's office.

Alex turned around and Jim looked up at once. Oh hell, thought Alex as he saw the look on Skye's face. He could feel Jim stiffen as he too looked at Skye.

It almost didn't register, it was so out of context. Alex sitting with Jim, folders between them. Jackets off. Coffee cups in front of them. Apparently in a meeting. She looked at one, then the other. Didn't look social. Been talking for a while. Even completely shocked and on automatic pilot, Skye's mind registered details and began computing.

"Alex?"

He just stared at her, forcing his face to reveal nothing until he saw how this was going to play out. It was one of his strengths that he didn't act before he assessed. Jim looked from her to Alex.

"Honestly Jim, why did you…"

She saw them sitting there. It looked like they were having a serious discussion. Did Jim call Alex in to subtly interrogate him? Did he want to do a personal assessment to supplement the written documentation? It didn't make sense. That was overkill. Automatically, her mind accessed other data...shifted her frame of reference...and, added to what she saw now, things were falling into a new pattern. And making more sense, she had to admit.

Jim and Alex could see her face change from pleasure, to confusion, to calculation, to conclusion, to complete and utter rage. She just stared at them both, her eyes dry and hot.

Skye was beyond fury. Events started to click in her mind like the tumblers on a safe.

Click...she looked at Alex...her initial suspicion of his interest. He was following her, all right. But not for a fucking date. No successful businessman with his reputation for direct, bold action would follow her around like some college freshman. Contrived. She thought so at the time. She just suppressed it like she did her other suspicions.

Click...she looked at Jim...his in-depth dossier...what a joke. No not a joke. This wasn't the least bit funny. He knew Alex personally and only told her...what? A cover story? Alex's cover?

Click...Alex's physical skills and capabilities...well trained by the best. She replayed him disarming the man with the knife. Living with cops was no explanation. But she swallowed it. She swallowed it whole. All of it. Lies. Liar. Liar.

Click...Jim appearing at Alex's hotel suite with a story about discrete messages from the desk clerk...damn...that didn't even feel right at the time.

Click...Alex disappearing and appearing at the Blythe estate at perfect times...very convenient...more like a partner than a naive civilian. He shows up on the terrace just as she is need of a cover. He knew her purpose. And he played her.

The safe in her mind opened. Alex was a covert agent assigned to follow her. She wasn't yet sure of his mission, but she was a smart lady, so she could guess. He was assigned before the attack, so unless Jim was clairvoyant, he wasn't there for her personal protection. He was following her to gather information on her and that usually meant she would either get pulled from the case or be cleared for continued action. She wondered which recommendation he brought in with his report.

Alex and Jim watched her as her brain processed the data in the context of this new bit of information. It was fascinating to watch, but neither man doubted they were in deep, deep trouble. Her anger was controlled, but they could see it mounting.

She looked at the faces of the two men. One her surrogate father and boss. A man she'd known her whole life. The other was her new lover, a man who just this morning was someone she thought she might be able to build a life with. It was her complete trust in these men that repressed her intuition. She should have listened to her inner voices. Instead she listened to her heart. Stupid, stupid, stupid. Well, she wouldn't make that mistake again.

Both men watched her. Watched her access the information in her well ordered brain, draw her conclusions, probably correct ones, then register how she felt. Deceived. Betrayed. Used.

"Damn you both. Damn you both to hell!" It was all she could get through her constricted throat. Her eyes were flashing, but her face was pale. It was the latter that had guilt and regret tearing through Alex.

"Skyler, sit down and we'll fill you in." Jim came around the desk, prepared to pull rank.

Alex didn't say anything because he wasn't sure what to say. He would let Jim take this for now. Jim knew her longer, better. Cold, hard fury collected in her eyes and she pierced Alex with a look that was as sharp as a shard of glass. Worse yet, he felt she was justified. How was he going to fix this? His wonderful, hopeful feeling from this morning was fading fast.

"Don't you dare treat this like business as usual, Jim," hissed Skye, her lethal glare lasering back to him.

"Skye…" Jim was sympathetic, but in this office, he was the director and she would hear him out.

She held up her hand. "With all due respect, sir, it isn't the lies. That's part of this job and I can accept that. It's the fact that if you were both lying to me that means you didn't trust me. For whatever reason you deceived me, the bottom line is that you didn't bring me into your confidence. That's something I'll never forget."

"Skye…," Jim tried to interrupt again.

"I'll complete this project. Then you'll receive my resignation."

"I won't accept it."

"Tough shit." She turned her blood-freezing eyes on Alex.

"And as for you, you goddamn bastard, if getting close to me was your assignment, then I hope you have incorporated in your report that you succeeded." She turned to Jim. "Did he tell you that he's been fucking me? Or was that included in his original assignment?"

"Skyler!" exploded Jim. Her anger was justified, but there were limits to his patience. "You'll conduct yourself with the dignity this job requires."

Alex stiffened, but smartly gave his director the lead. He was still assessing the damage. His insides felt shredded and could only imagine what was happening inside her.

"I'm sorry if that offends you, sir," she said 'sir' with venomous sarcasm. "Because what this man did to me most certainly offends me. I'm going in to take these invoices to Dan, then I'll be flying back to complete the mission. And you'd better call off your pet dog, because if he's still following me, I will kick his fucking brains into a teacup and he'll find out just how comprehensive his major medical coverage is." She turned and stalked toward the door. She didn't get two steps when Jim pulled her back with the call of duty.

"Special Agent Madison, you came in here with a report. Now report." Jim said, crossing his arms and transforming into her boss. Both his tone and his stance radiated authority and would accept no further insubordination.

Skye turned back to him, deliberately ignoring Alex who had yet to say anything.

"What's this man's clearance?" she demanded in a voice dripping with resentment.

"Level three, same as yours." She would not let herself be impressed. She would not let herself feel. "You'll give me your report. Alex is privy to everything."

That really pissed her off, too. Her report was delivered in a voice that could have converted bedrock to gas.

"I got the intelligence from the Tower of Terror this morning. This, combined with what we already have means we can move up the timetable. As a matter of fact, I recommend we coordinate a raid for next week."

"So soon?" asked Jim. Alex leaned forward, interested and impressed. He sure would like a piece of that action.

"I have reason to believe that they know we're close. If we wait much longer, valuable evidence could be destroyed. It's the information we want and that's more vulnerable than either the store of drugs or the money."

"Okay, Skye. You're Special Agent in Charge. It's your call." Jim nodded. Personal difficulties were set aside for the moment and separated from this new and excellent development.

Skye looked at Jim coldly. She was the ice goddess. Nothing, not even her own devastation, would interfere with her assigned duties. Both men in the room knew what it cost her to give that brief report in a stiff-lipped, but moderately civil tone. She never once looked at Alex. She never intended to look at him again.

"Indeed. I'll keep you informed." With that, Skye turned on her heel and walked out of the room slamming the door with the force of thunder.

"Goddamn it, how much trouble are we in here Jim?" asked Alex as he stood up. His first inclination was to charge out after her and tackle her before she got to the elevator. But Jim knew her best. Maybe he had a better, more dignified plan. Alex unconsciously rubbed his chest. His heart was beating fast and he was trying to collect the pieces that had flown off when she pierced him with her ice-cold stare.

"She'll complete the assignment," said Jim, taking a deep breath and blowing it out.

"You know that isn't what I'm talking about. We just put a nick in her heart. How the hell are we going to fix it?"

"Look, Alex." Then Jim finally gave into his emotions and ran his fingers through his hair. "I don't know. Tell me one thing before we talk about solutions."

"What's that?" asked Alex.

Jim turned a dark, penetrating glare on Alex. God, she must have learned that from Jim, he thought as he met the stare with a steady one of his own. "Was she just an assignment or am I right in assuming your feelings for her are genuine and sincere?"

Alex gave Jim a little ironic smile. "I've already been nailed by Hazel about my intentions. It's too much of a cliché to say they're honorable, so let me specifically spell it out. If I can ever persuade her to talk to me again, I'm going to ask her to marry me. I want a permanent, committed relationship with her. I'm in love with her."

Jim was stunned by his agent's completely unexpected reply, but he saw his sincerity and was a good judge of both character and situational probabilities. It took him a moment to assimilate what Alex told him and formulate his own response. "You have no idea how it makes things simpler on a personal level and completely messes things up on a professional one."

"Life is messy," retorted Alex, impatience in his voice. He was anxious to go after Skye. He wasn't sure how best to proceed and that was the only thing keeping him in the room.

"Indeed it is, son," agreed Jim, still working over the ramifications of what he had put into motion a few short weeks before.

"You need her to complete this mission," said Alex, his eyes burning and intense. "I need her to complete my life,"

"God, you're poetic," said Jim appreciatively. "So who's going to talk with her first?" They both continued to stare at the closed door. "You or me?"

"I hope you let me try first."

"You're not only poetic, you're the bravest son-of-a-bitch I know."

"Any suggestions?" asked Alex.

"Well, since we've done nothing but deceive her up until now, how about a direct, straightforward approach. Tell her everything. I had intended to do just that after I read and submitted your report, leaving your name out of it of course. And I would recommend punctuating that with groveling at the highest level," answered Jim.

"Flowers?"

"Not if you want to live."

Alex nodded. "I realize we're still in the office, but can I now speak to you as her godfather?"

"Certainly," Jim nodded.

"How come you didn't mention a dead fiancée in the dossier?" asked Alex softly.

Jim didn't respond right away. It didn't surprise him that Alex knew more than he had told him in the beginning.

"It's in her psychological profile records. I don't show those to fellow agents. It was personal, not professional, and really none of your business at the time."

"And now it is," said Alex, looking directly into the eyes of Skye's godfather. He saw the sadness and sympathy.

"Might be. I guess time and Skye will tell." Jim nodded, then went on. "Life makes us who we are…we're forged by fate. Skye was a happy, open, loving, good-natured child. She was always up to mischief and was intelligent enough to know just where the line was. Then destiny changed all that. In a single afternoon, her life changed…she changed. She literally saw her parents die and most horribly. The two most important people in her life. They were wonderful parents and closer than most families, always moving around. The reports said they burned to death. It was a firebomb and they didn't die in the blast. They didn't die right away. She was a witness to it all…from the initial blast through to the end." Jim had to stop for a minute and Alex was glad. His heart was beginning to labor under the empathetic pain he felt for her.

"We took her to counselors and they said she was coping fine, but she wasn't ever the same. They told us she was psychologically healthy and that was the most important thing, I guess," said Jim.

Alex found he was reacting both physically and emotionally. It was all too graphic. How much more horrible it must have been to have lived through it…as a child.

"After Angelina and Perry died," he continued, "she never really grieved. She was more in a rage. She tore through everything, diaries, files, papers. Looking for her parent's killers. She was only 15 years old and she was diving into newspaper archives to see if there were any names connected with her parents that could have been suspects. She was relentless and in the end, she failed."

"Then," continued Jim, "she turned her energy to other things. Her father's Cessna was her refuge. She would go flying for hours. You can't imagine the bad moments I had waiting for her at the airstrip. Pearl would take her to the airport sometimes and saw the same powerful, relentless attempt to escape the pain. We always held our breath until she came back safe. I wouldn't say she was suicidal, but she didn't care about the risks…she just didn't care. Thank goodness the old plane was as reliable as hell and she was amazingly skilled, even back then."

Alex felt some of his impatience fade. This information was important and revealing. He could almost see the girl…see Skye. And it shredded him some more.

"Her life took a real detour when Jeff wore down those well-built defenses and made her love him. She transformed. It was gradual, but the sunny, fun-loving child returned for an encore. He was such an incredibly amusing kid. Never really took anything seriously, and here he was relentlessly pursuing a girl who took everything too seriously. He had a strong will under all that engaging wit, and brought Skye around to his way of thinking."

"After her parents' assassination, she never let anyone into that special place in her heart…until Jeff. They had known each other for nearly their whole lives and he knew how to open her up. Unfortunately, it made her totally exposed for the lethal blow. After Jeff was killed, she completely shut that part of her heart down. I think she believes it no longer exists. She doesn't trust fate, so she has chosen to live life well, but not deeply. I know the rage is still there. It's why she continues to take such awesome risks."

"You don't have to tell me about how she takes risks," said Alex, remembering her fearlessly facing down the four men in the alley, never once considering running or calling for assistance. He recalled the challenging smile on her face when she confronted them, absolutely no fear. He also read some of the reports on her cases. She liked solo work and she liked danger. She would fly into danger with both confidence and unbelievable daring.

"Don't we both know it," said Jim, shaking his head. "It's not easy to love her when you know she thrives on putting her life on the line."

He looked at Alex intensely. There was a warning in the look and Alex nodded. He was beginning to understand that he had taken a step into a whole new world of complications and potential adversity. His heart stopped, then started again. He was ready and smiled at his boss.

Jim liked what he saw. Was satisfied. He decided to go on and finish what was in his own heart.

"She believes she's happy, Alex. She has great friends, a wonderful job, and a sister who brings her joy. I don't think she even realizes that something is missing. She's warm, kind, generous, and witty. But since Jeff died, something in her died too. She doesn't invest in deep personal relationships with men. Never."

Alex searched his heart and found that he liked that revelation just fine.

"She has several male friends," Jim went on. "But no one serious. No one she gives any part of her heart to." Then Jim relaxed. What the hell. Right now he felt like being more godfather than boss. "Good luck, my boy, but don't say you weren't warned. I've had to scrape legions of disappointed and heartbroken men off the sidewalk. They fall at her feet and she just steps over them. I don't even think she sees them. She's especially brutal with fellow agents. You realize it isn't only that we deceived her. When she settles down and sees the whole picture you're still going to have a great deal of trouble winning her over. She'll see you as a man with a gun, close enough to a cop to be one. If you think her anger is formidable, you should see her willpower in action. She's steel, son."

"Yeah, Hazel told me about Jeff and her pact with herself. No cops, no risk," said Alex.

"No passion, no life," continued Jim sadly. "I've always thought her bias in this area was hypocritical. She thinks nothing of putting herself in jeopardy. Scares the shit out of me sometimes. Hell, nearly all of the time. You realize she'll never give up this life. That you'll have to live with her peril as well as your own."

"The very thought of it terrifies me, but I'd rather live with that fear and her in my life, than give up my chance of happiness," said Alex.

Jim nodded. "If you're going to make this relationship work, then I suggest you get her to subscribe to that philosophy. And as her godfather, I wish you the best of luck. She's needed someone for a long time. I think she's just beginning to realize it."

"I intend to go in and get her," said Alex with determination. If she was steel, then he was fire. And fire could melt steel.

"Need back up?" asked Jim, letting some amusement back into his voice.

"I'll let you know."

There was another knock on the door. "Damn, I hate it when Pearl is on break. Come in!" he shouted and started back to his desk.

Dan came into Jim's office. "What the hell happened in here? Oh, excuse me, Jim. I didn't know you were in conference."

"Come on in, Dan. You know Alex Springfield."

"Sure do." Dan crossed the room and gave Alex a perfunctory handshake.

"I'll get out of your hair. When you have a minute, Jim, I'd like to talk with you," said Dan, his eyes sliding to Alex and a not-too-friendly look sliding with it.

"It's okay, Dan. If you're here as Skye's defender, then you should know that it's us she's angry with," said Jim.

"Well, I guess I wouldn't use the word angry to describe what I just saw. I was in central Wisconsin once. I saw a tornado coming across a cornfield. Should have ducked for cover, but it was just too fascinating to watch. All that power, all that destruction, all that dark, intense fury. Scared the beejeebers out of me."

"Are you trying to make a point?" asked Jim. Dan was one of his oldest friends, almost irreplaceable in the administrative details. But he had trouble staying on track.

Dan laughed. He looked at Alex. "That tornado had nothing on Skye. She isn't ripping things up in her path, but that's only because she's civilized. What did you do to her?"

Jim exchanged glances with Alex, then nodded. "Once the report has been filed with the task force, I'll share the information more broadly anyway. Besides, Dan can be helpful in patching up this little rift. He knows her well...very well." Jim folded his arms and looked over at an expectant Dan. "For one thing, she threatened to resign after this current assignment is wrapped up."

"What?" chuckled Dan, shaking his head. "Again?"

"That was temper talking...I hope. I told her I wouldn't accept it."

"She's made that threat before. Anytime she wants to take more risks than you believe are acceptable." Alex and Jim looked at each other. "We both know she'll never leave the department…especially as long as you're here." He sighed. "Okay. Fill me in."

Dan sat down and Jim and Alex reviewed the events from the last few weeks. When they were finished Dan was frowning.

"First of all, I'm glad you were there in that alley, Alex. I was on my way in here and ran into Greta Johnson from the Special Liaison's office. They just got the report from England on the interrogation of the four assailants and I told her I would bring it in. Three have clammed up pretty good. Professionals. But one is an addict. Easier to break. Quite easy in this case, actually. The person who hired them must not have known about the guy's addiction to crack and, of course, that person had no way of knowing about Alex." He waited a beat. "He or she was in the dark, just like the rest of us."

Did Alex detect a note of resentment?

"Get over it," murmured Jim.

"I already have," said Dan inspecting the tips of his fingers.

"What did they learn?" Jim prodded.

"Three of the guys got instructions to mess Skye up, take her down. But one had an order to kill…and Skye was the specific target. They must have figured that if they attacked both Skye and Alex, it would look more like a robbery gone bad. They had no personal contact with the individual who hired them."

Alex sat up straighter in his chair, as did Jim. It was the first they heard about the 'to kill' order. This changed things. Not that getting beat up was a pleasant prospect, but if one of the suspects had a kill order, then that put a new slant on the seriousness of the incident.

"Alex, you're on shield," said Jim without hesitation. "You'll coordinate her protection. In addition, I want you to run a parallel investigation on this development."

Alex had already established that. With or without Jim's permission, he fully intended to be Skye's shield until the end of the operation. Jim just made it easier.

"I'll write up the orders and put it through Operations," said Jim. "This puts the other problem in a whole new light. Dan. Help us out here. How do we convince Skye to allow Alex to get close enough to provide protection. In her current mood if she doesn't kill him on sight, she's likely to shake him off."

Dan leaned forward and looked at them both, like a professor delivering a particularly critical lesson.

"Skye's temper is a fearsome thing…something that comes from deep inside. Before her parents' death she was an open, happy kid. Absolutely the most precocious thing you can imagine. Have you met Sloane?"

Alex nodded and smiled. Somehow he couldn't imagine Skye that outgoing and vivacious.

"Well, the horrific circumstances of that event completely changed her. She became a controlled person. Tightly and finely tuned. Still warm, pleasant and funny, but with all of her emotions simmering under her guard. Everything is suppressed and like anything under compression, when released, you better run for your life. When Skye loses that control…when her temper gets through her powerful defenses, she's…well…very, very intense."

They all looked at each other and their accord was undisputed.

"However, right after she blows," Dan went on confidently. "She's at her most vulnerable. She's contrite, or her energy is down, or the temper blew some of the wall with it. I'm not sure why, but I would suggest you go see her sooner rather than later."

Jim was nodding. Dan was nailing it. He really was a good observer of human behavior and knew how to recognize patterns.

"Skye is tough, but she's fair. She'll respond to the argument that you were following procedure. She's an absolute nut for procedure. Actually use the word procedure or protocol. I remember when we took her to McDonalds for the first time, she marched right up to the person at the counter and asked for the protocol. It was hilarious, she must have been 4 or 5."

"Dan," prompted Jim.

"Yeah. Okay. Then there's her sense of obligation. She's very passionate about justice. I would go after the 'for the good of the mission' angle next."

Alex felt he should be taking notes. "This is good."

"Helps to know the quarry," Dan smiled. "Skye has a natural sense of humor and wit. She doesn't hold a grudge. Anger, once purged, doesn't stay with her long. If you can withstand the initial blast, get her to laugh. Once you have, she'll listen to you. That should work," Dan cocked his head at Jim and stroked his chin comically. "Of course there *is* Simpson in records…the exception that proves the rule."

"Yeah, he still scurries out of her way whenever he sees her in the building," said Jim. "Skye caught him kicking a stray dog in the parking lot. She hauled off and nailed him right in the shins. Told him that if she ever saw him kick a dog again, she would aim higher and all the stray cats in the neighborhood would come running."

"Nasty," said Alex.

"She was about 10 I think and she still glowers at him when she sees him. Now that's a grudge." The men looked at each other and laughed.

"Finally, work out a deal," continued Dan. "Actually make it sound like a contract. You're a lawyer...you know how to make it ring true. Be all business."

"Business...all business," said Alex. "That'll take some will power."

"I mean it." Dan leaned forward in his chair, his face serious, his eyes narrowing. "Off the record, and between us, Skye is dear to me. Like a daughter. What I tell you about her is so that you can get to her and give her the protection she needs. If she's pissed at you, she'll shake you off. No one could ever follow her to the end of the course at training school and I don't want her out there in the cold."

"I understand," said Alex.

Dan cleared his throat, looking uncomfortable. "The two of you...well, you need to work out something...civilized...ah, hell," Dan ran his fingers through his hair. "I know there's something other than a professional disagreement going on here and it's making me as itchy as hell. She would never have reacted this strongly if she didn't feel betrayed on a personal level." Looking out the window Dan said, "She ah...she called you a goddamn fucking whore who didn't have the skill to set up proper surveillance and had to use his dick instead of his brains to keep her in sight. Umm...I take that to mean you and she...ummm..."

"Yes," said Alex simply not at all daunted by the description delivered by the love of his life. "Our relationship is intimate." Alex deliberately used the present tense. He intended to patch things up, no matter what it took.

"Well, then you have a trust issue. That cuts even deeper than anger...and it's something I can't advise you on, Alex. I have three ex-wives. I guess my track record speaks for itself. You're going to have to address it in your own way."

Alex nodded. He understood.

"And one more thing. I've been Nancy's surrogate uncle for her whole life and on a deeply personal level, if you hurt her..." said Dan seriously.

Alex smiled, not at all offended by the implied threat, choosing to be touched by it instead. "First Hazel, then Jim, now you. How many people do I have to go through to get to her?"

"Legions, my man, legions. But you'll deal with her honorably or you'll not get an invoice through my department for as long as I'm at that desk," said Dan. To Dan that was the ultimate threat.

That wasn't much of a hazard to someone who had more money than the department right now, but Alex understood the sentiment and nodded. He got the picture. Now he was anxious to go get the girl.

"That's a deal I can live with." He stood and shook Dan's hand. "My intentions are honorable and thanks for the advice. I'll move on it right now. With your permission, Jim."

Jim nodded. "And Alex." Alex turned at the door.

"If none of this works, I would suggest hand-to-hand combat. She's good, but you're stronger. Take her down, and don't let her up until you have her cooperation. Our Major Medical Plan is the best in the nation."

"I'll take that as an order, sir." With that Alex went out the door to face the music.

CHAPTER 12

Skye was in her apartment chopping up vegetables for a salad. She chopped and chopped and chopped. By the time she realized what she was doing, she had enough salad for the entire Teddy Roosevelt middle school. And their staff. But when she put the debris in a big wooden bowl she saw that half of the vegetables were unrecognizable.

Her anger was keeping her from curling up into a little ball and going catatonic. She would start putting her thoughts in order later, for now she just wanted to...well for lack of a better word...die. No, that was way too melodramatic. She held up her knife and sneered...she wanted to kill.

Goddamn Jim Stryker. He wanted to check up on her, so her sends an agent from another cell. Doesn't just ask her a few questions or take the direct route. No. He has to send Clark Kent. Damn him.

And damn all men to hell. Well, that wasn't fair either. Not all men charmed her, pursued her, seduced her, had sex with her, used her. So damn Alexander Springfield to hell and back. What a consummate actor. A great special agent. Trained to play roles. Trained to lie.

God, she thought as she murdered another carrot, how could she have let her defenses down like that. Her instincts were screaming at her and she told them to shut up. In fairness to herself and her instincts, she allowed Jim to persuade her to believe something her heart was hoping for. She was predisposed to believe because Alex was just so...shit...hell and damnation. Her stomach seized on her when she thought of him.

Sloane had just called all a twitter...Alex had sent her a CD signed by that moron Terry something-or-other. Her sister was admonishing her not to blow it with this man sent from above. Skye didn't have the words or the heart to tell Sloane he was already out of the running.

Her knife poised in mid chop when memories flashed through her brain. Damn her photographic memory. She would just have to erase it. She knew she could do it. She could erase memory...she'd done it before.

His words shot through her mind like bullets on a pistol range.

"Is there any way...any way whatsoever, that I can talk you out of going to this party tonight?"

"You know that women in heels like that are every man's fantasy."

"Does that mean I get to kiss the princess?"

"You know if you waste too many of those, it makes a man crazy?"

"How about you call International and tender your resignation and we stay in this room for a week?"

She remembered practically every word. Were they all lies? Were they lines he scripted to get close, then stay close to her?

Then, of course, there were the blatant outright lies. She decided to replay them to fuel her temper.

"I thought I was being subtle, but I'm not very good at clandestine surveillance...Sam Spade, I'm not."

"I got all the wimp genes in my family...and they're pretty powerful. Saved them up over three generations. I want no more excitement in my life than anticipating the direction of the Dow Jones Average and nothing more life threatening than eating oysters at the New Jersey shore."

"Of course. Madison. I take it your parents were the Ambassador and her husband."

And I thought he was charming. Lying bastard. Her knife went down on the board again and she didn't even notice when it sliced her finger.

Her buzzer sounded. She wasn't expecting anyone. Still gripping the knife, she punched the intercom.

"What?"

"Landers message service with a package for Madison."

"What's the return address?" she asked automatically. The department used Landers exclusively, but she wanted to have additional confirmation. She never let random people up with out some verification, although if she hadn't been so distracted, she may have asked more questions. When she got the address of the Tower of Terror, she buzzed in the delivery person.

Opening the door without waiting for a knock, she saw Alex vaulting up the stairs. She almost had it shut again but he was quick and had his shoulder on it before she could swing it completely closed. She could think of nothing more ridiculous than a shoving match so she let him in. Best to get this over with, she thought.

"What the hell do you think you're doing?" he shouted. Why was he so angry?

"What the hell are you shouting about, you rat stinking lying sack of shit?

I'm in my apartment minding my own business. Now state yours, then get the hell out!" shouted Skye back.

"How did you know I wasn't an assailant?" he asked furiously.

"You said you were from Landers and you had the fucking address for the Tower!"

"Anyone who is on the inside could know that. And we're looking for someone on the inside. Procedure dictates that you don't open up until you confirm my ID through the security window on your damn door." Even through the cloud of anger, he congratulated himself for getting 'procedure' in right away. And Dan was right. It absolutely stopped her in mid-tirade. Hot damn. This might work out, yet, he thought.

Skye looked at his furious face. He was right…damn his worthless hide.

"You're right," she said quickly, anxious to get it out without too much pain attached.

Tough but fair, Dan had said. The man was a veritable genius.

"Oh…and for future reference, you lying prick, if you were an assailant, you'd be dead." Her voice was smooth, her smile wicked and before he could react, her knife was within a hair of his jugular. "You better hope I don't sneeze, you fucking asshole." She followed the comment with a string of snarling Italian.

"Okay. You made your point, now would you disarm yourself? You're making me very nervous." He looked deep into her flashing brown eyes. God, she was magnificent. And what he was feeling was more than lust…it was love. Everything she did magnified that fact.

"You should be nervous. You're in my apartment. You're uninvited and you're a lying, deceiving, unprincipled, amoral, whore," she said, snapping it out beautifully…convincingly.

"Ouch." He decided to cool this situation down, so instead of serious regard for both her righteous anger and her superior position, he smiled one of his best smiles. It was a blue ribbon special.

Skye completely pounded on the little flutter in her stomach until it ran for cover. Then she narrowed her eyes. "Do you have a reason for being here…telling more lies to get in, by the way. When are you going to start with the truth?"

"How about this. I'm crazy about you and your red hot snit is turning me on." He never took his eyes off hers. "Can I stay for supper?"

She almost screamed her frustration, but instead decided silence was her best weapon now. Slowly, deliberately, she lowered her knife.

When she stepped back, Alex relaxed and his eyes swept her luscious body. Suddenly he grabbed her arms. "Skye, you're bleeding. Where are you hurt? What happened?"

Thinking he was employing another ruse, she almost didn't look down, but the highly charged look of concern in his eyes had her following his gaze. Blood was all over the front of her old Embry Riddle t-shirt.

Alex took the knife out of her hand and started looking for the wound. When she found it herself, she lifted her finger. "Damn, this bled a lot. I didn't even know I cut myself."

Distracted by the blood that was pouring out of the cut, she went over to the sink and put it under the faucet. She breathed between her teeth. "*Merde. Ouch. Ciò duole.* Shit, this stings. *Arginato esso.*"

Alex came over and took her hand.

"Don't get grabby," she said angrily, pulling her hand out of his. The blood came pouring out of the wound again so she relented and let Alex guide it back to the running water. "This is all your fault, *l'idiota arginato.* Goddamn son-of-a-bitching idiot."

"I'm not the one with a sliced finger, sweetheart. There are better ways of committing suicide than bleeding out through your finger," said Alex, suppressing both his intense relief that it was only her finger and amusement at her anger. It would not be good at this point to have her think he considered anything humorous. He was still deeply in the penance phase of the mission.

"It's all your fault. I cut it chopping off parts of your body, you moron." She watched as the bleeding slowed down, trying not to react to his hand on hers or his warm body taking up room in her personal space. She could smell him...the scent of man...lover. There was that flutter in her stomach again. Did it have a death wish? She pounded on it some more and it backed off.

"Excuse me?" Alex asked. He didn't have to suppress any flutter. He highly encouraged his body to react. It helped turn up the heat.

"I was chopping vegetables and to give the exercise some added entertainment, I imagined they were parts of your body." She waited a beat looking at the water flowing over the cut on her finger. "The cucumber was particularly enjoyable."

Alex laughed. God, she was a package. Pure, unadulterated delight. "I should be flattered. Ah...what size was the cucumber."

In spite of herself, Skye snorted. "It actually was the size of an itty, bitty little dried up geriatric reject pickle."

It wasn't so much what she said as how she said it, in a little singsong voice. Like she was performing a Saturday Night Live skit. Alex laughed even harder.

"Do you have any first aid supplies? This looks like it could use some stitches," said Alex.

"I'm not going to humiliate myself by going to a doctor and having to admit I cut my finger chopping vegetables," said Skye irritably. She wanted him to be insulted, not entertained. Asshole. Bastard. Liar.

"You could tell him that you were brutally attacked," suggested Alex.

"I could tell *her* that, but then *she* would probably want to file a police report. Too much paperwork. Can't we just put a couple of those white strip things on it?"

He absolutely loved the sound of the 'we' in the sentence. He knew she didn't realize what she was saying. All the better.

"Sure. Here, hold it up." He grabbed one of her good kitchen towels and wrapped it around the finger.

"Honestly, Alex. Not that one!" exclaimed Skye.

"Huh?" Alex looked totally perplexed.

Men, she thought. You have a bloody cut and instead of using a paper towel, they snatch your good dishtowel. They need a rag to wipe their windshield and they take the guest towels in the bathroom. They were born without a complete brain.

"Never mind." She supposed she had something that could take out bloodstains. "The first aid kit is in the bathroom under the sink."

Alex walked by the bedroom and indulged himself by peeking in. Her sense of order was carried over into her living space. Everything was handsomely decorated, but not personal. This was where she slept. Virginia was where she lived. Looking longingly at the bed, he wondered if he had a chance in hell of ever getting her into it. He had to shake that thought out of his head right now, knowing there were many stages of atonement to get through before that was going to happen again.

As he entered the bathroom, he nearly groaned. He could smell her wonderful combination of scents. Maybe if he held his breath, he could get in and get out without giving in to the temptation of sniffing her shampoo bottle.

He located the first aid kit and brought it back to the kitchen. She applied pressure to the cut while he got out the supplies…working efficiently as a team.

"Excuse me," she said coolly when Alex had her all disinfected and bandaged. "I think I'd better change my shirt."

"Need any help?" asked Alex not even trying to keep the hopeful interest out of his voice.

Her response was a chilly silence and a stiff back. Walking over to her dresser, her eyes drifted to the bed. No, no, no, no. Not a chance. And least not tonight, some traitorous little voice whispered. She irritably shrugged on a new t-shirt. Not tonight. Not ever. She wished the thin shirt was armor. No matter. There was steel plating underneath. Turning, she went back to face her nemesis, knowing her major enemy was her own feelings.

"So answer my original question," she said stepping back into the living room. "What the hell are you doing here?"

Damn this little distraction, she thought, playing with the bandage on her finger. Taking a deep breath, she tried to recapture her mad.

Alex could see what she was doing and quickly moved in before she reconstructed the wall. Dan was right on target so far, so he thought he would keep to the plan.

"I'm here to explain."

"I don't care about explanations."

"Well then, let me put it another way. I'm here to report."

Her eyes stopped shooting daggers and he blessed Dan again. The report idea was his, but it was close enough to protocol to count.

"Okay, Alex," she said so coldly that the air conditioner almost shut off. "Sit down and report." No offer of wine, no niceties. But he was still in the room and he was still standing.

She sat on a chair. Damn, he was hoping for the couch so he could sit down beside her. Good tactical move on her part.

"What exactly is your title with the department?" asked Skye.

"Special Agent, same as you."

"And what cell?"

"Special Projects," he said. This was good. Straightforward questions, straight forward answers.

"Ah. The elite. That explains the competence in the alley." Her eyes flashed. "Damn you, you liar. I should have trusted my instincts."

"They were pretty much on target right from the very beginning. I couldn't believe you made me. It's never happened before. No one's even come close," he said with honest admiration and no enmity.

She shot down the little feeling of pleasure over the compliment. "So you improvised and sacrificed your body to stay close to your quarry. I guess having a snappy dick sure beats having a brain."

"I'll continue to take shots like that only because you deserve your anger," he said in a controlled voice. "But before I begin my report, I'll tell you that every single moment with you was completely genuine. Other than my purpose for being there, everything else I told you, everything else you saw in my eyes, felt in my touch, was truth. I regret the lies, more than you know."

"Oh, how convenient. Why should I start believing you now?"

"Use your instincts, darling," he said and smiled a soft, gentle smile as she struggled to keep his words out of her heart. "They're your strength. What do your instincts tell you?" His eyes were steady; his voice was creating a vortex of believability.

"How did it feel when I kissed you? Did it feel like a performance, when I held you, stroked you, made love to you?" His voice was hypnotic. She was beginning to fall under its spell. She shook herself again.

"Just shut up, will you, and report!"

He saw her weakening. It was enough for now. He told her about his assignment and gave her a concise summary of his conclusions. She was a good listener. He threw in 'by the book' and 'protocol' a couple of times, along with 'obligation' and 'the good of the mission.' He was quite shocked when he saw an amused smile creep onto her face.

"What?" he asked.

"You talked to Dan, didn't you?" asked Skye arching one of her beautifully shaped brows.

He wished he could lie, but it probably wasn't a good idea to lie to her again so soon. Besides, her smile was contagious. He smiled back.

"Damn."

"And you're trapped, because you know if I catch you in a lie so soon after you came clean, you'll be out of here."

"Christ, Skye. You're one savvy agent."

"So you and Jim and Dan laid out this strategy."

"I wouldn't call it strategy, just helpful advice."

"Nice evasion."

"So did it work?"

She waited a few moments, noticing the look of anticipation on Alex's face and wanting to stretch out the suspense. Then she sighed. "Of course it worked. No one knows me better than those two old soldiers. Clever bastards."

A vision of her bed flashed in his consciousness. "And have you forgiven me?"

"According to you, you haven't done anything to forgive you for."

"Oh yeah. That's right." Damn she was good at this. He wondered if he would ever win another argument again in his life. Well, if that was the price he had to pay, so be it. Maybe she would give him a pity win once in a while.

"Are we okay?" he asked softly, leaning forward and taking her injured hand in his.

"As it turns out, we're colleagues. Apparently, from what you have told me, you'll be coming back to London. As long as you respect my status as Special Agent in Charge and don't get in my way, we can work together." She sighed and shrugged. "At least we don't have to pretend anymore. I keep getting this flash in the alley after we leveled those poor unsuspecting thugs. Both you and I trying to be so casual, like neither one of us had special training. You were straightening your tie and I was trying to pretend that bruise didn't hurt like hell," she smiled at the thought. "Damn. Now you tell me one had a kill order? That seems a bit excessive." She said it without any concern, dismissing it as if it were just another interesting bit of data to be filed away.

"Will you take this seriously?"

"I don't have to. You'll be there watching my back. I can concentrate on other things. Operationally, this arrangement makes a lot of sense." She nodded and pulled her hand out of his…didn't yank it away, just pulled it out. "Since I wasn't privy to this information on me, I have to take some time to process it. Crime kingpins using my code name…I wouldn't mind it so much if they were saying things like that fucking Nancy Drew is one terrifying bitch—let's knock her off, but for them to refer to me as an accomplice. Shit. That pisses me off."

Alex was alarmed by her lack of unease. Suddenly he saw what Jim had seen throughout her whole career. She was treating a serious, life-threatening situation like a lark. It made him angry…and anxious.

"Someone wanted you off this case, maybe out of the department."

"Too bad I have some pull with the director…plus I've been sleeping with one of the departmental stars, it seems. You cleared me, right?"

"And that's it? You aren't interested in who might have done this?"

"Oh, I'm interested, all right. And as soon as we wrap up this case, I'm going to make it my personal mission to uncover the traitor who tried to set me up. Right now I don't want it to distract us. This operation is in its critical final stages and I'm going to ask you to step carefully when you're with my team. I understand Jim's need to consider all possibilities, but I can't operate thinking one of my team may be playing with the enemy. I trust them. That trust has got to be unconditional."

"All right, but I don't at this point. However, I'll respect your wishes and stay in the background. There will be only one Special Agent in Charge and that will be you."

"I'll decide how much I want to share with my team when we get to London."

"Agreed."

"And I'll call Jim in the morning and tell him to disregard the email and attached letter I sent an hour ago."

"I'm sure he'll appreciate that…although from what I gather, he has quite a collection of letters from you."

That made her smile. "A few. We have kind of a standing agreement that nothing I send will become operational until the obligatory three day cooling off period."

He was beginning to relax. He liked the sound of the 'we' and 'us' she automatically put into their professional relationship. Now for the next step…putting the 'we' back into their personal one. This was turning out all right. Maybe he could talk her into coming back to his place. He had a few business matters to take care of and would have to put in a few hours…but after that…

"If that's all." She stood up. "I have to call in to make final arrangements for tomorrow's flight."

"That's all the business," he said. Her cold, casual tone was his first clue that there was trouble brewing. "But I would like to get back to where we were before this all blew up. I would like to take you out to dinner. I think your vegetable mush is a lost cause. Then I would like you to come back home with me." He stood up and made a move in her direction.

"And what makes you think I'm going to continue a relationship, if that's what you want to call a couple of nights of great sex, with someone who lies to me?" Alex stopped, frozen. He saw her impassive smile, her cold eyes. "I had fun. It was a great release. I enjoyed it and I enjoyed you. But I was seeing a businessperson. A lawyer. Now you're a fellow agent. You're out of the pool of men I consider appropriate to have a relationship with."

She said it so coldly, with such an empty tone of finality, that Alex's temper flared.

"I'm not going to quit the Justice Department because you have a problem with it. I *am* a lawyer and a businessperson. I spent years building a successful practice and a fortune, what I thought was a good life. But after Rita was killed it wasn't enough. Not nearly enough. I joined to help bring down bad guys. I could no longer stand on the side lines."

"I can understand that kind of passion, that kind of compelling drive, Alex. I really can." Her voice was soft and compassionate. Skye could feel the heat and the pain. So it was his sister's death that was the catalyst. They had that in common. The deaths of someone close bringing them into the department. She was moved by his story, his motivation, but not by him. "Does your family know?"

"I've never told them, but they're cops." Alex shrugged, wanting to get back to a discussion of their relationship.

"And ultimately so are you," Skye said softly. Her eyes still impassive, her stance rigid. "And I don't date cops."

Ah, thought Alex. There was the real objection. He refused to be annoyed by her definition of what they had as dating. He knew she was deliberately trying to downgrade the importance of their relationship. For his benefit…or hers? "You know I can't stop. Justice means more to me now than anything I did before I joined."

"I'm not asking you to quit. Really," she said reasonably. "I believe we're very much alike. I joined to pay back the bad guys, too. We can be colleagues. I told you that."

Grabbing her, he drew her to him. She didn't struggle. She didn't fight. She just stayed still and cold and inflexible as steel.

"I want more. I want a whole lot more." He kissed her. She didn't respond. Didn't move. He had no idea how much willpower that took. His lips were warm and gentle. They were begging for a response. But she was forged of steel. She would not bend. She was protecting her heart at all costs. And it was costing her plenty.

"There is no more," she said softly, as he finally let her go. "I'm not going to change my mind. I will work with you, but I will not see you socially." Her voice was so cold, her demeanor so passive, he almost believed her. He let her go.

"I'll see you in London," she said without emotion. "I assume you've been briefed as to the location of our office?"

"As a matter of fact, I followed you there several times." Alex took a step back. He regretted the words as soon as he said them. Her already rigid posture got stiffer.

"Of course, I forgot. You were hot on my trail before you were hot for my tail."

He wanted to say 'good one' but thought it wouldn't be a prudent comment at this point. They hadn't broken eye contact. Alex looked into those cold, dark eyes. Devoid of any passion. Purposely veiled.

She didn't blink. She wasn't budging. Alex decided on a strategic withdrawal. He got a lot accomplished in his visit here. They were balanced again. He would wait for the rest of it. He had a lifetime. He could wait for it to begin.

"Okay. See you in London."

He smiled tightly and went to leave. As he opened the door he turned and looked at her. Rigid posture, lifeless eyes. "I know about Jeff, Skye. I know about the vow you made. I'm very sorry for your grief, sweetheart. I understand it. I come from a family of cops, and remember…we…we lost one. I know how it feels. After going through that, I know this as well…we must love intensely…cherish with extreme passion…because if life is going to be short, it will at least be powerful. If our life together is long and rich, that's a bonus. I'm not going to give up. Consider this a tactical retreat. See you in London."

The door clicked shut and Skye let out a long breath. She'd been holding it since he turned away. Holding herself in with it…remembering her vow and reliving the reason for it. It gave her strength. She just stood there staring at the door. Then she shook herself and walked into the kitchen to see what she could do to salvage the salad.

"Words," she said to herself. "Just words."

CHAPTER 13

They were assembled in their headquarters in London. Skye's team all stared at Alex. She had formally introduced them and gave a brief report. She told them everything…leaving out some of the personal information. But they knew Skye well and could fill in the blanks.

They now knew about the attempt to subtly frame her and could draw their own conclusions on who was behind it. Skye had seen Alex as a businessperson operating on a superficial level from the hotel room. This was the first she saw him as an equal in the field of intelligence gathering. He was concise, firm, and organized when he gave them his report.

"It was a very lame attempt. Too obvious and without merit," said Alex.

"Well if it was so lame, why were you here?" asked Barclay, offended that his leader was under suspicion for anything.

"Jim had to go by the book, Barclay," said Skye. "It's okay. This won't distract us. This is for informational purposes only. That part of Alex's assignment is over." Alex was surprised at her defense of something she was ready to kill him over a few days before. Then Dan's words came back. Tough, but fair.

"He's now here to provide additional security." They were all smart enough to know he was also there to keep his eye on their activities and since they knew it, she decided to get it out in the open. "And, I imagine, to keep an eye on all of you. Someone is on the inside trying to stop us. I suggest the best way to prove ourselves is to keep that from happening."

They all looked at each other. "Director Stryker thinks the leak might be one of us?" demanded a fuming Maureen, looking directly at Alex.

"Huh?" Lucas jumped at Maureen's outburst, letting the tiny screwdriver he was playing with slip from his fingers. "Is that why you're here?"

"No, Jim doesn't think the mole is one of you, and Skye most definitely doesn't think so, but I do have to consider the possibility. That's my job."

That brought a stunned silence, then Max laughed out loud.

"Nothing like a little overt hospitality to remove any need for secrecy and stealth. So you will be watching us at the same time you watch Skye's backside...ah...I mean back."

Linda glared at Max, then turned her penetrating brown eyes on Alex. "I suggest we not digress into what Agent Springfield is here to do," she said through clenched teeth. "I want to talk about the only real pressing thing he told us in his report. Someone wants Skye out, and from what he said, that someone has shifted his focus from an internal departmental investigation and removal to a more direct kill order."

They knew about the attack, of course, but they were alarmed when Alex told them that it was personal and potentially deadly.

Judy, always the mediator, looked at Alex and admitted, somewhat grudgingly, "I guess if the director hadn't assigned you to her, she might have been seriously injured. Or worse."

"That's true enough. For that reason, I'm willing to cut you some slack Springfield," said Maureen, cooling off a few degrees from her original reaction.

"Can't insult me with suspicion," said Max winking at Linda who all but gaped at him. "I thrive on it."

"I'm sure that's because your psychological profile indicates you're immune to personal attack and you derive your self worth from your own inflated ego," she said. She was a long way from letting Alex off the hook.

"Hey, if you say so, babe."

Barclay and Lucas went quickly back to their stations while Judy and Maureen stood back.

"So, Alex...you weren't just a filthy rich guy sniffin' after Skye? Hoping to score? I gotta tell you, I didn't make you for an agent," said Max ignoring the volcano by his side getting hotter and ready to erupt. He was inclined to think this elevated Alex's status, but in order for him to admit it, he would have to incur Linda's wrath. She was livid that Jim had sent someone over to investigate their SAC.

"I take it you have cleared her completely so we can get on with important work?" Linda asked Alex with fire in her eyes.

"I have indeed," Alex smiled.

"And how do you feel about this, Skye?" Linda took her eyes off Alex and looked at her friend. She knew there'd been an intimate relationship as well and was looking for signs of hurt. Skye was a master at hiding pain and she smiled at Linda and her entire team.

"Jim, Alex and I have patched things up."

"That's not how it feels in here to me," said Max bluntly, always able to read Skye just fine. "Feels like someone left a refrigerator door open."

"Well it was kind of a shock to find out I was an assignment and it wasn't my charming personality that attracted him," said Skye casually, but with a little trace of resentment that didn't get by her old friend Max. He stared at her a moment, then decided to say what was on his mind. It would help her in the long run, he thought. And what the hell, he was always incurring Linda's wrath. It was his joy in life.

"Get off it, Skye." He was the only one who ever did or who ever could talk to her like that. "We super agents don't sacrifice our bodies for the cause anymore. If he's boppin' ya, it's because he wants to. Because he can't help himself. The agent part of the body is up here." He pointed to the head. "The man part of the body is down here." He pointed to his crotch. "They're separate. He was using the man part in the bedroom or wherever he felt like poking' ya, and he just had to bring the agent part along cause the bloody thing was attached. See what I mean?"

Max and Alex instantly bonded. Max was his new best friend. Although Alex thought boppin' and poking' weren't exactly how he would describe their relationship, he really liked how Max explained it. Simple, uncomplicated, and quite true, actually.

Everyone except Linda instantly found something very vital to do. She was glaring, completely incredulous, at Max.

"You supercilious ethno-centrist! If that's your take on things, all that means is that you're way, way more man than agent," Linda spat out at Max. "As a matter of fact, the word dickhead comes to mind."

He looked at Linda and smiled broadly. "Why thank you very much. Hmm, an interesting physiological picture, but at least us mere mortals can spell dickhead…just what is a supercilious ethno-centrist anyway, cookie?"

"Stop calling me cookie, you pig. I swear you have the tact and diplomacy of a water buffalo."

"Yeah. Well, you know how I feel about diplomacy. Diplomacy is the art of saying 'nice doggie, good doggie'… while you're looking around for a handful of poison hamburger."

"Hey Max," said Linda, her voice soft and thin as glass.

"Yes, Linda?" He pronounced it Lin-duh again, just to get the glass to break.

"Did you ever stop to think and then forget to start again?"

"Jesus Christ. You sound like a goddamn bumper sticker," Max snorted.

Linda didn't want to admit that was precisely where she got it and was saving it for just the right moment.

"Yeah, well it's better than being a stumper dicker."

Linda barely reached Max's chin, but somehow they were nose to nose. Linda wasn't about to back off. Max looked directly into her flashing eyes, reached down, and kissed her lips. "Whoops, that was up here with the agent part. So sorry."

"Too bad dickhead is just a concept or that could have been great sex," said Alex grinning at his new compadre, who dissolved in highly charged laughter.

Linda gasped. "You two are far too prehistoric to be standing upright, you knuckle dragging cavemen."

Max and Linda glared at each other. Skye and Alex glared at each other and for a few heartbeats all one could hear was the frantic typing of computer keys by four other really, really busy agents. Skye wasn't sure they could even be hitting the right keys at that speed. Her lips twitched. Max's lips twitched. Then Linda's. Before another heartbeat there were gales of laughter floating through the office and all typing stopped for a good ten minutes.

"Okay," said Skye, feeling purged and much better. "Recess is over. Now that we've all met and greeted the new kid, bring me up to speed on what's been happening over here."

Alex was extremely impressed by not only the skill of the individuals, but by the coordination of their efforts. They were working with the local authorities, putting them on to individual drug users as well as the suspected drug suppliers. Phillip's Palm Pilot information was a treasure trove. He had much of it coded, but in such a simple language that Barclay was by it with barely a hesitation.

Skye reported on what they found out about Juan. Her instincts were correct and the fingerprints that Max preserved on the glass revealed a man who was complicated and dangerous. There were no current warrants out for him in any country they could locate, but he had served time in a Mexican jail for dealing drugs. Juan was Columbian, but as far as they could determine, his headquarters were not located there. He seemed to be an international figure who traveled and moved around a lot. Always managing to stay one step ahead of the authorities. He had been Juan Michallini for the last five years.

"He goes into an area, establishes a local contact, brings in massive quantities of drugs, then gets out before the law closes in on him. He's using a franchising technique," said Skye, summing things up.

176

"Kind of like McDonald's," said Judy.

"Exactly, except he distributes McDeath and his medium coke is not of the cola variety," responded Max. He was standing next to Linda who had decided it would be too surly to continue to hold a grudge against Alex. She even smiled at Max's comment.

"Do you think he has moles everywhere?" asked Judy.

"I do," answered Skye.

"If there's a mole in our operation, it seems all of our movements have the possibility of being thwarted."

"We can't let the idea of a traitor stall our operations. I would like to suggest we do just the opposite."

"What's your plan, Skye?" asked Max, now all business.

"I want to move our original timetable up by a full two months. Everything depends on speed and discretion. We have this big fish in our net now and we don't want to lose him. If we wait, all the information will vanish with him."

"But we have to know where to look…an important part of our mission is to locate the cache of drugs and that information," said Linda. "And we haven't got that yet."

"Not entirely true. I think I know exactly where that might be." Skye flashed a self-satisfied smile. "If we go in this much sooner than anticipated, we should catch them unprepared, before they can close down and cover up. I would like to schedule our raid for next week. It will take an incredible amount of coordination, but it will also completely throw off the mole and his or her partners."

"And no one will know except Jim, the people in this room, and our contacts in the local law enforcement agencies," said Maureen.

"Exactly."

"There are plenty of people out there we've been working with locally but the leadership is pretty tight. We haven't noticed any leaks so far, and we've been making a lot of discreet arrests, working our way to the mother load," said Linda, nodding her approval.

"I talked with Jim about it personally. Even if the mole finds out, it won't do much good. These kinds of drug operations take months to liquidate. We may not get it all, but we will dig up enough to take Juan this time. For twenty years he has been operating around the world like a man with a force field. His time has run out."

Max handed the list of assigned contacts to each individual for communication and coordination. "Does that mean Miss Tokyo and I don't have to serve another itsy bitsy sandwich?"

"That's right. You can quit today," she said, dodging as Linda threw a Coke can at Max's head.

As usual, Max ducked with incredible quickness and she missed. He underestimated his adversary, however, and failed to anticipate the assault of the three-day-old scones she hurled at him in a shotgun approach...all at once. Five missed, one did not. Nothing is more unyielding than a three-day-old scone and Max complained about his sore cheek all afternoon.

Later that day, Skye brought some ancient-looking parchment into the room and laid it out on the table. "Alex, our real estate tycoon, was able to use his contacts to secure the original architectural renderings of the Blythe estate. As you can see, it is far better than the drawings we were working with from various sources."

The team gathered around the table. "You'll see that according to these plans windows 1-25 are in the ballroom. This photo taken of the outside confirms that there are twenty-five windows. However, the other night, I counted the windows from the inside. There are only twenty-two."

"What an obscure thing to do. What possessed you to count the windows?" asked Barclay.

"It didn't fit into my well-ordered mind," Skye smiled. Barclay could always appreciate a well-ordered mind. "I walked to the area of the three windows from the outside. They have a state-of-the-art alarm system, while the rest of the house has 1970s technology. Also, the ground felt different under my feet. Spongier. Not that anyone would notice."

"You did," said Barclay, worshipfully, his admiration obvious.

"How do you do that? No one notices that kind of thing," said Max but he was smiling like a proud parent.

The look made Alex wonder about his and Skye's relationship. Max would often throw an arm around Skye's shoulder. But Alex noticed he did that with all the members of the team as well. Everyone, but Linda. Alex fought down a vicious little twinge of jealousy. Skye had a life before him. Besides, he and Max had just bonded.

"I think we have the lair identified. Now we need the warrants to go in. Maureen, have you and the local authorities gathered enough evidence to put through the paperwork?"

"Yes, I think so. I'm working with the prosecutors here. The Blythes are powerful people and their royal status puts them into a different legal position, but nothing will protect them from what we've gathered. We've had the house under surveillance for weeks and since the party we've been taking special note of the trucks from La Fleur Flower Shops," she continued. "You were right about them, Skye. What you saw, what you managed to put together. The estate has a greenhouse and acres of flowers, yet they get flowers delivered, twice daily...or at least something goes in and out in flower boxes. You thought that didn't make any sense. It does if you consider that the major stash of cocaine is located somewhere inside the estate and the deliveries are a cover."

Max took up the report. "Another nice deduction, Skye. As you suspected, the flowers at the party were from the greenhouses on the estate. The Blythes have exclusive hybrids. Very easy to identify. The trucks you saw the night of the party might have been full, but not of flowers."

Max continued, "We have had the 16 La Fleur shops across the city under surveillance. A very interesting assortment of people goes in and comes out with a little box of flowers. All upper crust. All in swanky cars and all really loving the bloomsters, some not even waiting to get into their cars to start the sniffing. Only thing is, it isn't the sweet scent of flowers they're taking up their nose."

"I went in and asked to talk with someone about flowers for a wedding. Maureen went in to get some flowers delivered for a sick friend. They don't do weddings, or deliver. They're the only floral shops in London who do neither," added Linda. "In the opinion of the experts in the field, it is impossible to survive, much less thrive, under those circumstances."

Maureen smiled and nodded. "Bottom line is, yes Skye, we have enough to move in. It'll be tight because we have to find people to issue the warrants who will be both discreet and are not on Phillip's lists."

"How do the names of the people entering and leaving the flower shops check out against Phillip's list?"

"Perfect match, so far."

"So we have the bee hive and the distribution system." Skye nodded, a surge of anticipation making her eyes bright. "We go."

They all looked at each other. This was it. All the planning, the data gathering, the analysis, the coordination. Now the pay off was near.

"Of course this is just one of the arms of Juan Laimenteir. Hopefully, with the data we get from the raid we can go right up the arm into the brain. It isn't the drugs we're after, it's the intelligence."

Skye straightened and stretched. That was the important business. Now she needed to get to other, more peripheral concerns.

"There's one other thing. Part of Alex's continuing assignment is to uncover why there seems to be so much interest in me. We're still not sure if they have targeted me personally because they want to throw things off on this case by removing the Special Agent in Charge; if I know something from another operation; if I offended a passenger or something else related to my job at International, or if they just want turmoil within the department. It could be a combination since this part of me," she pointed to her head, "is Special Agent in Charge. This part of me," she pointed to her heart, "belongs to the airlines. And this part of me." She pointed to her hips, "is personal and now off limits." She looked right at Alex who was standing by his new best friend Max watching her work.

Alex choked on his coffee and Max pounded on his back. "Don't feel too bad, my friend. You got a lot farther than any other special agent ever even dreamed of."

Alex looked at all the grinning faces and grinned back. "Are there...ah...no secrets here?"

"None. We operate on openness," responded Skye, her arms folded in front of her, her lips twitching. "You're lucky you weren't disqualified right from the start."

"Ouch." Alex put his hand over his heart.

"Lower," said Max under his breath.

"Dan Dickson is on the line, Skye," said Judy with a smile.

Skye's face lit up. "Put him on speaker."

"Hi Dan," Skye began.

"Hi ya, Nancy. How's Ned?" Laughing, Skye looked over to Alex. "Sitting right here."

"Good. I'm glad you're finally working together on this."

Skye took the lead in getting the conference call underway. "Dan, Jim has informed me that you have some more information."

"Yes. We got it from a file you downloaded from Phillip's Palm Pilot," Dan answered. "You may wish to take me off speaker."

"I'm not going to filter this. There's been enough of that already," said Skye, not quite able to keep the edge out of her voice.

"Sorry, Nancy, but that's the way this business runs sometimes. None of us can get overly sensitive when it comes to security. Sometimes if it walks like a duck, quacks like a duck and looks like a duck, it's a duck. And sometimes it isn't."

"Understood, Dan," she smiled. Leave it to Dan just to lay it out simply and logically. That duck thing was one of his favorites and the whole agency knew it. Her whole team was smiling with her. She looked at Alex. He'd been caught in the middle and Dan was sending her a message to get over it. She could see that Alex caught it too, and appreciated the sentiment.

"It isn't my job to draw the conclusions or the strategic initiatives from this data but I will tell you, even if Jim doesn't, that it was my recommendation you come in. Someone has been trying to get you expelled from the case. I think since that didn't happen, you will be in further jeopardy. Jim is putting that recommendation into the mix. He wasn't ready to pull you when the original data surfaced because you were getting such great results. Besides, Phillip seemed to have built a rapport with you that would be difficult to duplicate."

Max and Barclay snorted and Lucas looked up from the report he was reading. To him this was one of those boring people meetings that someone would summarize later. He just wanted to know what the snorting was about.

"Rapport. Is that the same as droolin' all over his shoes?" asked Max.

"Exactly," said Dan easily.

"Well, I'm still here," said Skye.

"True, thank God. After Alex submitted his report, everything on that issue will wait until the conclusion of your operation. He saw no evidence of any unusual movement on your part, no private meets or movements unrelated to the operation, no clandestine correspondence. He had you under...ah direct surveillance during the time contact was being made with the other side. You are completely cleared." With each word, Alex could feel the temperature in the room go down a degree. He liked Dan, but sometimes he was clueless. "Hey and Jim tells me you tagged Alex. That's my girl!" said Dan. That helped immeasurably to warm things up. Maybe Dan wasn't so clueless after all.

Skye smiled and looked at Alex. Skye's team beamed and looked at Alex. Lucas didn't look up. Beaming doesn't produce a sound and he was still looking down at his reports.

Dan cleared his voice. "There's other information to report relating to you specifically."

"Go on," said Skye.

"In Phillip's personal files, we ran routine name checks through the text portions and as expected, your name was on several," continued Dan.

"Please elaborate."

"Most of it was routine correspondence. Invitations, his guest lists, notes to himself about your dates...and a little inventory of changes that he would like to initiate…your hair is too untidy, your appetite is too robust, your love of the lower classes is far too obvious, your acknowledgement of servants is appalling and your language is too colorful." Everyone in the room had to suppress a comment, but Skye knew they would lay latent and pop out later when they were all alone.

"Sounds like I need a great deal of work."

"According to his criteria anyway. While this is interesting, and I'm sure is now fodder for your team's usual feeding frenzy, the only interesting thing to pop were copies of a couple of emails he sent to his mother about you…here let me get the exact copy. 'She will be very valuable to us. I will seduce her and take her into our confidence. We'll then be able to turn her and bring her into the operation. Assets: She'll be able to smuggle valuable papers into the country on her person and use her knowledge of Customs procedures to get in larger shipments of drugs and cash.' Sounds like they were going after you at the same time you were going after them." They could hear Dan shuffle papers. "Here's the interesting one, quoting again. 'I mentioned the possibility of bringing my pilot into the operation to J. He said no. Violently. The man is not very cooperative. Since you think my plan is a good one, I introduced S to J. last night so he could see for himself. He nearly killed me later, telling me I was an imbecile. I am not, and if you are agreeable, I would like to take him off our preferred guest list.'"

"Now there's a threat," mumbled Max.

"So you think J. is Juan and the original meet was the trigger that set off the scheme to frame me?"

"Yes."

"But I barely remember the introduction. God, Phillip introduces me to a hundred people every time we go out. When I gave it some more thought, I remember meeting Juan at the Dali Exhibit, but there was no recognition."

"When you're guilty, your perception is skewed…you become paranoid. Juan in his self-centered way, thought you recognized him and wanted you far, far away," said Maureen.

"According to Jim, the date of the email corresponds with the beginning of the set-up. Within the week, your reports were being sent to a drug dealer under the nose of MI5. I can only speculate that the person who sent them knew that someone in the intelligence community over here would be informed," added Dan.

"But if he recognized me, knew what I was doing, why didn't he tell the Blythe's?" asked Skye.

"He knew he was cooked the moment he saw you…probably before if someone on the inside warned him of your team's arrival. He wanted a few more good months out of them before he disappeared and when he saw you, he knew you were closing in."

"Closing in, but still governed by laws, procedures, principles of evidence, and seizures. He knows building a case takes time and he intends to take it. You can be sure he has an escape plan," added Alex.

She shook her head and blew out a sarcastic little sound. "Just when was Phillip going to get to the seduction part? I wonder what he's waiting for?"

"Maybe a warm reception from you?" asked Max.

Skye ignored Max. "If Phillip wants me on the team, I know for certain he has yet to make that proposition."

"He still thinks he has time," said Judy. "I think it reinforces the idea that Juan is going to leave them out there to hang and disappear soon."

"That makes it even more critical we move fast," said Max.

"Skye," said Dan. The use of her real name punctuated the seriousness of his position. "It's obvious someone wants you out of commission. The personal attack on you in London was an escalation of that wish. I've strongly recommended to Jim that you be placed in a safe house until we figure out why. Everything there is set, you can come in."

"Unacceptable Dan. Your thinking is too sentimental," said Skye.

"Acknowledged. I freely admit I don't want anything to happen to you. But if you want to take sentimentality out of it, you're too valuable. I have the figures right here on how much it cost to train you. Add to that the astronomical amount that has gone into your flight training. You're one of our most valuable assets."

"And you helped raise me." Skye said, smiling now. "Put your figures away, you don't fool me a bit with that one. You're a sentimental softy."

Dan chuckled. "Well, there is that. Be careful what you say in front of your team, Special Agent. They might think you got your job through nepotism."

"I'll not be taken off this case. It's been mine from the beginning. I won't hide away. The danger's incidental." Skye said with finality. Her team looked at each other. Incidental? There had been a kill order on her and she treated it like a minor inconvenience. In reality she didn't treat it at all. It wasn't a variable she gave any weight to. There was admiration, but also deep concern.

"I want you in, Nancy, but it's Jim's decision." He hesitated a moment, then went on. "I was a pall bearer at your father's funeral. I'm chilled by the thought that his daughter is in the same kind of jeopardy. It gives me many sleepless nights."

Alex looked at the rest of the team. Their eyes revealed that security was going to be on everyone's mind until the end of this operation. Alex was finding it hard to take a deep breath. This was reality and it was getting more and more dangerous for the woman who held his heart.

Skye appeared to be the only one unfazed. "Low blow, Dan, and completely off the subject. There have been no other incidents since that evening. It was unsuccessful, so it could be that they'll back off."

"You're right. I apologize to you and your team for the sidetrack into personal indulgence. Nancy, be careful. And Ned, watch her back. Anyway, here's Jim. He wants to talk with you."

"Skye? You on speaker?" asked Jim.

"I am."

"Dan told you about his recommendation?"

"He did," she said coolly.

"Now, don't get pissy with me. I have to make decisions on the deployment of my people. I have to weigh your contributions to the case with the potential for injury or loss of life," said Jim dispassionately. Skye didn't mind his detached tone a bit…this was more like it even though it sounded cold after Dan's emotional outburst. She knew Jim felt the same way about her, but he would never formally weigh his personal feelings in the equation.

Her team was just enjoying the pissy comment. She got pissy a great deal but because it was Jim who brought it to her attention, she couldn't do a thing about it…except get pissier.

"Agreed," said Skye, her tone only a notch above civil. "May I make a case for my continued presence here?"

"No need. I'll not be pulling you. I need you there. Alex, your job is to cover Skye's ass. I want you close. If they're out to discredit her, or stop her, they may turn up the heat and I want you there to keep the ground around her clean. You all have worked too hard and too long on this."

Alex had a comment about her ass on the tip of his tongue, but wisely kept it to himself. He would be glad to cover her ass and be as close as he possibly could.

"I can take care of myself, sir. I don't want to be taken off this case," said Skye between clenched teeth, "and I don't need a watch dog." This was definitely moving up on the pissy scale and her team liked the show.

"I suspect you'll have five or six of them over there."

Max started barking like a dog. Judy rolled her eyes, Barclay and Lucas laughed and Linda slapped Max over the head.

"Thanks, Max. Linda, will you throw the man a bone?" asked Jim.

"How'd you know it was me, sir?" asked Max, grinning. He didn't have Skye's rapport with Jim, but he was highly regarded and he knew it.

"Your bark had a Brooklyn accent," explained Jim. "Anyway, you'll report any incident directly to me. I expect with heightened security, there shouldn't be an overly high probability of a successful attack in the future. One more near miss, though, Skye, and I may have to reconsider. For now…status quo. Okay, report on your plans to accelerate the timetable. Have you briefed your team?"

"I have," and Skye gave him a complete, concise report, with members of her team adding their comments and insights.

When a team works closely together for months, even conversation over a few beers turns to work-related topics. Over drinks, however, there's less structure and informal explanations can be shared. The team had plenty of questions for Alex and Skye. They were in a back room of a local pub. Whenever they were in a public place, they kept their voices down and spoke in cryptic or general terms. Something Dan had said was on their collective minds all day and they didn't even get their first beer down before Max, always the team spokesperson, brought it up.

"So Skye. Tell us how you made lover boy. You just couldn't believe anyone that pretty could be anything but a covert special agent for the Justice Department?"

"Actually it all started as a fluke at the airport." She proceeded to tell them the whole story, with Alex laughingly interjecting his point of view when things got too one sided.

"Ever been made before?" Max asked Alex.

"Never."

Max nodded his approval. Of both Skye and Alex. He thought they would make a dandy couple. "What was all the Nancy and Ned crap? Some kind of new code or something?"

"Well, you know my code name is Nancy Drew. That's because I was a nut for Nancy Drew mysteries when I was a kid. Dan bought me nearly every copy ever published," explained Skye.

"Who the heck is Nancy Drew?" asked Barclay. "I thought that was you."

"Well, it's my code name, but before that it was a series of books about a female detective," said Skye.

Alex smiled. "My sister had every one, but I always preferred the X-men and the luscious, curvaceous Storm to the cute and charming Nancy."

"That explains your perverse appetite," sniped Skye.

"For the luscious and curvaceous," Alex countered, raising his eyebrows and grinning at the hooting Max.

"Nancy solved every crime in about 200 pages," said Linda, rolling her eyes and getting the conversation back on track before the tangent got Skye and Alex engaged in mortal combat.

"Well then, who's Ned?" asked Max.

"Ned Nickerson was her stalwart and virginal boyfriend," said Lucas. When Skye looked at him in amazement, he smiled. "My sister had every book too, and she would read them out loud from the back seat of the car when we went to Montana on vacation. I liked them."

"Well, who the hell would want a virginal boyfriend?" scowled Max. He only read comic books as a kid.

"I loved how Nancy would put clues together and find the perpetrator," added Judy, ignoring Max's question.

"With her best friends Bess and George," added Maureen. They all grinned at each other like reading Nancy Drew was a secret rite of passage.

Max shook his head thinking they were all goofy. "So that's how you got started with the investigating thing, Skye? I suppose if you would have read books about dinosaurs like other normal kids you would have been a paleontologist." Max shrugged, pretty proud he got his tongue around that word after his third Guinness.

"You obviously read Mickey Mouse and Daffy Duck," sniped Linda.

"No. Superman and Dick Tracy," Max said puffing out his chest. He made a mental note to look into this Nancy Drew thing for his nieces. They were always trying to uncover their brother's secrets, and maybe this would give them a clue. If the team liked them, that was better than a critique from Amazon.com. Buying for those girls always had him baffled.

"I never heard of them either, Max." Barclay's idea of a good read was *Quantum Physics: The Reality of Time Over Matter*. As a kid, he had the complete set of the *Encyclopedia Britannica* and would read them from A to Z, then start again going from Z to A when he was feeling a little racy. He always resented the fact that there had been no Internet when he was a boy. It was the feeling of the team, however, that had there been the Internet and PC's when he was a kid, he would still be in his childhood room.

They wondered what Phillip thought he had that could turn Skye to become a working partner in their nefarious activities. Chocolate, pancakes, shoes, a new Beechcraft Bonanza. The guesses got wilder and the laughter got more hysterical. Finally Skye broke it up.

"Time to get to bed, children. We have a lot of planning to do. I'll see you all back at the office tomorrow morning," said Skye.

Max offered to walk Linda back to the little apartment she was renting. They had both consumed more than their usual limit of Guinness since they knew this was their last night to indulge in play. They would need to push the work out at an incredible pace for the next few days. Linda looked down the dark street and then up at Max.

"Well I suppose a half-in-the-bag bodyguard is better than none," she said, although the edge was off her voice.

"Exactly, so allow me to walk by your side and protect you from flying scones," said Max.

"I was talking about me, you moron!" she said as they walked off laughing.

The others scattered. Barclay went back to the office. He had a cot there. Sometimes he would get up in the middle of the night with a brainstorm, and it was best he be right there with his computers. Judy and Maureen shared a place and decided it was a lovely night for a walk. To everyone's shock and surprise, Lucas had picked someone up in the bar.

Alex took Skye's arm. "As your official watch dog, I think a cab is a better idea than a walk." She nodded. He was doing his job.

"Skye. I didn't want to talk about this with the rest of the team present."

"You know how I feel about secrets."

"This isn't a secret. They all know how I feel about you."

She sighed. "What is it?"

"I would appreciate it if you would move into the penthouse suite with me," said Alex.

"God, give it up, Alex. I'm not moving into your suite!" Skye got into the cab Alex had hailed.

"I'm not talking about cohabitation. The place is so big you can have your own space. Your own room, your own balcony."

"Not a chance." She was going to stand firm on this one.

"Afraid you will give in to temptation?" Alex taunted. He thought that might work. He really wanted her close, both the special agent and the man.

"Why, you got chocolate up there?" she asked sarcastically. Temptation was exactly what she feared.

"Every night on the pillow, but I was talking about this." He grabbed her so fast; she didn't have time to react. Pulling her to him, he kissed her, hard, hot, and hungry.

"Get off me you horny bastard, or you're going to have to explain to everyone tomorrow how you got a black eye and swollen balls. I wouldn't want to go through the humiliation if I were you." Looking down he saw her hands were actually fisted, cocked, and ready. He laughed and let her go…for now.

"I'm responsible for your safety. It would be easier if we were closer at the hotel," he explained reasonably, trying one last shot.

"Wrong. I'm responsible for my safety. You're responsible for watching my back. And we're plenty close enough." She moved over closer to the far door.

"Okay." He thought it had been worth a try, now back to business. "Then I'll either come to your suite or you'll come to mine for a briefing. We can do this tonight or tomorrow over breakfast. Your choice."

Skye looked at her watch and Alex's mouth twitched.

"I saw that," she said. Skye hated getting up in the morning and Alex knew it. "Let's do this now. In my suite. And you have to leave when I ask you to. No grabbing."

When they got to her room, Alex realized he should have insisted on his suite. Midnight Seduction. He sniffed. He was sure of it.

Alex steeled himself against the onslaught to his senses and drew in the professional agent. He went over all of the safety procedures. She would still have relatively free movement, but he was in charge of this aspect of the operation.

"Do you want to come up for a drink? Tuck me in?" he asked with a seductive smile when they had finished.

"No, Alex."

"The drink part or the tucking me in part?"

"Alex, I will not set foot in your suite for the duration of our stay in London. I have one more rotation before I want to go into the estate with the warrants. I have a ton of paperwork to complete…"

"Those are all excuses. Those things have always been a part of your life. I just want to squeeze in there. Where I was before," he looked at her with his burning blue eyes, directly, steadily.

She looked up at him. "No, Alex."

"How about dinner tomorrow night? You have to eat." He thought maybe a bit of logic.

"I'm going out with Phillip." And she was glad.

"Why? You have everything you need."

"I want to see if I can feel any change in his attitude. He may telegraph any intentions they have of moving. There may be panic or tension that I can detect. I'm a thorough person, Alex."

He couldn't argue with her reason for being with Phillip. It was actually quite logical. He didn't like it, but he couldn't argue with it.

"How's your finger?" He thought a little diversionary tactic would work.

"What?"

"You know, where you sliced it chopping up my body parts."

"It still hurts like hell." She stood up and indicated through her manner that the briefing was over and he had to leave.

"Can I kiss it?" He stood up too and gazed down at her.

"Goodnight, Alex" She opened the door. He walked through it and stood in the hallway until he heard her lock and chain the door.

"Good night, Alex. Go to bed." she said through the door.

"Okay," he said staring for a minute at the closed door, wondering what the odds were of him being able to seduce her and going to bed in her room. He gave his head a little shake. Not good. He pulled the key for the room across the hall out of his pocket and let himself in. Then he called the room next to Skye's.

"You in place?" asked Alex.

"Sure am. This place sure beats my room downtown."

"See you in the morning, Max."

"Sure thing, Alex."

"Tell Linda sweet dreams." Alex smiled into the receiver.

"Ah...just how...?"

"I'm a super secret agent, remember."

"Sure. Okay. One more thing...man to man." Max's tone was serious.

"Linda must be in the bathroom."

Max snorted. "Yeah...well...anyway. I've known Skye ever since we met each other on the rifle range in Colorado. She's a special woman. And this is the last time you'll get this mush from me. If you mess her up, your dick is mine."

"I get the picture." How many guardians could one woman have, particularly a woman who probably didn't need one?

"That said, super special agent, I'm going to give you a bit of guidance. What's your clearance?"

"Level three."

Max whistled. "I'm impressed. I think then I can trust you with this." He lowered his voice to a stage whisper. "When she speaks Italian, duck for cover. When she speaks Spanish, it's all business. But when she speaks French, turn down the sheets and prepare to be eaten alive."

Alex laughed, delighted. "Thanks for the advice. How…ah…well…" He had been wondering this ever since he saw them work together at the estate. "Have…ah…oh…never mind." He usually didn't have this much trouble with words.

"If you're asking me if I ever rode her, no Alex, I never have. I love Skye, but I also love pizza and the Green Bay Packers. It's always been Linda for me. I love her madly…more like I'm mad to love her…and if you ever share that with the little China doll, I'll tell Skye that you said women shouldn't be allowed in the cockpit."

"There's an incentive to be discreet. Don't stay up too late," chuckled Alex, relieved.

"Oh I intend to stay *up* all night." They both laughed a uniquely boy laugh and rang off.

When the man with the breakfast cart came into Skye's room the next morning, he looked around as if he thought someone would be there. He knew no one had been in the penthouse suite. The Big Tipper must be out of town. Then came a knock on the door and he smiled.

"Who is it?" asked Skye.

"Max."

"Max?" She peeked through the security hole and opened the door. He was holding a cup of coffee. Thoroughly confused, she let him in. "You're here early."

She signed the check absentmindedly and the waiter closed the door, shaking his head. Just then, Alex came out of the room across the way and knocked on Skye's door. He smiled at the waiter. "Hi, Chuck." The waiter gaped.

Skye opened the door and Alex pounced on her, grabbing her around the neck and shoving her back in the room, kicking the door closed behind him. Chuck fled.

Max was eating the garnishes off Skye's plate in apparent nonchalance. Only Alex saw him put his gun back in his belt. Good man. He was quick. Alex let her go, but there was anger in his eyes. She was so shocked, she didn't even react.

"You did it again," he said angrily.

"Did what again?" She was still stunned.

"You opened the door without proper safety procedures. Shall we go through this again?"

"Max was here."

"And if I had a gun and not just my hands?"

"You do have a gun," she said reasonably, loving to win any part of an argument she knew she was going to eventually lose. Alex closed his eyes and took a deep breath to calm himself. He couldn't believe after their conversation the night before that she just opened the door without taking the proper precautions.

Skye stared at him and was about to argue, but couldn't. He wasn't her lover this morning; he was a member of her team with a job to do.

"Alex, you're right. I'm sorry."

Max almost choked on a slice of orange. He thought Skye was going to pound Alex, but she took her rebuke like a...hell he was going to say like a man, but then Skye would have to pound him. He always admired her class. When she was wrong, she just admitted it and moved on. He was always half in love with her, but he was always all in love with Linda. So, he thought he should just give his new friend and colleague a hand and leave them. Now that Alex was on duty, maybe he could get back to his room before Linda had a chance to get dressed.

Skye coldly went to the cart to replenish her coffee. She could admit he was right, but she didn't have to warm up to the idea, or to him.

"Skye. Lighten up with him, okay? He put me up next door and got the room across the hall for himself." There, he thought, when they both scowled at him. I just stirred it up for you Alex, old boy, now toss her and get on with the making up part. "See you two at the office."

"What did you do that for?" asked Skye when Max had left.

"I wanted to be close," Alex said in a low voice. "You're the most precious thing in my life."

"Damn it, Alex. Stop saying things like that. It's not going to get me to capitulate."

But she took his arm when he offered it and gave him a smile when he stood behind her and let his eyes work their way up her back. It almost felt like fingertips. He caught the softening around her lips and eyes. He wasn't going to say anything about his new room arrangement, but it appeared as though Max knew what would hit the heart of his leader. He owed Max, all right.

191

The next week was a flurry of activity. Skye flew out and back, and had another date with Phillip. She reported no difference in his attitude, except they had a discussion about the benefits of low-heeled shoes. She was going to be so glad when they threw his ass in jail and she would never have to talk with him again.

Wherever she went, Alex was there. She didn't always see him, but she could feel him. He could be practically invisible. It was impressive. She knew he was there, but others did not. And that was the idea.

Everything was set for Tuesday night. The Inspector would come with the warrants and serve them. Skye and her team would be on the scene acting as a surveillance back up until it was their time to go in. It was going to be a great victory for the good guys.

CHAPTER 14

Skye leaned casually against the car, one leg propped up against the bumper. It was the kind of provocative pose one sees on calendars in car repair shops across the nation. She had no idea what a picture she made in the moonlight. She looked all business as she kept her eyes on the main house. "Damn it, where are those warrants? They could be shredding in there."

"It's after 1:00 a.m., I would say there's a lot of bedding in there," said Alex.

No reaction. And he thought that one was pretty good. Skye had on a midnight blue one-piece jumpsuit that fit her like second skin. Her gun was tucked into a holster at the small of her back.

"You get those jumpsuits specially made, or are they Government Issue?"

"You talking to me?" She turned to him as if she just noticed he was there and scowled. If she thought looking fierce was going to discourage him, she was totally mistaken. It only fueled his interest and the interest of his sensual nature.

"Trying to. Well?"

"Well what?"

"I just wanted to know if you get those specially tailored?" He loved pushing her buttons.

As a matter of fact, one of her dearest friends had them custom made, but she didn't think he needed to know that. "What are you now, my fashion consultant? What's your point?"

"I don't really have one except that you look absolutely ravishing in it."

He smiled a devastating smile meant to hit her heart. It did, but she wasn't going to let it in. Not a chance. No way. God, he said some unbelievably lovely things at the most unexpected times. She clamped ruthlessly down on the fluttery, traitorous feeling in the pit of her stomach.

"It's just a goddamn jumpsuit."

"Then it must be the body inside." Now that would have worked on all the other ladies he had ever known.

"Like you're ever going to see it again." She made a little sarcastic noise in her throat and turned back to the house.

"Please. Don't take away my reason for living." He came a little closer when she pushed herself off the car and went over to the open window of the car.

She reached into the front seat of the car, deliberately letting the fabric stretch over her firm, round butt.

Skye heard him moan out loud and almost...almost...smiled. Damn it. She wasn't going to let him get to her. She straightened out the expression on her face and it was perfectly impassive when she reached for a basket of fruit on the passenger side. Alex was treated to another eyeful before she straightened up and went back to leaning against the car. He took another step forward.

Skye had snagged an apple and was polishing it slowly, rubbing it along the outside of her jumpsuit against her abdomen.

"Lucky fruit," he said as he watched her slowly move it to her lips.

"You should see what I can do with a banana." She raised her eyebrows. This was good. She was getting playful. Her natural good humor was a formidable force...and his ally.

He was nearly next to her now. "Oh, to be an apple. Maybe if something happens to me tonight and someone gets a lucky shot, I can come back as your apple."

When he saw her unconsciously stiffen, he could have kicked himself. Damn, he wanted the words back as soon as he said them.

"I'm sorry, sweetheart. That was really the wrong thing to say," he said in a gentle, sympathetic tone. He felt bad for hurting her, but the fact that she reacted like that gave him renewed hope. If she truly didn't care what happened to him, then why did she go so rigid and still? He saw her shake it off and resume her casual air.

She bit into the apple and chewed. She really didn't want to care, but she was hopelessly attracted to him. She wasn't over her anger. After all, what he did to her was monumental. Still, when he talked about something happening to him, it chilled her to the bone. It should have strengthened her resolve to keep him at arms length, but somehow, it was melting it.

She took another bite and noticed he had stopped talking. Turning, she caught him staring at her.

"What?"

He just continued to stare. What she was doing to him. Leaning there. In that over-the-top sexy jumpsuit; biting into an apple like a modern day Eve. Well if he was going to fall out of the Garden of Eden, by God, he was going to enjoy his last moments. He started to reach for her.

"What?" she said watching him like a cat. "You want a bite of my apple?"

"No, actually I want a bite of your neck."

"Go to hell!"

"Been there, it wasn't so hot."

"And you think that was a clever comeback?" asked Skye.

"Sorry, it comes from hanging with two preadolescent boys," responded Alex.

"Well, at least they have an excuse for acting like one."

He reached over, snatched the apple, and threw it into the trees. Alex had a great deal of patience, but he had reached his limit.

"What the hell did you do that for?" asked Skye.

Instead of answering her, he pulled her to him and kissed her. After her first rigid response, her arms went around his neck in apparent surrender. He should have sensed the attack coming, but he was too caught up by the feel of her soft, full lips, and her rigid, but wonderful body against his.

Skye's foot silently snaked around the back of his leg and she pushed. At the same time she took his arm and twisted it behind his back as he went down. She flipped him, pinning him with her knee up against his lower spine and bending his arm further up his back. It all happened in the blink of an eye. Alex was down in the grass, smelling the sweet, dewy fragrance of it with the woman of his dreams on his back.

Shocked but smiling, Alex pondered his plight. While uncomfortable, the position wasn't painful. She was definitely holding back a bit. How sweet. It just didn't get any better than this.

Alex wondered if he was just a little perverted, because he was really, really getting turned on. He was just about ready to tell her, when he had a better idea. He thought he would show her. Bending his knees, he used his superior size and strength and her desire not to inflict real damage to his back, to reverse his position. She was still on top of him, but she was sitting on his lap and he had her fingers wrapped in his.

Skye's jumpsuit was very thin and so was his. She felt the obvious pleasure his body had with this wrestling match.

"Oh, for Christ's sake, let go," she growled. "You're sick."

"Just keep moving, will you? Only could you move more rapidly in an up and down motion."

He was laughing now and making little sexy movements with his hips. He had his hands around her trim, firm waist. It magnified the obvious nature of his desire.

"Let me up, you fucking asshole!" she snapped, more alarmed by her own body's response than his movements.

"Hey, I didn't start it."

"You did too, you goddamn son-of-a-bitch. You self-centered, lying, stinking sack of shit!" She tried to pull away now, but she only managed to lever them into a sitting position. She was still, very firmly planted on his obviously aroused lap. "What, all the blood from your brain drained into your fucking cock?"

"Do you have a problem saying penis?" Oh, he was enjoying himself now.

"No. Do you have a problem being one?"

"God, you're sexy when you talk like that. It really turns me on."

They rolled over once more. Now he was the one on top and he had her arms pinned above her head. He decided that now might be a good time to give her a thought-provoking kiss. He touched her lips with his. When he didn't get any resistance, he lowered himself over her and deepened the kiss. She let him in. Her hips moved up and down exciting him and fanning the flames of his desire. Her capitulation seemed imminent. She couldn't fight him and her body. Wrong. The man just didn't learn.

He nearly passed out as Skye's knee came up ruthlessly between his legs. He immediately took a defensive posture and slowly rolled off of her. He went into a semi-fetal position. He couldn't even breathe for a full thirty seconds. Couldn't get any air in his lungs.

"Tell Mr. Penis, Mr. Knee says hello!" she growled and neatly rolled away from him.

He just lay there for a while on his back, trying to control his breathing. Suddenly, she went from triumphant to contrite. She wanted him off her, but not immobilized. They were expecting a warrant soon, for God's sake.

She rolled over on her side and then sat up, looking at him trying to catch his breath.

"Uh, sorry. I didn't mean to get so rough. It's just that, well..." she started to giggle, "I do have a temper, I guess. And. Well. Are you okay?" She was laughing hard now. She crawled over to him, stood up and offered her hand. Still laughing. Alex scowled up at her. Women had no idea.

"Here, let me help you up." She wiggled her fingers.

"I'm not sure I'll ever be able to get up again," he said through clenched teeth. But he took her firm hand and heaved himself up. He stood for a while with his hands on his knees. "Next time go for a head shot, will you?"

This struck her as very funny and she had another fit of the giggles. "That's what I thought I was doing. At least I thought I was going for the brain center." She was really enjoying herself now.

Even though his crotch was burning, the sound of her laughter was the medicine he needed. It put her one step closer to him whether she realized it or not.

He straightened up gingerly and watched as she looked at him with shining eyes.

"Come here," said Alex, looking her up and down.

"Oh no. If you think I'm going to give you the opportunity to pull me down again, you're an idiot."

He stood there with the moon giving light to his beautiful face. His hair was mussed and was moving slightly in the breeze. He wore it long and it gave him the look of a highwayman. All she wanted to do was go over and kiss him, touch him, ravish him. There was definitely a part of her that liked the feel of him again as they rolled around on the ground. She was hot and sweaty and wet and she needed a few moments to corral those familiar feelings and put them away where they belonged.

He blew out a lungful of air and stretched his back.

"That was fun."

"You started it," she repeated weakly. "You sure you're okay?"

"Yeah. I think I'll live."

He wanted for all the world to rub the sore spots, but didn't dare touch them, or she'd go off again. He liked her laughter. Found it to be music to his ears. But there was a limit. He smiled at her and started for her again.

"You'll regret that when you want a baby and we find you knocked all the little guys out of competition. I know for a fact, I heard them screaming retreat. How are they supposed to swim to glory when you scare…"

She stared at him with such a thunderstruck look on her face; he stopped in mid sentence and laughed out loud.

"What are you talking about?" she said finally,

"Didn't Hazel tell you about…you know," he smiled playfully, "the birds and the bees? The egg and the sperm? It's how babies are made."

"Are you a lunatic?" She was too stunned to even back away when he reached for her. Too shocked to resist when he kissed her gently.

"You do want babies, don't you?"

"What the hell are you talking about?" she asked breathlessly. He could actually feel her shudder. "Why are you talking this way?"

"Because I'm in love with you. I have been since I saw you walking though the terminal of Dulles." The words just popped out of him, like a cork from champagne. He hadn't intended to be so blunt. But there it was. His cards were on the table.

'No, no, no, no,' her mind screamed at her. While his words slammed into her and surrounded her, she forced back that little lick of pleasure working its way up her spine. She was ruthless to that budding feeling of joy, telling it to back off. You'll not let this affect you. You'll not respond. The voice whispered inside her. He said he loves you. He loves you. Loves you. You.

She continued to stare at him incredulously. Her eyes registered horror. He could feel her denial, could almost hear her rejection of his heart.

So, he just stared at her with his intense blue eyes exploding with passion, and just a hint of humor. He hadn't meant to say it, but now she would have to deal with it. And from her expression, the only way to go from here was up.

Finally she couldn't stand the tension anymore. She broke eye contact first and brushed the dirt from the front of her jumpsuit in quick, angry stokes.

"Oh for crying out loud. Aren't you the romantic. Grab me, take me down, roll around in the dirt, babble about babies, then throw in a little love talk. How am I supposed to react to that?"

"I hadn't meant to just blurt it out, but I left the candles and soft music in my other jacket."

He put his hand on her cheek. Just a light touch. Now wasn't the time to press it, to pressure her. He would give her time to think. To assimilate. To accept.

"Look, this isn't the time or place for this," she said. But she didn't shake his hand free.

"This is the perfect time and place for this."

"We're waiting for a goddamn warrant."

"So?" asked Alex.

"So? So?" Skye threw up her arms in frustration.

"Waiting for warrants will always be a part of our lives. So will my love for you."

"Stop. Now. I mean it. We just can't talk about…about feelings here," countered Skye.

"We are talking about it here," said Alex, reasonably.

"Well, stop it."

"Why, is this a 'no love' zone or something?"

"You really are a crazy man." She was actually backing away from him.

"Maybe it's your heart that's the 'no love' zone."

"Don't even go there. Just back off."

"No."

"No?" She was incredulous. "No?"

"You may be able to control your feelings. Turn them on and off. But pardon me if I can't."

Suddenly his eyes flashed fury. He lowered the hand that was on her cheek and started brushing off the dirt and grass from his own clothes. If he didn't keep his hands busy, he was either going to embrace her unwilling body, or strangle her.

"God. Where is that fucking warrant? We should be halfway through the wall by now," she snapped as she looked down the road. She really needed to end this conversation. Headlights would be greatly appreciated now.

"Quit trying to change the subject."

"Quit trying to change me." There. That stopped him. He just stared at her for a moment.

"Christ. This has to be one of the strangest conversations ever uttered on this planet. Can we just rewind back to the apple?" he asked in a hopeful voice that was filled with an absurdly affable tone.

A little snort of laughter escaped Skye.

"What was that?" His smile was warm and noncommittal. Friendly.

"Just letting some air out."

"And you wonder why I love you? You're the most incredible package. Come on." He came closer, as if that little sound was an invitation. He was crowding into her personal space. "Come on." He gently bumped up against her and planted a quick peck on her lips. Lips that were quivering with the effort not to smile. "Admit that you want me." He didn't embrace her but his hands rubbed up and down her arms. "A little."

"Okay. Okay." She sighed broadly. There were limits. Even to her iron will. She looked him straight in the eye. She never did shy away from either a fight…or capitulation.

"Here's the deal. I'll work with you and in the spirit of tolerance and good will, I'll do so without animosity. We can work out our differences amicably."

"Okay…" he drew out the word. Even though she made it sound like a formal contract, he would take what he could get.

"I'll admire your talent."

"Talent. Check."

"I'll be duly impressed by your considerable mental acuity." She smiled.

"Mental acuity. Is that like brains?"

"Yes, that's like brains," she snorted.

"Brains. Check."

"I'll continue to laugh at your absurd manner and your stupid jokes."

"You'll continue to be entertained by my urbane style and astounding wit. Check."

"I'll communicate with you in a cordial manner." Her lips were twitching, winning the battle to smile at his absurd and urbane manner.

"Cordial. Check."

She wished he would quit being so darn cute.

"You really are cute." It was out of her mouth before she could stop it. She really hadn't intended to say that. But he took it up and put it in the agreement.

"Cute. Check." He liked how her face and voice were softening. He knew she hadn't meant to say cute. It was a wonderful feeling to have her just blurt out what she was thinking. It was so rare for her to spontaneously say what came into her head. She was so guarded. So controlled. Cute wasn't really what he had in mind. But he would take it. He smiled. Cutely, he thought.

"Maybe I'll even allow a bit of lust to creep in. You are, after all, one incredible, edible package." It was the cute smile that finally did her in.

"Edible. Check." He stared at her. His love was pouring out of his eyes and he lifted his eyebrows expectably. This was getting better and better.

He momentarily mesmerized her. She stared back at him. So close. So wonderful. So. What? Suddenly she stopped and got very quiet, very serious.

He knew the moment she closed back up. He could see it in her face, her eyes, her posture.

"I just will never, ever allow myself to fall in love with you." Her jaw set in a stubborn line. Her eyes went cold. He heard a trace of regret there, but it was ruthlessly erased by her determination and single-mindedness. "There. That's the deal."

"Coward," he said in an equally controlled voice. Enough, he thought. He wouldn't allow her to just throw his feelings back at him.

"What?" She nearly growled.

"You heard me. You're a fucking coward," said Alex, staring right into her blazing eyes.

She put both palms to his chest and shoved. He didn't budge. She struggled with her need to smash her fist into his face. She stared up at him. His eyes had lost the trace of humor and tolerance. They were now flashing with passion and aggravation. She knew if she met his heat with her own, it would only fan his temper and intensify his frustration. She deliberately and calmly stepped back and held his gaze.

"I guess I can live with that," she said coldly, keeping her voice steady. Being called a coward wasn't pleasant, but she was determined not to lose her temper. It would only shove a wedge between them and she really didn't want that. She didn't want that at all.

He continued to stare down at her. She continued to return his gaze. Her pulse was throbbing in her temples. Her throat was tight and dry. The wall she'd built around her heart was cracking, but it was constructed by her will and that was more powerful than the bombardment it was being subjected to now. It held. She blinked. She turned away from his gaze...turned away from his love.

"Look, this is such bad timing and this conversation is beginning to sound like a badly written Broadway melodrama. Let's just change the subject and get back to business."

Alex was wise enough to quit while he was ahead. She blinked. There was a part of her that couldn't stand up to his superior forces. He would wear her down. He was confident of that now. He would bide his time. So, he simply nodded and turned his attention back up to the house.

Skye watched him change back to the seasoned professional. Impressive. She ruthlessly suppressed the part of her that was disappointed he didn't press the point. He didn't continue to pursue her. Good. That was good. Right? She could fight the good fight, but she needed his cooperation to do it. She stared at his broad, rigid back.

First he tells me he loves me. Then he's willing to drop it when he faces a bit of resistance? Some grand passion. She mentally shook herself. I don't believe I'm having this internal dialogue, she thought. I get what I want, then I get miffed because he respects my wishes? Get a grip, Skye.

She took a deep breath. Okay. Back to business.

If she only knew that as he continued to stare at the building, his mind wasn't on business at all. It was on strategic planning, all right, but not the sort that served warrants and brought down bad guys. He was planning something far more important to him.

Even though he wanted to continue to attack her defenses, he realized it was the wrong tactic. All right, he thought. What kind of initiatives would work? How could he turn that bit of lust in her heart into a trap? Use the respect and admiration to forge a bond, then turn that bond into something irresistible. He smiled. She thought he was cute. Well, my darling Skye, he thought. You haven't seen anything yet. He had to keep himself from rubbing his hands together. She had formidable defenses, but they had never been assaulted by his best effort. His reserves were barely tapped. Look out, you steel-hearted goddess. Prepare for the breach. Alexander Springfield is going to come after you on all fronts.

Just then, they saw headlights and their conversation was over for the time being. They stood side by side as Inspector York and his team drove up with the necessary papers. They had worked out everything in his office that afternoon. To continue to protect their cover, Skye, Alex and her team were not to be a part of the initial wave. They would not go in until the Blythes, their guests, the servants, and all the other household inhabitants were out and off the premises.

All business. Any thought of personal trials no longer had a place here. They had to go in without distraction and without personal friction. Skye got on her phone to Linda, Max, Barclay, and Judy. Lucas was on his way with some special equipment he was picking up at the airport. Maureen stayed at the office in case they needed access to any paper files there.

"The inspector is here. Call in the rest of the team. They'll serve in exactly ten minutes. At this point the U.S. team is to observe and advise. We're not to interfere with Inspector York and his people." The estate was so huge, the inspector had a team of twenty-five men and women just to watch the doors.

"Let's go," she said turning to Alex. "Can you walk?" she asked softly with a bit of humor back in her voice.

Alex smiled and nodded. "Of course. But if you would rub it, it would feel better faster."

She laughed. It was a start.

They all got into their cars and started up the long drive to the main entrance. Some of them veered off to the left and right to cover all exits.

Inspector York and several of his lieutenants knocked on the door of the mansion house. Even though it was the middle of the night, it was answered almost immediately.

"Great staff," Alex mumbled to Skye.

Skye held a radio and Inspector York kept her informed of their progress. Now, she knew there would be silence until they completed their phase of the mission. She and her team were to stand ready, and stand back. He would contact her again when he had something to report. Until then, they had to content themselves with visual only. Most of her team had field glasses and were watching the windows and doors. Preferring to look at the big picture, she stood and watched from her vantage point just outside the active perimeter.

"It isn't easy waiting in the shadows," she said, knowing he would understand her burning impatience.

"Part of our life will always be in the shadows, Special Agent," he said softly, feeling the same frustration.

Skye was jolted by the pleasure it gave her to be able to share her thoughts, her feelings, with someone who she…who she what? She remembered the feeling of wanting to be able to share with him before. Had she always known she could? Yes. Her instincts were right on target, at least. She could be grateful for that.

"We'll have our chance. And the satisfaction of making it happen," she said.

"And we'll know." He smiled easily down at her. The blue-eyed highwayman. Dashing and a bit dangerous. "So, now that our cards are all on the table, I can ask. How do you feel about your boyfriend being busted tonight?"

She snorted. "I just wish I could be there to see the look on his face. Egomaniacal, self absorbed, narcissistic, vain, conceited snob. My only regret is that I won't be there when they mess up his impeccable outfit with hand-cuffs that are not fur-lined."

"Whoa now. Don't hold back. And I thought it was true love."

"In his dreams." She gave a mock shudder.

"Yes, I imagine it was." Alex chuckled.

Skye liked the sound. The tension between them ebbed as they stood side by side, in an identical stance. Arms folded, back straight, legs slightly apart. They looked like a couple of generals, surveying their troops and waiting for battle. It was an awesome sight. One not wasted on her team as they gathered at the perimeter. They all watched and waited for their turn inside the house. Even Max was subdued and poised. Soon, it would be their time to act, and they were well trained for the moment.

They were all watching Skye and Alex as well. Some money had exchanged hands and Max was holding the pot. The team started a pool as soon as they had left the office that afternoon. Max had Thursday. He knew it wouldn't be long before they patched up whatever was between them. That much tension always led to an irresistible pull and then to really great sex. Plus there was the victory euphoria after the raid tonight; that would turn them both on.

Linda was thoroughly disgusted by their discussion of her friend and leader's sex life, but she had taken Friday. She grinned, knowing she was going to win. She was logical, after all. Today was Tuesday. They would be in the house until at least Thursday. Then there was the post victory celebration and the after effects of that. Yes. Friday was the earliest they could have their personal celebration. She agreed with Max on principle, he just got his timing a bit off. Not that she would admit to Max that she agreed with him on anything. Pig.

The lights began going on all over the house. It was a sight. One after the other, the windows glowed from the inside. Scotland Yard and British Intelligence had an army of people in there. Skye noticed with satisfaction that the windows between the library and the ballroom were still dark. Three windows. The secret room. She felt the rush in her stomach.

Alex read her thoughts. "Looks like you were right, Special Agent. No easy access from the inside. As soon as they get the people out of there, we can go in and take a look. If I know Inspector York, they'll wait for us."

She nodded and smiled. "We're ready. We have the equipment to make holes in the walls but we probably won't need to use muscle. Lucas is a genius with hidden devices. We want to be sure they haven't set any traps."

"Makes all the months of work worth it," he said reading her thoughts again.

"All the deception, the lies, the cons."

"You love it," said Alex. "You were born to it."

"Don't ever turn it on me again," she said casually, but she meant it.

"I hear an 'or else' in there somewhere."

"We've already established the consequences. Just don't make me hurt you again." Skye's lips twitched.

"The only way you can hurt me is to keep yourself from me."

He said it so matter-of-factly, never taking his eyes off the house, she almost missed the implication. It gave her insides a little quiver. Why did he do that? How could he do that? Bastard. Maybe she should pretend she didn't hear him. Or at least didn't understand.

When she didn't respond, he smiled.

"You heard me. But just go ahead and pretend like you didn't. Or that you don't know what I meant." He shifted his position slightly as the first of the officers in the house started taking people out of the front door. "I love you, Special Agent. And that's no con."

He left her practically gaping after him as he went over to talk with Max, Linda, and the other field agents. Her eyes narrowed and she hoped he felt the little daggers she aimed in his direction. How dare he love her when she so distinctly told him to cut it out?

Alex smiled to himself. The battle had begun and he intended to wage it until she surrendered. Or until she took him down. He was a man with a great deal of ammunition and a whole warehouse full of reserves. He had confidence in his ability to do battle and win. The stakes were high, but he was a skillful combatant.

Just then they all turned and there was no more thought of love, cons, battles, victories, or anything personal. Shots were fired. Officers in danger. Everyone instantly turned all business and stood at full alert. As one, they pulled their own weapons, although there was no danger to them. They knew they were only the backup, but they were ready nonetheless.

Alex moved to stand near Skye again. He looked appreciatively down at the Glock .357 she held in her capable hand. It was an incredible firearm with a magazine capacity of seventeen.

"Get a new gun?"

"This is my business attire. The other one is for dates with filthy rich tycoons wearing Rolex watches."

"Ah."

The activity at the house had definitely heated up. There were no more shots fired, however. And no call for backup. Skye's team relaxed and reholstered. All was quiet except for the shouting of the prisoners and coordinating calls of the lieutenants in charge.

Then they heard Emily's voice. Most of the culture and all of the aristocratic haughtiness were absent from her tirade. "Take your filthy, low-class, hands off me you cock-sucking faggot."

"My, my. She has expanded her vocabulary," said Alex, chuckling a little.

"Not too enlightened, either," snorted Skye.

Just then, Skye's radio cracked and York's voice was on the air. "We're into the clean up now. We have most of the major players. Sir Phillip and Lady Emily have already been taken to central command for questioning."

She smiled. Even though they were unprincipled drug dealers, they were still Sir and Lady. Nice and proper. She really did love the Brits.

"And Lord Henry?" asked Skye.

"We're trying to get into his study now. The shots you heard came from there. The door is locked."

"I understand. But I heard three shots. Either the man has very poor aim, or you're going to find more than one dead body."

"Roger that."

They indeed did find more than one. Franklin lay in the room with Lord Henry. Henry killed his driver, then turned the gun on himself. Either he didn't want to face St. Peter on his own, or Franklin did something to piss off Henry before he decided to end it. They would never know. And in reality, they didn't really care. Henry became his own judge and executioner. The only regret was that he died with information that might have been helpful in expanding the investigation.

It was almost an hour later before Skye and her team stood in front of the wall she knew was a barrier between her and the room on the other side. The windows on the outside turned out to be a facade leading nowhere. Behind the curtains was a solid wall of cinder block. They could go through that way, but she wanted to keep the damage to a minimum.

"Have we had no cooperation from any of the staff or from Emily and Phillip as to how to get into the room?" Her hands ran over the wallpaper. Made to look old, but too smooth not to be of this century.

"No one is saying anything. All got lawyers right away," said Linda.

"Okay, let's bring Lucas the Great in here to do his magic."

It took Lucas all of 12 minutes and 27 seconds to locate the device that would get them into the room. Her team timed it. They had a pool. There was one whoop and Max handed the money over to Judy.

"If you kids are finished playing, shall we get to work?" smiled Skye. Her money was on 10 minutes, 25 seconds. Lucas must have been confused by the fussy rose pattern of the wallpaper. She should have factored that in. "Lucas, you lead the way and let us know if it's safe to go in there."

"Yeah. Thanks a lot. And if there are bombs instead of mechanical booby-traps?" asked Lucas.

"Then we're all pretty safe out here, judging from the thickness of that wall." She grinned at him.

He grinned back. "You're just pissed 'cause you lost the pool."

"Damn right."

Lucas nodded. He would have it no other way than to lead them into an environment he deemed safe. He was always first into a room. It made his geeky heart sing. Geeks of the world rarely got this kind of respect. Skye knew that and gave him not only respect, but genuine admiration. He would have gladly fallen on a bomb to protect her.

Lucas took the flashlight and found three very cleverly hidden traps in the first few feet. He moved with confidence, as if he had planted them himself. He disarmed them all assuring Skye that while explosives weren't used, there were several nasty flash fire devices that would have destroyed all the evidence and most of the people within a 20-foot radius.

"All clear," he said after 15 more minutes.

"You're a hero," said Skye. And when she said it, he felt like one.

She went in without hesitation and turned on the lights.

Jackpot. There were shelves containing cocaine bags everywhere. This wasn't the lab, but the warehouse. She imagined that they would find the packaging and distribution center in London. The computer lab in Washington had uncovered several addresses under phony names in the London area from the data she collected from Phillip's computer. He thought he had the locations hidden under enough layers of codes and passwords, but the Washington people were up to the task and started running information to Scotland Yard earlier that evening. The clean up there would be under the jurisdiction of the British authorities. She wanted this room. Not because of the drugs, but because of the information she might get from the bank of computers and file cabinets in the corner. Her team moved immediately in that direction.

Skye smiled at Inspector York. "The drugs are all yours. We'll provide you with copies of everything we find over there. Nothing will leave these premises without your signature or the signature of your assigned representative."

Not much for protocol, Inspector York acknowledged the official exchange of power and other niceties, then he slammed Skye on the back and grinned from ear to ear.

"Nicely done, my fine sweet girl, nicely done." He was a good four inches shorter than her and his eyes crinkled with delight.

Max snorted loudly. Skye hadn't been called a fine sweet girl in…well…never. He thought she was a bit overly sensitive in this area, but he waited with the rest of the team for an explosion.

Instead Skye lowered her lips to York's cheek and gave him a loud smacking kiss. "Thank you my wee old man."

Inspector York paused for a second while her words sank in. Then laughed uproariously. "Let's get to work. The faster we wrap this up, the faster I can get you drunk and stretch the truth about my youthful exploits."

"Done." Then Skye turned and it was all business again.

Everyone had an assigned task. Barclay and Lucas went to work on the computers. Linda, Max and Judy took the file cabinet. Inspector York and his people took charge of cataloging the drugs and placing them into evidence. Skye reviewed their findings to determine their relative importance and cataloged everything along with a priority number. Maureen stayed in constant contact, having already witnessed the booking and questioning of Lady Emily and Sir Phillip. They remained mute, but several servants were singing a pretty tune.

Alex watched Skye with her team. The easy rapport and mutual regard was obvious. She was a master of motivation and a natural leader. They all knew their jobs and she got out of their way, not insulting their years of training and expertise by telling them what to do. No job was too big or too small if it helped the success of her team. She would risk personal safety, or serve them coffee. In her mind it was the same. They would all die for her.

As he watched them work, he gave some more thought to his original assignment. Someone inside or outside the department wanted her out so they set a trap. One that Jim was too smart to fall for, but it could have taken Skye out of the game. It seemed to him that this would have changed things considerably. It was her relationship with Phillip that got her into the estate. Then she speculated about the possibility of a room and located it using deduction and her uncanny intuition. It was her instinct the night of the party, that among all the guests, she found Juan. It was she who gathered all the intelligence from Phillip's computers, made the flower shop connection and it was she who was the leader of this team. It was her plan and she was instrumental in the execution. Yes. It would have been a slower, less effective investigation without her. The British authorities may have someday come to the same conclusions, but proving it would have been difficult. He could see the wisdom of wanting her out and it made his blood run cold. Was she still in danger? The investigation had three fronts, the Blythes, Juan, and the mole in the department, and she was critically important in all of them. He was determined to stay close.

Alex was assigned to back up Skye in the cataloging, but excused himself to look through the rest of the house. He wasn't really a part of her team, so he wouldn't be missed. He wanted to look at the crime scene in Henry's bedroom. Henry just didn't strike him as the type to take his own life.

Shooting someone else, well that he could probably do to save his hide, but not do damage to himself. It was out of character. And he remembered a detail from the architectural plans. His mind was always programmed to see the details.

CHAPTER 15

Juan was livid. He had been in Emily's bed when he heard the sounds of the raid. He knew instinctively what was happening and pulled on his pants and shoes and gathered up his personal possessions. His fingerprints were all over, but according to his contact, the authorities already had those. That didn't worry him, they had no provable connection to the cocaine trade...just that he had been a guest of Duke and Duchess. Hell, this whole operation was ending badly. He had just talked to his contact a week ago and he thought he had two more months to get things transferred. He needed to tie off some loose ends here, then get back to London and go underground. The flash bombs would take care of the evidence if they ever uncovered the secret room. Lady Emily would hang tough, Phillip didn't know enough and he would take care of Henry before he left. Then maybe in a few years, he could come back to the room and clean it out. He had always been a long range thinker.

"Okay," he said, looking into Emily's startled, frightened face. "You know the drill. We talked about this. You'll say nothing. You'll scream ignorance. Your husband may have been a part of this, but you know nothing. Save yourself. You have your personal accounts in the Caymans. They won't touch those because they don't know about them. Your lawyers will get you out of this, and in a few months you can go off somewhere to recover from the shock. It will be awhile before we can meet up again, but we will. Understand?"

He wasn't sure any of this was true, but he knew she would cling to the plan like a lifeline. She would not roll over. It wasn't in her nature.

She did understand. As frightened as she was, she was even angrier at the authorities for bursting into her home like this in the middle of the night. She was a Duchess and believed in her heart that she was above the laws that kept the common people in their place. She pulled a robe over her nightgown. They would certainly leave and come back at a more civilized hour.

"I'll go down and tell them to come back later. Then I'll get properly dressed and call the lawyers. I should be home by this evening. You go, Juan. I can't have the authorities finding a man who is not my husband in my bedroom this time of night." She walked swiftly to the door and with purpose went to give the barbarians a piece of her mind.

Juan had seen a lot in his years, but this woman's delusion was beyond his experience. Since it worked in his favor, however, he accepted it. He had one more job to take care of, then he was out of there. He walked swiftly down the hall, reaching inside his jacket pocket as he went.

When he got to Henry's room, Henry and Franklin were running around, shouting in a panic. Henry ordered Franklin to bring the car around while he got dressed. Again Juan shook his head at this breed of human. Henry was actually expecting his driver to bring around and drive the getaway car. Juan stepped into the room and locked the door behind him.

"That won't help!" screamed Henry. "Those people have master keys and battering rams. Franklin, now!"

Franklin turned and started toward the door. He never saw the gun that killed him. Two shots right through the brain. Henry looked on in horror.

"What the hell did you do that for?" he asked incredulously. "Now who is going to drive the fucking car?"

"I am."

"You are?"

"Yes, and I'm going alone."

Juan looked over to the left. The door to the hidden passageway down to the garage was open. Henry had shown it to him a few months ago when they discussed escape plans. Henry just laughed. My dear Juan, he had said, my family has had escape plans for generations. People periodically get a bit testy about the aristocracy and storming the castle has been a dark part of our history. In modern years it has allowed the master of the house complete freedom of movement, if you get my drift. Juan did indeed. And he filed the information away as a contingency plan. Now was the time to put the plan into action.

In one swift move, he grabbed Henry's hand, put the gun in it, placed it in his ear and blew a large piece of a startled Henry's brain across the room. Now Lady Emily and Sir Phillip could blame everything on Sir Henry and there would be no one to contradict them. A loose end neatly tied.

Smiling, Juan went through the well-concealed door, secured it, and settled in to wait for the grounds to clear. If they discovered the secret room on the first floor, he assumed he would hear a flash and screams. Then there would be emergency vehicles all over and mass confusion. He figured he could blend in and make an escape then. If not, he would just wait it out. He was in no hurry.

Alex stepped into Henry's room. It was a good thing he had an excellent memory for architectural details, because it wasn't all that easy to find from the hallway of the secret room. He looked around the beautiful old suite. The bed was huge and because Alex was a fan of antiques, he could appreciate both the value and the beauty of the piece.

He looked down and saw the white silhouettes that were the universal indication of a body's last location. The blood strains were massive, both located near the head.

He stood over the white lines and turned his body, standing in the positions the silhouettes indicated. Men usually didn't shoot themselves standing up. And it seemed that Franklin fell forward from a spot near the door. It was possible that Henry stood in front of the door, shot Franklin twice, then walked back to the middle of the room and shot himself. But not probable. Then there was the mystery of Franklin. Why call in your driver and then shoot him if you're planning on shooting yourself? And he knew that when people shot themselves, they usually did the deed sitting or lying down. When one thing doesn't make sense, it could be the inability of the investigator to get into the mind of the killer. But when two things didn't make sense, it pointed to another explanation. Wisdom learned on the knee of a cop.

He looked carefully around the room again, the positions of the bodies no longer important. He pulled the memory of the charts and diagrams of the estate from his well-trained mind and placed himself in the picture forming in his imagination. Turning left and looking toward the right side of the fireplace, he mentally measured three feet in the direction of the windows to the outside. He walked directly to the spot on the wall and knocked. It was hollow.

He smiled grimly. "Gotch ya."

Juan almost jumped out of his skin when he heard the knock on the wall. He took his gun out of his pocket and didn't stay to listen. The mechanism to open the door was well hidden and that gave him time. He got up and made his way carefully down the steep stairway. It wouldn't do to fall and break his leg on the stone stairs.

Alex heard rustling behind the door. Either Henry had a real infestation problem, he thought, or the rat was of the two-legged variety. He debated trying to find the lever to open the passageway, but decided it would be quicker to get to the other entrance. It was in the garage, he remembered from studying the plans of the estate. As he raced down the hall and to the stairs, he pulled out his radio.

"Skye!"

She responded immediately. "Where…"

"Get Inspector York and his team down to the garage. Henry didn't commit suicide, he was murdered and the killer is coming through a passageway that leads to the garage."

"Understood. We'll mobilize from here."

Alex grinned. His kind of woman. No questions. No skepticism. No argument. Just unquestioning action. There was always time for explanations later and she knew it. God he loved her. Probably the only time she was this compliant, but he would take it.

He ran through the massive foyer and out the front door. Everything started happening at once and from where he stood, it was like watching a movie in slow motion. He saw Juan run out of the garage toward a car parked by the old stable. He saw Skye, the Inspector, and their teams pour out of the building. Because Skye's legs were longer than the rest of them, and she was in superb physical condition, she was crossing the lawn at a ground eating pace and was well ahead of the pack. She had her gun drawn, but had not yet spotted Juan.

Juan saw her, however, and grinned. He couldn't believe his luck as he raised his gun in her direction. He didn't think he would have the chance of taking her out personally.

Alex had to make a split-second decision. He was close enough to Juan to take him down, but not before he got a shot off. Skye was closer and with her body silhouetted by the light from the front terrace, she made a perfect target. She spotted Juan then and went right for him, raising her gun. Just waiting to get in range to take a shot. Goddamn her. She wasn't going to jump for cover. Alex veered to the left and launched himself at her just as he heard gunfire.

They went rolling, but because the grass was thick and Alex protected her body with his, she only had the wind knocked out of her. Juan took a few more shots that spit into the lawn just above their heads, then jumped in the car and raced down the long drive. Inspector York was on his radio to all cars in the area. He stopped briefly to be sure Skye and Alex hadn't been hit, then ran to his car. Containment was almost certain, but his team jumped in their vehicles to pursue him from the rear.

"You okay?" asked Alex with apprehension. He felt the bullets whizzing by and was pretty sure they'd missed.

Lying on the ground with Alex on top of her, Skye took a moment to figure out how she got in that position. She had the wind knocked out of her and was trying to get a full breath into her lungs. Both of them were breathing heavy. When she finally was able to speak, she was spitting mad.

"*Prendere via da me, lei figlio di puttana.* Get off me you goddamn son-of-a-bitch. What do you think you are? Bullet proof?"

Yup. She was okay, he thought with relief as she continued to curse at him in Italian. Then he noticed the feel of her breasts against his chest as she worked to get her breathing and wrath under control.

"I could ask you the same thing." He was looking straight into her eyes now, and they were as dark as the sky above them. Instead of stars, there were sparks of fury showing in their depths.

"*Che lo pensa lei fanno.* What the hell did you think you were doing?" Skye hissed when she found her breath. Struggling a bit and intensifying his gratitude.

"Saving your sweet ass," he said, covering her mouth with his before she could start insulting his ancestry. He also took the time to secure her knees to the ground with his leg, so she couldn't use them as a weapon again. With his lips locked over hers, her words were completely muffled. And there were a lot of them, he was sure.

Maybe it was the air of danger, or the after effect of hearing gunshots. Maybe it was her natural competitiveness, Alex knew he sure didn't give a damn why, but suddenly she was the aggressor. She rolled him over and nipped his lower lip, then locked her lips on his and pushed against him, pinning him to the ground with her entire toned-up, turned-on body.

Alex completely lost track of time and space. This was good. This was very, very good. By the time they came up for air, neither one of them was sure exactly why they were on the ground.

The applause had them spinning back to reality. Skye turned her head and with as much authority she could muster lying on the ground kissing the hell out a fellow agent, she commanded, "Back to work. Show's over."

"Are you sure?" Max asked and got an elbow from Linda in his side.

"Now!" insisted Skye, resting her elbows on Alex's chest and smiling down at him.

"If you're sure you don't need any assistance," said Max, chuckling.

"Does it look like I need any assistance?"

"No ma'am."

"Then carry on."

"Ah. You too."

Skye's team walked slowly back to the house. They knew they would get explanations later.

"That counts," said Barclay. "I think that this should definitely count." He had tonight in the pool, never really thinking about timelines. He was just a geek who picked a day at random.

"No it doesn't," said Judy. She was stuck with Saturday. After what she just saw. No chance in hell. But because she was a romantic at heart, she didn't begrudge the dollar she threw into the pot.

"That was a post-attack adrenalin rush. Not a conjugal connection," said Linda.

"What the hell is that? Are you talking about fucking?" snorted Max.

"Okay...so it wasn't...you know. But they were rolling around on the grass," persisted Barclay.

"He pushed her down to keep her from having her head blown off," said Judy, wanting to sigh a little, but thinking that it wouldn't be too Special Agent-like.

"That was the reason they were on the ground in the first place, but their lips were locked and it wasn't mouth-to-mouth resuscitation," said Barclay.

"I still say Thursday," said Max.

"Friday," said Linda.

"Okay, China Doll. Then how about we get together on Saturday and talk about it?"

"I'm from goddamn San Francisco. I'm not Chinese. I'm American."

"Okay American Doll. How about we get together on Saturday and talk about it?"

"In your dreams."

Linda threw him a withering look, but he could see her eyes dance a bit. "I think I'm wearing down her resistance. What do you think?" Max asked Lucas as they went back into the house. Lucas wasn't even sure what Linda was supposed to be resisting, so he just shrugged. He wanted to get back to the secret room. So much good stuff.

Back on the ground, Alex and Skye were finally catching their breath, winded more from the kiss than from the run across the lawn.

"That'll teach you to save my life," she said, smiling into his eyes. She'd felt the bullet whiz by her ear and knew he had made the right decision. She was never one for staying angry at good judgment, even though she would have liked to have taken a shot at the man herself.

He tightened his grip, thinking of what might have happened had he not been there.

"Would you mind telling me what you were doing running right at a man with a gun instead of diving for cover?" asked Alex.

"It's not easy to get all this body to change direction."

"You really terrify me," he said, brushing an errant curl off her cheek.

She had her chin cupped in her hands and was looking down at him curiously. It never occurred to her that taking risks and putting herself in jeopardy was anything to be too concerned over. She never really thought about it much. She decided to change the subject.

"Is that a gun in your pocket?" she asked smiling. He recognized the evasion and decided to drop it. For now.

"Nope." He waved his, still in his hand. "Are those apples in your shirt?" He bumped her elbows away so she fell back onto his chest.

"Christ…back to apples," said Skye, knowing she should really get up and move out. But he did save her from a bullet, after all, so she gave his luscious lips a quick kiss instead.

"Can I take a bite?" he asked, loving the taste of her.

"*Vous êtes mon héros*. Let's go back to work. I want to hear your report and I think the rest of the team should hear it, too."

Just like that. The bullets whizzing by. The run across the lawn. The shock of being airborne. All neatly put away. Back to business. She was definitely going to drive him insane. But he was sure she had said you're my hero in French. Things were looking up in the romance department.

"Besides," she nimbly jumped to her feet and snatched her gun off the lawn, "I think they need something besides us to talk about."

She smiled and held her hand out to help him up. "*Comment d'une main, un partenaire*"

When he looked confused, she translated. "How about a hand, partner. "

Partners. Colleagues. Maybe friends, she thought. When he took her hand in his, she felt she could work with him on this level.

"Did you just switch languages?" he asked, reluctantly letting go of her hand after she hauled him up.

She frowned. "Maybe I did. I always think in English…I guess I did go from Italian to French."

"Did you just call me partner?"

"For now."

"Can I brush the leaves and grass stains off your uniform, partner?" he asked hopefully.

Then again, maybe not, she thought. She shook her head and walked purposefully back into the house, snapping the safety back on her gun and putting it back in the holster. He walked behind her, enjoying the view.

They worked through the night and well into the next day. Skye was like a one-woman cheerleading squad, encouraging, celebrating, applauding. Information poured out of the machines and everything was cataloged. They didn't stop to evaluate and assess, that would be the work of people back at the department, but they knew good data when they saw it.

They also knew that they would be closing up the operation here and going back to the United States. Hot dogs, driving on the right, watching football played the way it should be played. They were homesick and now they were going home and going home in triumph.

The only dark cloud was the fact that Juan got though the net. A troubled and somewhat humiliated Inspector York returned to the estate with a new team in the morning. The roadblock stopped him, but one of his bobbies was shot and Juan got through to London. The woman was hanging on to life in the hospital. They had all the exits from the city blocked off and hoped to catch the shooter soon. Instead of the expected recriminations, all he got from Skye was sympathy and concern.

"I'm so sorry, Inspector," she said. "You must be exhausted. Why don't you go on back to London. We've plenty of help here." He had spent the night at the hospital with the husband and family of the officer. "You'll want to be with her."

She understood leadership. She understood compassion and concern. The Inspector nodded, wiped his gentle eyes and decided things were in good hands here. Very good hands. He went back to the hospital and was lifted by the fact that the officer was going to make it. He called the news back to a pleased Skye and went home for a bit of a rest. He knew the rigor of the celebration was going to take some stamina.

Skye and her team were flagging a little when they went into their twenty-fourth hour, so she sent them to various rooms in the mansion for a much-deserved rest. Might as well have her team sleep in sixteenth-century luxury, she thought. It saved them a commute and was a practical solution. Max was delighted because it might still get him the pool. He kept an eye on Skye and Alex, but unfortunately they never snuck into a room together. By early

Thursday morning things were winding down. Alex had returned to London on Wednesday night to help coordinate the search for Juan.

She also assigned Alex the task of reporting to Jim. He spent all of Wednesday and into Thursday on the phone, fax, and computer. He made good use of the time, taking care of some business as well. Reviewing faxes, directing various projects in the pipeline, finalizing the agreements for buying and selling property. He chose excellent staff and could leave them to their jobs, but he had a dozen calls to return when he finally got back to his hotel. He wanted to keep busy. Very busy. Every time he let his mind wander it would go back to Skye. Skye looking at him in the moonlight. Skye leaning over Barclay sitting at the computer patting his back. Skye rolling around on the grass. Skye running with her weapon up, racing head-on toward a man with a gun and murder in his eye.

Alex tried to lie down, but didn't stay in bed long. An hour or so after he fell asleep, he woke up in a cold sweat. The image of Skye running across the lawn, gun up, then taking a hit and flying back under the impact of a hail of bullets was fading, but was still present enough to give him the shakes. He saw the blood. He felt the anguish. He knew it could happen. His pounding heart whispered, *Rita*. It had happened to his sister.

Alex didn't go back to bed that night. He paced; he worked; he dozed in the chair. He would come to grips with the fear, but for the first time, he realized the source of Skye's nearly phobic resistance to getting involved with him. To letting her heart go. To letting herself go. He considered for a moment that perhaps the noble thing to do would be to let her walk away. His heart skipped. Nah. No way was he giving her up. He smiled at himself in the mirror as he was shaving. Look out Skye, he thought. I know more about what I'm up against now. It gives me more information and a better chance of flanking your defenses. God, I'm a good agent.

Congratulating himself and feeling better for having talked everything out with himself, he called room service and ordered a huge breakfast. The Inspector had told him there would be celebrating and he should fortify himself. He intended to do just that and start Operation Seduction as soon as possible.

Skye had called sounding tired, but triumphant. They were going to drop everything by the office, then join their wonderful colleagues and friends at a private pub in London to debrief and get drunk. Telling her he would meet her at the pub, he rubbed his hands together, smiling diabolically. Get her a little drunk. Not too drunk, but enough to be open to his fatal charm.

Juan was holed up in a London flat he owned under one of several assumed names. He paced and fumed until his contact in the Justice Department finally called.

"This one was too close. I know you didn't have a lot of notice, but Jesus Christ Almighty, I didn't get your message until I got back here. A lot of good it did me then. I was in Paris with Lady Emily. She had an itch and needed new clothes with her usual steady diet of sex."

He listened to the person on the other end of the line.

"Okay. Okay. So I couldn't keep my dick away from her. She's like forbidden fruit to a farm worker like me. The last I heard the timetable for the raid was in a few months and we were liquidating. I thought we would have another month to sell or transport the shit and at least that to get the computers purged."

"No use worrying about that. Those empty-headed Blythes didn't know what hit them. It's the only good thing about this fucking mess. We won't have those blithering idiots to deal with anymore. On the other hand, your fucking agents cost me big time, and I'm taking it out of your cut."

Juan paced back and forth. He had to get rid of some of the excess manic energy that came from the close call and the kill. He could still smell the blood and feel the adrenalin. His partner on the inside was fanning some of the flame by threatening him.

"What are you going to do about it, you fucking asshole? Turn me in? Just remember we're attached at the hip. What happens to me, happens to you."

"Don't yell at me. These are your fucking people. Don't worry though. The stuff is pretty well protected. Tell me what you know."

"What! Goddamn it. They found the fucking room? Who would have thought that ball buster would find that room...the room the royal bitch and her brain-dead husband said was invisible...no one had detected it ever...in a century...impossible to detect. Your fucking agent comes there one goddamn night and makes the flower trucks, the goddamn room, and me. What is she? Fucking clairvoyant?"

He listened some more and paced in fury. He wanted her. And he was going to bide his time until he got her.

"All right then. All right they found the room. Damage control. The stuff should be cinders by now. It's a shame, but not a catastrophe."

Juan's head nearly exploded when he heard.

"What! Why didn't those flash bombs go off? They should have turned half the team into fucking torches. Tell me why I didn't hear any screaming."

More shouting from the contact fueled his anger further.

"I thought you were going to get that bitch off my back? I look up tonight, and there she is racing across the lawn at the estate with a gun in her hand. I would have taken care of her myself, but some big guy knocked her to the ground. I think I missed."

"I expect you can do something about her over there when she gets back to the States. I may make one more pass at her before I get the hell out of this fucking town."

"No, I'm not sure. I know she recognized something. She's the only one who can make the connection. Don't you think she would have told you by now if she'd remembered? What's she saying?"

"Do you think you might be out of the loop? Yeah, yeah, I know. I forgot you *are* the fucking loop."

Juan knew that he needed his connection in the Justice Department, but right now he was furious. His contact was blaming him for everything that had gone wrong.

"The goddamn code was your idea, hot shot. We've been working with it since we began our little adventure together. I'm beginning to wonder if you're not as smart as you think you are if this one babe can bring us down with what she knows."

"I know it was years ago, but you're the one who told me she has an incredible memory."

"Okay. So it was bad luck that we met in February. The stupid over-bred son just brought her up to me and I had to take her hand and kiss it. Yeah, yeah, I know I was pushing it when I asked her to dance but I just wanted to see her eyes…to see if she remembered…she didn't or you would know it."

"Now tell me where they'll store the fucking evidence before they bring it over. I'll have it destroyed for sure this time. Direct action."

"No, I'm not going to stay put here. It's too hot. Had to shoot a cop."

"My fault, my ass. I had to run because another one of your fucking people made me in this supposedly secret passageway. Fuck it. We need to do some work at the Washington kitchen, anyway. We got a lot of the stuff out of the room and it should be over there by now. Might as well be Washington streets."

"I'll call you in two hours and give you the details of my trip."

He slammed down the phone and prepared to change his hair, eye color, physical appearance, and identity. He still had a great deal to do and was impatient to get on with it.

CHAPTER 16

They were all gathered again in the private pub off Trafalgar Square. In the age-old tradition of soldiers, cops, and special agents, they regaled each other with their version of the events. They drank too much beer, ordered endless shots, toasted themselves, and laughed off the tension. They toasted everyone they knew, every prominent person dead or alive. It took extra time, because they were a team of both Brits and colonials and their list was long. They weren't quite sure about what to do with Benedict Arnold and Paul Revere, but in the spirit of international relations, they drank to their health with hearty goodwill.

Skye ordered her team, including Alex, to stand down. She was sure everyone involved in the cartel would be too busy running to care much about her right now. Plus she was certain that since the bust was behind them, they would give up on stopping her. Alex was not about to allow anyone to bring down their guard, however. They had quite a row about it when she returned to the hotel. In the end, Inspector York and the head of MI5 had assembled a small army to watch and protect them from outside aggressors. Alex coordinated everything until he was satisfied that for this one night, they could step back. They were safe and it was a good feeling.

Linda and Max were hanging on each other and hugging the jukebox, singing their lungs out with the Beatles. They were sipping their pints enthusiastically and exchanging wet smacking kisses when they finished singing "Come Together." What was happening to her world? Skye thought. When they started bickering over the words to "Lucy in the Sky With Diamonds," she relaxed and knew everything was going to be all right.

Alex and Inspector York were playing darts in the corner. They hadn't hit the target in over an hour, and the barmaid refused to go over to replenish their mugs. Undaunted, someone brought them a keg which they promptly tapped and were in the process of draining. Skye watched them in her own haze of beer blur and smiled. At least she thought she was smiling. She stopped drinking hours before, never allowing herself to lose control. The officer sitting near the bar thought the smile was directed at him and nearly fell off his stool. He would have come over to press his advantage, but the feeling in his legs had deserted him long ago. He just smiled back and hoped she would be able to make it to him.

When Alex finally managed to hit the bull's eye, the game ended with much cheering and bowing.

Alex spotted her and thought he had better tell her soon that he had never seen anything lovelier than she looked right now. Smiling, her foot tapping to the music. Her hair was out of its constraints and forming a cloud around her face. He was sure he was on the verge of passing out and didn't want to miss the opportunity to talk with her, so he studied the path and began his journey.

She was a vision. He couldn't feel his body, so maybe he was dead and she was the angel sent to greet him. Thought he should tell her she looked just like an angel. He snorted. Yeah. An angel that could kick a giant's ass. He frowned. Where did the image of a giant come in? Maybe she was like Cinderella or something. Did Cinderella have a giant in her story? None of these thoughts stayed too long, however.

He worked hard to focus, then even harder to move his feet. He knew he was getting closer to her, because she was getting bigger. Her smile was his beacon. His guiding light. His current target. Those lips. That neck. He suddenly realized he was standing in front of her and she was leaning back with her elbows on the bar and her chest was right in front of him. What a chest. He swayed only a little then looked up into her incredible brown and amused eyes. She was still smiling and that was a very, very good sign.

Skye watched him cross the room. She was sure he was nearly incapacitated, but he managed to walk a fairly straight line. What control. She was enjoying her pleasant buzz not having a need to see how much she could consume before falling off her stool. Plus, she didn't have all that testosterone egging her on into oblivion.

Alex was an awesome sight. Grinning like a fool, his hair in disarray due to the hundreds of times his fingers combed through it during his fierce battle with the inspector. He looked just as splendid in his casual jeans and flannel shirt as he did in his expensive hand-tailored suits. Better, actually, because she could see his muscles more clearly, especially on his arms where he had rolled up his sleeves to defeat the bloody British.

His slow progress allowed her to watch him as if he were in a movie. God. That face. Gorgeous. And that body. It didn't help that she knew exactly what was beneath those well-cut jeans. In his case, the clothes didn't make the man. No, sir. The man definitely made the man. He filled out whatever he wore perfectly. As a matter of fact, even naked, he filled out his skin perfectly. She had to admit, to herself only of course, that she liked how he looked in the shower. Just remembering his lean, muscled body made her hot.

She looked down at his hands. She loved his hands too. They were a wonderful combination of strength and tenderness. They could disarm a felon or make her moan with pleasure with the same competent finesse. Why was she breathing so heavily? And why was it so damn hot in here?

Then suddenly, he was standing in front of her. Grinning disarmingly and conquering her without a single word. His arms. Those superb, muscular arms slid on either side of her as he braced himself against the bar. He leaned over and positioned himself right above her.

She was now sitting in the circle of those arms and her chest brushed his. The contact was electric. Even in his advanced stage of inebriation, he felt it. She definitely felt it. She was practically sober, after all. Although in this place, her sobriety was a relative thing. She moved forward, intentionally teasing him by pressing her chest more firmly into his.

Blue eyes seared brown eyes. Lips smiled. Brains switched to automatic pilot. Heat poured from one to the other. He slowly lowered his head until their lips barely touched. The world around them ceased to exist. There was no one in the room but them. Sounds faded. All she could hear was the beating of her own heart. Or was it his? They were too close to each other to tell. Their hearts seemed to be beating as one.

His head came up. He licked his lips and then came back down for seconds. His mouth gently touched hers in the sweetest, most loving, most arousing kiss she'd ever experienced. There was so much love in his tender kiss, the poignancy of it brought tears to her eyes. She couldn't fall in love with him. She wouldn't let herself. Her heart felt like it was growing too large for her chest. Damn it. Was it too late?

Alex pulled back, noticed the tears, and with Herculean effort, stood up. "Someone hurt you, baby?"

"Not yet." If she let herself feel, let herself go, she knew she was headed for heartbreak.

Alex frowned, trying to process her response. As he pulled back to contemplate, he listed badly to the left. Chuckling, Skye slipped her arms around his waist and brought him back to lean against her. Pain or no pain, she wasn't done yet. She was going to allow herself this treat. Tonight was a celebration and he was her reward. She swallowed the ache in her throat and blinked back the tears.

He kissed her again. Just barely touching her lips. Something was trying to get through the cloud coating the conscious surface of his brain. Were those tears he saw in her eyes? Was someone hurting her? He pulled back again and frowned. Yup, those were tears, all right. He would just have to kill the man who made his girl cry.

"I'm gonna have to kill the sonnavabitch."

"Who?"

"Who? Who made my girl cry." He looked around the room fiercely and saw a likely prospect grinning at Skye from the other end of the bar. He looked down at her arms around his waist.

"Can't move. Trapped."

When his brain caught up, it occurred to him that it might be himself he would have to kill. Was he hurting her? He frowned even deeper. Damn. He shouldn't have had that last shot. Double damn. He shouldn't have had the last fourteen shots.

"I'll take care of him myself, cowboy," she said and blinked the tears away. She never let tears fall. Ever. She couldn't believe his kiss, his love, conjured them up in the first place. A very good reason not to drink. She was a woman who liked to be in control. Needed to be in control. Drinking made you mushy. Made you needy. Made you soft. But what the hell? It also gave you a special dispensation for acting uncharacteristically uncontrolled. She put her hands on his face and drew him back down to her. Her team wasn't going to remember anything past midnight, anyway. The kiss was a great deal hotter this time. Her long, strong legs as well as her arms went around him.

Alex nearly drowned in the combined impact of ale, Scotch, and desire.

"Could you do me a favor?" he whispered in her ear then became distracted and he started to nibble her neck. Actually, he only thought he whispered it. The four men beside Skye turned and said "sure." They were drunker than he was, though, so the chances of them being able to do anything were pretty slim.

"Of course," she said softy. Feeling the residual tingle of his lips on hers and his mouth tracing the curve of her neck made her inclined to do just about anything for him. Just about. "What do you want?"

"Besides having my babies?"

He straightened, looked down into the depths of her soul and shot one right to her heart. The serious look on his face made her shift and lower her legs. Teasing was one thing. Leading him on was quite another.

"I thought we'd already covered that ground."

"Oh yeah…that's right. We covered that all over the ground." He couldn't seem to recapture his thoughts and decided to just stare into those brown eyes for the next few days.

"You were asking me for a favor?" she prompted when it appeared he wasn't going to proceed on his own.

He really was getting to her. She was feeling all hot and gooey and tender hearted. Could it be…no. She wasn't going to go there. Wasn't even going to finish the sentence. She could be fond of him. That was allowed. Okay. She was so, so fond of him. But that was going to be it.

Skye still had her arms around him and he returned the favor, taking his off the bar and pulling her to him. His face reflected a successful retrieval of his thought. He leaned over and whispered in her ear, again.

"Could you tell me where I am and where I parked my car?"

The feel of his breath on her neck sent shivers through her body. She instinctively raised her chin as he brushed his lips over the wonderful spot on her neck that he considered his. All his. Only his.

Alex heard the moan coming from her throat and completely forgot he was in a public place. His hands started to work their way to the front of her jump suit. Was there a zipper or buttons? He was pretty sure he could do a zipper. Managed his own an hour or so ago, didn't he? Hoped he'd remembered to get it back up after be completed his business. He stopped nibbling her neck and took a quick peek…great. Accomplished two tasks in his quick reconnaissance. His was up and hers had a zipper. His hands went in to unwrap the package.

Reluctantly, Skye decided to break it up before they became the floorshow. Being drunk on desire was as intoxicating and mind numbing as alcohol, but a little bit of discretion made it through the mist. She gently pushed his hands aside, slipped her hands between them and pushed. God, he was so strong. He was as hard to move as a brick wall. But he got the message and moved himself.

He grinned down at her and raised an eyebrow. "Got a plan?" he asked boyishly.

"Yes."

"Good." He looked around, swaying as the quick motion made him dizzy. "Got a car?"

"We'll walk."

"Not sure I can."

"Lean on me."

"Hot damn. That works for me!"

"Come on," she said, sliding off the bar stool and grabbing him around the waist.

Alex particularly liked the sliding off the stool part since she performed that incredible feat between his legs. Took him a minute to pull himself together.

Skye laughed at the play of expressions that breezed across his face. She turned him toward the door before he forgot where he was and tried taking down his pants.

"Come on. Fresh air will help."

"I'd rather breathe in Midnight Seduction."

"No."

"Can we go back to your place and get it and you can spray my pillow?" Skye looked up at him. The idea that the cover boy for *Business Week* wanted her to spray his pillow with her perfume was so incongruous. So outlandish. So sweet. So endearing. So, well, indescribably nice. She pulled her eyes away from his face and shook her head to clear it.

Stop it right now Skye, she thought. *Pull yourself together.* She shoved Alex toward the door. Get him back to the hotel, pour him into his bed, and give him a quick friendly kiss goodnight. Okay, so maybe treat yourself to a long, lingering, fond kiss goodnight. Maybe a couple of kisses and a chance to run her hands over his chest and down his butt. Then out the door. He was sufficiently incapacitated that he wouldn't remember it in the morning, anyway. Where's the harm? She could give her body a treat and maintain her pride. She could have her cake and eat it too.

It took them another half hour before they made it to the street. She had to firmly tell him no more drinks when his new best friends wanted him to join them in another toast. They laughed their way through the room, enjoying the easy camaraderie and the feeling of a job well done.

Alex had sobered up a bit by the time they got outside and the fresh air did help. His eyes automatically took in the sight of four solid guards tracking them and on the job so he slid comfortably back into his stupor. He looked over at Skye...felt her arm around his waist. He thought he might be able to walk on his own, but he didn't want to enlighten her. She seemed just fine with the idea of him leaning on her. It gave him tacit permission to keep bumping up against her firm, generous breasts. He just loved the feel of those firm, generous breasts. And if his hand would once in a while work its way up her shoulder and rub against her neck, well, he was a good man, but no saint.

He would have to pay for the sin of taking advantage of her charitable nature later. For now, he was getting all he could.

Once, he turned and pressed her up against the side of a building. Just to give her a little kiss on those man-killing lips. Just to test the waters, so to speak. She laughed and spun him around until they got back on track. He didn't like that spinning part much but he liked the laugh a whole lot.

He moved his hand up Skye's back again. She was being really nice tonight. Smiling and kissing him and letting him bump up against those firm, generous breasts. Where did she get all that tolerance? Was it something he said? He tried to remember. She was mad as hell at him. Let's see. When was that? That was a few nights ago. Gave him a real shot where it hurts the most. Oh man. That hurt. He stumbled at little looking down at himself.

"What?" She felt him stagger and smiled up at him. She was enjoying the rather intimate walk back to the hotel. It was a warm night and she was woman enough to appreciate the feel of a really strong, well built man wrapped around her.

"Mr. Penis just had a flashback."

"What?" That made her laugh out loud and she nearly stumbled.

"I was just thinking why you aren't mad at me anymore and Mr. Penis wanted to remind me to be very, very careful not to rile you up again."

"I'm still mad at you," she assured him shaking her head and giggling. She was sure this made perfect sense to him. "But don't worry, I would never kick a man when he's down."

"Whew. That's a relief. Mr. Penis assures me he's down, alright." Then something crept into his mind. He actually stopped walking and she had to prod him along.

"Hey. I saw you kick a man while he was down. You went right for him. The Klingon ball bust." He shuddered. "Scary."

"Close enough," Skye said under her breath.

"I really have to lie down," Alex warned.

"Soon. We're almost there."

She weaved him through the lobby grateful there weren't more people around. He kept greeting everyone like someone running for public office. She managed to get him into the elevator and to the 24th floor.

"Where's your key?" she asked him when they got to the penthouse.

"In my pocket, where's yours?"

She rolled her eyes and propped him up against the wall while she went through his pockets. She found it and slid it through the card slot.

"Isn't it funny how they still call them room keys instead of room cards?" he frowned. This one was worth pondering, but by the time she took him by the waist and led him into his suite, the thought had escaped him.

"Want a drink?" he asked in what he perceived as a hospitable tone of voice.

"No."

"Want something to eat?"

"No."

"Want a TV?" He laughed uproariously. How clever can a man get and not be on the stage, he thought.

"You're stalling," Skye said with mock sternness.

"You bet your ass I am." He took her in his arms and smiled down at her. "Speaking of your ass. Want to fool around?"

"And what if I said yes?" she asked, raising an eyebrow.

"Would scare me to death," he snorted. And a thought flashed through his brain about a plan. Something about Operation Seduction. But he lost it.

"Would you like to visit the bathroom before I tuck you in?" Gently pulling out of his arms and leading him toward the bedroom.

"Somebody in there?"

"No, nobody is in there."

"Why visit?" asked Alex. She raised an eyebrow again. "Oh. Gotchya. Yup. Sure could empty out some of this beer."

She led him to the bathroom connected to the master suite and waited until she heard the toilet flush. She turned and saw Alex standing in the doorway, one arm on either side of the door jam holding him up. He was completely, magnificently, gorgeously naked and her entire body flooded with desire. It was a good thing he was way too drunk to notice.

"Wanna take a shower with me?" asked Alex.

"No."

"Stay?"

"All right. Just to make sure you don't fall in there and kill yourself."

"Okay."

He turned cheerfully and almost didn't stop spinning. He did manage to step into the shower and figure out how to turn it on. From the sound of his yelps and curses, he either couldn't find the hot or couldn't find the cold. She peeked in to make sure he wasn't scalding himself and smiled. Couldn't find the hot. Well that should sober him up. She decided to stay and watch the show. He would never know and it was such a wonderful show. Kind of like a pornographic comedy.

He looked at the soap as if he was trying to figure out what to do with it. She was afraid he was going to eat it when he raised it to his face. He was just smelling it. Idiot. He threw two over the top of the shower before he decided on the third one. He seemed to be talking to himself, but when she took a closer look he was actually having a conversation with his, well, the manly parts of his body. Then he just leaned there with his hands up against the wall and his head under the shower. She was about to go in after him when he stood up opened the door and stepped out. He smiled at her with a goofy look of triumph on his face. Then he remembered and turned to shut off the water. He only managed to find the hot water so when he caught a towel on his third grab, she went around him and turned everything off.

"Come on," she said, smiling. "Let's put you to bed."

"Hot damn! Let's!"

He walked over to the king-size bed where she'd already pulled down the coverlet and blanket. He shed his towel along the way and fell face down on the soft bed. He was a bit sideways, but she considered it a victory that he was actually in there at all. He appeared to have passed out.

He was so appealing, so magnificent lying there. What the hell, he wouldn't know, she thought. She learned over, covered him up, smoothed his wet hair and tenderly kissed him goodnight.

His arm shot out and caught her hand completely by surprise. She let out a startled cry and tried to remove it from his grasp. But he caught his quarry and he wasn't letting go. His grip was amazingly strong. He was a man who wanted her deeply no matter what condition he was in.

"Don't go, Special Agent Madison," he mumbled softly and turned on his side toward the center of the bed. Her hand went with him and she found herself sitting on the side of the bed, one arm resting over his naked waist. It appeared he had some life in him after all.

"I wanted to be sure you were safely back in bed. Mission accomplished." She tried to pull her hand away, but it just made his grip firmer. Plus his other arm was beginning to snake around her waist and pull her down.

"Safe. I don't want to be safe. I want you." His eyes, heavy with fatigue and drink, held hers. "Love me."

"I can't."

He pulled her toward him, his eyes never leaving hers. There was such desire in them. Such longing. He was too vulnerable. She shouldn't be seeing this. Her lips touched his. She hadn't realized that he had let go and her body finished the journey to him until she had both hands on either side of his lovely face. She kissed him with all the regret and unhappiness she felt.

"I can't," she whispered to him again.

"But I used your soap," he grinned, happy as a clam that he remembered something important.

"Excuse me?"

"I found the one you use and I used it. I can smell it. I can smell you. I love you."

That one got through. She had no defenses left. She was tired, tipsy, and trapped by her fondness for him...there was no way she was even going to think the "L" word.

She bent down to him again and kissed him deeply, lovingly, passionately. His arms came up and circled her.

"Don't. Don't love me," she whispered when she came up for air. There were tears in her eyes again, but he didn't see them.

"Too late." His eyes were closed now. She was still locked against his chest by his arms, but she could feel the power ebb out of them. She could leave now. She should leave now.

"Stay," he said, practically in his sleep. "Stay."

"I'll stay."

The battle was over. She surrendered, deciding she couldn't deny her need for him, even though she would continue to deny her love.

He smiled, sighed, and gave into his body's need for rest. He heard what he needed to hear. It was good enough for now. He slid into the stupor he'd been keeping at bay for the better part of the evening.

CHAPTER 17

When Alex opened one blurry eye late the next morning, the first thing he saw was one of Skye's blue jumpsuits thrown over the chair. The rush of pleasure quickly gave way to excruciating pain. Not moving his head, he sent an exploratory arm across the bed to see if she was there. She wasn't. Good. That meant he could go through the humiliating process of lifting his head without an audience.

He raised his head off the pillow, groaning out loud as his mind screamed in protest. There was nothing in his brain but agony. Maybe if he just lay here, he would die. That would solve everything. He closed his eye again. The room was spinning badly and he had no desire to move out of his bed to get sick. He was too uncomfortable to go back to sleep. He was too uncomfortable to get out of bed. What to do.

Then he smelled it. Coffee. Maybe he could find the will to go on living if he could get some into him. How to accomplish this without moving was the monumental task before him.

"Good morning," came a fresh voice from the mist.

"Quit shouting," he croaked and immediately regretted it. His own voice echoed painfully through his brain.

He thought he heard a chuckle. He would have to kill her. He knew that now. As much as he regretted having to do the deed, it was inevitable and justifiable.

"Run," he suggested out of a sense of fair play. "You're a dead woman walking."

Again, the chuckle.

He opened the eye again. Shit. Even his eyelids hurt.

"Want some coffee?" asked Skye.

"Got a straw?"

"No. You're going to have to move."

"Can't," answered Alex.

"Is that the legendary Special Agent Springfield talking?"

"No. He's not in here."

232

"Just how many brain cells did you kill last night?"

"All of them."

"Well, you're going to have to move sometime. They're going to want to vacuum in here and make the bed."

Just the mention of a vacuum made his head throb.

"If anyone uses a vacuum in my presence today, I'm going to buy this hotel and fire everyone."

"Ah, you're getting better already. You're talking in complete sentences."

Skye sat on the edge of the bed and waited for Alex to get the courage to lift his head.

"The sooner you move, the sooner I'll be able to get these aspirin in you."

"Extra strength?"

"Both the coffee and the aspirin."

He opened both eyes and slowly lifted his head. After the initial rush of pain and nausea, he turned his body. Skye had pillows ready and plumped them up behind his head. She wisely refrained from any conversation as Alex closed his eyes and settled back. He reached out and she placed the tablets in his hand. He sat for a while contemplating the wisdom of putting anything into his stomach, then put them in his mouth. She handed him the glass of water and he was able to wash them down. Taking a few deep breaths, he reached for the coffee. He still didn't have his eyes open, so she placed the mug in his outstretched hand.

After a few sips, he sighed and let the pills and caffeine do their work.

"Thanks, sweetheart. I think I'll let you live now."

"I'm grateful," she said with laughter in her voice.

"Unless you get chirpy on me again. Then all bets are off. I hate chirpy and cheerful when I feel like shit."

"You feel that well, do you?"

"Add sarcastic to chirpy and cheerful."

"Done." He felt her start to get up and the same arm that got her the night before shot out and grabbed her hand.

"How do you do that? You have radar or something?" she asked, looking down at his hand firmly gripping her wrist.

He opened one eye again. "I have the instincts of a jungle beast." He took another sip of coffee and opened the other eye.

She was grinning at him. Fresh and beautiful and, most importantly, not mad. The 'not mad' part hit him after he flushed the resentment for her good mood out of his system with more coffee.

"You…ah…spent the night here last night?" He closed his eyes again and tried to remember. It hurt.

"I did," she said cryptically, smoothing the sheets and smiling sweetly. She was really enjoying this. It would take awhile before he remembered what went on and that put her at quite an advantage. Her natural inclination to tease, dormant for a while, became powerful. And irresistible. Almost as irresistible as him. His hair was pretty much unsalvageable without a total shampoo. His eyes were puffy and bloodshot. What she could see of them. They had only been open briefly. And he still smelled like the soap he chose last night. She decided on the same soap this morning. Seemed only fair.

He rubbed his eyes and smelled the soap on his hands. He sniffed his forearms. It was her scent. Did that mean he got lucky? Very, very lucky? She did seem different this morning.

"Did we…ah…?" He peeked at her through his thick, dark lashes. His headache was subsiding to a dull throbbing. It was Skye that was getting to be a real pain now.

"You don't remember?" she asked in mock distress.

"Okay. You got me. Did I get lucky?"

"Define lucky."

"Goddamn it Skye, did you let me make love to you last night?" His fingers shot to his temple. Whoa. That put the pain right back to the front page. Skye took pity on him and stood up.

"You couldn't even walk straight last night, much less shoot straight."

Alex didn't know whether to be relieved or disappointed. He decided to be disappointed.

"Shit. Could you fill in some blanks, here? I remember some kissing, I distinctly remember some really good kissing. That was you, right?" he teased. He could get in a few shots too, he decided. He opened his eyes and she nodded her confirmation.

"Then you let me bump into your delectable breasts."

"What?"

"On the walk home. I remember bumping into you as often as I could."

"You son-of-a-bitch. And I thought you were having trouble navigating."

"Well, that, too. Damn. How much did I have to drink?"

"Not that I was your keeper, but I think you and the inspector stopped counting at 22 or 23."

"Did we have fun?"

"We had a wonderful time. Really. It was a great feeling to celebrate. And you had a lot of people to toast."

"So why aren't you mad anymore? Was it something I said? Something I did? Something I didn't do?"

"Maybe I just don't hold a grudge," said Skye.

"That's not what Jim says. He told me about Simpson in records."

"Simpson is a complete ass. You," she kissed him on his pounding forehead, "are just a pain in the ass."

"I can live with that," said Alex.

"Could you have a little breakfast?"

"So why aren't you mad at me anymore?" Alex wasn't going to be diverted.

"I decided that it would hurt me as much as it would hurt you. Someone once said resentment is like drinking poison and expecting the other person to die. It was just too painful to carry around in my heart." She smiled tenderly down at him.

"Does that mean you'll let me touch you again?" he asked, hopefully.

"Perhaps."

"And make love to you again?"

"We'll see," said Skye.

"And love me?"

"Not a chance."

"Thought I might be able to slip that by you."

"I'm not the one with the hangover. Now. How about some toast?"

"I'd rather have you."

"One step at a time. First you'll want to feel human again."

"I'm getting closer. And I'll take the toast," said Alex gratefully.

"I leave you to your recovery. I'm going back down to my room to get dressed."

"Let me call and have all of your stuff moved up here," Alex said taking another sip of the strong, black coffee.

"No," said Skye firmly.

"It makes perfect sense. We can use this room as our headquarters."

"Nice try."

"I thought so. Come back soon?"

"Sure, as soon as I get dressed and check in with Jim."

"I think we should take the day off."

"My intentions exactly." She knew her team would be in no shape to do anything for at least a day. Everything in the office was boxed, printed, and ready for special shipping. She would be taking everything with her in cargo on her flight the following afternoon. There was nothing more to do here but tie up a few loose ends and that she intended to do on her next flight over.

"Maybe you should just stay here. We could get naked, watch a few videos, call for room service. Take a nap in this nice big bed?" Alex shifted in the bed. His head was beginning to fit his body again and he was hopeful of a full recovery.

"Why do I feel like Little Red Riding Hood?"

"Haven't a clue."

"Not a good state of affairs for a Special Agent."

"You haven't told me how you like my idea."

"What makes you think I like any part of your idea?"

"What were you planning to do today?" challenged Alex.

"The Victoria and Albert Museum, horseback riding in Hyde Park, and tea at Butler's Bridge." The thought of horseback riding made him wince and made her laugh out loud.

"What's wrong with looking through that book over there and then riding me? We can have tea in bed." Alex smiled.

"You really are feeling better."

"Not really, but I'm planning on it."

She gave him a quick peck on the cheek and left the room. The smile formed slowly on his lips. He would settle for that. For now.

By the time Skye returned at noon, Alex had chosen life over death. After she left, he got up, nearly crawling to the bathroom for a long, tepid shower, stepping over soap, brushes, sponges, and little plastic bottles that were scattered over the bathroom floor. God, what happened in here? He vaguely remembered he had an audience last night and smiled. If she liked looking, she would like tasting. He grabbed the used soap in the dish and smiled even broader. Her soap. That was really sappy. But maybe she liked the fact that he used it. She sure was nice to him this morning. He took another whiff and unwrapped a bar of his own.

By the time he was dressed and on his third cup of coffee and second plate of toast, he was even brave enough to let the maid in to vacuum. When he heard Skye let herself into the suite, he was in a real mood to celebrate. It had finally hit him that she stayed last night. Okay. So Operation Seduction was supposed to end up with the two of them naked and sweaty and panting. But she stayed. That was real progress. He could build on that.

"You look like a picture," he smiled leaning against the bedroom doorjamb and drinking in the sight of her.

He had no idea how long it took her to paint it, she thought gratefully. She'd stood in front of her closet for nearly twenty minutes trying to decide on the look she wanted. This was very uncharacteristic of her. Either she would wear her uniform, or jeans, or her jumpsuit or whatever the situation demanded...but what did this situation dictate? This was ridiculous. That's what it was. She grabbed a red knit dress. Held it up. No, too suggestive. She threw it over her chair, another uncharacteristic move. She took out a pair of slacks and jacket. No. Too business-like. Damn why didn't she bring more clothes with her? Then she pounced on the pretty one-piece jumpsuit. It was a wonderful color of teal and she had the perfect shoes to go with it. She didn't realize she was acting like a woman in love.

After the monumental clothes decision came the how to wear her hair decision. Must be sleep deprivation, she thought. She'd better get it together before she got in the cockpit tomorrow. After playing with it for another twenty minutes, she decided to just leave it down and put a clip on the side to keep it from falling in her face. The fact that Alex liked it down was...well...coincidence. Now, for the lipstick shade. She frowned.

When she walked into his room, she had the casual look of someone who had just thrown on some clothes and run a comb through her hair. He walked toward her, his eyes reflecting both desire and appreciation. Score. Everything worked.

"It's good to see you alive and alert."

"Relative terms."

Alex came over and gave her a chaste kiss on the cheek. She smelled like...oh hell...like Midnight Seduction. Scamp. He almost threw her on the sofa to be kissed into submission. Chill, he thought. You have time. He smiled. She smiled.

"Tell me," he wondered. "Did you not have a lot to drink last night or are your powers of recuperation something medical science should know about?"

She laughed and went over to help herself to coffee.

"I celebrated, but stopped at relaxed. You didn't stop until you went through intoxicated, inebriated, drunk, smashed, and witless."

She took a strawberry from the plate and tasted it. Her stomach wasn't 100 percent, either. Just a little jittery.

"Talk to Jim this morning?" he asked, working to keep his voice casual.

"Yes, I did. Actually I had a very busy morning." The fact that most of it was spent getting ready to come back was her little secret. "Ready for a report?"

"Let's sit down. I'm recovered a bit, but my knees still remember the twenty-fifth toast."

Laughing, she sat down on the sofa.

Alex casually sat beside her and watched as she drank her coffee and ate a strawberry. He sat back against the corner cushions and crossed his legs, a perfect gentleman.

"Okay Special Agent in Charge Madison. Report. What exactly happened last night from the time I innocently walked into the pub and said hello?"

"Oh no. If you're going to be idiotic enough to drink yourself into oblivion, don't expect me to fill in the gaps. It occurs to me that the Brits could have won the war if they had just taken the colonials to a pub for a drink. The inspector called me from there less than an hour ago...his team are still at it and they wanted me to know they found a ladder in the storeroom so that he can deliver my first passionate kiss."

"What did you tell him?"

"That he was far too much man for me."

"So are you going to tell me if I was man enough last night?"

"No."

He smiled his most devastating smile and his blue eyes, having most of their color back, held her gaze.

"How about I tell you things and you tell me if I remember it correctly?"

"Okay." His gaze held hers. He had the most incredibly sexy voice, deep and sensual.

"Let's see. There was a dart game and a keg."

"Correct."

"You were sitting on a stool watching me," said Alex.

"Among other things." He raised his eyebrows. "Correct," she said, smiling. She liked the mood.

"I think there was some kissing in there somewhere."

"We were feeling particularly lighthearted." Then she remembered the game. "Correct."

"You and me."

"That's right."

"It was really good kissing," said Alex, his hand coming up behind her going right to a curl and running it through his fingers.

"Now that's a value judgment and not strictly a factual question."

"Really, really good kissing," he said, sure of his facts, his voice low and arousing.

Skye smiled, her lips around the strawberry. Alex's voice was almost hypnotic and Skye had to take another bite of the strawberry to break the spell he was casting over her. If she only knew that what she was doing with the fruit was very sensual…that Alex's reaction to her lips making those little sucking noises on the berry was both physical and potent, she would have stopped it and thrown it in the corner. Or would she have?

"Okay." She nodded slowly and cocked her head. "Some would say the kissing was both tolerable and skilled."

God. She was delightful. He inched a little closer.

"There was a walk and a lot of bumping."

"Indeed. And I found out this morning, when you thought you were dying and were in a confessional mood, that much of that was intentional."

"Oh yeah. That I remember. Firm, generous breasts."

"Let's get over that."

"Easy for you to say."

"Alex."

"Skyler."

She took a deep breathe of mock exasperation. "Back to the questions."

"Okay. There was a very cold shower. Did you do that?"

"No. That was self-inflicted. You couldn't find the hot water and I wasn't inclined to show you where it was."

"Did I at least ask you to join me?"

"That you did."

"I'm glad I didn't forget my manners."

"That's up for interpretation. You were buck naked when you asked me."

He roared with laughter, then regretted it as his head objected strongly to the move. He winced and Skye took pity on him. She put down her coffee and half eaten strawberry. "Did you take more Tylenol?"

"Double the legal limit."

"Good, then come over here and turn around." She laid a pillow on her lap and tapped it lightly. He followed her direction gladly, hoping it meant some touching. It did. She gently, but firmly started to rub his temples. "Close your eyes."

"Shall I think of palm trees and warm breezes?"

"Shhhh. Think of pleasant things."

He thought of her naked.

"Working?"

"I'll give you two weeks to stop."

She chuckled and continued the process of kneading the ache out of his temples, neck, and shoulders. Her cool touch and tender fingers did more than a whole bottle of Tylenol and he meant to tell her, but at the moment he wasn't even earthbound. If he hadn't been in love before, he would have tumbled now. He was completely hers.

Skye could feel him relax. She was shocked that she wanted to trace her lips over the same route her fingers were taking. Her thighs were beginning to go liquid. She saw flashes of him standing in the doorway naked and asking her to take a shower, coming toward her in the pub with so much tenderness on his face, smiling like an idiot at her soap, the longing look in his eyes before he fell off to sleep. If he had been trying to weaken her resistance, he was succeeding.

He moaned with pleasure. The sound went through her and right down to her liquefied lap.

Alex was drifting. He could smell her, feel her fingers on his flesh, see her in his mind's eye. Laughing. Returning his kisses. Standing alert in the moonlight. Drifting.

He was floating. Every ache was rubbed away. Her fingers were magical. She was here with him. He thought she would stay mad at him forever, but she admired him. She thought he was edible.

Alex had no idea the picture he presented her. One arm was resting across his chest, the other was laying over the side of the sofa. His legs were crossed at the ankle and casually propped up on the arm of the sofa on the opposite end, while she continued to rub his breathtakingly handsome face. She looked down at his hands. In repose, they were fine, long fingered, capable looking hands. She'd seen them lift a glass, grasp a gun, work a computer keyboard, brush her naked breast.

"You were watching me," he mumbled. His eyes opening and seeing her soft brown eyes looking into his. She hadn't expected him to open his eyes and he caught her tender expression before she could lower the veil and raise her eyebrows in question.

"Hmmm? Did you say something?"

"Last night. You were watching me in the shower." That memory and the affectionate expression on her face when she thought he wasn't looking was all it took to strike the match to the smoldering feeling of hunger that was churning through him.

"*Vous avez été très bu, quelqu'un devait être votre ange de gardien,*" she said in a warm, sultry voice.

"What?"

"You were very drunk. Someone had to be your guardian angel. I wanted to be sure you didn't fall and kill yourself. Do you know the statistics...."

She didn't finish the sentence. He turned around, wrapped his long fingers around her neck, and drew her to him. His lips cut off the statistics on shower injuries and she never went back to the thought. French, he thought. That was definitely French he heard. Alex sat up, removed the pillow that lay between them, and drew her into the circle of his arms all in one smooth motion.

"Here or in the bedroom?" he whispered huskily when he drew his lips back. She stared at him. He held his breath. She smiled. His heart turned over and his body sang the halleluiah chorus.

"You feeling well enough?" she teased.

He looked down, then looked up with a wicked smile. "I think we have another party in us."

She laughed and threw her arms around his neck as they went tumbling off the sofa. There was a lot of floor and a lot of pent up desire. Her carefully chosen outfit went flying and she nearly got hysterical when she found that his underwear was on backwards. He was both enchanted by her enthusiasm and touched by her quiet need for compassion. He would give her his love, his body, his life.

After the first sensational stretch of foreplay and love making, they finished the strawberries and opened a bottle of champagne. They decided videos in the room were a good idea after all. Skye loved Jackie Chan movies and Alex had the whole library of them. They made love again in the bed. In the shower. And then again on the sofa before they ordered steaks from room service.

"Red meat," she said heartily, "and lots of it."

From the big lounge chair on the balcony, Alex watched the sun go down on the best day of his life. He had her wrapped in his arms. She was finally beginning to tire. Good thing, he thought. He wasn't sure he could sustain the pace much longer. She was a passionate woman, a tireless lover. She was able to both give pleasure without awkwardness and receive it without guile. He was completely mad about her. And he was convinced that there was a significant part of her heart that was his. She may not label it as love. Not yet. But he was content to wait until she did. Bloody hell. He was just plain content.

Skye melted into Alex's body and sighed. She hadn't thought about work all day. Most of the time, she hadn't been thinking at all. Alex's body was all a woman dreamed of, a fantasy of shape and textures. He was a generous lover and a considerate man. Passionate and demanding, but not selfish. Wanting pleasure, but taking pleasure in her release as well. She'd never experienced a day like today. She wouldn't think about tomorrow, not yet. She felt like Scarlett O'Hara. Tomorrow is another day. A sigh of absolute contentment escaped her and she drifted into a safe place, securely held in his arms.

Alex looked down at her face. Her eyelashes brushed the tops of her cheeks, her mouth was turned up in a little smile. Her hair, never too tame on the best of days, was a riot of waves and curls. He buried his nose in it and smelled the scent of her. It would have scared her witless to know how much he loved her and the fact that he was more determined than ever that she would be his. It was no longer an option. It was no longer a dream. She was made for him.

He kissed the top of her head tenderly. "Skye?"

"Mmmm?"

"Sweetheart, do you want to spend the night out here or shall we go to bed?"

"Bed."

She turned, nestled into his chest, sighed, and went back to sleep. Well, he thought as his arms went tighter around her. He supposed he could get her in there eventually. For now, he was content to sit on the balcony, watch the day turn into night, smell her hair, and drift a bit.

Alex's eyes flew open. Damn. It was the phone. What the hell time was it anyway? He wasn't wearing anything but his robe. From the stiffness in his arms and legs, he must have been lounging there for quite awhile. It was dark and the stars were out. Skye stirred and mumbled something unintelligible. The phone rang again. He would have ignored it, but he had Special Agent in Charge Madison curled up on his lap.

He kissed the top of her head. "Skye? Darling? I have to move."

She snuggled deeper. "Okay."

"No, I mean I have to get up." He gave her a little shake.

She sighed and sat up slowly, forcing her eyes to open. Then she heard the phone too, and she got up quickly and ran to the sound of the ringing. They had been quite enthusiastic during one of their rounds of lovemaking and the table with the phone had upended and scattered. She found the cord and followed it to the receiver. By this time, Alex had reached the extension in the bedroom. They both answered at once.

"Skyler Madison."

"Alex Springfield."

"Well, which is it, and what took you so long to answer the goddamn phone?" said an irritated Jim Stryker.

"Well it depends on which one of us you're looking for and it's the middle of the night here, Jim," said Skye, coming to alert when she heard Jim's voice. At least she thought it was. The clock on the coffee table had taken flight at some point, too and she couldn't see the bedside clock from her vantage point.

"It's only a little after midnight there."

"Well, we've had a few busy days," said Alex. "Which of us is your target?"

"I need to speak to Skye. Have her call me." And he hung up.

"Just a minute, let me get her," Alex said mockingly to the dead receiver. Skye started her search for the portable secure cell phone unit.

"Where is the damn phone?" She never woke up happy, even in the best of times. "It better be important. I swear if he's just calling for a routine report, I'm going to take back his birthday present and exchange it for wool underwear."

"Good thing it isn't a two-way video hook up." Alex stood in the doorway shaking the phone in his hand, looking at her disheveled appearance. He thought she looked adorable, but she probably wouldn't want to be seen in public.

"I can only imagine," she said as she grabbed it from him and speed dialed Jim's number. "If I look anything like this room, I'm going to have to spend an hour in the bathroom before I go out in public. Christ, couldn't you have shown a little more restraint?"

Alex laughed out loud and started to put the furniture back where it belonged. He didn't think it would be prudent to mention that she was his cohort and willing partner in the demolition of the décor.

"Jim?" She got through to him and mostly listened. All Alex heard was "Shit. I knew it... That's precisely why... We have a great deal to talk about... No idea... None of your business... Talk to you tomorrow."

She disconnected and sat down, deep in troubled thought.

"What is it? Can you tell me?"

"Our office was fire bombed an hour ago."

"Christ! Anyone hurt? What about all the evidence?"

"Not seriously, thank God. The special couriers weren't scheduled to arrive until morning and both guards sustained only minor injuries from flying debris. They were in the hallway outside the metal door."

"Oh, hell. All those months of work. Darling, I'm so sorry. At least you've brought down the London connection."

"Alex," she said, looking up at him with a self-satisfied smile. "The data is safe…all the evidence we gathered is intact."

"What?"

"Yesterday, I personally took everything we gathered, placed it in a paneled truck, and stored it in a secure location. Only Jim and I knew about it."

"Your team?"

"No."

"Inspector York and his team?"

"No. No one."

"You knew someone was going to go after it."

"I suspected they would. They hid it well, but we found it. They had the room rigged to blow, so we disarmed it. This was the only option left. All those months of work and it would have been destroyed in one night."

"Fine bit of effort, Special Agent."

"Yeah, but that also means someone who knew our office location and our assignment wanted everything gone. It narrows down the field considerably. It has to be someone on my team or someone with a level three clearance or higher which narrows the field even more. The exact location of our offices is a very tightly held bit of information. No local contact was ever there…we always went to them."

"Someone could have followed you."

"To the building, sure. But not inside."

"How did they get in to fire bomb the place?"

"They didn't. Ground launcher into the window."

"Very effective."

"It would have been. The windows were safety glass and bullet proof, but nothing reinforced. Hell, all terrorists have this kind of equipment. Wee probably will never find out where the equipment came from. We need to find the who, not the how anyway."

"You going to the scene?"

"Yeah. I want to supervise the forensic work. The how should give us clues to the who."

"I'll call Inspector York. You go start the process of transforming into a public creature."

"Thanks. You coming?"

"Of course. Where you go, I go until Juan is caught."

"I'll meet you in the lobby. I need to go back to my room to pick up my purse and gun."

"I'll take a quick shower. Shall we say a half hour?"

"There's no real rush. The evidence isn't going anywhere."

She stood there, in her robe and her tangled hair, wanting to say something. He gave her a moment to decide if she was going to.

She decided action was better than words. She walked up to him, put her arms around him and gave him a long, passionate kiss. He held her for a moment. Just one more moment to extend the time of sweetness.

"Thanks for a lovely day. And night," she sighed and he tightened his grip on her.

"I know you don't want to hear this, but I'm feeling it, so you may as well know. I love you, Skye. Completely. You don't have to love me back. Just don't keep yourself from me." He said it simply, almost matter of factly. This is the way it was. No mystery. No ambiguity. Simple fact.

"Okay," she said simply, then lifted her chin and met his kiss with one of her own.

She left him for the second time that day to go back to her room and change. He decided that she was going to move in with him when they returned to Washington D.C. First things first, however. He dialed the inspector's number then went to take a shower and put on some clothes.

CHAPTER 18

The place was a complete mess. The investigators knew it was a grenade launcher that put the fire bomb through the window and had a line on some local suppliers, but there were hundreds of unregistered pieces on the street, and it would take either a lucky break or months of arduous leg work to track them all down. There were no witnesses and very little forensic evidence remained. Skye looked at the black hole that had been their London headquarters. It wasn't a huge loss, just some standard equipment, computers, and a refrigerator, but it was her team's symbolic home and she felt violated. Thank God all of the files and important papers and disks were safe.

Alex conferred with the inspector and made himself useful gathering the relevant data Skye needed to complete her report. She liked the feel of their partnership. It helped her deal with the stress and anger. It was a good feeling knowing she could count on him so she put the personal emotions away for the time being. She would think about them on the flight home. One great benefit of the long flight over the Atlantic was that it gave her a great deal of quality thinking time. She suppressed all thoughts of her attraction to Alex and its ramifications until she had time to decide what to do.

"Done here?" asked the subject of her deeper thoughts.

"Yes. They're doing a good job. I want to get the van from the secure location and have new couriers assigned for its transport. I just talked with Jim and he gave me the names and numbers of the people to use. As soon as I check them out, they'll accompany the cargo to my flight and check it through Customs."

"What can I do?" She liked that. He knew she was in charge. No battle with his ego, just easy camaraderie.

She hesitated for a moment. It wouldn't even have been detectible, except that Alex was supercharged when it came to her actions and reactions. She decided in that split second to trust him again and handed him an envelope. It was another sign of the healing of their ruptured relationship.

"In here is a location, a map, and a signed receipt. It's for a secure car storage on Covenant and Le Pont. I need you to pick up the evidence and bring it over to the airport. The location of the cargo dock is in there. The couriers will be there to take it from you and over to Customs."

Alex smiled. "Thanks. I know what this means."

"Well, at least I know where you were last night at midnight."

Alex slipped all the information into his pocket. "When is your team going back to the States?"

"They leave tomorrow. We're going to reconvene for a debriefing and strategic planning on Thursday in D.C."

"Have you talked with them?" asked Alex.

"Yes. I called each of them and let them know what happened here. They now know the information has been saved."

"Are you coming back to the hotel?"

"Yes."

"You'll need protection while I'm gone. Either you call Max, or I'll arrange for one of these officers to escort you."

"I'd rather not pull Max all the way out here. How about we arrange for a couple of these uniforms to drop me off on their way back to their station house, then secure protection in the hotel until we can reconnect?" She really didn't want anyone to accompany her and he knew it. She was certain she could take care of herself, but Alex was in charge of this part of the operation and she wouldn't argue with him. It wasn't worth it. He appreciated her cooperation.

He went over and two young officers immediately volunteered. They were a bit too enthusiastic to Alex's way of thinking, but at least he was certain they wouldn't let her out of their sight. He chose a more seasoned officer to accompany them and stay with Skye.

"Stay close to these officers, Skye," he commanded, looking into her face for confirmation. He read cooperation, barely. "Will you come on up for a nap before you fly out?"

"I need to sleep. I won't take off in this state of fatigue. If I come up to your room, well, one thing may lead to another," she smiled with some regret.

He held up his hands and smiled back at her tenderly. "Just sleep, darling. I promise. I'll guard the door."

"Said the fox as he sat outside the henhouse door." Skye's eyes said yes, however. She would trust him there, too. "Okay. I'll meet you back in your room."

She watched as he drove away. Sure was nice to have someone to rely on. She shook herself before she went any further down that path.

Skye saw a bakery across the street and thought she might snatch a pastry before going back. Talking to the two young officers, she convinced them that she would meet them at their car in fifteen minutes. They looked at each other. The big guy told them not to let her out of their sight, but they figured she was only going to be across the street and they had a few more people to interview. They nodded their assent and Skye jogged to the curb. The traffic was light, so she ran across the street with little trouble. It took her a few moments to make her selections, then she stood outside to eat, thinking she may go back in and get a few extra pastries for her bodyguards. She looked up into the sky. It was going to be a beautiful day for flying.

Juan watched him from the front seat of his rented luxury car. Damn if fate must have just felt like handing him a bonus card. All the evidence of his operation and any connections he had was dust…and now, there she was. It was the she-bitch and she was looking up and licking her fingers. Perfect target. He hadn't really planned on this, but sometimes opportunity just comes up and bites you in the ass. He was checking out the destruction of the office in the daylight, making sure everything was incinerated. Looked like a perfect pinpoint hit. So there, you bitch. Take that. Then like magic, she materialized. Right there across the street.

There she was, in the flesh, and her watchdog had just set off in a car. Juan had his tickets for a flight out of Heathrow, but he had just enough time for a little side trip. Right into the body of the slut who did nothing the last few months but make him miserable and who just cost him hundreds of thousands of dollars.

When the light changed, he stepped heavily on the gas and headed for the bitch. There was a gleam in his eye. He didn't get to kill people himself much anymore, and this would make three in one week. Fate had blessed him.

Skye heard the roar of the car's engine. Her reflexes and incredible radar made her spin and assess the danger and in a split second run like hell in the opposite direction. The car was speeding down the empty street with Skye streaking out in front of it. She was used to running full out and she was keeping some distance between her and the car while she looked for options. An alley. To her left. She could almost feel the heat of the engine when she swerved into the alley, barely slowing down.

The car didn't make the turn as smoothly and ran into the side of a building, scraping paint off the passenger side and slowing it down. Juan rammed the car down the tunnel-like alley, garbage cans flying from its front bumper. Both he and Skye saw the back of the alley at the same time.

"I have you now," he growled in triumph. The back of the alley was a tall brick wall. No way in, no way out. He accelerated, anticipating the kill.

Skye didn't look back; she didn't need to. The sound of the car's engine told her he was very, very close. She resisted the temptation because she knew it would slow her down. Besides, her escape wasn't behind her, it was in front of her. Her mind looked, processed her alternatives and sent the signals to her muscles. Jump, leap, grab, pivot, propel, land.

In one smooth, flowing move, practiced hundreds of times on the training course, but never executed in a back alley, Skye jumped. She leaped toward the lower rung of a fire escape using every inch of her considerable height, grabbed the metal rung, brought her legs up, pivoted her entire body, threw herself over the brick wall and landed with the grace of a cat, knees bent on the other side. Safe from harm. The vehicle no longer a threat, she drew her weapon, but by the time she climbed back up, the driver had wisely given up the chase and was making his exit.

"There will be another day," growled Juan. "Even a cat only has nine lives."

Skye flexed her muscles, replayed the series of moves in her mind, smiled in self-congratulations and went to alert the inspector that she had another little incident to look into.

Skye gave her an account of the event, the license number, and the make and model of the car.

"Will you want us to send Jim Stryker a copy of this report?" asked the inspector. She had sharp eyes and a no-nonsense manner. Skye trusted that if Juan was still in the area, he would be apprehended. She decided to leave it to the local officials. She had a plane to fly.

Skye handed her business card to the inspector. "No. For my eyes only," she said. She wasn't going to give Jim an excuse to pull her off this case. No way. She was going to go into phase two of this investigation and nail the bastard. He was going down. He ran over her cinnamon raisin scone and he was going to pay.

When Skye got back to the hotel, she went directly to Alex's suite. He was already there, making one of his endless business calls. Moving to the mini bar, she poured herself a glass of mineral water. Running away from crazed lunatics driving lethal cars made a woman thirsty.

When Alex finished, he came over and gave her a light peck on the cheek.

"Mission accomplished. Where have you been? I was beginning to think you weren't coming."

"Just gave myself a little workout," she said casually. Withholding information wasn't exactly like a lie. "It helps me sleep. You said no sex, just sleep, right?" He nodded regretfully, put his hands on her shoulders and pointed her toward the bedroom.

"We can both use a nap." He was true to his word and only lay down beside her as she slept in his big bed. She could go unconscious almost instantly. No tossing. No turning. No dreaming. Just closed her eyes and zoned out. What talent.

At 4 p.m., he kissed her awake.

"Five more minutes," she muttered as she rolled over and went back under. The snooze alarm was made for her. When traveling, she would set the alarm, ask for a wake up call, and program her cell phone to play the "Battle Hymn of the Republic," all at ten-minute intervals.

Five minutes later he kissed her ear and annoyed the hell out of her. "Darling, you have to go fly a big plane today."

"Coffee," she croaked and let her eyes close again.

By the time he came back into the room with the coffee, she was laying on her back blinking at the ceiling.

"What are you doing?" asked Alex.

"Turning on my brain and tuning into the information station."

"I brought fuel."

"God bless you and all your ancestors."

"Remember that next time you want to rip my face off."

She looked at him and smiled. "And it's such a pretty face."

She really could be nice. Very nice. She had on one of his t-shirts and it was very becoming, he thought. Of course she could wear a cow-patterned seat cover and it would be as fetching as hell.

Taking the coffee, she smooched the air at him. He smiled back at her, enjoying the intimate moment. She had the most adorable habits. That turning on the brain thing. Either she was one of a kind, or he had never run across her species before. She was a constant delight.

"Want some pancakes?" he asked.

"Want my undying gratitude?"

"How about your love?"

"Alex."

"Yeah. Okay. I'll take the gratitude and shut up."

"Smart man."

"Want a ride to the airport? I thought we could go together."

"Love one. Let me go put my uniform on and I'll meet you in the lobby." She really was getting annoyed with having to get dressed just to go down to her room to get dressed all over again.

Alex went over to the closet and opened the door. Her clothes were hanging there and her suitcase was on the floor.

"Your girly things are in the bathroom."

"You went down and packed my stuff?"

"Actually I had one of the staff do it. I didn't want you to think I was pawing through your underwear." Alex waited a minute for the flash of irritation he knew was coming. While she was sleeping, he had decided it was the most practical thing to do. Best use of time. Good business practice. After the deed was done, he thought she might interpret it as male dominance and find it too personally intrusive. If she'd done the reverse, how would he have reacted? Well, too late to put things back now. He would just have to face the consequences like a man.

She frowned at her clothes in his closet. Wasn't she just thinking with exasperation that she was tired of dressing and running down to her room? Here was the perfect solution. This was great. Now came the question of the day. Was she going to let him know how delighted she was to see her uniform in the same room where she woke up? She was used to split second decisions, but this was more important than the average life or death alternatives she faced in the field.

This might define their relationship. There was such a thing as precedent. He was a lawyer. He understood that kind of thing. Besides there was the fact that she might have been able to sleep five maybe ten minutes more if he would have told her earlier what his intentions were. If he would have consulted with her. Inconsiderate of him. Overbearing. Insensitive. She sighed...silently and internally, not showing the slightest sign of her inner dialogue to the man of her dreams. Thoughtful. Caring. Sweet. Lovely. Perfect. These inner dialogues were becoming far too inconsistent. She was going to have to get in the air and give this some thought.

She moved her gaze from the closet to his face. She calmly took another sip of coffee. He folded his arms and calmly waited for the tempest. It was way, way too calm in the room. Finally she decided the best course of action was no action at all. With great care she set down her coffee, got out of bed, walked to the bathroom, and shut the door.

Alex didn't move until he heard the shower running. What was that all about? Nothing was a greater mystery to a man than no reaction at all. Chilling. He shrugged his shoulders and went to order pancakes.

Alex was on the phone when she came out of the bedroom a half hour later and completely forgot whom he was talking to. "I'll call you back later," he said to a stunned real estate dealer, who thought the negotiations were going well. Alex had no way of knowing, but his abrupt disconnection saved him over $100,000 when the deal was completed the following day.

He had seen Skye in her uniform before, but mostly from a distance and in a crowded airport. And maybe it was the contrast between the tousle-haired, sleepy-eyed, beauty in his t-shirt who he had last seen and this regal goddess of the air. Her make-up was impeccable, her finely tailored suit was snug against her incredible curves, and the modest length of her skirt did nothing to hide the immodest length of her legs. She'd done something magical with her hair so that it was now sleek and smooth and in some kind of knot at the back of her neck. It made her face extraordinarily striking. She looked confident, competent, and completely aloof. Was this the siren in the three-inch heels? The woman who walked naked around his bedroom? The woman who cuddled in his arms on the terrace last night? Yes, she cuddled. There was no other word for it. The woman standing before him didn't even look like she had a heart.

"What did you do with the woman in my t-shirt?" he asked, then looked down at his phone as it started to ring. He tossed it on the sofa and let it ring some more.

"Pardon?" she asked. Her look of confusion would have impaled him had he not known there was a naked woman under all that polish.

"You look, well, different."

"Different?" She looked down at herself. She knew she had on a uniform and her hair was pulled back, but she felt the same on the inside.

"Never mind. Come over here and have some pancakes." He pulled the chair out for her.

"Yum." That was better. Only a woman with a heart would say "yum" and eat pancakes.

Because she had a lot of length and she was incredibly active, she could always give in to her appetite. She ate with relish as Alex updated her on the activities of her team and the crime scene.

"Are you on the 6 o'clock British Airways flight?"

"Nope." He walked over to the desk and picked up a copy of an email. "I got the last first class ticket on International Airlines Flight 127."

"Outstanding! British Airways, eat your heart out." She had such a look of pleasure on her face he nearly forgot himself and grabbed her. The way she looked, he felt he should ask permission. Maybe put it in writing. She finished everything on her plate and everything edible she could find on the tray, then sighed with satisfaction. "That was great. Let me go put on some lipstick and we can get moving to the airport."

She stood up and turned when he said her name. He came over to her and lightly kissed her. She tasted like maple syrup and smelled like heaven. He smiled. "Thought I should get that in before we leave. I'm not sure if it's quite proper to kiss the captain of your flight before, during, or after takeoff."

"I'm not sure what the protocol is on that. I've never kissed or had sex with a passenger before." There was something about that fact that Alex liked. "But it's a long, long flight over the Atlantic." She ran her hands up his chest and around his neck. "I think you can do better than that if we have to abstain from kissing for the duration."

Her eyes closed and she touched his lips with hers, parting them and playing with his tongue as he teased it through her teeth and into her mouth. His arms enfolded her and he realized that with his eyes closed, she was the same, wonderful package. He squeezed her tight and put 3,000 miles of passion into the kiss.

"That's the goodbye kiss," she said, breathless and hot. "Wait until we break the long abstention with the hello kiss at the other end."

"One more like that and I won't need a plane to fly over the ocean." He went for her lips again and she put her hand on his chest.

"I wouldn't want to injure International's bottom line by providing alternatives to commercial flight." With that she turned and went to put on her lipstick and grab her flight bag, purse, and hat. In the false bottom of her flight bag was her gun and special license to carry. Both Captain Madison and Special Agent in Charge Madison were ready for work.

They met Max in the lobby. He had filled the trunk of their limo with boxes of the team's personal items bound for the cargo hold. Alex was going to transfer them at the airport when he checked on the evidence containers. Skye had informed her team that the office had been bombed, but that the evidence was safe.

"See you Thursday morning, Max," Skye said shaking his hand.

"Ah, Skye?" asked Max.

"Yes?"

"I just wanted to say how glad we were to have you as the SAC. The data that we busted our balls for would have been up in smoke if you hadn't been thinking ahead. Never occurred to any of us that it would be in any danger. You're the best," said Max.

She smiled. "That was a real nice speech, Max. Now what is it that you want?"

"Well fuck my duck...my mom could do that too."

"Do what?"

"Read my mind."

"I'm not your Mom," said Skye.

"Not hardly."

"Max..."

"Well maybe sometimes when you fold your arms and frown."

"Max..."

"This isn't easy."

"I really can't read your mind. You're going to have to verbalize it." Skye crossed her arms and stared.

"Right there," he said, looking at the expression on her face.

"Right there what?" asked Skye.

"You coulda' been Mom."

"The fact that you had one astounds me, Max. I have to go. Spit it out."

"Well... ah...okay. Here it is. I noticed you and Alex are...ah..."

"It was Friday," Skye laughed.

"Damn. Damn. Double damn."

"It isn't going to break you, Max."

"It isn't that. I gotta go back and tell the China doll she was right. This hurts, Skye. This really bites."

"Buck up, Special Agent. I think you have a contractual obligation to be bold and daring."

"Yeah, but this is different. Can I just fly home with you?"

Skye laughed again. "Get the team packed up and we'll see you in D.C."

"Hey," Max's face lit up. Hope springs eternal. "What exact time was it...could it have been after midnight?"

"Goodbye, Max."

"We never specified the time zone."

"See you Thursday."

"Okay. But I warn you, Linda is going to be impossible to work with for awhile."

For you, maybe, she thought. Was there something brewing there? God help us. She put on her hat, lowered the brim to the exact regulation angle and went out into the sunshine.

Connie and Bill were at the gate with the rest of the crew. They were standing apart and had a look of deep concern on their faces. They had been discussing something and when they looked at Skye, she knew it had been her they were talking about. She could guess the topic and smiled. They would be filled with worry about her emotional state over Phillip's arrest, his father's murder, and his family's disgrace. They would never know that she helped bring them down.

Never much for subtlety, Connie came over, took Skye's arm, led her over to where Bill was standing and launched into a tirade. "Are you all right? Did you know anything about that creep's other life? What scum. I never did like him. Sorry if that hurts your feelings, but it's a fact. I tried calling your room, but there was no answer. You weren't there were you? Bastard!" Connie rarely swore. Bastard was her limit, so Skye knew she was really furious.

Bill held up his hand to stop Connie's flow of pent up dialogue. "Which question should she answer first? You have to take a breath if you want to have a conversation." He turned to Skye. "Are you all right?"

To their utter amazement, Skye laughed at the two of them. "Thanks for your concern. I'm touched. Really. But as I said to a friend a few nights ago, I just wish I could have been there to see the look on his face. Phillip was an egomaniacal, self-absorbed, narcissistic, vain, conceited snob. I was only polite to him because he was a friend of my mother's family." A small lie, but an expedient one.

"See, Connie? I told you. Skye is too smart to fall for someone like him," said Bill.

But Connie's highly tuned radar went right to another fact, missed by Bill. Phillip was a dead subject. Dead and buried. She moved right along to other things. "What friend?" she demanded with her eyes narrowed. "Male, right?" She could sniff out romance at 10,000 feet. Plus Skye hadn't been in her room or returned any of her calls. And there was that glow.

"As a matter of fact." Her voice trailed off as the man in question walked through the terminal. He had changed into business attire after helping agents load the cargo. His impeccable suit was tailored to his wide shoulders, his blinding white shirt a stark contrast to the tan he sported year round. His hair was perfectly groomed. He was from head to polished toe the image of a successful man. He had a confident stride that added power and life to the picture. Skye wasn't too keen on all the female attention he was getting as he walked in her direction. He's mine, she thought. That beautiful specimen is mine.

Connie saw something in Skye's eyes and whirled around. She slapped her hands together and with breathless anticipation asked the question. "Oh please, Skye. Please, please, please tell me that's the friend. He's male. God! I would say he was the prototype for male."

"As a matter of fact," she said again, smiling her professional pilot smile at him, creases forming on either side of her mouth. Controlled. Contained. She would make it up to him later. Right now, she was the captain of this aircraft and she had to be all business.

Alex smiled back. Reserved. Restrained. Being an attorney and businessperson who had presided over hundreds of negotiations, he understood perfectly the need to be in control in professional situations. He wouldn't do anything to crack her veneer. He admired it, actually.

But neither of them could do anything about their eyes. They flashed, burned, and sizzled. Connie and Bill saw it all. They knew Skye very well. Both of them started their day with a feeling of concern for their friend. Now they couldn't wait to get her alone and away from the airport to pump her for every single intimate detail.

Alex's gaze swept over Skye standing straight and tall at the gate. He nodded slightly, then went to a seat and unfolded his *Wall Street Journal*. He was hoping to catch up on the business news. Pursuing criminals and drug dealers was one thing, but pursuing Skye had consumed an incredible amount of his time. And thoughts. Even now he was looking down at the front page and hadn't even finished the three-word headline. It was the hat. She looked so smashing in that hat. It was going to be a long, long, flight.

"Connie. Quit gawking. That's an order," said a smiling Skye. But Connie had just recognized who he was and with the light of dawn all over her face, she beamed.

"Bill. Do you know who that is?"

"No. Some TV star?" He didn't watch a lot of TV and they frequently had celebrities in first class.

"That's the guy we saw in Dulles…when was it, about a couple of weeks ago?" Was it only a couple of weeks? Skye thought. "We were ranking guys."

"*You* were ranking guys," Skye corrected.

"Right. Anyway, he was hanging by the gift shop and I showed Skye the perfect man for her. And this was the man. A faultless 10. And you said you weren't going to meet the perfect man for you in an airport. But God, Skye, were you wrong. He's the perfect man. Is he nice? Intelligent?"

"Tell me," said a beaming Bill. "Is he a 10 all over?"

"You two better chill out before we take off or the cabin temperature will never stabilize." Skye looked at her watch, a signal that a change in topic was in order. "Shall we board? Time to get this bird off the ground."

"Destiny!" sighed Connie, wedging in one more word before getting down to business. Bill nodded, took Skye's flight bag and they went on board.

No, Skye thought, not destiny. Not hardly. Actually, his job was to follow me. She looked once more in his direction and found he was staring at her. Flashing one last smile at him, she went to begin her pre-flight protocol.

Alex caught the smile and let it flow through his system. God, he liked watching her take command. When she talked, people around her listened. He noticed a very good-looking copilot take her bag. He half expected her to grab it back from him but she didn't. They looked relaxed together and seemed to have an easy rapport. He made a mental note to ask her about him. When she turned and smiled, he hadn't realized he'd been staring.

"Quite a dish, huh?" said the man seated next to him. There was one lurking in every airport waiting to make the person sitting next to him in the plane consider spontaneous sky-diving. If the man's ticket proved to be 6B, Alex would be forced to embarrass the captain by shooting a passenger in the head. He also had a gun in his briefcase, with special papers. He would use it.

"I wouldn't mind tasting it either. They sure do make stewardesses beautiful, like they have a stewardess farm somewhere. Except of course those dogs they have over at..." The man went on and on. Alex wondered at what point he should tell the moron that they're now called flight attendants and that the 'dish' he was referring to was his pilot. Asshole.

"Yes siree bob, I remember when we were flying home from Vegas, me and the guys from the club, and there were these two babes." Alex almost winced. "Well they were real friendly and knew we had a stash of fresh money in our pockets. I hear some of these tootsies are pretty easy. I wonder if that tall drink of water is looking for a real man? You know all of the boy stewardesses are fruity as hell."

They called for first class boarding and the man made no move to get up. Alex turned to him. He should really tell Skye and unleash her on this little piss ant, but she had a plane to fly. "The woman you're referring to is the captain of this aircraft and I suggest you keep your mouth shut. Her boyfriend owns a gun and is a real nut case."

The man's eyes went wide.

"A girl pilot?" He looked down at his ticket. "A girl pilot? What's that all about? Never should have given them the vote, that's what I've always said." And he turned to the woman on the other side of him to tell her what he thought of having a girl pilot. Alex smiled as he heard the woman slice him into little pieces.

He had to duck to get into the plane. Connie, positioned at the entrance, was working first class and couldn't wait to show him to his seat. Alex looked left and saw the love of his life expertly checking the instruments, talking in a low, commanding tone to the copilot. Even though no one on the plane knew of their relationship, he was absurdly proud to be her lover. Well, he thought as he looked at Connie's beaming face, almost no one on board. Some things you just couldn't hide from a perceptive woman. He returned her sunny smile with one of his own.

"May I take your jacket, Mr. ...?" asked Connie.

"Springfield."

"Mr. Springfield." Connie escorted him down the narrow aisle and took his jacket. Ah. The feel of beautiful material, she thought, as she ran her hand over the cloth.

"Call me Alex," he said, sitting next to the window.

"That I shall, as soon as we land and we're out of the terminal, Mr. Springfield. Our captain insists on strict protocol in the cabin. She can be a real stickler for procedure."

"An admirable attribute for a captain."

"Right you are. And we certainly want to keep our captain happy. May I get you something while we wait to pull away from the gate? A drink, a magazine, our captain's favorite flower?"

"A Scotch, the latest *Fortune* and..."

"The white gardenia."

Alex beamed and Connie nearly swooned. How did Skye stand the voltage? "And your name is Ms...?"

"Oh, you can call me Connie. And call me anytime. The call button on this aircraft is right there to your left."

She came back in a flash with his drink and magazine and he didn't see her again until they were in the air. He knew from his surveillance that she and Skye were friends. He shook his head. They were so completely different. Connie was short, open, outgoing, and bubbling over with words, thoughts, and expressions. The mystery continues.

At the moment they left the ground and the airplane lifted into flight, his body pressed against the back of his leather seat and his mind flashed to a picture of Skye in the cockpit. Her hands firmly on the controls, her eyes seriously assessing the instruments, her mind completely focused on the task. Competently bringing the giant machine and its human cargo safely up into its specific corridor. She was up there. She was taking the risk. She was meeting the challenge. And he was sitting back here totally, completely turned on.

Flying from an island nation meant they were almost immediately over water. There wasn't much out there to look at, so he just concentrated on the surreal experience of being in the plane his lover was piloting. A few weeks ago he had been sitting in his office, running his business and performing special services for the Justice Department. Not an average existence, but a relatively predictable one. Now his world was spinning as fast as this plane was flying. Everything felt new, different, exhilarating. He felt the pull of gravity, the sound of the engines. All that power was being controlled by the woman who just hours before had been naked in his arms, nearly incoherent with pleasure and weak from sated desire.

He loosened his tie and tried to think of something else, but then her voice, sensual and serious, surrounded him and she was saying something banal about the temperature and the destination and time in flight. But her low, seductive voice made it sound erotic. Shit. He was going to climax right here in first class. He drank his Scotch in one long swallow and wiped the sweat off his face. Maybe if he thought of the design of his new building. Let's see, how many stories? 36? Or was it 63? Christ! It wasn't working. Damn, why didn't she stop talking? And why was it so damn hot in here?

The older and blessedly silent woman sitting next to him, patted his hand. "Don't worry. This airline has never had a major accident. Maybe if you have another drink it will help you sleep. Then before you know it we'll be in Washington." She smiled at him with compassion. He automatically smiled back, but all he could hear was Skye's voice.

"...I hope you enjoyed yourself while in England and that you'll give us the pleasure of serving your needs again in the near future. Have a nice meal and sweet dreams. We'll see you on the other side of the Atlantic." No matter how professional Skye tried to sound, her honey-coated voice always came through as sensual and provocative as a woman on the other end of a telephone sex line. When she repeated her message in Spanish, then French,

Alex ran his hand over his face and nearly moaned out loud. He shifted in his seat. The pleasure of serving your needs? Was she talking to him? And why had she felt compelled to repeat the whole thing in French? Damn her.

The woman in 6B was able to get Connie's attention. "I believe this gentleman could use another drink. Make it a double, dear, and bring the same for me."

Connie grinned at them both, understanding his discomfort completely and loving him for it. "Do you need ice with that, sir?"

"A bucketful." He grinned back. When Connie brought their drinks, he sipped his and found it did help. That and a few deep relaxation techniques suggested by 6B. When he felt in control again, he settled in for a nice, pleasant chat with the woman who turned out to be a retired private investigator. She completely captivated him with stories of her youth and they both were a bit tipsy by the time dinner was served.

Later in the evening, Skye walked back to go to the lavatory. Connie had been giving her and Bill reports every half hour or so. It seemed he was being charmed by the woman seated next to him. Connie said they were having drinks, laughing, and getting quite cozy with each other. The last report was 6B had her hand on his arm and was flirting shamelessly. Short of ditching the plane into the ocean, Skye meant to put an end to this woman's fantasy.

When she saw that the woman was beautiful, but over 65, she swore that Connie was going to pay big time for this one. She walked slowly through the cabin not wanting to disturb the sleeping passengers. She saw Alex and his companion quietly chatting and nodded to him noncommittally when their eyes met. They lingered a little longer than she had intended and she almost ran into a man's elbow sticking out in the aisle before she deftly avoided it and went into the lavatory.

"Was that the pilot?" 6B asked. She was a P.I. for many years and could detect a connection when she saw one.

"Indeed."

"Now I see why you were a bit distressed earlier, dear. I think I'll try to get some sleep now. Did you want to visit the lavatory before I settle in?" She asked so innocently, he almost missed the subtle gleam in her eye.

"Yes, actually, very much."

Getting up, the spry older woman let him out. "I can certainly understand an urgent call," she chuckled. It was a delightful sound and a perfect backdrop to Alex's feelings.

He walked past the flight attendant's station and smiled in at Connie. She'd seen Skye go by moments before and got the message loud and clear. He waited outside the door until it opened and Skye walked out into the narrow corridor. 6B was the only one awake now and she was being discreet, so he put his arm out in front of Skye. She looked up and smiled. The vibration from the plane's engines sent little tremors though her body…at least she assumed it was the engines.

The aisles were very narrow and as they stood face to face, they were almost touching.

"Good evening, Sir," she said, smiling her International Airline captain's smile.

"So, who's flying the plane?"

"Oh my. I knew there was somewhere I had to be."

Connie was talking into the cockpit intercom. Suddenly the plane banked ever so slightly to the left and Alex, always ready when an opportunity presented itself, found himself pressed against her body. He could feel her heartbeat, reveled in her quick intake of breath. He braced his hands on either side of her for balance. "Must have wanted to get around a cloud."

"The only explanation." Their lips were only inches apart. His breath mingled with hers. His eyes held hers for a few seconds, then he stole a kiss from the captain of flight IA127. Just a brief, soft, infinitely sweet kiss. He straightened and said to her, "now I'll have sweet dreams."

Pushing herself off the cabin wall, she smiled and nodded. "It was a pleasure to serve your needs." Turning, she went back to the cockpit. Alex went into the lavatory feeling like an addict who just got his fix.

"Nicely done," said 6B when she got up to let him back into his seat.

"I thought so," he said as he settled in, closed his eyes, and dreamed of making love to Skye on a cloud.

"So, have you done the deed with that positively gorgeous man, yet?" asked Bill in the cockpit.

"Why is everyone so interested in my sex life?"

"Because, Captain, we didn't ever think you were going to have one. I personally told Connie that you might just be waiting for Mr. Right and she told me that was a fairytale and she prefers to have a 'mister right' now." He laughed heartily. His happy, carefree style was a great foil for her more serious, no-nonsense attitude.

"Just because I want to keep my personal life private doesn't mean I don't have one. Check the course and the heading, then call in the wind and sky conditions. That's a pretty solid bank of clouds over there."

"So are you going to answer my question?" asked Bill, doing everything according to her specific instructions, perfectly in rhythm with his captain. "Have you and Mr. 6A done the horizontal mamba?"

"Damn it, Bill. This is going on the flight cockpit recorder. Please check the fuel gauge and oil pressure." Skye's eyes were constantly scanning.

"Which no one will hear unless we're beyond caring," answered Bill.

"Oh, really. And you were saying you have been cheating on Carter all these years with that flight attendant from Northwest?"

"Hey!"

"And you don't wear underwear on international flights because of that awful rash?"

"Okay, Okay. I get the point."

"Don't worry, darling. Our one night of passion will forever be our little secret, as will the child we made. She'll be happy in the convent school where we placed her." Point made, score another one. Skye grinned.

"Doggone it, Skye!" exclaimed Bill, horrified. Bill never swore in the cockpit. He really didn't want his grandmother in Topeka to hear him cuss if the plane went down and the black box was recovered.

"No one will hear unless we're beyond caring," smiled Skye, tapping one of the instruments that seemed to insist on sticking. "Make a note to maintenance. The altimeter is possessed again."

"Just tell me and put me out of my misery. Carter will be pumping me for details the minute we get off the plane and he sees that look in your eyes."

"No. Now check the pressure gauges on the fuel and communicate our ETA to International," said Skye.

"Is that a 'no you haven't done it yet' or 'no you aren't telling me?'"

Skye smiled cryptically and didn't say another word.

"All right. You asked for it. I'm going to sic Carter on you directly as soon as we land," threatened Bill.

"You're scaring me." Skye did a little shudder and the flight data recorder picked up another chuckle from the copilot.

Several years before, Skye had introduced Bill to his partner, Carter. Carter had been Skye's date at an International Airlines holiday party back when he was still hiding his sexual preference. He was the marketing director for International at the time. Wickedly handsome, reserved, with a sharp wit, Carter was the perfect companion. They got to know each other because he was offered the job as the on-camera personality in a series of ongoing TV and print commercials for International Airlines after Skye had turned down the offer. He always said she was responsible for his celebrity status. His face was nearly as recognizable as a major movie star.

Skye smiled at the memory of the moment she knew that she was no competition for Bill. She'd introduced them and they casually shook hands. Then Bill flew into one of his manic gossip fits and had them both laughing until they could hardly stand up. By the end of the evening, she knew she was going home alone.

Carter and Bill had been together ever since and they both thought of her as some kind of pet project. Bill was always trying to fix her up with someone and Carter was always just trying to fix her. One was obsessed with introducing her to every eligible man placed in the 8-10 category, according to Connie's scale, and the other was forever pointing out how to dress for maximum impact or ways to manage her fly-away hair other than brushing it into submission, pulling it straight back, and spraying it down. Carter was the one who had her jumpsuits tailored to fit like a second skin. Remembering Alex's reaction to how she looked in them, she had to admit Carter was a genius.

Alex woke up as the flight attendants were coming around and handing out warm, damp towels. 6B looked perky and fresh, and was reading a novel with a man and a woman clutching each other and gazing with what looked like rapture, but could have been pain, into each other's eyes. He stretched, gratefully took the towel, and rubbed his face and hands vigorously.

"Youth," snorted 6B. "If I did that, half my face would come off and the other half would scare you to death."

He smiled at her from behind his towel and rubbed again.

"Allow me to let you out. You'll want to get all cleaned up so that lovely captain will be impressed. She came by while you were asleep. She thought I was too. Stood and watched you for quite a while. She'll give you many sleepless nights, my dear, but she'll be worth it."

"She already has, and she already is." So she watched him while he was sleeping. He filed that one away. Pleasure was definitely connected with that picture.

6B sighed. She just loved love.

Bill took the intercom and made all the appropriate announcements this time. Skye was busy with the tower. Connie came over and handed him his jacket and briefcase.

"I hope you'll fly with us again, Mr. Springfield. I'm sure you wouldn't want to fly United, unless it's with the captain." It took Alex a minute to register the meaning of the old joke. 6B got it right away and laughed out loud.

Alex was one of the first people off the plane. After going through Customs, he bid a fond adieu to 6B, then walked up and down the crowded passageways of the terminal to work the stiffness out of his legs. He knew it would take Skye extra time to shut everything down and go through her post-flight protocol. She hadn't even looked up when he passed the cockpit door on his way out of the plane.

He leaned against the wall near the exit from Customs, not wanting to sit down again for a week. How did Skye stand it? He looked around at the several clusters of people greeting passengers from her plane. His sweep of faces stopped on an incredibly handsome man leaning against the opposite wall, waiting patiently and reading a magazine. Nearly everyone who was on the plane had disembarked and made it through Customs. Who was that guy waiting for? He looked vaguely familiar. He was sure he had seen him somewhere. Of course. He was the pilot who starred in all the commercials for International Airlines. He didn't appear to notice as people stared at him when they walked by. His handsome features were impeccably groomed and he had a way of standing that was both relaxed and poised for action. He had an athlete's body—well toned, but not bulky.

Alex looked at the door again. He was sure all the passengers were off now. That left the flight crew. Maybe he was waiting for Connie. Then Connie came through and went directly over to a very tall man in the corner of the gate. Alex thought he recognized him too. Maybe he played pro basketball. The only people on the plane now were Bill and Skye. Mr. Commercial Man folded his magazine, stood up and looked down the tunnel expectedly.

Alex's eyes narrowed. He never thought that Skye might have someone meeting her. They hadn't discussed an exclusive relationship or where they were headed when they reached Washington. She certainly had a life before him and except for his presence in it now, it would be the same as before. He had just assumed. Assumed what? He knew little of her life over here. There had been no liaisons in Washington since he had been following her, but she had been consumed by this case. Her dossier certainly didn't list her current lovers. Maybe he was just one of many.

He straightened. To hell with that. If she was going to keep a stable and he was just one of her studs, then…then what? His testosterone almost pushed him into leaving. A man had his pride. He looked over at the stud by the wall again and frowned. Why did he have to be so bloody flawless?

Then he saw Skye and Bill enter the gate area. Skye looked like she just stepped out of a shower after a good night's rest, put on her pressed and polished uniform and was ready for a day of vigorous activity. Damn. She looked good. Fresh and animated. Like she was anticipating something. Or someone. He hoped it might be him. But he was making assumptions again.

Skye started to look around expectantly and spotted Commercial Man. She called out his name in a delightfully surprised voice and threw her arms around his neck. Carter, as she called him, put his arms around her, kissed her soundly on the mouth and then laughing grasped Bill's hand. He didn't take his arm away from Skye's waist, however, as the three of them chatted excitedly. He heard Phillip's name and saw Skye shake her head. Commercial Man kept his arm around her. Alex's attention seemed to narrow down to that arm.

Suddenly, Alex could feel his blood boil. He never understood that term until now. He was going red hot from the inside out. Not only was his lover fresh as dew, she seemed to only have eyes for that guy. She said his name with such obvious delight Alex wanted to thump his fist in his handsome face. They stood close looking very comfortable together. She almost looked relaxed, not all tense and bothered like she seemed to always be with him.

She chatted spiritedly with this Carter person as he reached over and straightened the wings on her uniform. It was far too close to her breast to suit him. This was no Phillip. He was constantly touching her. Goddamn it. Alex pushed himself off the wall in a rage. That Carter guy had just playfully touched her earlobe and patted her hair. That was his earlobe and his fucking hair. If she thought he was going to put up with sharing, she was delusional. He didn't share and she was going to discover she couldn't play with him like this.

Just then she turned and saw him. Her bright smile faded like light after dusk. She looked around alarmed. She saw his fury. What had happened? Something with the case?

Bill turned and saw him as well. He recognized jealousy when he saw it and tried to get Carter's attention. Carter was completely oblivious and still had his arm around Skye's waist. He had been telling them about a new restaurant he wanted to take them to.

"So," Alex heard the prick say. "How about I pick you up at 8 o'clock and we can check it out. Then you can stay over and go on down to Virginia in the morning."

Carter looked over at Bill who was making faces at him. "All right with you, Bill?" He had a deep masculine voice, the kind that was the favorite of commercial voiceovers. He couldn't decipher Bill's eye motions and jerky head moves.

Alex stopped in his tracks, his hands fisted in fury. Why the hell was this man asking Bill if it was all right? Was Bill Skye's lover, too? Goddamn her black heart. It made sense. They flew together frequently and come to think of it they were very, very friendly. Why the hell was everyone so casual about it? What had he walked into?

The expressions crossing Alex's face were really alarming Skye. Something was very, very wrong. "Excuse me Carter," she said and pulled out of the circle of his arm. "Let me talk to this man for a minute. Then I'll introduce you. Bill, why don't you fill Carter in on the excitement in London?"

Bill was going to fill him in all right, but it would have nothing to do with the situation in London.

Alex was close enough now to hear her. Now he was 'this man?' He was about to turn and leave before he tore someone's head off, when she put her hand on his arm. "Alex? Tell me what's wrong. Something with the case?"

She looked concerned, but nothing close to uncomfortable or guilty. Of course, why should she feel guilty? She made no promises. She wouldn't even tell him she loved him, damn her. What he just assumed was exclusive for him…her body, her passion, her desire…wasn't something she agreed to withhold from others. She was always up front that there was something she couldn't give him. Well maybe that had more to do with the fact that she'd been giving it to someone else. The thought of it ripped his heart out and left him bleeding into his gut.

He went from the agony of rejection to the hostility of betrayal and she just stared at him. He wasn't going to make a scene, but he wasn't going to leave without telling her what was on his mind.

"Look, Skye. Nothing is wrong with the case. This has nothing to do with business. It's personal. Very, very personal. If you can't understand what's wrong with this picture, then I'm going to have to think about whether or not I can live with this."

She was so confused she didn't even know what questions to ask.

She shook her head to clear it. "I have no idea what the hell you're talking about. I feel like I entered the theatre in the middle of a movie." She put her hand on his arm and could feel him pulsating with temper. "We can talk about this later when you've filled me in on the opening scenes. Can we postpone this little drama until you have time to debrief me? I want you to meet someone. More importantly, I want someone to meet you." She looked back at Carter and Bill. Then up at Alex. "Could you be civil for a few minutes, then I'll go with you to talk about what has you in a lather."

"Sounded like you and pretty boy were making plans for a little overnight stay. I wouldn't want to intrude," snarled Alex.

All Skye heard was pretty boy. "Pretty boy? You mean Carter? Well yes, I guess he's pretty, but you don't have to say it like that. Don't worry about him. I can meet up with him later. And it doesn't have to be tonight. He's flexible. He always has some idea or other. I have stuff over at his house in case I don't want to drive to Virginia."

Bill was filling Carter in on what he thought was happening and Carter was enjoying himself immensely. He was trying to decide just how to play it when Alex's sharp blue eyes pierced him. He said in a low voice. "This is really wonderful, Bill. He's absolutely right for her and it looks like he thinks so too. If looks could kill, I'd be in my coffin, headed for the Immaculate Garden for Eternal Rest. Holy healthcare. I hope I have my insurance paid up. Looks like he wants to pound someone. I wonder if I should tell him, 'Not the face. Not the face.'"

"All right…she's bringing him over. Now you can see what all the buzz is about," said Bill.

"I can already see. He's magnificent. And he's so jealous. Didn't like me pawing his girlfriend, huh? I wish I would have known he was back there. I would have squeezed her butt. Should I blow little air kisses to Skye?"

"I wouldn't recommend it. It looks like all that fuel needs is a match," observed Bill.

"Yeah. Come to think of it, she probably would have pounded me if I squeezed her butt," replied Carter.

"Hey. You're the guy who actually had a date with her."

"Yeah…well, that was when I was a bit more conflicted. Oh my. Now Skye is getting fired up. Maybe we should call 911. All that heat around all this jet fuel could be a conflagration ready to happen," said Carter.

"You mean fire?" asked Bill.

267

"Didn't I just say that?"

"Honestly, since you have been doing the *New York Times* crossword puzzle, your vocabulary has become almost unintelligible," answered Bill.

"Unintelligible. I actually think that one was in Monday's puzzle."

"I wish they wouldn't be so civilized." Bill nodded toward Skye and Alex. "It would be a lot easier to eavesdrop if they shouted."

"Honestly, Alex, what's your problem?" Skye was beginning to rally her own temper.

Alex had become the immovable object. He didn't want to get any closer to the grinning Carter. He would have his hands around his throat if he made one crack about Skye that was intimate or sexual. He knew it. Just an hour ago, he thought Skye was his. Or at least that as much of her as she was ever willing to give right now was his. And now? Well now he needed time and space.

Skye could feel him pull back. "Is it Carter and Bill?" Alex didn't seem bigoted, but some men were very petty about such things. It was starting to make her mad. He looked like he was going to clobber Carter any minute. She was very, very disappointed in him.

"And you think I shouldn't have a problem with them?" Alex looked from them to her incredulously.

"I really thought you were a better man than that." She put her hands on her hips and frowned at him, her brown eyes flashing fire. They were two of her closest friends and she wanted desperately for them all to like each other. She was confident they would. Maybe that was why she was feeling so disillusioned. And disappointed. She was hurting but she could feel the anger bubbling and ready to take over. She knew all this lover business was going to complicate her life.

"You mean you thought I would just accept it?" He could see the disappointment and disapproval in her eyes. When had she turned him into the heavy? How much was a man supposed to take and still be a man?

"Alex. Not all love affairs fit into your obviously narrow definition," she said like she was talking to a very naughty child. "And speaking of narrow, I can't believe you're so narrow minded."

Alex felt himself slipping. Jealous rage seethed through every inch of him…all the way to the top. She was going to drive him crazy. His lips could still feel the sweet goodnight kiss she gave them in the plane she was piloting. She'd watched him in his sleep. Now she was hugging another man and wanted to rub his face in it by introducing him? Damned if he'd let her. The fact that they were in a public place was the only thing stopping him from taking them all out.

Skye took a deep breath, pushed her disappointment aside, and looked him straight in the eye.

"Alex, listen to me. This is not the time or place to talk about this so I'll make it simple." She put steel in her tone so he would know that this was a nonnegotiable item and he got the message, loud and clear. "If you can't accept them and what they mean to me, then we absolutely have no future together. It will be business only. Only. Understand? I'll see you in the office on Thursday morning."

"You mean that?" There was a smoldering resentment in his eyes that would have frightened a less courageous soul.

"Yes. I mean that." He was hurting her so badly. Why was he doing this? It wasn't just that she wouldn't give up her friendships for him. It was that he was either so selfish or so intolerant or some combination that he wasn't the man she could have a deep and lasting relationship with. Her heart was being bombarded and big chips of it were flying in all directions.

"Both of them?" He could see the agony in her eyes. Why was she making him feel like a heel? She was the one hurting him.

"Of course both of them, you narrow-minded, intolerant, prejudiced son-of-a-bitch." She snapped as her words came out in a tumble of broken illusions.

Alex was far too angry to trust himself any longer. He absolutely knew he was going to hit someone if he didn't get out now. He could feel himself losing control. He looked at both men who had completely stopped any pretense of talking and were just staring at him. He glared at them in disgust.

"Skye?"

"Yes?"

"Go to hell." Turning, he walked down the corridor and into the nearest bar.

Skye just stared. She'd never been so hurt and disappointed by anyone in her life. How could she have been so wrong about him? She thought he was perfect once. Man, was she wrong. He wasn't even close. She'd let her desire blind her to his flaws. Now she felt like a fool. That was just another turn of the knife sticking in her heart. Or was it her back.

She could feel a lump forming in her throat and her eyes started to burn. No. She wasn't going to break down. He wasn't worth it. It was better that she found out now, before she got more deeply involved. Hell, she was already more deeply involved. But she was also devastated. She looked down. And he forgot his briefcase. She picked it up and looked around. She was miserable.

Carter and Bill came up and flanked her. "Sorry you had to witness that," she said unhappily. The wretched feeling of abandonment was creeping in. "I thought I knew him. I thought I could…well…never mind."

"He sure is over the top for you, gorgeous. He was hotter than hell on a holiday," chuckled Carter.

"It doesn't matter." She looked down at her hand lovingly rubbing the side of the briefcase. She immediately stopped, aghast at her feeling of loss.

"Shall we put her out of her misery, Bill," sighed Carter with a lot of compassion and a bit of laughter still in his voice.

"I think so, Carter. She looks like she's ready to jump head first into a jet engine."

She looked at the two of them and frowned. They obviously didn't know what she and Alex fought about.

"Go after him Skye. He's crazy in love with you. And you have his briefcase, for God's sake."

"Crazy is the word. I don't know what came over him, but I can't go after him." She looked at them, the misery on the surface of her face. "He wouldn't even come over and meet you guys. Bigoted asshole."

Bill and Carter looked at each other. "I don't think so," said Bill.

"He said he couldn't accept you in my life," said Skye.

Carter laughed out loud and the more Skye frowned, the harder he laughed.

"Did you hear me?" demanded Skye.

"Of course he wouldn't, you silly girl. He thought we were, ah…that I was…ah…well to start with that I was straight."

"But you're not!"

"He didn't know that," said Carter.

"But he was so angry and he said…"

"Can I put a different spin on this?" Carter asked. "I'm waiting by the gate. He sees me. I'm an Adonis. I'm man's image of perfection. I'm…"

Skye's lips quirked and there was a flutter in her stomach. Hope. "I get the picture."

"Okay. Then he sees you and Bill come through the door and you're all but pawing me in public. Kissing and hugging and throwing your arms around me."

"Pawing?" said Skye.

"Okay, petting. But to a jealous eye it would look like pawing. Anyway, you were being real affectionate to the prototype of male hunkdom," said Carter, his eyebrows raising, encouraging Skye to see a different picture.

"But we're friends. And you aren't interested in me that…" Her voice trailed off and her face brightened a bit. "He was jealous. The son-of-a-bitch was jealous."

"I think she has it, Carter," said Bill, his eyes dancing with humor. Carter continued.

"Then I say to you, do you want to come over and spend the night. Then I ask Bill if it's all right and boom. He thinks Bill gets a little action, too."

"Oh, God. Oh, God," said Skye, laughter bursting out of her. Her face transforming from miserable disillusionment to undiluted amusement. "Then I said he was narrow minded and I wasn't giving you up. And that I keep things over at your house so I can stay when I don't want to go home to Virginia."

"Oh, for crying out loud Skye. I can't believe he didn't go postal!" cried Carter.

"I think he was about to. He told me to go to hell. To hell!" Now she was holding her sides she was laughing so hard. "And he never forgets his briefcase."

Carter and Bill watched her enjoying Alex's state and began to feel sorry for their fellow male human.

"Okay. The only question is do we tell him now, or tell him later," she asked, trying to sober up and think.

"I saw him head into the Rusty Nail. He's probably drinking himself into oblivion right now," said Bill.

"I really should take him his briefcase," she smiled impishly. Her eyes met theirs and arm in arm they headed for the Rusty Nail.

Alex was on his third Scotch in ten minutes. A record for him. He was hoping to anesthetize the pain in his heart. Damn her. First she makes him fall in love with her. Then she gets mad at him and he has to win her trust all over again. Then she's more wonderful than any dreams he had of her. More than any man had ever dreamed of. Then bam. Right between the eyes. Whore. Bitch. Trollop. Did anyone say 'trollop' anymore? Why didn't anyone tell him about the Carter and Bill show? Nice looking guys, to be sure, but what have they got that I haven't got? Beside the fact there are two of them. He groaned and threw back the rest of the Scotch, motioning the bartender for another.

The man slowly walked over to serve him, trying to stretch out the time between the drinks as best he could. This was a guy on a bender and it had to be a woman. He looked behind Alex and saw Skye. Yup. A woman.

Could he share? His love was so new, but it was powerful. Was one third of Skye better than no Skye? Depended on the third he got. He snorted. He kept seeing that man's arm around Skye's waist. Could he share? Oh God, he didn't want to lose her. He ran his fingers through his hair. Most of the anger was gone and that let all the hurt in. Maybe in time she would dump the other two. Maybe they should talk. Work something out. He thought of her soft skin, her smiling lips, her beautiful brown eyes. He looked up in the mirror over the bar and his mind had conjured her, standing right beside him. He frowned. And he could smell her, too.

Then he felt her firm grip on his shoulder and looked at her long, slim fingers. Okay. He would talk. He would find out which third was his before he made a final decision. Turning around on his bar stool, he stared at her looking so unhappy, she took pity on him. No more teasing. No more misunderstanding.

"Alex. Did you forget something?" she asked in a soft, gentle voice.

"Yes," he said, a bit drunkenly. "I forgot to tell you I love you and I don't want to share. Choose just one and make it me."

"No. I mean some *thing*." She held up his briefcase and he looked at it. She was touched by his words and decided to store them away for later.

"That's my briefcase."

"You left it at the gate."

"Thanks." He looked at Carter and Bill. "Let's talk." They smiled sympathetically and nodded. The way they were all looking at him, he felt something must have slipped by him. He got off the stool and they went to a corner booth. Bill and Carter sat opposite Skye and Alex took the seat on her right.

Shaking his head to clear it, he said, "Sorry I yelled at you, Skye. I guess I am narrow minded, but it was more like I was making assumptions." He looked at Bill and Carter, obviously at ease with each other. "How do you two do it?"

"Do it?" They looked at each other and burst out laughing.

Alex didn't get the joke and scowled at them. They must both have an IQ of a zucchini. Combined. He looked at them and then at her. "What? You like them good looking and stupid?"

That set them off again and Skye joined them this time.

His mind, blurred by Scotch, fatigue, and temper, was just not firing on all cylinders. He felt like he fell into an alternate universe. These idiots looked like humans. Why weren't they acting like humans?

He turned back to Skye. He saw humor in her eyes. The mad was gone again. Good.

"Which third do I get?" he asked simply. Bill and Carter howled. Skye looked at her friends with indescribable relief. They were right.

"And when do I get it?" If he was going to be entertaining, he might as well go all the way. He felt his temper slipping again. Bill and Carter were wiping their eyes as Skye saw the thundercloud forming. She decided to enlighten Alex before he lost it again.

Skye took Alex's face in her hands and turned it toward her. Slowly, gently, she kissed his tight-lipped mouth.

"You're pouting."

"Damn right. I think I'll go out and find two women and we can have an even match."

Now she was beginning to get where the fury came from. She didn't like the thought of him with anyone else. Bill and Carter were just sitting back and enjoying themselves. Bill had his arm across the back of the booth.

She kissed Alex again, more persuasive this time, and he lost himself in desire. He put his hand around the back of her neck and deepened the kiss.

When they came up for air, they just looked at each other.

"Now that was hot," said Carter with appreciation.

Alex turned slowly and looked right into his fabulous hazel eyes. "I think we're going to have to renegotiate the deal here." His fist came down hard on the table. Fury and resolve were in his eyes.

Skye turned his face back to her. She looked him in the eye.

"Sober up and look at Carter and Bill. Here's a dime. Buy a clue. Your dense-o-meter is running." Sometimes Sloane provided her with just the right thing to say.

Alex turned to look at them. He leaned back in his chair and looked hard. Carter and Bill looked at each other, smiled, then looked back at Alex. The seconds ticked by and the night turned into day. Alex's eyes opened a bit wider, then looked at Skye. She was grinning broadly and she raised her eyebrows at him. He looked back at the guys.

"Are you saying that Bill and Carter are a couple and neither one of them want you?"

Bill and Carter laughed. "Skye, honey," said Carter. Alex frowned at the endearment, not quite ready to concede his original impression. "It isn't that you aren't desirable, sexy, and a real great package, it's just that, well, you don't have a chance."

Alex covered his face with his hands and leaned on the table. He tried to shake out the fog in his brain. He lowered his hands and gave them a sheepish look. Replaying the scene with this new script had everything falling into place much more to his liking.

"You're gay?" he asked.

"Yup!" they both said.

He shook his head again. His grin started slow and gathered momentum as it transformed his face and made his eyes sparkle.

"But neither of you are wearing purple. You could give a guy a sign." Alex was getting over the initial shock and letting all the relief flow in. He was feeling intoxicated, but it had more to do with release of the vise that had been squeezing his heart than the Scotch.

Bill and Carter laughed.

"Purple isn't my color. But let's see. How do we convince you, besides the obvious? It has to be persuasive, so he doesn't think we're a couple of straight guys conning him," Bill said as he looked at Carter.

"I talked Skye into highlighting her hair," said Bill.

"I have all of her uniforms tailored," said Carter.

Alex laughed. Bill and Carter joined him. "Okay. I'm convinced. Now, how about I buy you two a drink." They spent the next two hours talking, laughing, and replaying the scene at the gate. Alex, Carter, and Bill bonded instantly, now that there was no danger of them giving him competition with Skye. Each time they told the story, it got funnier, or maybe they were just getting looser. Skye, in her uniform and staying with Diet Pepsi, enjoyed the show. Bill went and changed out of his uniform so he could join in the wine draining ceremonies. The boys went through two bottles of wine and were on their third when a phone rang. Four people diving for their respective cell phones was the picture of the new millennium. It turned out to be Alex's phone, which they located after much digging. He straightened as he listened. Looking at Skye meaningfully, he said little.

"Well guys," he said when he rang off. "It's been a real pleasure, but I have a meeting and I intend to take Skye with me. Unless you two have a problem with that." They looked at each other and shook their heads in unison, smiling. "No problem."

"Then I'll see you next Wednesday at Fern Hill," said Alex.

"Sounds great. Skye, you going to be the fourth?"

"Not a chance. I don't play." She dug her car keys out of her purse. She was definitely the designated driver.

"Honestly, with your long arms, the arc on the club would be a mile. You could be a great golfer."

"You boys go ahead and chase a little white ball. I plan to take the Cessna for a spin. You two have a ride home?"

"We'll finish these and take a cab." She nodded and gave them each a kiss. Alex smiled this time.

They went out and took the employee shuttle to Skye's car. "Was that Jim on the phone?" Skye asked Alex.

"It was. He knew we landed a few hours ago and was wondering what the hold up was," said Alex, breathing in the cooler air outside to clear his head.

"Let's go report. Then I need some sleep," said Skye, finally yawning. Alex was beginning to think she was a robot.

"Sleep with me at the townhouse?" asked Alex, smiling. He had all three thirds of her and he was a happy man.

She smiled and nodded, "Eventually."

"Can I have my hello kiss now?" asked Alex. And it was almost ten more minutes before she steered the car toward Washington D.C.

CHAPTER 19

Skye's cell phone rang while she was processing more information on Juan. It had been over a week since they returned to Washington and her team was busy cataloging all the information they'd gathered in England. She'd flown back and forth to London twice and had virtually moved into the townhouse. Nothing official, just a gradual slide into his space. Alex was delighted and she was content.

More had come in from Columbia, including some fuzzy old photos. Skye was in Alex's large study, looking at the photos and sipping a cup of coffee. She was alone, wanting to wait up for him rather than go to bed solo. Alex had a business meeting, then a lot of legal briefs to review. He had neglected much of his work while in London, so he was going to do a marathon in his office.

"Skyler Madison."

"Skye?"

"Max?"

"Skye. I got something I gotta tell you. Show you actually." She didn't like the tone in his voice. It didn't have the usual brashness. It was like he was about to tell her something she didn't want to hear. Something that would hurt her.

"What is it Max? You sound stressed."

He chuckled at that. "Yeah, I guess I am. I need to talk to you."

"Sure. Shoot."

"No, I mean, well...could you meet me? I've got one more thing to check. Oh man, Skye. This is bad."

"Max. You're scaring me. Tell me."

"No. Meet me at my place in half an hour. Come alone, okay? We've got to talk this out before we do anything."

Skye went to the closet and got her jacket. Unlocking the desk she grabbed her gun and pushed it into the pocket. She thought about leaving a note for Alex, but figured she could call him if she was going to be late. Max sounded like he wanted this meeting to be just between them.

Alex would be furious with her if he found out she left the house. His security system was state of the art, so he went to his office only when she guaranteed she would stay in for the evening. Well, this breach of his security procedures was necessary. Max wouldn't have called her and asked her to come alone if it wasn't important. He could be her protection when she got there. Unless he was the traitor, a small nagging voice whispered. Well, if he was, she was armed and would take him into custody.

An hour later, Skye waited and paced on the front stoop of his house. It was so unlike Max not to let her know he would be late. A trap? It didn't have the feel of one. No prickly feeling in the nape of her neck. No feeling of something being off. She let her mind wander through the possibilities. Had he found out something about the mole? Did he want her to come alone and not tell anyone because the person she might tell was the person who was the traitor? The small voice that whispered that it might be Max himself pierced her heart.

She punched Linda's cell phone number to see what she knew about Max's movements. She didn't elaborate and Linda didn't ask for any explanation. It was common enough for Skye to be looking for Max late at night.

"He said he was going to the office to check out something on the Internet."

"Why didn't he use his laptop?" asked Skye.

"He would have, but he sat on it again and the LCD screen was cracked. Lard ass."

Skye laughed. "You know his ass is as tight as a bow. He's in great shape."

"Okay...then he's a tight ass," said Linda.

"I think I'll go over and see if he's there. Maybe he left a trail."

"Yeah, of cookie crumbs. Is it important? Is there something I can do? Shall I meet you there?"

"No thanks. Go on back to what you were doing. Maybe I'll just wait until morning." Skye wanted to tell Linda about Max's call, but she remembered the tone of his voice. She would keep it between them for now, but it felt horrible not to be able to confide in Linda. Could she be the mole? No. Max sounded distressed, but that would have sent him over the top. Still, she rung off without elaborating

Skye gave him fifteen more minutes, then went back to her car and drove to the office trying several more times to call, both Max's cell phone and the office number...no answer. She kept telling herself he probably lost track of time. Damn him.

Max had been working on the information they had gathered from the hidden room. Juan had left considerable evidence, they were sure of it, but it was very cleverly coded. He would have no way of knowing it hadn't been destroyed in the fire so he wouldn't be on the alert. No one but her, Jim, and her immediate team knew they still had the evidence. Max had been poking at it when she'd left the office that afternoon. What had he found? Maybe evidence identifying the mole. She suddenly felt cold. Maybe it was someone she knew. Knew well. Maybe that was why Max sounded so subdued. Almost compassionate. Like he knew what he suspected would hurt her. Or had hurt him.

Pulling up in front of the building, she was happy to see Max's car parked haphazardly in the lot. She looked up and saw the light in the office.

Bastard, she thought. He better have a good reason for not meeting me. If he was cruising through baseball scores and eating Oreos, she was going to kill him.

As she walked up the stairs, a creepy, tingly feeling started up her spine. It still wasn't like him to be late and not call her. Her cell phone had been on.

Then she remembered something else. When Max worked on the computer he did so without any overhead lights on. It was a quirky habit and one that drove her crazy. She kept telling him it was bad for his eyes and he kept telling her it gave him more focus and the colors were better, or something. She only half listened to him, but the why wasn't important. If he was in there working on the computer, all the lights wouldn't be on.

Instinct had her removing her gun from her pocket and taking off the safety. She walked quietly up the final flight of stairs and down the hallway. Everything looked normal but she kept the gun out in front of her, sweeping it from side to side, ready for any confrontation.

She entered the office, crouching low, and keeping her gun raised. Now she knew something was wrong. The door wasn't locked and secure and she couldn't hear Max. He always sang along with the tunes on the radio. He knew every word of every song from the fifties to the present. Oldies were belting out of the radio but there was no live male voice joining in.

Then she saw them. Two scuffed leather boots were lying just inside the inner door. Skye rushed over, sweeping her gun around the room.

Oh no! No, no, no! Skye's mind screamed the word over and over. The boots were attached to her man. Max was lying face up and there was blood. So much blood. Oh shit. Oh shit. His chest had three huge holes in it. She knew he was dead, but leaned over and checked for a pulse anyway. He was already starting to cool down. Her mind registered the fact that even if she would have come an hour earlier, it still would have been too late. Small consolation when she looked down at the open eyes and sprawled body of her friend. Her friend. Not just a colleague. Her eyes burned and her throat closed.

With effort, she took out her cell phone and left the office to make the call. Bringing the forensic team in for one of her own nearly broke her. This was now a crime scene and she had work to do. She would let the enormity of the loss sink in later.

She leaned against the wall, her knees unsteady. Oh God. Max was dead. She said she was going to kill him. That random thought shoved a dagger through her heart. She could hardly feel her fingers as they dialed. Steady, she thought. Steady. Go through the motions. Don't let it in. She called Detective Brighton from the Washington D.C. Central Division. She was their local liaison and would give it top priority.

She informed a shocked and horrified Jim who told her he would call in the team agreeing to let her call Linda. Skye steeled herself and punched Linda's number for the second time that night. Skye could hear the awful sound of Linda's ragged breathing as she tried to process what Skye was telling her. They were both working hard for control. Linda suppressed the sobs until she could be sure Skye was all right.

"I'm on my way. Are you in any danger?" asked Linda in a tight voice.

"No. I'm sure there's no one in the office. I'm going to search the perimeter."

"Oh my God, Skye. Wait for back up. Don't move from there."

"I'll be careful."

"By the book. Damn it, Skye, you wait for backup. Don't move." Linda's voice broke, and then became stronger. "You stay near Max, Skye. You stay with Max."

'Go by the book' Skye repeated to herself. The goddamn book. Secure the scene. Wait for backup. She cocked her head and listened. There wasn't a sound or a whisper of air moving. Fuck the book, she thought as she started walking down the hallway. If the killer was still in the building, she was going to find him. Skye methodically went through all the offices, the closets, even out on the balconies. She was conscious of the fact that people would be there soon to dust and search everything, so she minimized her contact with all the surfaces. Nothing.

She went back to the scene of the murder. It took all of her will and self control not to go to Max or at least cover him. She could hardly breathe from the weight in her chest. In her mind flashed images of Max's face. His smile. His expressions. His voice. That wonderful voice with the Brooklyn accent. All the pictures rushed into her head at once. She saw an empty bottle of Coke near his desk. She swallowed hard. It looked so totally undisturbed.

Then she looked down and noticed the big hole in the front of his computer. Whoever shot him, destroyed his computer as well. What had Max been looking at? What was he checking out? Suddenly cold with another realization, she looked over at the box that held all the backup disks. Gone. She knew all the original documents were back at central. Those would be safe, but all of her team's work up to this point was on Max's computer and on those missing backup disks. They would have to start all over again and it could take weeks to find the one thing that Max had obviously stumbled upon. Plus the killer was now on alert. If it was Juan, he now knew what they had and would be working hard to cover his trail...or eliminate it. And what if the mole could get to the originals.

She dialed Jim's number again. He was on his way to the scene. "Jim, Max must have found something important. The disks are gone and his computer is totally destroyed. First order of business...make and secure new copies of everything we brought over from London."

"Understood."

"We'll have Barclay and Lucas start working on it right away."

Jim hesitated.

"What?"

"I will inform Dan of their existence and have him assign the duplication and security of the original disks to someone else, Skye. Your team will be given copies only."

The thought of someone from her team doing this to Max would have broken her heart if it hadn't already been numb from grief and shock. She didn't fight him.

"Then I want Barclay and Lucas to go after what can be salvaged on Max's computer. It looks completely destroyed, but they are incredible with lost causes."

"Agreed. You all right, Skye?" asked Jim, his voice thick with compassion.

"Yeah. For now."

She cracked only once the rest of the evening. When Linda arrived, the steel in her resolve almost broke under the weight of their combined grief.

They sat in the lounge softly talking, holding each other, and laughing over Maxisms.

"Oh, Skye, I thought we had time," sobbed Linda as Skye held her. "I loved him. And I thought we had time."

"I know." Skye was finding it very difficult to breathe.

"And he knew. He would ask me out, we would get together and then he would call me China doll or something, and I would get mad and slam him. But he knew he was wearing me down. We were thinking about moving in together when this case was finished."

"He was a patient man and he was crazy about you. He loved you since we went through training together."

"I know," said Linda with one last shudder. "We just ran out of time."

When they both knew they could hold it together, they went out and joined the rest of the team. They wouldn't rest until they evened the score. Their colleague and friend had fallen in the line of duty and there would be no greater purpose in their life right now than finding his killer and finishing his work. They were convinced that one would lead to the other.

The forensic team was moving around the room when Alex's car screeched to the curb outside the office. He raced up the stairs and glanced around until he found the face he was looking for. Skye was right in the middle of the action. They had taken Max away, but the pool of blood was evidence that violence had been done here. Skye was conferring with a D.C. detective, who was intently listening to something she had to say. She was Special Agent in Charge tonight and she was one impressive sight. Even casually dressed, her air of authority attracted people to her to confer, share information, and ask for direction. Her team was all there, subdued, shocked and sad. Linda looked devastated. He went over to her and she gratefully accepted his embrace.

"I'm so sorry, Linda." He told her what he had sworn to Max he wouldn't repeat. He felt Max wouldn't mind at all. It seemed to help.

"Go to Skye," she whispered. "This is killing her."

Skye's eyes were filled with sorrow and there was blood on her clothes, but her face held only grim determination. She was holding everything in. She would turn the grief into anger and the anger into action. It was her pattern. And with each blow, she would build the wall around her emotions stronger and tougher. Skye felt his eyes on her and turned. She saw compassion and sympathy. She also saw that he was furious. Was it directed at her? Oh bloody hell. Of course it was. She hadn't called him. Excusing herself, she went over to where he was standing.

Alex stared at her. Sympathy for her loss was warring with a seething, burning anger. He couldn't explain why it was so potent but he would suppress it for now. It wasn't the place or time. "Skye. I heard. I'm so sorry. Do you know anything?"

"No. I'm at the stage of gathering all the information I can," her voice was soft, her tone impassive. "Then I'll look for patterns, relevant data, connections. There are many tracks. I'll find the one that will lead us to Max's killer. I need to get everything in before I can start to process."

God, that was cold, he thought. He could see her turning off and closing up. "Coming home tonight?" he asked, his tone beginning to take on its own cold edge.

She looked at him with dead eyes, then slowly shook her head.

"No. I'm going to stay here until we get everything set up. The sooner we start, the faster we get to our solution. We discovered more damage in the other offices. We're going to set up our headquarters in the conference room down the hall so Maureen, Lucas, Barclay, and Judy can start salvaging files, equipment, and computers the police have cleared."

Silence followed. Alex continued his internal war. Did she have to sound like a goddamn instruction manual? Only his compassion kept him in check.

"What can I do?"

"I'm not sure right now. I'll have something." She looked back at the crime scene. "I'll be working on assignments yet tonight. You may as well go home right now. There's nothing you can do here until the crime scene team gets all they can."

"Call me?" he asked finally.

"Yes...I'm...I'm sorry I didn't call. I was...it was..." Skye stepped back when Alex's hands came up to take her to him.

"Jim informed me. We'll let this one go." For now, he thought as she nodded and turned back to the scene...into the scene. The look on her face was both fierce and determined. Max's killer was going to be found. What scared him was that she was making this personal. That would make her not only relentless, it would increase her inclination to take chances.

When Jim arrived Alex pulled him aside to discuss the arrangements for Skye's protection. He hadn't wanted to admonish Skye about taking off without someone at her back while she was dealing with the details of Max's death. But the fact that she was in this building alone and the killer could have been present not only chilled him, it angered him. They decided on a 24/7 surveillance and Jim called in some of his best shields. When he felt

282

everything that could be done had been done, Alex went back home to begin his own hunt. He had taken Max at face value, trusting both Jim and Skye to know their man. Now he wanted to use his own resources to find out what he could.

Skye didn't come home that night and when Alex finally dragged himself to bed near dawn, he found he couldn't sleep well alone anymore. He kept rolling over, expecting to be enveloped in her warmth. Finally, he gave up and got up.

When the sun came up and she still hadn't called, Alex could feel his blood begin to boil. She hadn't left a message for him the night before either. When he arrived home from his office, he was frantic with concern. Skye was gone and so was her jacket and gun. Jim hadn't heard from her either and she wasn't answering her cell phone. Just when he was about to go out looking on his own, Jim had called with the news about Max and was surprised that Skye hadn't contacted him. Alex waited for Skye to do just that. When it was obvious she wasn't going to, he drove to the crime scene. He realized now that he was one of the things she placed willfully on the outside. Nothing got in.

By 8 o'clock he had just about run out of compassion and was plunging into resentment when Linda called. They were scheduling a team meeting for noon.

"Where are you?" asked Alex.

"I'm at my apartment. Skye sent us all home about 3 a.m."

"She still there?"

"I assume so. She asked that I call everyone. She's meeting with Max's family first thing this morning. To…to make arrangements and everything. Oh, Alex. I still can't believe he's gone," cried Linda.

"I know Linda. I'm so sorry. I know what you had was special."

"He was a pain in the ass."

"He would have been the first to admit it was his special talent. See you at noon."

"Alex?"

"Yes?"

"Find Skye. I've known her since we trained together. She's a hunter and she will not rest. It's her special gift, but it's also her curse. Her determination is something that will drive her, but it's dangerous. Alex, she has taken this all in and let none of it out. Find her, please. I don't have the strength right now to help her. You'll know what to do."

He hung up the phone slowly, chilled, hoping he was up to the task. Find her. Help her. Strapping his gun to his belt, he knew nothing was more important to him.

When he pulled up to Max's house a half hour later, he saw his intuition had been correct. Her car was there. He spotted with satisfaction the two agents stationed across the street and the one at the entrance to the property. When he approached, she took a defensive stance and asked him to present his identification. Even though he was impatient to go in and find Skye and was pretty sure she knew who he was, he took out his ID. She called it in, then nodded. The other two agents were out of their car and standing at the foot of the driveway. Alex decided he liked their thoroughness.

Walking around the brick path, he saw the back door standing ajar. Damn her. Like she was inviting someone in. Maybe that was exactly what she was doing. Putting herself into the path of the killer. Inviting him or her in. The hunter presenting herself as bait.

Alex found Skye meticulously, respectfully, and sorrowfully going through all of Max's things. Her face was filled with personal grief but there was plenty of fury there, too. He entered silently and wondered if she would have heard a brass band. He knew it wasn't fair to see her so unguarded, but he wasn't interested in fair at this point. She was the hunter and she would not rest. She was a hunter who would pour her soul into the task. It was up to him to be sure it didn't kill her.

She picked up, searched, and replaced with great care, all of Max's things. Alex knew precisely which items held memories for them both. She would touch them a bit more reverently. Linger over them a little longer. Alex's heart was touched. She loved him. Not as a lover, but as a brother. She'd let him into her heart and now he was gone. A small smile touched her lips as she looked at a framed picture he had on his desk. It was a can of coke. She turned it around, took it out of its frame, looked between the cardboard and the picture.

"Nothing," she said softly, sadly. "No clues. No secret messages. He didn't have time. He didn't know he was going to die." She turned and looked at him with haunted eyes. "I keep thinking maybe he left something behind. Something for me to find. I have this strong feeling."

"The heart of the hunter," murmured Alex. So she knew he was there all along.

"Huh?"

"Something Linda said."

"Oh, she called you about the meeting?" Skye picked up another framed picture. This was of a hot dog. Her movements were very slow now. Fatigued.

She looked tired to the bone. Her hands shook a little when she saw a Nancy Drew book sitting on the desk. The note stuck to the front cover said *For Jenny*. His favorite niece. Skye picked it up and closed her eyes against the intense physical pain.

"Have you slept?" he asked.

She shook her head and gently placed the volume back on the desk.

"Have you eaten?"

She shook her head again.

"Will you let me in?"

She looked at him and blinked some of the fatigue out her eyes. The guard was back up. Maybe a little chipped around the edges but firmly intact.

"I'm not hungry," she said ignoring his last question. "I'm meeting his family here at 9:30. I haven't seen his mom and dad since our graduation. They're flying in from Arizona. They retired there a few years ago. His sister's picking them up. She lives in Arlington." Her sentences were short and choppy, like a robot with a preprogrammed format. She picked up a picture of a woman with three little kids and a dog surrounding her. "Max gave them that dog. The dog's name is Max." Her hands shook again and she placed the picture gently back on the desk.

Alex simply didn't know what to do. He was brought up in a family where emotions where right out in the open. When his sister lived at home, there was weeping and wailing over the death of a hamster or a sentimental moment. And they didn't let his dad watch "Saving Private Ryan" without a box of tissues by his side, because he lost it every time. There was always laughter and loving and loud explosions and tears. Skye's reserved reaction was something beyond his experience.

"What can I do?" asked Alex.

"I have pretty much finished in here. You could take the garage."

"No. I mean what can I do for you?"

She looked at him again. Her face was unreadable.

"You can search the garage for me."

"Skye. I'm not going to search the garage for you."

She stared at him again. Nothing.

"Okay. I'll come by later today and do it then."

He started the mental process of counting to ten. To lose his temper here, in Max's home, on the morning after his brutal death would not be appropriate. Then it was like Max gave him a shove from the grave. He didn't even get to five and his anger popped the cork.

"Goddamn it, Skye. You can't do this alone!" he shouted.

Skye didn't act like it was unusual at all to shout in Max's den. As a matter of fact, a rotten attitude felt right at home here.

"I'm not alone, you moron!" she shouted back. "I have an entire team of people and the D.C. police department behind me. And what the hell are you so pissed off about!"

"Because you're standing there like a robot, hardly breathing, much less feeling."

"I'm not a robot you insensitive son-of-a-bitch. I'm working a case in an efficient manner," retorted Skye.

"You don't come home. You don't call."

"Oh for God's sake. You sound like some frustrated house spouse on *Days of Our Lives.*"

"*Days of Our Lives* doesn't have frustrated housewives anymore. They're completely out of vogue. They get multiple lovers."

"What the hell are you babbling about? You read that in your fucking *Wall Street Journal*?" shouted Skye.

"Why the hell didn't you call me last night?"

"Jim called you."

"That's not my fucking question. Why didn't you come home?" shouted Alex.

"I didn't come back to your townhouse because I was busy."

"You went somewhere."

"Huh?"

"You changed."

"I went to my apartment to shower and change. I didn't think I should greet Max's family with his…with his…"

She closed her eyes and started shaking. The forces of her emotions were gathering power and her will was weakened by exhaustion.

Alex was holding her before he knew he had moved. He could feel her violent shaking and tried his best to absorb some of its horrific grip on her body.

"Come on baby. I'm sorry." He murmured in her ear. "I'm sorry. Let some of this out, sweetheart. You can't keep it in. It will kill you."

She didn't say a word. She just moaned like she was in terrible pain. Her breath was coming in gasps. His heart ached for her.

He held her and kissed her and rubbed her back. He led her to Max's huge leather recliner and sat down with her in his lap. Not a tear. Not one tear did she allow to fall. The force of her will was making a comeback and was channeling the sorrow into fury. With one shuddering, gasping breath, she won the battle. Her breathing started to even out and the vicious shaking was reduced to a few weak shudders.

"This is why I didn't come to your townhouse last night." She never called it home. But that was something they would deal with later, too. Her eyes were too bright. Too big. Too empty. But at least there was some life back in her...he could feel it.

"I can't explain it, but I didn't think I could deal with Max's death mixed in with...with..."

"With what you feel for me?"

"I can only fight one battle at a time." Part of him was completely exasperated by her need to deny her feelings for him and part of him was elated that there were strong feelings there to deny.

"So, you feel you have to suppress your feelings for me and that doesn't leave a lot left to suppress the heartache you feel for Max."

He could feel her nod. He put it so well. "Just too much stress on the heart," she sighed.

"All right. I need you to come home. To stay with me. I need you period. So here's the deal. I'll lay off the love talk for now. Okay?"

She nodded again "I don't know how you got to understand me so well in so little time," she sighed.

"Because I..."

Skye raised her head and looked at him reprovingly.

"Because I...read a lot?"

"Is that where you picked up that tidbit about *Days of Our Lives?*"

"Skye, darling..." he started, then paused and looked at her. "Is 'darling' allowed?"

Skye narrowed her eyes. Then gave him a weak little smile and shrugged her shoulders. He took it as a good sign. Not letting the joy of this little victory show, he continued.

"Skye, darling, sometimes you make me so crazy, I don't even know what I'm saying. I'm sure I have no idea what anyone is doing on *Days of Our Lives.*"

"You can ask Hazel when you see her next. She watches it, tapes it, has her red hat ladies over, and discusses it. She's an authority."

"Is kissing allowed?"

Alex could feel Skye relax. This was going to work.

"I think kissing is required."

Alex pulled her closer to him and they shared a wonderful few minutes wrapped in the arms of Max's leather chair.

CHAPTER 20

During the next few days, the activity level was high. The team was determined to do their best by Max. His parents and his sister and her family were grief-stricken, but proud of their son and brother. Hundreds of people came to pay their respects. Several of his former students came, all grown up with memories and stories. He worked with the Big Brothers group and all of his little brothers from over the years were there. He specialized in taking boys with special needs. One in particular, who was hearing impaired, brought pictures of all the games they had attended. Linda and Skye remembered him well. When the young man was assigned to Max, they had laughed thinking that if he couldn't hear Max, he couldn't be corrupted by him. He was now a fourth grade teacher, just like his mentor, for a special school for the hearing impaired. Inspired. Encouraged. Skye looked at all the faces. Max's legacy was alive in all the people he touched over the years.

Alex stood with his arm around Skye through it all. She was reserved, respectful, and outwardly calm. Only Alex could feel the tension and see the anguish when she thought she was unobserved. When she delivered the eulogy, it was moving and fun, and poignant and sentimental. There was only one pair of dry eyes in the house as she stood tall and straight and captured Max's character and spirit through her carefully delivered words. Alex knew how much it cost her. She did it for Max.

As the days went by, her workouts became increasingly more brutal. She would run for miles instead of jog. She pushed herself until she fell into bed exhausted and numb. Often in the middle of the night, Alex would reach for her and she would come to him gratefully and passionately...losing herself and her misery in the rejuvenating feel of his body merged with hers. He would pour his energy into her. And she would lay for hours, awake, but restful in his arms.

"I'm taking a short vacation," Skye explained to Bill, Carter, and Connie. She was due for a little time off and she told them she wanted to explore her relationship with Alex. It was a good cover and one they not only accepted, but heartily approved of. She virtually moved in with Alex, although it was still his kitchen, his bed, his sofa, *his* place. They would drive down to Virginia to visit Sloane and Hazel and because she was a consummate actress, they only thought she was distracted by love. They were delighted by her somewhat preoccupied manner.

Bill and Carter loved playing with Alex. Sometimes Skye would come home after a run and find the three of them screaming their heads off at the TV or playing video games. Alex gave them investment advice, and they gave him 'how to handle Skye' tips. Since all three of them were clueless on that topic, no real insightful or working plan ever materialized. Skye just enjoyed hearing them bounce around the house.

Phillip and his Mum had been released from jail on bail, but the inspector called in periodically to report the progress of the case. More and more of their dealers were caving in and the elite users of the product were deserting the sinking ship like rats. The case was going well.

The D.C. police had few clues on Max's death. Some wanted to believe it was a random robbery gone bad. Some held the theory that Max was the mole and Juan shot him in a falling out. Max had called Skye to set her up, to ambush her and something went wrong. Maybe he changed his mind. Skye decided not to use this hypothesis as a possible scenario when developing her case. She had copies of all the crime scene photos and forensic reports, and would stare at the information for hours, trying to find a clue.

A week after the murder, Jim called a meeting of her team. It was unusual for the director to bring in everyone and facilitate the meeting himself, so they knew it was important. Skye and Alex arrived first, followed closely by Linda, Judy, Barclay, and Lucas.

"Anyone know what this is about?" asked Skye.

"Maybe they found out something about Max's killer."

"We'll find out soon enough."

Just then Maureen bustled in followed closely by Dan and Jim. This was going to be big, Skye thought, as she saw the grim look on their faces.

"I won't keep you in suspense," began Jim. "Please take a seat. This is about Max."

Maureen remained standing. In her arms were several folders. At Dan's signal she distributed them and explained.

"Dan and I have been working with Tower personnel on Max's personal computer, his laptop, and with the Washington D.C. police department on physical evidence." She stole a look at Skye and took a deep breath as if to steel herself. "I want to warn you before we go any further that what we have found is both disturbing and highly incriminating."

Skye looked at Jim. "You've reviewed the data?"

"I have."

"And..."

"I'll let it speak for itself." It was Jim's style to never sway a team prior to their assimilation and assessment of the data. He didn't want to influence their conclusions and perceptions by registering an opinion before they had time to formulate theirs.

"First, I want to show you the transcript of an email Max sent just before his murder. The address on the document is no longer in use. We're trying to track the receiver, but we have little luck in doing that kind of trace...we may be able to find a location, but even that is questionable." Maureen proceeded as she did in the courtroom. "Please look at Exhibit A." They all did as she requested. There were gasps of surprise, then the room went cold and still.

Everything is in order for Operation Freedom, and none too soon. My usefulness as your informant has come to an end. They are getting too close and the director's pet bitch isn't going to let this go. She's fucked her way to the top and now she's on her back with this new hot shot. He looks like he is going to fall in line and be a problem as well. No matter. I'm out.

I'm going to take care of that ball-busting bitch, then say farewell to her side slut Linda. God they were easy to play. I was always the best agent. Always. I just wish they could appreciate the amount of effort it took to keep from blowing their fucking faces off all these years.

I'll meet you in the Bahamas for my final cut, then I'm going to disappear. I just might buy an island and finish out my days seeing how many of the natives I can ride before I check out.

The team was stunned into silence.

"No. This isn't Max's style. Someone wants us to think so, but he didn't write this. This is how he talked, but this isn't how he wrote," said Skye, tossing the paper back on the table in disgust, her stomach in knots, her head starting to ache.

"There's more," said Maureen keeping her tone impassive and clipped. "Exhibit B is the bank accounts in the Bahamas that were traced to him and C, D, and E are what we found in his safety deposit box." They each paged through the documents. Huge balances in numbered accounts, phony passports, credit cards, and a one-way ticket to Nassau scheduled at 10 a.m. on the morning after he was killed. The name on the ticket was the same as the name on the passport and credit cards. Exhibits F through J were pictures of the interior of his car trunk revealing a disguise kit. Max was a master at changing his appearance.

"We think that he did indeed plan to kill Skye, then clean out his box at the bank on his way to the airport. There was also one hundred thousand dollars in cash in the box. As you can see, the passport picture has him blonde, bearded, and blue eyed. All the necessary materials for the transformation were in his car."

"This all could have been planted," insisted Skye. "We already know it's a favorite ploy of the mole...he or she tried it with me. That didn't work and neither will this. That picture on his passport could have been taken during one of our training classes on disguise."

No one else spoke. They were studying the documentation and letting Skye take the lead. Jim looked at Alex, and Dan reached over and took her hand.

"Honey, I know you were close, but you have to consider the possibility Max was the mole. He had the contacts to get these things done. He would have known how to play the angles. No one knew you better and could get around your usual instincts."

"I couldn't be that wrong," Skye's heart was breaking, mostly because a part of her was being influenced by the evidence.

"Is that ego talking?" asked Jim in a controlled voice. He wasn't sure what he was prepared to believe, but the physical evidence was strong and persuasive.

"No, it's Special Agent in Charge Madison talking and I'm going to find Max's killer. First to put him away, and second to clear Max's name. This is hideous. He didn't die to be a fall guy for the real mole."

"There's more." Dan looked stricken, but he pulled out a folder and laid it in front of him. "I'm not going to show you what's in the folder. Until we have conclusive proof that Max was the mole, I want to assure agents their privacy even after death." He looked at Jim. "We accessed his personal profile containing all the psychological testing we require and had three independent forensic psychologists look at it in the context of...well betrayal, anger, loyalty, and possible instability. They were unanimous. Max had a problem with authority and with...well," Dan looked both uncomfortable and terribly sad. "With women in authority in particular. They feel that if…that's still *if,* Skye," he said when he saw her expression. "If he was the person who betrayed this department and wrote that email, it would have been because of his jealousy of your success, of having for his entire career been outshined and beaten…by…ah…a woman. His ego was his Achilles heel. Everyone has one and the psychological profiles tell us what they are. His anger and resentment would have been directed at you, Skye. Specifically." He looked at Linda who was too shocked to react. "And he would have reveled in his ability to…to, oh hell…seduce another strong and capable agent."

"You led them and contaminated their findings by setting the context," Skye countered.

Judy found her voice. "He was a little chauvinistic at times, Skye."

"He could be a narrow-minded asshole," said Maureen who had never forgiven him for calling her babe when they first met.

"Some would say it was part of Max's charm," Skye snapped back.

Linda came to her feet slowly. "I think we would all agree that charm and Max in the same sentence is a real stretch, Skye. Max could be an insensitive, opinionated, tactless boor," she looked at Maureen and gave her an achingly sad smile. "A narrow-minded asshole. What those three forensic psychologists missed, however, was the multidimensional man…they missed the part of him that can't be defined, described, and analyzed. He knew his flaws, his shortcomings, and his impossible ego…and he worked hard to be a better man…every day. Max was a work in progress…and I sincerely believe the strong women around him were the reason for his growth, not his destruction." She looked around the room, her eyes dry and burning, her voice just above a whisper. "So are you going to believe what you know in your heart and gut, or are you going to accept the fucking evidence?"

There was complete silence in the room.

"Well, he did kind of grow on you after awhile," said Maureen swiping angrily at a tear she had allowed to escape.

"And he was just sort of rude to everyone…kind of an equal opportunity asshole," added Judy.

"So…who are we talking about?" said Lucas as he looked up from his printout and opened the file Maureen had placed in front of him.

To Dan's amazement, the entire team burst into gales of laughter. Purged and energized, they all got to their feet. "Let's go catch a killer…and find a slimy, gutless, half-assed traitor," Skye said and they all filed out leaving the folders lying on the table.

Dan looked at Jim after they had left the room. "Do you think they're in denial? The evidence is pretty compelling."

"Dan. I liked Max. Very much. But I sincerely hope that it turns out he was the mole, because if he wasn't, then it's very likely it's one of those people who just walked out of here. I don't see that as any less devastating to Skye. Or any less dangerous."

Skye reassembled her team in the new space assigned to them and they attacked the evidence with renewed determination. Over the next few days, they spent countless hours on the original investigation trying to recreate Max's breakthrough. Barclay was their best bet for that early break. He worked 24/7 to try to reconstruct what was on Max's computer. It was painstaking work. Without Max's usual banter, the room was subdued and quiet. They were all pushing themselves to the point of exhaustion. Linda came back to work, even though Skye gave her the option of taking some extended personal time. They all had one purpose now. To find Max's killer. All other reasons for their work were secondary.

Barclay had been working on Max's office computer. He'd just finished a delicate round in the sterile room and Skye was looking at what he'd found. It looked like nothing to her.

"I don't know if these are file names or codes. I did uncover that one of the last searches concerned something about a password. He must have used it because he went another layer down. That's where I got all of this," said Barclay.

"These lines could be file names or codes? All it looks like is a long string of letters and x's. Mostly x's," said Skye.

cxxrmsxxxuesoxxcloxkstaxxxxsexignxxsterioxxclxxsxadxxxungaloxxxcre txxkxwistexxraxsheelsxaxxwordxxxeglxnmxstxxywhixxxringrexlilaxhidd xnalxumxxxdyboxxrixxelxxxjxwelcluxxxppixgtxuxk

"They are. There are big gaps in the data. That's what the x's represent. There had to be more, a lot more. But I couldn't get any more than this. Sorry, Skye. These remaining letters could be random or they could have been words or phrases. First we've got to get the file names. Then I'll be able to work my way back. The file names are the critical door."

"So if we can figure out what these letters represent, we can open the door?"

"All we have is a shadow of some of his work. If they were the names of the files, they were located behind multiple codes and passwords. The disks we are working on were much more sophisticated than Phillip's work…the difference between kindergarten and a graduate course in advanced quantum physics." This had been Barclay's favorite course, but he knew many people would avoid such a thing. "I taught Max how to work the system. He was looking for a key, a pattern."

"Like a cryptic device. Know the key and you can unscramble the code," said Skye.

"Exactly," responded Barclay. "It looks like Max may have found the key and was experimenting on some of the files. He was a smart guy, Skye. I know everyone saw the smart mouth first, but he had an incredible memory."

"I know," said Skye, tightly.

"The damage to the computer jumbled the words and phrases. It's going to take me weeks to see if there's any cryptic pattern. My problem is I'm sure there are missing parts. Letters, words, maybe whole phrases. If we only had the key."

"What kind of things are keys?" asked Linda.

"We're not necessarily talking about a sophisticated process. It would have to be something accessible to all the parties who would need to unlock the files. In other words, something that would make some sense to the person setting it up. Random words and numbers are too difficult to remember. For example, if I wanted the two of us to be able to communicate and I wanted to lock the door to everyone else, we may get together and say American Presidents. Then our key would work through the names of the presidents."

"But if anyone saw the pattern…the names of the presidents, it would be pretty simple to open the files," said Skye.

"True. But there's another step. You would scramble the names in some kind of random fashion…front to back, numbers to letters, letters to numbers. I could crack that in no time. The brain is a logical instrument and even when we think we're being totally unpredictable, we aren't. That part's not as easy to explain. That's where you trust me to do my job."

"You're the best," said Skye. "I don't need to know how you work to know you'll get it done." She stood up and stretched. "I'm not even sure how the TV remote control works, but I trust it to change the channels."

"Well, you see, the technology is relatively simple…" said Lucas, looking up from his desk. He had been working to reconstruct the hardware.

"That wasn't a question Lucas. Let me think it's magic," said Skye.

"Cool. It's magic."

"Right."

"Now get me the key and I'll make magic," said Barclay.

"Fair enough. Is that the list of words?"

"Yeah."

"I think I'll go flying. That will help me think. I can process my random thoughts better," said Skye.

"Like a computer."

"Precisely."

"Have a good flight."

Alex walked in just then. "Going flying?"

"Yeah. I need to think."

"Need a lift?"

"Sure."

"Then can I watch?" asked Alex.

"Watch what, exactly?"

"Watch you take off. It really turns me on. Knowing your hand is on the throttle. Lifting off. Leaving the ground. God it makes me hot just thinking of it."

"You're sick."

"So sue me."

"I can't. I don't know a good lawyer." She gave him a wicked grin and got into the front seat of his truck.

Skye did her preflight check, then taxied on to the runway waving to Alex. He was leaning against the truck, his hands in his pockets, looking for all the world like a fashion model on a shoot. Her heart melted as she took the yoke in her hands. She flew by instinct, like a bird. Good thing because her mind wasn't strictly on the instruments today.

He was looking at her thinking she belonged in a different age. When aviation was in its infancy and men and women flew from town to town strictly by visual landmarks and performed daredevil shows and ran cross-country races. Biplanes. Barnburners. Fearless pioneers in love with the sport. Today, it was a means of transportation. Back then it was a love affair with the air. Yes, Skye was a throw back to that age. She was an intuitive flyer. Not a commercial pilot today. She didn't just fly the plane, she felt the plane. And he was completely infatuated with the notion.

He watched as she lifted, banked, and waggled her wings. Then he drove back to the city to get to work. He saw the agents at the airfield. Diligent and ready for danger. They would make sure she got back to town safely. No one had gone after Skye since the incident in the alley with the four thugs, but he wanted to be sure she was secure.

It was a glorious day for flying. Skye decided to take the plane inland. She often would fly out over the ocean, but today she felt like heading west.

When she'd achieved altitude, she trimmed her wings and relaxed. Looking out over the land far below, up to the endless blue sky, she opened her mind. Taking the paper with the hodgepodge of letters out of her pocket, she stared at them. The x's represented spaces that could have been letters, but may not. They may have been spaces between letters.

cxxrmsxxxuesoxxcloxkstaxxxxsexignxxsterioxxclxxsxadxxxungaloxxxcre
txxkxwistexxraxsheelsxaxxwordxxxeglxnmxstxxywhixxxringrexlilaxhidd
xnalxumxxxdyboxxrixxelxxxjxwelcluxxxppixgtxuxk

With the pattern planted in her mind, she went back over the case, inch-by-inch, fact-by-fact. She'd been flying for over an hour when she suddenly sat up straight. It was like a light bulb went on. Literally. Like a damn comic book light bulb went on over her head. Something in her brain clicked. Then other flashes. Other conversations. Other clues. She could see it. Hot damn! She knew what the key was and it made perfect sense now why someone wanted her off the case! Her specifically. Turning the plane, she headed for home, anxious to put it all together. Excitement surged through her veins and there was a satisfying sense of exhilaration. They were going to put this all together and get the bastard who took down Max.

Suddenly all hell broke loose. She could feel the yoke buck and jump violently. Her engine was making popping noises and more alarmingly, her foot controls were unresponsive. She was cool as she looked over the land below. Taking a deep breath, she cleared her thoughts. Then the engine died completely. Her plane had just transformed from a motorized aircraft to a glider without power. Okay. She would have to land without power. She had wings and the altitude gave her time. Time to think, time to plan, time to locate her spot.

Skye scanned the horizon, instantly assessing and calculating. Her mind was clear, her hands steady. The complete silence was a bit unsettling, but strangely powerful. It was challenging her. Panic, the silence screamed. Be afraid. A smiled parted her lips. It was her against gravity and as formidable as gravity was, she was going to win the battle. She reached for her radios. They were still working just fine. Chalk one up for birdwoman. She quickly assessed what controls she did have. She had no way to get to any airport and land safely, so she opened the frequency for emergencies only.

"Mayday. Mayday. This is Cessna N6657U. I'm flying without power and without ailerons. I'm declaring an emergency. Please be advised. My current altitude is 7000 feet and position," she looked over at the Global Positioning Unit that was not working. She looked out for a landmark. Nothing. She grabbed her father's old beat up compass. She never flew without it...damn the ground was coming up fast. "I'm approximately 25 miles due west..."

CHAPTER 21

Linda, Barclay, Alex, Lucas, Maureen, and Judy were pacing in the office. Skye had called them from the Crane Medical Center and told them all to stay put, she was coming in. All they knew was something happened and she'd declared an air emergency.

"What could have happened?" asked Lucas.

"I saw her take off and nothing seemed to be the matter with her or her plane," said Alex anxiously, telling himself that if she was making phone calls, she had to be all right.

They all looked to the door when they heard Skye taking the stairs to the office two at a time. She came roaring in, filled with kinetic energy and adrenalin. Looking at their concerned faces, she smiled a cocky, brash smile.

"The son-of-a-bitch broke my plane and grounded me. When we catch up to him, you're all going to have to stand back and let me take the first shot. And we're going to get him, because I think I've found the key. Give me some alone time and I'll bring you what you need to nail this guy's ass."

"Before you do any ass nailing, do you want to tell us what happened?" Alex stood up, doing a visual inspection. She was dirty and the elbow of her shirt was ripped, but no signs of any blood. The tiniest scratch on the top of her hand seemed to be the only injury. For the first time since she called in, he relaxed. "Sit down and take a minute to fill us in. We've been pacing ever since you called."

"Can't sit. Too fucking wired. You should have seen it." Skye was pacing. Her arms moving all around. "No power. No controls. My aileron wire sheered off. I was wrestling with a dead bird. But she's my sweet, sweet baby. She took me down. Of course when you're 7,000 feet off the ground, there really is only one way to go. I still had a little bit of control in my rudders, those wires stayed with me until I hit the ground. And damn. We hit hard. I would have been able to pull it out, too, but the goddamn farmer put a goddamn fence right in the middle of the goddamn field. Flipped me right over. Shit. I could see the horizon looping through the windscreen. Just like

299

when I do the loops in the air, except I was on the ground. Sheered my wings right off. Linda, get me a Diet Pepsi, will you? I need a drink."

"Sounds like you really got off on it. Makes me wonder why you didn't do this sooner," said Alex wryly, covering both his relief and his horror.

"Well. You know what they say. Any landing you walk away from is a good landing," said Skye.

"Is that what they say?" asked Linda as she handed the glass to Skye. Her hands were shaking and the ice made clinking noises on the side of the glass. When Skye took it from her, the little noises instantly stopped. Skye's hands were rock steady.

"So did the farmer pull you out of the wreckage?" Barclay asked, sitting down. Skye was his idol and he always liked to listen to her exploits. Gave him a voyeuristic rush. Not that he wanted her life. He liked his nice safe existence just fine.

"Sure as hell did. Scared the shit out of him, too. I had to apply maximum leg pressure to get out of the cockpit. I was kind of hanging from my seat belt. My dad used to say, fly it until the last piece stops moving. Well, he would have been proud of me today!" She took a long swallow of her Diet Pepsi. The image of the barn burning, daredevil fliers of old flashed into Alex's mind again. All she needed was a leather cap, goggles, and a long white scarf.

Then suddenly there were tears in her eyes. She realized what she'd just said. Mentioning her father was something she rarely did. As a matter of fact it was Alex's influence, she was sure. He was always so comfortable talking about people in his life who had passed away. Damn, what was wrong with her? The tears were gone as quickly and quietly as they had appeared.

Everyone in the room pretended not to see them. They knew why they were there. She'd inherited both the plane and the love of flying from her dad and he hadn't been with her for fourteen years.

"The asshole is after me. Me personally. At this point in the investigation, there's no point in getting the Special Agent in Charge. There's something in my brain he or she doesn't want to come to light. Mine." She tapped on her head for emphasis. "I thought it might have been something I saw or uncovered in England. Something that Phillip said or did. Maybe something Max and I knew from training or cases we shared. I've been racking my brain for days."

They looked at each other. No one wanted to remind her that it usually took weeks, sometimes months, to uncover evidence, make connections, and draw probable conclusions. There was a whole unit back at the department headquarters specially trained for this deductive function. Skye was always so impatient. She also had a great track record of being faster.

"We're going to get this fucker now!" She was on a tear, pacing, and sipping. "First he tries to discredit me within the department. Nothing too direct, just a bunch of sneaky ass attempts to get me pulled off this case. Then the shit sends some goon squad that couldn't take out a carload of senior citizens. Then there was that car incident in London, but that was so lame it hardly bears mentioning. Then Max, and now my plane. Well, he's cooked now."

"What car incident?" her team said as one.

"I'll tell you later. Like I said, it's hardly worth mentioning. But now…now he has sabotaged my plane. I loved that plane. Plus, until the NTSB determines that it was deliberate, I'm grounded."

"That's a relief," said Lucas under his breath.

"I've never been grounded for anything in my life. It's like half my soul has been put into a cage."

"But if you got the plane down successfully, how can they ground you?" asked Judy.

"Routine. Officially it's a crash."

"A crash!" Judy exclaimed. They had all been picturing a soft landing and maybe a little flip. Like a carnival ride.

"Well, it was a bit hairy," she continued, dismissing the horrified looks on the faces of her team and the cold distracted look on Alex's face. "Anyway. The NTSB will ground me until they clear me. I'm sure getting sick of this pattern of having to be cleared."

"That shouldn't take long, should it?" asked Linda.

"Not with Jim's contacts. But I'm going to ground myself regardless until we get this case cracked, so let's get going on these disks and papers."

"Ground yourself?" asked Barclay.

"I'm not putting any souls under my protection in jeopardy because some Cretan has a bug up his ass and wants me to die. So I'm on the ground until this brain barfs up what someone is so anxious to hide. The fact that I'm grounded could work in our favor. If I can't fly, I can work on this 24/7."

She stopped pacing for a minute. "The mole made a big, big mistake. If he or she had just settled in and let it lie, I might have taken my mind down a different track. But this is personal. He's after me and what I know. This is good. Since I take my brain with me wherever I go, I can work on it all the time. I'm going to go back to the beginning through my personal journey on this case. Then I'm going to tie in this fucker and when I do his balls are mine. I'll be in my office."

She went in her office and slammed the door.

"Ohhh. Now he's done it. Before she was determined and focused. That was bad enough. Now he has really pissed her off. He's going down, whoever he is. Hard. And soon," said an awed Judy.

"Anyone know about a car incident in London?" asked Alex in a cold, controlled voice.

They all looked at each other and shook their heads.

He slowly rose and walked toward Skye's office. He opened it and walked in, closing the door with deliberate care. No slamming here.

"Excuse me. I think the Special Agent in Charge is going to have to barf up an explanation as to why her team wasn't informed of a potentially relevant incident," said Maureen.

They all looked at each other, and in memory of Max, the pool was defined and wagers were made.

Alex walked in and caught Skye in mid pace. She was going to wear a hole in the rug, but by Christ, she was going to remember what her adversary was trying to cover up. It was in her brain. That meant it was accessible to her. He was hers now and she just needed time to find the right track. And she needed to be alone to do it. First, get the key, then get the guy who tried to put her into the ground. She was staring at the paper in front of her and muttering.

She frowned over at Alex.

"What do you want? That door was closed. I have to be alone to think."

"It's important." If she hadn't been in a temper, she would have seen the look of controlled anger in his steely blue eyes.

"Okay. What?"

"How come neither I nor any member of your team has seen a report on a car incident in London?"

"What the hell difference does it make now?"

"Exactly. Had we known about it earlier, we may have been able to interview witnesses, get some forensic evidence."

"There were no witnesses. Except about 25 garbage cans that flew in every direction. The paint samples were from a 2002 Lincoln. The license plate number was NS179746. The car was located at Heathrow. Since we already had very heavy security there, I figured we were covered."

He just stared at her.

"What! I'm a trained agent and as Special Agent in Charge, I decide what is relevant. To have pursued that line of investigation would have been distracting and fruitless."

"And Jim might have pulled you off the case and placed you in a safe house." They both knew the real reason she kept her mouth shut.

"Well there was that. Drop it will you? I have work to do."

Alex took Skye by the arms and shook her. "You'll never, ever withhold this kind of information from me again."

She brought her arms up swiftly in between his and pushed out violently, breaking his hold, then turning and planting a foot in his stomach, she sent him into the filing cabinets.

Her team heard the crash from the outer office.

"Hand to hand?"

"Definitely."

"3 minutes, 17 seconds. Barclay is the winner!" Barclay never won the pool. He always selected times and days totally at random. He was delighted. Wanting to press his luck, he suggested. "Shall we go another round and bet on when he exits, how he exits, and maybe if he exits at all?" They all cringed when they heard another solid crash.

"I think maybe you better quit while you're ahead. Let's see what we can find in these files. Then send them over to Geek World."

"Hey. I resent that," said Barclay.

"You get to take the information over."

"Hot damn. Let's move it." Barclay loved Geek World.

Alex had Skye pinned to the wall. They were both breathing heavy. Her eyes were the deep dark chocolate color that indicated rage of the highest order.

"I'm Special Agent in Charge. I make decisions based on my best judgment every day. I'll only tell you what I want, when I want," she hissed, struggling against his cast iron grip. "And the only reason you're still standing is because I need your expertise."

The fact that he had her effectively incapacitated, with little hope of escape made him laugh at her bravado. She really was fearless.

"You withheld information for your own personal reasons. Your protection is my job. Had I known about this incident, you may not have been in the air today. We may have taken added precautions with your plane." He pinned her hands above her head when she tried to use them. "You obstinate, stubborn, thick headed…"

"My point exactly. You would have restricted my movements. I won't be caged," she interrupted.

"Fuck that." He shoved at her again.

"Fuck this!" She stomped on his instep, spun and caught his chin with her elbow, then grabbed his arm and with leverage and strength born from fury, she flipped him into the center of the room. He didn't lose his grip on her hand, however, so he brought her down with him and rolled over on to her. This time he had her pinned to the floor and wasn't going to let his guard down again.

"You're not only the SAC, you're my lover. And as such I have a right to know when the body I love has been a target," shouted Alex.

"What?" she spit out indignantly. This was just about the most ridiculous thing she'd ever heard. "This is an office of the Justice Department. This is not your bedroom. Get the hell off me and show a little respect for the job. Show a little respect for me."

"I'll let you up if you promise to keep me informed of everything, Special Agent in Charge." He really liked the wiggling. She was beginning to feel his response. She ceased wiggling immediately.

"As a professional courtesy. Please." He lowered his head and kissed her neck. "I do respect you. More than you know." He kissed her throat. "But darling, I also love you." His voice started to lose its anger. He was running out of irritation and moving into exasperation. "Do you know what that means?" His voice was husky with emotion and his eyes went the color of the sky on a cloudless day. Her favorite color. She melted. He felt it.

"Means you come in and beat me up?" she said, kissing his lips as they made a pass over her face.

"No. It means that what happens to you, happens to me." He looked directly into her eyes. Into her heart. Into her soul. "That I know you understand."

"Low blow." And what was worse, she knew he was right. And what was even worse than that he knew she knew he was right. She nodded slightly. That was okay for now.

"No lower than stomping on my foot," he said changing the mood before he ripped off her clothes. "It hurts like hell."

"Want me to rub it?" she said sweetly, a smile forming on her lips. The storm was over and he could see the sun peeking though. He felt it was now safe to let her go. He did so, but she was no longer inclined to get up.

"No. That would make my crotch jealous."

"I could hit that again on my way up."

"How about we finish this tonight?"

"Are we into the making up phase of the program?" She put her arms around his neck and drew her to him, turning her churning temper into desire and pushing it all through her lips into the kiss.

"Most definitely," he said and lost himself in another passionate kiss.

Linda held up her palm. "All quiet.

"Either one of them is dead or they're making up."

"We'll know soon enough. If you hear an ambulance, go unlock the door."

When Alex came out of the office five minutes later, they were all very busy not looking at him or Skye. They were far too busy to see Alex limping slightly and Skye's hair coming out of its clip.

From all the suppressed smiles in the office, both Skye and Alex knew precisely that they had been the targets of another pool.

"It was a draw," Skye said simply and calmly closed the door.

Linda looked up at Alex. "Nothing like a bit of physical exertion to even out a temper. Need some ice?"

"I can get it," said Alex.

"Okay."

"And I think we'll watch the Special Agent in Charge more carefully from now on," said Alex meaningfully. Her team nodded, then he filled them in on the London incident.

"We'll all take shifts on that duty," said Linda. She was determined not to lose another friend.

"I'll take the midnight to 7 a.m. shift," said Alex.

"Oh, man," said Barclay, still euphoric over his windfall, "I wanted that shift."

"Shall we arm wrestle for it?" asked Alex pleasantly, knowing he outweighed Barclay by seventy-five pounds and had arms the size of Barclay's thighs.

"Nah. I concede. Wouldn't want to hurt you." Barclay never took his eyes off the screen.

Well, what do you know? The little nerd was getting a sense of humor. Another one of Skye's small victories.

"Thanks," said Alex.

"Don't mention it," said Barclay.

"Back to work."

A half hour later they all looked up again as Skye strode back into the room. She had the look of an expectant mother ready to announce the big news.

"I have it. I have the key and, I think, one of the reasons someone wanted me off the case."

She gave Barclay the paper. It had been transformed. All the spaces had been filled in. All the words had been unscrambled and all the phrases had come to life.

He looked down and frowned. This was the key all right and his admiration knew no bounds, but how did anyone who had not originally written them see the pattern?

The team looked over his shoulder. Alex smiled. Linda and Judy smiled. Lucas was as clueless as Barclay.

"I don't get it," Barclay said.

Linda looked up. "I don't know how you ever in a million years went from this," she pointed at the original paper, crumpled and dirty from its trip through a farmer's field, "to this." She pointed at the list without the x's and with dashes between the words.

charm--statue--song--clock--staircase--sign--mysterious--clue--shadow--bungalow--secret--oak--twisted--brass--heels--password--lane--glen--mystery--whispering--red--lilac--hidden--album--shady--box--bridge--lost--jewel--clue--tapping--trunk

"To this." She pointed at the long list of neatly typed titles. "But I think we have them."

Secret Of The Old Clock
The Hidden Staircase
The Bungalow Mystery
The Mystery Of Lilac Inn
The Secret At Shadow Ranch
The Secret Of Red Gate
The Clue In The Diary
Nancy's Mysterious Letter
The Sign Of The Twisted Candles
The Mystery Of The Brass Bound Trunk
Clue Of The Tapping Heels

The Clue Of The Broken Locket
Message In A Hollow Oak
Mystery Of The Ivory Chain
The Whispering Statue
Haunted Bridge
The Case Of The Lost Song
The Secret Of Shady Lane
The Clue In The Jewel Box
Clue In The Old Album
The Secret Of The Whispering Walls

"Would someone fill me in?" asked Barclay looking at all three papers. He was totally impressed but not sure why.

"These are all titles of Nancy Drew books. The codes will be based on them," said Skye. "In that original communication when the drug supplier was talking about Nancy Drew, he wasn't talking about me like we thought. He was talking about this code. Remember they found the phrases 'we will use N.D. to verify our routes' and 'use Nancy on this one'? We thought they were setting me up, but they didn't think of doing that until later. They were referring to their coded communication."

They all looked at her. She knew they wanted to know how she put it together. One of her tasks as SAC was to teach and to train so she took them through the process.

"There had to be something in my brain that was vital to this case."

"How about everything," said Lucas.

Skye smiled at him and made his day.

"This information wasn't exclusive to me. Many of you on this team remembered the series. But someone, the mole probably, knew about my particular interest because of my code name."

"And we don't have your analytical, photographic brain," said Judy. "I see the pattern now, but I would never, ever have perceived it on my own."

"Thanks, Judy. I think we can say the person knows me, or about me, and how I work."

Alex was really enjoying the show. He had to stop himself from swinging into a couple of verses of "My Girl."

"The key had to have been something that Max knew or would recognize. He was a brilliant detective and even when you think he isn't...wasn't...," Skye had to stop a minute and Linda wiped her eyes. "Wasn't

307

concentrating…he was taking things in. Remember when he asked us at the bar what all the Nancy and Ned stuff was about?"

They all nodded sadly.

"He absorbed it. I suspected he saw one of the words and something clicked. You said one of his last searches had something to do with password. We assumed he was looking for a password for a file."

She took a deep breath. "He had a copy of *Password to Larkspur Lane* on his desk. It was a gift for Jenny." They all nodded and remembered when Skye had given it to the girl after the ceremony. Jenny was already reading it in the back seat when they left the gravesite. They also remembered the inscription.

What it takes to make a little girl strong is a heroine like Nancy. Uncle Max.

"He must have called someone. Someone he thought could help him. Or someone he suspected. The individual killed Max and thought he destroyed the work. He took the disks but he didn't count on our Barclay's thoroughness." Some would have said, compulsive-addictive, type A, anal-retentive personality disorder. But not Skye.

"When I'm up in the air, maybe it's the solitude or the altitude, I don't know. I see things more clearly. I stared at the paper and thought about the various elements in the case and it was just there. Fully formed. I only had to confirm it, which I just did. You know I have always told you find yourself a special place to think. Max's place was in the big leather chair in his den. The book was right there on the desk. He made the connection."

Barclay was looking at the list. "Good God, how many did she write?"

"These and more. I'll let you continue the research. These are the ones I could remember off the top of my head. We have the key and now we're going to go into all the copies of the original disks and we're going to find the person who is responsible for Max's death."

They nodded. They would work now with renewed energy and vigor. It was rewarding to see progress. Skye had provided them with valuable clues and they were well trained on following them up.

"This is perfect," said Barclay already working the keys to his computer. "I can get the complete text of these volumes and start working. It's a perfect cryptic devise. Common enough not to attract attention. From what you tell me, easily acquired. Books are easy to transport. All they would have to do is have the same volume at both ends of the communication and they could hide information very effectively. This will still take a great deal of time, but it will no longer be a trial and error, random search. We'll be able to go right for the data."

"I have the complete set at home. I'll have Hazel send them over." She turned to Barclay and gave him a determined, confident smile. "Now make your magic, Harry Potter."

"Who?" asked Barclay.

"Harry Potter, the little wizard?"

"Never watch Saturday morning cartoons."

"Books, movies, cult hero."

"Well thanks. Sounds like he's a nice person to be."

"Just break this for me."

"And for Max."

"Yes. For Max. Let's nail these bastards."

While Barclay, Lucas and Judy worked with the disks, Linda and Alex wanted to discuss other matters with Skye. Most particularly her safety and finding the mole.

"Linda, nearly everyone at the department has heard Dan call me Nancy from time to time, but I would say relatively few would know that it's my code name and that I have a special affinity for the series. I was getting too close to the people who used the books for encryption, so they wanted to take me out of the game. Why don't you put together a list of names. I think Jim told the story at my initiation and once at a department holiday party. It hurts to have to make a list of people we know and trust, but let's get started."

"Alex," Skye continued. "You can check alibis. Make it subtle. We can start eliminating people. You know, who was out of the country, that sort of thing."

Alex nodded. He intended to make the search thorough, concrete, and anything but subtle.

Later in the day, Alex and Skye went out to the site of the crash. Alex's stomach clutched and his heart nearly stopped when he saw the wreckage scattered for a quarter of a mile across a field of clover and grass. Earlier when Skye was telling the story, the abstract picture was hard enough on his nerves. This was horrific.

"How's that for fieldwork?" asked Skye mockingly, sincerely hoping she didn't do too much damage to the farmer's field.

Skye didn't know that the farmer was already down at the local bar sharing his story with all his friends. About the plane coming in as quiet as a bird.

Then breaking up into pieces. He hadn't wanted to take his truck out there, thought he would find body parts lying around with all the metal. But his wife was calling 911 and he had his civic duty to try to help, so he took the truck and went to find the biggest piece. When he got there, he could hear someone cursing and pounding. Then the door flew off and a woman got out. Darnedest thing he'd ever seen. Must have been over six feet tall and a ravishing beauty to boot. Here is where his friends and neighbors assumed he was embellishing a bit. Not lying, exactly, but stretching the truth a tad.

Not a scratch on her. Like she had a force field around her or something. If she'd been an alien, he wouldn't have been more shocked. Gave her a ride to the Medical Center in town. She was as nice as could be. A bit chatty, perhaps, but concerned for his field. It was only in grass this year anyway. She had wanted to pay for his time, but he wouldn't hear of it. It was a once-in-a-lifetime adventure and it had fallen right in his lap.

Jim stood in the field looking at the carnage. He wanted to be on hand during the investigation. His stomach was still in a knot. Pieces of Skye's plane were spread out in a trail of twisted metal. When he saw what was left of the cockpit, he had visions of Skye as broken and battered as her plane. He saw Alex's truck pull up and went over to greet them as they made their way through the long grass. "Skye. Alex. I thought I would come take a look for myself. Jesus Christ, Skye. Are you okay?"

"Not a scratch."

Alex held up the hand he was casually holding. The abrasion was a red line crossing the top of her hand.

"And this?"

"Got that getting into the farmer's truck."

"Ah."

"Well, from the preliminary report it was definitely sabotage," Jim said. "Everything was expertly rigged to snap after you were in the air for an hour or so. Maybe the perpetrator thought you would fly your ocean route."

"I'm just glad I turned the other way." She could feel Alex's hand grip hers tighter. She was sorry he had to be so connected to her, so connected to the things that happened to her. The wreckage did look horrible from this angle.

"Sorry about the plane, Skye. Maybe it can be repaired." The three of them stood and watched the team from the NTSB study and gather pieces as small as a pencil.

Skye laughed at the ludicrous thought. "That would be like trying to put together a puzzle with no pattern, no directions, and half the pieces missing. It's gone, Jim," she said softly, sadly. "It's gone."

Memories of her dad in the cockpit. Of her needing a pillow to see out of the windscreen. Of taking her lessons. And when things in her life were dark and bleak, of taking it up and soaring through the endless sky. The pain and agony left on the ground. The hours she spent, using the air space to let her mind wander. To ponder complicated problems and find solutions. Her plane. A big part of her life. Her inheritance from her dad. A place where there was no heartache. Freedom. Her protection against reality. Her safe place.

Skye tried to suppress the wave after wave of pain. It was coming in on her too fast. Too powerfully. Her father, mother, Jeff, Max, and now her beloved plane. Alex looked at her face, turned her into his chest and held her. He could see it coming, even if she couldn't.

Skye's chest hitched twice and then she found herself sobbing against Alex's chest. Alex held her shuddering body close. Neither Jim nor Alex knew quite what to do. Jim had known Skye her entire life and could count the times he saw her cry on one hand. Not even when she broke her arm as a child. A few tears, then she would wipe them away. But to lose herself in this kind of sorrow. It broke his own heart and it was tearing Alex's out.

Skye's body shook from the violence of her grief. This plane was part of her connection with her father. A connection that would be forever lost to her. Jim's eyes met Alex's. Someone was going to pay and pay dearly for this.

Alex signaled Jim that he would take care of her. Jim nodded gratefully and touched Skye's shoulder. "I'm so sorry, honey," he said, turning slowly back to work in the field.

She didn't even hear him. She was so lost in her anguish. She couldn't seem to get through it. It was so thick. So dense. Then she saw Max's face. Oh God. He was dead. The pain was horrific and was weighing her down. She wouldn't have been able to stand if she hadn't felt Alex's arms around her through her sorrow and bottomless grief. In fact, it was those arms that gave her the strength to give in to the pain. To let it out. To finally let it out.

Alex stood looking at the pieces of the plane. His jaw set and the muscles in his face tensed. Skye could have been in pieces, just like the plane. If it weren't for her cool head and her incredible skill, he would have been the one standing here trying to cope with the grief.

Alex held her a little tighter, his magnificent daredevil. Her bravado and audacious temperament not diminished by her sobs, but punctuated by them.

He kissed the top of her head and whispered words of comfort to her.

Skye didn't hear the words, but she could feel the soothing tone of his voice. The indescribable tightness in her chest began to ease a bit and she was able to breathe.

Finally, she could cry no more. She was weak and exhausted. Instead of being held by Alex, she was now being supported by him. He reached down and swept her up in his arms. She nestled against his broad chest and buried her wet face in his neck.

"I can walk," she sighed.

"I know." He carried her to the truck, opened the passenger's door and gently placed her inside. She leaned back against the headrest, her eyes closed, her cheeks wet, her profile in stark relief against the setting sun. He was more in love with her than he ever thought he could be with anything or anyone. He stared at her for a moment, then closed the door and got in behind the wheel. Skye sighed again.

"I wouldn't have been able to do that without you there," she said softly, gratefully.

"I'll always be there," he said brushing his lips over hers. She opened her red swollen eyes. Tears were still swimming in them. She touched his face.

"I would have carried around that pain and it would have eaten at me from the inside." Her breath hitched again. "It's been my way. You've changed that. You've changed me."

Her words penetrated his heart, making it beat faster, fuller. She was getting closer to acknowledging her love. Closer to letting her heart rule her head. He wanted to tell her he loved her. Wanted to ask her to love him back. But he decided to wait. He wouldn't press it now. It wouldn't be fair.

"He was with me," she whispered. "Dad was sitting in the seat next to me the whole time." She reached in her pocket and pulled out the compass. "The only thing I have left," she said. "It was my dad's. He gave it to me when I made my first cross-country solo flight. It was in my hand like my talisman." She closed her fist around the precious keepsake. Then she closed her eyes and slept.

He buckled her in and kissed her wet cheeks.

"And for that I'll forever be grateful," he said. He took one last look at the pieces of the aircraft, shuddered, and drove his daredevil home.

CHAPTER 22

Alex woke up and automatically reached over. Damn. She was up again. She hadn't had more than a few hours of sleep a night since Max died. She just couldn't turn off her brain. That incredible brain. Some nights he would find her pacing in the den, going over the last few months day by day. She had replayed every conversation she'd had with Max. Sometimes she would be in the weight room, pumping iron until she exhausted herself. Once he had found her at his big desk, just staring at Max's body in the crime scene photo.

He thought she would sleep tonight. She was so exhausted. He put her to bed after carrying her in from the truck. They made sweet, gentle love and she fell right back to sleep, curled up by his side. Now she was up again. The clock read 2:47 a.m.

He got up and put on a robe. She was going to take something, goddamn it. She was losing weight and even though she was a master at concealing them with make-up, there were circles under her eyes. She had incredible endurance, but she wasn't pacing herself for the long haul. Skye was the hunter. This is what Linda wanted him to watch for. The hunter now had a guardian and he was awake.

He found her staring out the window in the library. He knew she loved this room. It overlooked the gardens, but that wasn't what she was staring at. She was in her brain. And in that uncanny way she had, she also knew he was standing there. She always had all of her senses working, even when she was lost in her thoughts. She didn't even turn around.

"I'm going to tell you something about me and how I process and how I think," she said softly as though she were just waiting for him to enter.

"All right. Can I get you something?" Maybe he could slip a sleeping pill into her peanut butter sandwich. She loved peanut butter.

"No, thanks. I'm not hungry." Funny, she thought. She hadn't been hungry for a long time. Then she smiled. "Maybe pancakes later."

She turned. The moonlight was coming through the window and she was a magnificent sight. Her hair in disarray, her tall, slim body wrapped in a robe.

Her lovely, haunted face pale full of shadows and angles. She was a vision in black and white.

"Do you want me to turn on a light?"

"No. I want it to be dark."

"Can I hold you?"

"All right." She came over to him and he took her hand and led her to the sofa in front of the fireplace.

"Want a fire?" He knew she liked to stare into flames when she was thinking.

"Yes."

He pushed the remote and the propane made a little whooshing sound as it lit the logs laid out in the hearth. Skye stared into it awhile, then came into the circle of his arms and pulled her feet up beside her. There was a fragility about her tonight. The fact that she found refuge in his arms touched him. He wanted to tell her how much. To tell her he would hold her and love her forever, but he had made a deal with her and he was going to keep it. If she was as perceptive as he knew her to be, she would feel it. Because it was powerful, it radiated from him every time he looked at her, touched her, made love to her, or just held her like this.

"My brain is an instrument. A tool. Most people see the body first. Hard not to, there's so much of it, but I'm really more proud of my brain." No preamble, no introduction. She had something to tell him and she was going to do so efficiently. It was her way.

Alex had a lot of things to say to her about that, but he was going to let her get it out. He just held her and settled in to listen.

"My mind is like a safe. Behind the door to the safe is the answer to a problem. First, I formulate the problem, then I work to open the safe. When I start the process I don't have the combination. I don't know the numbers or the sequence. All the data and facts and bits of information I gather will give me that combination. They'll click into place. But I have to try hundreds of different combinations and configurations. The combination is there. It takes patience and persistence to find it. When I do, the safe opens and there's the answer."

"I've seen it work," said Alex.

"I have difficulty when I don't have all the pieces. I can't get the door open if I don't have all the possible parts of the combination. My brain can't take the leap. It's too methodical."

"That's why it's very nearly always right."

314

"Thanks," Skye continued. "For the last week, I've been gathering all the pieces and I want to start processing. I'm usually best able to do this in the air. But now that I don't have flight. I'm going to need a place. A safe place to put this all together. I think it's all in my brain. I just need to find the right combination. My plane, the air. That has been my safe place."

"I'm sorry darling."

"I know. Anyway, there's a point to all this." She turned and gave him a quick peck on the lips. "Thank you for letting me get to it in my own way. I can feel your muscles tense every time you want to interject a comment. You've been very disciplined."

"Go on," he said, deliberately tensing his arm muscles so she could feel them through her thin robe. She chuckled softly and settled back in.

"I need a new place. A place where I feel completely safe…a place I love and where I know I can fly. Or at least my mind can."

"And that would be…."

She snuggled. "Right here."

The impact of her words went straight to his heart and took his breath away. He never saw this one coming. Never thought she would give him this astounding gift. He heard love. He was sure he heard the word love. He didn't move for a minute, letting it sink in. Reveling in the warm, wonderful feeling of it. Wanting to remember this moment forever.

"You can breathe now."

"Right."

"Alex?"

"Yeah?"

"And you don't have to lay off the love talk anymore. The dam broke this afternoon. I'm not even sure I can rebuild it."

"Are you saying you love me?" His head was spinning, his voice was soft and low. He had waited a long time to hear her say this. Had he interpreted her words the way he wanted to hear them, or the way she honestly meant them? He held his breath, anticipating the answer.

"I don't know. I only know I'm not going to fight it anymore."

"Close enough." He turned her in his arms and kissed her with all the love in his heart. She felt infused with it. It was like the source of life itself.

"I love you to distraction, Special Agent. And I always will." It felt good to say it. She loved hearing it.

"No matter what?"

"No matter what."

"Guaranteed?"

"Want it in writing?"

"Know a good lawyer?"

He chuckled and kissed her until she couldn't feel her toes. He was very ready to consummate this new phase in their relationship, but he knew there was something more. That all this was leading her somewhere and she wasn't yet there. He looked down into her credulous, trusting eyes and put a lid on his lust. There was plenty of time for that later.

"Now that you have laid all the groundwork, tell me what keeps you up at night."

She smiled. He was the most incredibly wonderful man. He looked so good on the outside, one might miss the heart and soul. The handsome face and sculpted body were only the wrapping for the real gift inside. And he loved her. No matter what. Guaranteed. So now to the one thing she never, ever shared with anyone in her life.

He saw something big coming. He had lawyer's instincts and cop's eyes.

She took a deep breath and went to her safe place, nestled in his arms. Her voice turned softer, lower, more solemn. He waited.

"There are sometimes barriers to my thinking process. For example," she peeked up at him and smiled. "When I knew there was something about you that went deeper than what you were sharing, what you were telling me. I had all the pieces and they were lining up. But my trust in Jim was a barrier."

"Darling." He hadn't intended to interrupt, but this was still a sensitive area. It killed him to think there might be the slightest breech in their trust.

"Don't worry, I've patched up that little wound and there isn't even a scar."

"Sure?"

"Really. I only bring it up, because in that case I allowed my trust to stop the natural flow of my reasoning. My instincts were correct."

He kissed the top of her head. "They were indeed, and you'll never know the gratitude I feel for your pardon and absolution."

"I'm no saint."

"Thank God. Never thought you were. I just think you're an angel."

"God, you say the strangest things. Anyway, my point is, I think I haven't been able to get to all the answers in this case because there are several barriers."

"You've already cracked more of the case than anyone thought was possible. You're stopping the drugs, seizing the money, and uncovering valuable data to be used in prosecution."

316

"Yes, but we haven't found Juan. We haven't identified the mole. And, most importantly, we haven't found Max's killer."

"It's only been five days."

"There's a sense of urgency here. I need to process the data, and the more I try to put it all together, the more afraid I am that I've constructed barriers."

"Trust again?"

"Of course, but I've programmed myself to factor that in. In this case the suspect list most certainly will contain people I thought I could trust with my life. The more I've been thinking about all the component parts of the investigation, the more I'm convinced there's a vital fact that I and only I have."

"I agree." That fact made his blood run cold. Stop her, stop the process. Someone had already tried. Several times.

"And I think that vital piece is behind a barrier, because it just isn't where I can get it. I've been trying and trying. I believe I've relived every thought and reexamined every idea I've stored in my conscious memory." She sighed. She was tired and she had an incredible tension headache. "Am I making any sense?"

"Yes, I'm following."

"I've thought this all through and I'm going in to get the information from behind a barrier I know is there because I put it there myself and I need you to help me."

She was very, very still. He had no way of knowing where she was going with this, so he let her say what she needed to say without prompting. This would be a night of unforgettable revelations, private disclosures, of unqualified trust, of forging a bond that was both as delicate as glass and strong as iron.

He had no idea he would be the source of her freedom from her self-imposed personal nightmare. When she took a deep breath, he could feel the shudder, deep, deep inside her.

"This is like exposing my jugular to a predator. I've never told anyone in my whole life what I'm going to tell you now. You've seen me naked, but that's nothing. Nothing compared to how unprotected I'm going to be tonight. Right here. I'm trusting you to stand by me. Can you handle this? Do you want me to go on?"

He could feel her heart. Steady. True. Trusting. Waiting.

"Skye, darling," he said solemnly, knowing she was taking the step beyond love into unconditional surrender. "I'll love you until I take my last breath. I'll always consider it the most important task of my life to protect you, to cherish you, to make you happy, to serve as your shield."

"To be my safe place?"

"Always and forever."

Their hearts beat as one. She was ready.

"I'll need you to stand by me on this one. I'm going on a journey into my own mind. There's something in my brain that's so important that I've become a target." She felt him stiffen and went on quickly.

"I think I know *where* it is, even if I don't know *what* it is." She stared into the fire, her eyes becoming haunted again.

"There's a part of my brain that isn't open, Alex. It's been locked down for over fourteen years. Deliberately. Thoroughly. By my own will...my own action." Skye's voice went softer. Alex waited when Skye hesitated, knowing she was tapping into that incredible reserve of willpower.

"After...after I saw my mom and dad blown up in Rome, I shut that portion of my brain down. Those terrible memories. I had intended to let that time stay locked away forever. It seemed best...for me. The counselors and psychiatrists Jim sent me to tried to help me, but I was a determined person even back them." She felt his arms tighten and it helped.

"I have to get this out before my throat closes up." She took a deep breath. "I lied to all those people and to all the people I loved. Always telling them what they wanted to hear. I cried on cue. I told them I was coping with seeing my mom and dad burning alive in..." Skye's voice broke.

Her obvious anguish was killing Alex. He didn't know what to do. Should he let her go on? This was beyond his experience and certainly beyond his training. He tightened his grip around her as she started to shudder. He let instinct guide him. She wanted a confidant, a safe place, not a counselor. She was too smart for them. So he drew her on to his lap and let her find her own words.

Tears were falling from her eyes but she started again. "I told them I was dealing with it, describing it, describing my feelings. I was a textbook case study. That's mainly because I got my responses and words from a series of textbooks I researched. I talked them into the illusion that I was taking a healthy course of action." She tilted her head back and looked at him. He almost stopped her. It was agony to see her tortured face. "I was lying, deceiving everyone, and no one knew. I don't remember. I built the wall solid. You're the only one besides me who knows. And Alex," she whispered in a shaky voice. "I think it's the barrier I need to cross."

She looked right into his eyes and he found that it was he who wasn't breathing. To trust so completely was a tribute to her courage and character. Her need to sacrifice her peace of mind, her equilibrium for her friend, for her job, was the definition of valor.

"Alex, I didn't remember then and I don't remember now. I didn't feel anything but rage. The trauma was horrific, but my reaction was to bury it. I suppressed everything through the force of my will and have kept it locked away by that same mental resolve. I didn't allow myself to remember, think, feel. No one knew that because I knew the words. The platitudes. The overused clichés about traumatic stress. I expressed thoughts from the writings of others. The counselors believed the deception and said I was coping just fine."

Skye continued, stronger now. "For fourteen years I've completely blocked the memories of that summer. The whole summer. There's nothing there because to remember that time means I have to remember the day it happened. To remember means I have to feel it, see it, smell it. I'm so afraid that fourteen years of repression will be unleashed and I might lose control. I need someone here when I go through the barrier. I need someone to come in after me if I can't find my way back. I need you."

She was now at the point of her evening's deliberations and she was shaking with the implications of her plan. Of the enormity of the risk. "Alex, I'm very much afraid that the missing piece of information is in that block of suppressed time. I've tried looking everywhere else in my mind. It's the only other place it could be. I have no moral alternative. I have to go back. Oh Alex, help me. I have to go back there and I don't know what will happen to me."

She was crying now. Not the racking sobs that tore at his heart earlier, but the infinitely more agonizing tears of a broken and battered soul. "I need you to help me. I need you to come with me. To open my mind. I can't go there alone. I'm too afraid to go alone. Tomorrow, Alex. I want to go through everything again, then I want to crash through the barrier and find the missing number in the combination. Oh, Alex, please help me."

The tight fist in his chest that had gripped his heart was spreading to his entire body. His need to be with her was a physical ache, a tangible throbbing pain. She was hurting and he had a gripping need to absorb it. To diminish its hold on her. She was weeping and shaking from the effort of getting this out. For the first time in her life she was turning to someone.

He took her face in his hands and kissed the tears. They were salty on his tongue and they fueled a burning desire to make them stop, and to lessen the anguish he saw and felt. "My darling. I'll go with you anywhere. I'll be by your side. You're not alone," he promised and he put that promise into his eyes for her to see. To believe.

And she did. Her gratitude, her trust, her pain, all swirling through her. He was kissing her and she was responding with all the passion that was in her trembling body. They came together, both of them wanting to diminish the ache in the other's heart. Fighting together to take on years of pain and suffering.

"That's enough for now, baby. I know what you're asking. I know what you're planning. Now rest," he said simply. "Let me help. Let me love you."

He was making love to her. It wasn't just sex. It was more than their bodies mating. It was the anesthetizing comfort of two bodies, perfectly in tune, coming together to turn pain into pleasure. He removed her robe while kissing, touching, stroking her body, everywhere he thought might arouse her so she would have weapons to fight the demons.

She wanted him. She wanted to take her protector and give back to him some of the heat, the love, and the passion he gave to her. They were both demanding and giving. Generous and kind. They were untamed and human. Physical and emotional and in the end they were one.

The storm passed and they lay in each other's arms, sweating, sated, and utterly secure. She'd used all the reserves she'd stored up and was slipping into near unconsciousness. He watched her go. Let her go. They had work to do together and she would need to sleep. He shifted so he could cradle her in his arms for a lengthy siege. She wasn't going to go anywhere until he said she could. He was now her designated defender.

Just before she slipped away, she gave him one more magnificent piece of herself.

"I love you," she murmured into his chest. Then she was gone. The jolt her words gave his already electrified system spread throughout his entire body, then flowed back unerringly into his heart.

"I know, my darling," he whispered as he kissed the top of her peacefully sleeping head. "I know you do." Then he grabbed the afghan from the back of the sofa, covered their naked bodies and followed her into an untroubled sleep.

CHAPTER 23

When the sun came up, Alex eased himself from under Skye. She barely moved, but expressed her disapproval with a little frown. He looked down at her. She'd shed over a decade of tears in the last 24 hours, yet she looked serene. He leaned over and gave her cheek a little kiss. He couldn't resist.

He showered and dressed, and then called Linda and told her Skye would be working at home today.

"Thank God," said Linda with feeling. "Is she okay? I mean the crash and everything."

She crashed all right, thought Alex, but not with a plane. "She's fine. She just needs to step back and take a day to think and put things together."

"Well, you know what my ancient ancestors said. When you're standing at the edge of a cliff, a step forward is not progress."

"No wonder the Chinese culture has survived for thousands of years."

"Damn. You're as bad as Max. I'm half Vietnamese, you dolt."

"Hey, just because he's gone, doesn't mean I'm your new whipping boy."

They both laughed. "That felt good, didn't it?"

"Yeah. It did."

"What's so funny?" asked a groggy, barely conscious voice from the doorway. He turned. His precious package was wrapped in his robe. It worked, except it was on inside out.

"I'll tell you later. Ready for some coffee?"

"Can I have it intravenously?" Her eyes closed and Alex was afraid she was going to go back to sleep standing up. Chuckling, he went over and led her to the big overstuffed chair by the window. He gave her a little shove and she went into the chair without a great deal of grace.

"I like the inside out look."

"Huh?" She looked down, then looked up and him and grinned. "Kind of makes a statement, doesn't it?"

"That it does." He bent over and gave her a quick kiss. "I love you unconditionally, though, so the statement be damned."

"Thanks." She said it so sweetly that it took away the sting of her not repeating the words back to him. Almost. In his heart he had the words from her last night and that would fuel him for a long time. So he would wait.

"Pancakes with that coffee?"

Her smile lit up the day. He went over to the phone and pressed "1" for the kitchen. "Pancakes and coffee for two in the master suite. Make that pancakes for two and coffee for an army." He laughed. "I'll tell her. Thanks."

"What?

"Cynthia says you have lost weight. You haven't been eating. She'll bring enough of both for an army and you better prepare for the campaign."

"She's sweet."

"That she is. And I wouldn't cross her if I were you."

"I don't intend to. You know, I could get used to this filthy rich stuff."

"You after me for my money now?"

"Hell no. For your pancakes."

She stretched and yawned and shook her head to clear it. "I actually feel good this morning. Alex?"

He hadn't taken his eyes off her; she was such a lovely picture.

"Yes?"

"You're the reason." That warmed him more than the coffee.

"Was it the listening part, the protector part, the loving part, or the sex part?"

"Actually it was the mattress part. My body seems to respond well to sleeping on top of you."

"I'm flattered."

"More like flattened."

She got up and gave him a quick pat on the cheek on the way to the bathroom. She looked into his eyes for a long moment. Her gaze was clear and composed and there was a tranquility that he hadn't seen before. Or that she hadn't let him see before. She was opening her heart to him and he liked the feeling. "I'm going to take a shower. If the coffee arrives before I'm done, you can bring me a cup and scrub my back?"

"For that you need to press 2."

"Ah. I see. And just where is that button located?"

He pointed to his lips. She laughed and gave him a more thorough kiss.

While she was in the shower, Alex contemplated whether to call Jim. He and Skye were going into her mind today to find a clue. He was convinced of it. What if the clue pointed to someone very near the top? Or at the top? He thought they should keep everything between the two of them for now.

After breakfast and another short detour to the bed for a fast, hot, pancake-fueled session of lovemaking, they sat in the library on the sofa they'd slept on the night before. Skye had her fingers entwined in his. She asked if this could be the spot where they would work together that day. It was these small gestures of trust that settled into his heart and made him a happy man.

She turned to him and opened a thick file. She took a pad and pen from the sofa table. Serious and all business.

"We're both cleared for the day. I'd like to start by just thinking out loud. Running through the process, creating a mind map. Okay?" asked Skye.

He nodded.

"First of all. Where were you the night Max was killed?"

This came so out of the blue that he just stared at her.

"Pardon?"

"It was a simple question." Her face revealed nothing. Her gaze was steady. Penetrating, in fact.

"Are you serious?"

"Do I look serious?"

He considered her for a moment. He was really fuming, but it didn't help to fight her on this. Once she got on a track, she didn't go to another one until the end of the line.

She could see his anger. Didn't blame him for it, but it couldn't be helped. She was a logical, methodical investigator and she was going to take this in a logical, methodical pattern.

"I was working in my office." He noticed she wasn't writing anything down. Yet.

"Can anyone confirm that?"

"I was alone."

"Did you make any phone calls that would be logged on your bill?"

"Yes. I called L.A., Denver, and my parents in Chicago." She looked down at the top paper in her folder. The muscle in his jaw tensed and he said in a barely controlled voice, "that appears to be a copy of my phone bill."

"It is."

"Then why did you ask?"

"To get confirmation." This wasn't going the way he planned. Not at all.

"You don't honestly think I had anything to do with this, do you?"

"No, of course not. And I've just eliminated you. You fit all the criteria, but you have an alibi."

"If you don't think I did it, then why the hell are you wasting your time asking me these damn questions?" He couldn't keep the irritation out of his voice.

"Being investigated without your knowledge by someone you're sleeping with really bites the big one, doesn't it?"

He stared.

She stared.

He smiled a small ironic smile.

"Touché," said Alex.

She nodded, then looked down and in an exaggerated movement, took the top page and tossed it over her shoulder.

"Now that we have that established, I would like to bring you, and only you, into my confidence."

"Okay. I am your protector, after all."

"That will be later. When we go exploring my mind. For now, how about sidekick?"

"Too western."

"Partner?"

"Too FBI."

"Any suggestions?"

"Husband?"

Skye's eyes nearly popped out of her head. She shook her head as if to clear it. And gave him such a horrified, incredulous look, that he was almost insulted. Like a kid looking at the pile his cute little puppy left and being told it was his job to clean it up. He didn't have two heads, after all. He hadn't meant to say it, but he liked the idea. And he meant to show her he liked the idea. He had intended to withdraw the suggestion. Now he decided he was going to leave it out there on the table. Deal with that offer, Special Agent in Charge Madison.

Skye couldn't believe her ears, and she couldn't believe he didn't say something like 'only kidding' or 'oops' or anything to deflect the shock. It looked like he was going to for a second, then decided to dig in his heels and let it stand. Well she wasn't going to let it intimidate her. She was in the middle of an important operation. Dunderheaded idiot. Didn't he know that?

"What was that? A proposal?"

"I do believe it was."

"You have the most screwed up sense of timing. We're in the middle of an investigation here."

"We're alone in a room in our home, after a night and morning of sharing breakfast, a shower and a bed…and this sofa. I think it's perfect timing."

She just stared at him again. He was losing it. He was definitely losing his grip.

"Well, since it's my investigation, I set the agenda and proposals are not on it."

"So your answer would be…"

"First of all that was no kind of proposal, that was a sneak attack. And secondly, I've already told you, I'm not going to commit ever, ever, never to another cop."

"I'm not a cop."

"You carry a gun and you think you're bulletproof. Close enough."

"But I don't like donuts and I don't wear a hat," answered Alex.

"I don't believe we're having this conversation in the middle of an investigation."

"Are we being taped?"

"Drop it," said Skye.

"Like a hot potato."

"Okay. So back to the file." She looked down and he took the opportunity to slide in the last word.

"So was it the fact that it was a lousy proposal or was it the timing?" asked Alex.

"Shut up! I mean it. You're getting dimmer than Phillip."

"Ouch. Is that any way to talk to your guardian?"

"Sidekick."

"Okay. Proceed."

Taking a deep breath and referring to her meticulous notes, Skye continued. "Here are some of the assumptions I'm working with, based on all the data. First of all, I think there's no doubt there's someone on my team or in the agency who is dirty."

At his nod, she proceeded. They were both back to business now. It felt good to her to have a close confidante she trusted to unload all that was in her mind. He could help her find the patterns, the gaps, the flaws. They made a good team.

This fact wasn't lost on Alex and a separate strategy was working on another level in his mind.

"The individual has been using the Nancy Drew code for years. Barclay is really cooking now. He's finding accounts, locations, and names. Well, it's a windfall. He received my complete set of Nancy Drew books yesterday and has been using them to decipher codes from codes. The mole and his or her contact have been using specific pages in specific volumes for a relatively sophisticated communication system. It's no match for Barclay, though. He's been cracking into numbered accounts all over the world. I think Max must have stirred things up a bit because the accounts have been very active this week. Barclay goes in, freezes what he can, but in several cases, the accounts have been closed or moved in the last week."

She looked up at Alex with the most melancholy look on her face. "Of course if the mole is Barclay, he could be doing the cleaning out himself."

Alex nodded. He understood both the suspicion and the pain.

"Anyway, someone is preparing to disappear. Actually that's the good news. If it is Juan moving the funds, we have him on the run and we may be able to trace his trail. If it's the mole who is divesting, then the theory that it was Max has been disproved, reinforcing my assumption that the traitor killed him. From what we're seeing with the consolidation and liquidation, our mole will reveal him or herself just by not showing up for work one day."

"Anyone so far?" asked Alex.

"We've been following up with anyone calling in sick or requesting vacation time. We had one possible lead yesterday. Someone called to go to his Mom's funeral. When we called Records, it turned out his mother died eight years ago."

"She'd be pretty ripe by now," said Alex.

"Anyway, they found him in a No-Tell Motel with his girlfriend. We found a man cheating on his wife, but no mastermind."

"Bet he thinks twice next time."

"No doubt."

Skye sat for a moment looking down at the folder. Alex could see her mind getting back on track. "Anyway, this person needs to be a level three or higher or needs to be a member of our team to have access to the information used to work this case." She went on, her 'report' voice coolly detached. She was in her element. "My second assumption is that Max wasn't the mole." Alex nodded, trusting her instincts.

"My third assumption is that Max knew his killer and knew him well. Actually trusted him."

"Based on?"

"Mostly knowledge of Max. He was a careful, intelligent agent. Someone got close, very close." She'd reenacted his last moments in her mind several times a day. "He was working at the computer. His killer walked in and Max turned. He stood up." Skye swallowed the lump in her throat, cleared it, took a deep breath and proceeded. "Max stood up and said something, asked a question or made a wise ass comment. The killer knew that Max had discovered information that was significant, raised a gun, and shot him. Juan or anyone he or the mole would have hired wouldn't have gotten that close, nor would he have been able to shoot Max without some kind of struggle. Nothing was disturbed in the office, other than the bullets through the computer.

"The fourth thing," Skye continued, "is a judgment on my part based on intuition and knowledge of Max. I didn't believe then, and don't believe now, that he was setting a trap for me. He had a tone in his voice when he asked me to meet him. I've replayed the conversation several times in my mind. It was compassion. Not anger. Not disbelieving. He was going to tell me something he thought would hurt me and he was sorry for it. I was the only one who talked to him and I have to go with my instincts. His killer is someone I like, admire, maybe even love.

"Next, the person had to know about Nancy Drew. This really could be anyone. I certainly don't think it was a coincidence. The fact that Dan has called me Nancy since I was 8 may have trigged something in someone there at Justice sometime over the last 20 years or so and they selected the code because of it. Or maybe it was a clever random choice and the mole, when he or she realized that my code name was Nancy Drew, decided it was too risky to have me on the case. I might see patterns simply because I was so obviously connected with the books. He or she would have cursed their bad luck and then proceeded to do something to thwart me. The cause and effect relationship may be there, but I have no way of knowing which is the cause."

She looked down at her folder and removed three pages. "There are twenty-seven people in the department that would have direct knowledge of my code name and would also know of my involvement in the case in London. Most of them I know very well. It would break my heart if any one of them turns out to be the mole. God Alex, even Pearl is on this list. She knows everything about me. And the other members of my team. Several people in the Tower. And Dan and the personnel in Records.

"Next, I need to consider the fact that someone has been trying to get me off the investigation. For awhile I thought my knowledge of the Nancy Drew series was what triggered the need to take me off the case and then later take me out completely." She didn't like the look in Alex's eyes, so she went on rapidly. "But now I don't think so. That kind of knowledge is too general and not specific to me. So why me in particular? That has been whirling around in my head and occupying my thoughts. The investigation is independent of my presence. I hope to think there would be something lost if I weren't the Special Agent in Charge, but the investigation wouldn't stop. So it comes down to, what do Juan and this mole think I know? It has to be inside my brain. And since it isn't in the conscious part, well..."

She shuddered slightly, but Alex saw it, felt it. "We have work to do on that," said Alex.

She smiled grimly. "And we'll get to that momentarily. I hope it will be the only other piece I need. Then the combination will be there and the answer will lie behind the door."

"Darling, have you considered the cost? I'm not a psychologist, but it seems as though you blocked the memory partly for self-preservation. What will opening it up do to you? Why not investigate other leads and wait for other developments?"

"We want Juan. We want the mole. We want to break up their partnership. I have a feeling we're almost there. We can't wait, not if we want to catch them. They're on the move. It's not enough for me right now to just stop them." Alex could see the eyes of the hunter flash with anticipation of the kill. Skye looked down at her folder. "Hell yes, it's worth the cost."

Alex just nodded. He would let her take the lead.

"Now comes the hard part." She turned to the photos of Max. Tears formed and spilled out of her eyes and onto her cheeks. "Shit." She took the tissue Alex handed her.

"Shit, shit, shit! Once this stuff starts, does it ever end?" She blew her nose and wiped the tears from her face.

Alex certainly hoped not, but he kept that to himself.

She reluctantly handed him the picture. "Pretty tough to look at," she said miserably and sniffed again. Alex looked at them. He had seen crime scene photos hundreds of times, but never a friend. As it always did, Alex had a flash of Rita. She would have photos like these in a file somewhere. Skye knew what was going through his mind and touched his hand.

"I'm sorry Alex. I know this is tough. I just don't know how else to do this. It's important." Alex nodded and took a look at the shot. Skye had circled Max's right hand with a red marker. In the next picture, the hand was the only thing in the shot. The first finger of the hand was pointing, the thumb and other three fingers in a fist.

"I had them blow it up. Alex, I think Max did leave me a clue. The police think it's nothing. That his hand just fell like that or that he's pointing at the computer that was shot, but he's not. Look at the larger picture. There's nothing in that corner he's pointing to but Lucas's old computer…the one he used for spare parts."

"Could he have wanted to tell you it was Lucas?"

"I don't know. God Alex, I'm devastated by this investigation. Lucas has no alibi…no one has."

"Linda?"

"She answered her cell phone when I called. We all communicate using cell phones and that means physically any member of the team could have been anywhere when we called them in. I assumed Linda was home because that's where she said she was. Her fingerprints were all over his unit, but that wouldn't have been unusual…so were Lucas's and Barclay's. Maureen and Judy…God, Alex…they all fit much of the criteria."

Alex took her hand and looked her in the eye. She was distraught and the worst was yet to come.

"This is your job, darling. Don't torture yourself," Alex said.

She nodded and smiled gratefully. "I'm just glad I could eliminate you so I would have someone to talk to. No offense."

"None taken." Alex looked down at the picture of Max's hand and studied it carefully.

"I'm sorry Alex, but here it comes." He looked up, saw the signs, and quickly took his sobbing investigator in his arms. She started crying in earnest now. Alex took the folder from her capable hands and just held her. She cried with such quiet sorrow that Alex had to blink a few tears of his own out of his eyes. When she finished, she sighed.

"When this case is over, I'm going to take two weeks and go dry out someplace." She reached for the folder again.

"Can I come?" asked Alex as he kissed her on the end of her nose. She wrinkled it in a funny little gesture.

"No one has done that since I was 7."

"No one has been able to reach it. Well, can I?"

"Of course. I wouldn't want to leave my mattress behind." The thought of him, alone, for two weeks was going to distract her too much. She had to put it out of her mind for now.

"Can we make it a honeymoon?"

Whack. Just when she had it filed away for later, he hits her again with something out of the blue. He was lucky she didn't just break his neck and be done with it.

"Alex. Drop it right now."

"Okay, okay. Consider it dropped."

She was glad he agreed to do so before she had time to analyze that little fluttery feeling in the pit of her stomach. Too many pancakes, she thought.

She took one last long shaky breath and went back to the picture of Max's hand. "I haven't been able to connect a thought to this picture. I only know when I look at it something clicks in my brain. It's like a camera taking a picture. It only happens when there's something significant. Like when I was dancing with the man who turned out to be Juan. Something clicked."

"I've seen you do that. It's fascinating."

"As long as I'm thinking out loud, I've given that dance some thought as well."

"I still get cold thinking of him with his hands on you."

"Down, boy. You can growl and snap later. Anyway, I thought it was instincts kicking in, but when I reflect on it, my reaction was more of a click. A memory click, not an instinct of warning or a slime meter going off in my head."

"Slime meter?" asked Alex.

"Yeah, when a guy comes on to you and he's slimy."

"Hasn't happened to me lately."

"Well, all women have them," said Skye.

"That would explain why it hasn't happened to me lately."

"Well, anyway, that wasn't what went off. It wasn't so much how he looked. It was the voice. I remembered the voice."

"Didn't you say you had met him earlier? We decided that was what set off the attempt to get you off the case."

"It wasn't from our earlier meeting. All he did at that event was kiss my hand and smile. It was so fleeting that nothing clicked at that time. My memory of him is from back. Way back. But I can't make a memory connection. I'm afraid it's behind that wall. And that would fit better into the pattern. That combination. He met me and thought I might have remembered his face. I didn't. Then he overplayed his hand and had a conversation with me at Blythe's party. That's when it clicked. The irony is that if he would have just stayed in the background, I never would have singled him out, and the fingerprints would never have been taken."

"That's why we're going to go back there, behind the wall...to find the voice?"

"Yeah." She shook off the apprehension and looked back down at the picture of Max's hand. "I was looking at this picture and something about it was talking to me. That click in my head. Max had a split second before death to leave me something. Couldn't be too obvious or the killer would have altered it. Oh, Alex. Max is counting on me to see it. It's the hand, I know it. He knew his killer. He was working on the Nancy Drew connection. He wanted to talk to the killer about it. He was shot. He fell back and in that last instant he drew one finger up, like he was pointing."

"Looks like he could have been indicating the number one. Like when teams win a game. They raise the one finger."

"I thought about that. Number one. Number one. For one horrible minute, I must admit I thought of Jim. He's number one at the department."

"Skye."

"I haven't been able to eliminate him, Alex. He was in his car when he answered his cell phone. He was logged out of the office at Justice and we have no way of knowing where he was when he took the call." Alex saw the tortured conflict in her face. No wonder she wasn't sleeping. He remembered he hadn't called Jim that morning. The way things were going it was only he and Skye who were in the clear. Hell.

"It could be sports. Max did like to go to games. One summer he and a little brother he was assigned to went to every Senators game. You met him at the memorial service, remember?" Skye stopped. Something clicked in her brain. When things did that she added them to her file of possible connections. Part of the combination that may open the door to the answers.

"Skye?" She blinked like the lens of a camera. Click. He could almost hear her brain register something. It was spellbinding to watch, so he remained silent while she filed it away.

"Yes. I have to just let the bits and pieces fall into place." She closed her folder. "I need to get away from this for awhile, stir it up, then let it settle again."

"So in the meantime, tell me again why I was one of your primary suspects."

"Why should I do that now?"

"I just love how your mind works."

"Okay. One, you're a level three or higher clearance." She ticked off the list on her fingers. "Two, Max knew that I would be devastated if it was you. Three, your alibi was weak. Four, you have lied to me before."

Alex winced on that one, and she gave him a wry smile.

"Five, Max knew and trusted his killer. You two had a great rapport. Six, you knew Nancy Drew, very well, actually. Seven, while all your operations appear to be legitimate, you're obscenely rich. Number eight, and here was a kicker, open for interpretation." She paused and looked him in the eye. He was very glad he was innocent at that moment. "You stopped me from shooting Juan."

Alex's posture immediately straightened in defense. "Have you forgotten he would most probably have shot you first?"

"I said it was open for interpretation."

"And you have told no one?"

"Not a soul."

"Now is this where the music in the background reaches a crescendo and I'm supposed to transform into the evil doer and wrap my hands around your neck?" His smile was genuine, his tone teasing.

"I figured that if you were the guilty party, I'd be dead by now. And I also figured if you were the guilty party, I wouldn't want to live anyhow, so what was the difference."

That shot Alex for a loop. It wasn't often she could zing one in that would knock him flat, but this one definitely pinned him before he reached the center of the ring.

"You mean that?" he asked, looking for the truth of it in her eyes.

"Yeah, I think I do," she smiled without pretense.

He stared at her and waited for a few seconds. "Then back to that proposal thing."

"Alex. Not now. I'm just too mushy."

He looked at her long, lean body, dressed in jeans, boots, and a rust-colored sweater that hugged her curves like his Porsche hugged the road. There wasn't one thing mushy about her. But he understood and would put the matter to rest. For now.

"Okay. Then instead, let's tick off eight good things about me."

"I only needed one."

"Which was?"

She smiled and pointed to her heart and sent Alex over the moon.

CHAPTER 24

They wrote notes of their discussions and some of their conclusions. Putting their heads together for something other than kissing or hand-to-hand combat was stimulating and exciting. But they both knew they couldn't postpone Skye's great experiment any longer.

"Now on to the main event," she said when she clicked her laptop shut. She looked at him with both apprehension and hope. "You ready?"

"Are you?" asked Alex.

Nodding, Skye closed her eyes and tried to steady her jumping nerves. Alex pulled all the drapes, casting the room in dark shadows. She sat on the leather sofa. A place she was beginning to think of as her refuge. Alex was pacing like a caged cat.

"Are you sure about this darling? I'm not a professional. What if I can't get you back?" he asked with concern obvious in his tone.

"Or what if I morph into a raving lunatic?" she smiled softly. "Honestly, Alex. I think I'm basically well adjusted."

"What about a sedative or a glass of wine?"

"For you or me?"

He just looked at her with a little exasperation in his pretty blue eyes, a darker shade because of the dark room and his deep concern for her emotional well-being.

"You did say you were mushy."

"That was my heart. I'm definitely not mushy in the head."

"No. I would say that's as hard as stone."

"Maybe I'll have a glass of wine after. But not now. Alex. I need you to sit."

"I can't stand to see you hurting. It tears my heart out." He sat down next to her, put his arm casually around her and pulled her to him in a gesture that had become automatic in the last few weeks.

"Do you want to change your mind? I can try to do this on my own." She pulled away from him, turned and looked him in the eye. Intense. Questioning. Concerned.

"Good God, Skye. Promise me that's one thing you'll never do." His gaze was intense. "Promise me, damn it."

"All right." Skye nodded, then shifted to look into his face. "This is how I'd like to do this. I want to go back to the day my parents were killed and move forward. It's been years since I've even let the tiniest memory from that day into my consciousness, so it may be very bad. Can you stay with me on this?"

He nodded, not sure at all if he could. He guessed he'd rather go back in that alley with those four thugs than take on this assignment, but she was determined. And there was no way he was going to let her go there without him.

She smiled at him reassuringly. "Just hold on to me, okay?" He opened his arms and she went into them. Like coming into a safe harbor. She closed her eyes, laid her head on his shoulder, and purposefully and relentlessly started her journey back.

Nothing happened for a while. Alex watched her carefully. He knew this was her show and he was just her safety net. He let her take it at her pace.

Skye was 15. She was graduating high school early and was begging to be allowed to enter Embry Riddle, a college in Prescott, Arizona specializing in aviation. She'd been flying solo for ages and she wanted her license on her 16th birthday and not a day later.

Her mom and dad were in the front seat. Dad was driving. He was so handsome. Laughing at something Mom was saying. They were all talking in Italian. He was in his suit. The gray one that matched some of the gray that was beginning to pepper his wheat-colored hair. Her mom was dressed for work as well. Always lovely. Very Italian. Stylish and full figured.

Skye begged them to stop at the bakery. Please, please. They laughed because she'd started her growth spurt a year earlier and she'd shot up from 5'2" to 5'7" fueled by constant hunger. Maybe a basketball scholarship. She wanted to fly. Always hungry. New shoes. No one would recognize her. Aunt Hazel. The baby at home. Sloane. The thoughts were getting all jumbled. She had to straighten them out. Her subconscious didn't want to continue, so the memories started piling up. She forced her mind to obey.

She took a deep shuddering breath. They stopped at the bakery. She knew they would. Dad handed her the lira. Winked and said to get something sweet for Mom. She'd been trying to lose the extra weight she gained with Sloane.

The bakery. The smells. She could smell the pastries, the bread. What to select. One of each? She took too much time to make her decision. She should have been back in the car. Leaving the bakery, she turned to say '*ringraziarlo molto'* to the nice man and now everything was happening in slow motion. She saw the blast first, then a split second later, she heard the terrible roar. The burning car. Her mom and dad still smiling. Burning. She screamed and screamed and screamed. Someone from the crowd grabbed her and wouldn't let her go to them. She wanted to go save them. "Let me go! Let me go!" She fought them, several people now. But they were too powerful. She could only watch as her parents disintegrated in the fire.

"No, No, No. *Ciò che succede?* No. No. No. What's happening?"

Alex's Italian was very rusty and there was no way he could keep up with her words. But there was no mistaking the tone of shock and the agony in them. She was moaning now. He held her tightly. This was getting bad and it was only the beginning. Suddenly she jerked violently and tried to get up. Her eyes were open, but they were completely unfocused.

"Oh il mio Dio. Oh il mio Dio. Me ha lasciato va. Loro devo risparmiare. Sono sul fuoco. Me ha lasciato va. Oh my God. Oh my God. Let me go. I must save them. They're on fire. Let me go. *Ciò è mia Madre. Mio Padre. Dio per favore, caro. Ho bisogno di risparmiarloro. Voglio morire, troppo. Per favore. Per favore. Per favore. Me ha lasciato va a loro.* That's my Mother. My Father. Please, dear God. I need to save them. I want to die, too. Please. Please. Please. Let me go to them."

She was screaming in Italian. He could understand some of it. "Let me go! Please. Please. Let me go to them! Oh my God." This valiant child. This tormented, grief-stricken child inside the body of the woman he loved. She wanted to save them. To run to them. Skye was screaming and trying to get away from him, but his strong arms gently held her.

Skye was fighting him. She still had incredible strength and he could hardly keep her subdued. The look on her face was something he would never forget in his entire life and would continue to define his devotion to her happiness. No child should have gone through what she went through. No child should have seen what she saw. Through the look in her eyes, Alex saw not what she saw, but what she experienced. He saw the agony, the hopelessness, the utter devastation of a childhood. The trauma that made her withdraw from commitment. From love.

For Skye, to love was to risk this suffering. For her, to love was the prelude to pain. For her, the price of love was the possibility of this happening again. He could now understand that for her to love him took courage beyond description. He was humbled by it. Tears sprang to his eyes for the child and for the woman she'd become. And for the powerful force her love must be to be able to push through all this pain. He realized that he may not have been able to take on the demons if he had been in her place. Thoughts of Jeff and the added trauma of a wedding dress unused raced through his mind as well. God, the heartache.

Alex held her tighter. "I'm here. I'm here. My darling. Hold on to me. I'll never leave you. I'll love you and help heal your heart. You're my life. Skye? Skye?"

She was sobbing now. Sobbing against his chest and moaning. Then she slipped her arms around his waist and held on tight. She knew he was here. He just held her tightly until the storm passed. "*Madre... padre... Lo manco così molto... L'amo,*" she whispered. "I miss you so much...I love you."

She forced herself to go forward to the funeral. Then she stopped feeling the pain. Stopped feeling anything but anger. The only thing that helped was flying. She flew every day. She flew until she ran out of gas. Twice, she had to incur the wrath of the airport owner because she came in on fumes. She was Amelia Earhart, Bessie Coleman, Dora Dougherty Strother. She wasn't Skyler Madison. She stayed with the airport memories. If the memory she needed was in her brain, this was where it most likely would be. Except for school the following fall, she rarely went out of her room.

Pearl was there smiling, driving her. Taking her turn along with Dan and Jim. Skye held on to that memory for a while before moving forward again. It was a respite that she desperately needed.

She remembered when she was a little girl and she wanted to be a detective, not a pilot. After she had finished reading and rereading each book in her Nancy Drew collection, she'd moved on to other crime fiction. She was Kay Scarpetta, V. I. Warshawski, and Kinsey Millhone. But Nancy Drew was where it started. A memory. A memory was trying to force its way to the surface. She felt strong arms around her. Alex's love got through, traveling with her through time. She knew she was safe. Safe and loved. He said so. He would never leave her.

Alex heard her again. "Safe. Safe," she said over and over.

"Yes, my darling," he said softly as he continued to hold her shaking body. "You're safe."

Her mind wandered through days, weeks, months. Drifting. Searching. The hunter.

Then she had it. Fully formed. Damn if she didn't remember. She was at the General Aviation airport. Someone was picking her up. She wasn't sure who. Wasn't important. A man was there with a Nancy Drew book under his arm. He was holding it. Holy shit, it was Juan. She was sure of it. The voice. It was the voice! She went over to talk with him. The face was 14 years younger. It didn't even look familiar. It wasn't the face. It was the voice. He said his little girl loved the series. He left it on the table in the corner of the terminal. She saw it. He walked out and forgot it.

"Holy shit!" Her eyes flew open.

Alex saw Skye in them. Not the child but the woman. Not suffering, but animated and excited. She tried to jump up, but Alex held her tight. She'd been very, very still for almost an hour. His arms were cramping, but he never moved. He knew she was on a hunt. Then he saw the look of triumph. Of victory. Of complete exhilaration. He smiled. It worked.

"Alex, let me go. I'm okay. I found the key. The clue. The memory. And if we're very, very lucky we have the bastard. Get your keys." She rubbed the tears off her face. "We have to go dig my logbook out of the wreckage."

Alex knew that voice. It was the woman he loved on a mission. He was so relieved to have her back, he almost got an elbow in the face when he didn't immediately release her. She jumped up, grabbed his hands, and pulled him off the sofa. She gave him a big smacking kiss and started for the door, pulling him in her wake.

"I'll thank you later and get all mushy and lovey and we can have a bottle of wine and I'll get rid of this stomach ache and we'll share stories, but now we have to get moving. Barclay said they're liquidating. They may be doing that with their drugs too. We've got to go get them. Now!"

Alex grabbed his keys from the foyer table and they ran to the truck. Words were running out of her like water. Alex was loving every minute. Explanations would be forthcoming, he knew. For now, Special Agent in Charge was back and ready to roll.

"Do you think the logbook is still in the fuselage? I didn't take it out yesterday. I got kind of hysterical. Happening a lot lately. Anyway, Jim may have it or the NTSB, but we'll find it and then we may just have them."

Alex nodded. They would have plenty of time to talk about the other issues later.

"So tell me, what's so important about your logbook?" he asked as they drove as quickly as possible to the scene of the crash.

"Log books are required for all airplanes. There must be an unbroken record of all the flights taken in that aircraft. It stays with the plane, not the pilot. So when Dad...well when I inherited the plane, the logbook came with it. I always wrote in it when I landed."

She told Alex about seeing Juan. "I know it was him. It was me specifically they were after. He must have known I saw something that day. He had no way of knowing I had suppressed it. He left the book and he said it was for his daughter, so I ran out to tell him. He was just leaving in a taxi. So I remember thinking, Nancy Drew super detective will find out where he went and send him the book. Kind of a clever civic duty kind of thing. Anyway, I asked the lady who was standing at the taxi stand if she heard where the man was going. And she told me."

"And you remember?"

"No. We might get it out if I could be formally hypnotized, but we may not have time. This is better. I wrote the address in my logbook."

"Did you ever send it?"

"No, because by the time I got back to the terminal someone had snagged it."

"Who?"

"One memory at a time. I'm not up for going back there tonight. Ah…did I hurt you? I seem to remember some elbows flying."

"Your mattress absorbed the blows just fine." She had a powerful swing. Maybe he wouldn't expose his naked body for a while. Then he looked over at her face. No, he thought. She would definitely see his naked body tonight. He would just make her kiss the bruises. With that on his mind, he accelerated the pace.

The logbook was exactly where it was when she hit the earth, under the passenger seat. She was glad to have it back. It was filled with her father's notations, her girlish script, and finally her more adult handwriting. Every flight they ever took together. Alex watched as she got on her cell phone and told her team to saddle up. The logbook was clutched in her hand like a special charm. The address was being checkout out by Barclay.

Skye was paging through the book, smiling nostalgically, when her cell phone rang.

"Skye Madison." She listened and looked over at Alex giving him a broad grin and an enthusiastic thumbs up.

"The building is a warehouse. The same corporation has owned it for 18 years. Hi Ho Silver. I think we might have them, Alex." She leaned over and covered his face with kisses.

"I think I'm going to really like being your sidekick."

The warehouse was dark and deserted looking on the outside, but the surveillance team Skye assigned reported a flurry of activity inside one of the offices. No one had been in or out.

Alex and Skye hurried back to the townhouse to make calls and to secure the proper papers to search the inside of the building. Skye was on the phone with a judge shouting about probable cause and finally threw the phone to Alex.

"Here. You speak law. Talk to him."

"What's his name?"

Skye looked down at a piece of paper. "Hamilton Baker."

Alex got on the phone.

"Hello Ham. This is Alex Springfield. How's Beverly? And did Ham junior get that scholarship? Great news. I'm sure you are. So about the search warrant. Yes, we can fax that information over to you. Yes, I'm acting as consultant. Yes, she's a bit excitable. Maybe we should adjust her medication." He ducked as a pillow from the sofa flew by. "I'll have someone there to pick it up. We'll be executing it first thing in the morning. Thanks, Ham."

He rang off, turned, bowed, and was buried in a hail of pillows from every corner of the room. What was it about decorators and those little pillows anyway?

Everything was in place. Jim had been informed. None of his people would be in on the serving of the warrant or the arrests, the local authorities would do that, but Skye's team would stand ready to sweep the building once the arrests had been made. Clues to Juan's location and the mole's identity might be in there...it might be all over by the next evening.

Alex would be with them. He was a tacit member of the team, anyway. Since he was so chummy with the judge, she sent him over to get the warrants. That would pay him back for that medication crack. He would be up all night, making copies, delivering papers, blah, blah, blah. She laughed. Skye remembered the look on his face when she told him his part of the operation. Well, she was Special Agent in Charge, was she not? She knew he had hoped for a bottle of wine and a sexual celebration. It wasn't until he left that she realized she'd just cut off her own opportunity for said celebration. Oh well. She planned on having two weeks in paradise with him. She told him so and from his grin, he considered the bargain acceptable.

Alex had called several times. Everything was falling into place, but he had more drafting to do. Now if they could only locate Juan and the mole. She had a strong feeling that when they got one, they would get the other. They were connected.

She was feeling a bit bummed out by midnight. She didn't want to go to bed alone. TV was boring. Her team had instructions to get a good night's sleep. She decided to go down to her safe sofa. Alex wasn't there, but his presence was. And tonight, that was enough. Lying down, she let herself drift. There was one more door in her mind to open and the hunt began again.

She continued to let her mind wander, drifting through everything in her file, through every conversation. Drifting through time. Alex kissing her on the end of her nose…someone else used to do that when she was little. Going back. Back to the airport. Back to the memory of The Voice. She sighed. Come on brain. What's the combination? Drifting. Moving forward. Max. Such a nice man. A good man. A funny man.

She hadn't realized she had drifted right into sleep until she woke up with a jerk, bathed in sweat. Her mind was screaming, "No! No! No!"

She ran down to the office and got on the Internet. Pushing the mouse around, she got into the search engine and typed in American Sign Language. The young man who was Max's little brother had taught Max to sign. They used to have all those secret conversations and laugh at their private jokes.

Each letter had a different sign, using the fingers. The computer screen loaded a visual of the letters. When she saw the one with the single first finger pointing up, she laid her head on her crossed arms and sobbed. When bitter anger replaced heartbreaking grief, she went up to the den, got her jacket and her gun, and dialed the familiar number.

"This is Skye. I'm sure you have been expecting my call. I want to meet with you. Just you and me. Name the place. I'll be there."

Skye left through the rear of the house and easily evaded the surveillance team Alex had arranged for her protection. To hell with that. She was doing this solo.

CHAPTER 25

Skye knocked on the door of the apartment, waited until he let her in, then slapped him hard across the face. "That's for Max, you son-of-a-bitch."

Dan had been watching out the window for signs of a backup or her guards. He didn't see any. He knew she would be like her father and come alone, but he wanted to confirm it. He wasn't sure how skilled the team of guards was. Not as good as his Skye. He smiled. They might eventually realize she was gone, but this wouldn't take long. Either she would let him go, or she would be incapacitated. He intended on leaving later that month, but her discovery would push his plans forward. Unfortunately it would cost him plenty. Damn his luck.

Skye took a deep breath and tried to see the man she'd loved as a member of her family her whole life. He stared back.

"For old times sake, Special Agent Madison. Please report."

She knew his meaning. How did she figure out it was him?

"You started buying me the books twenty years ago, and that coincides with the time the codes were set up." Click.

"You have three ex-wives and you have a pattern of marrying young women. You need money to compensate them for marrying much older." Click.

"Ouch. Accurate, but it hurts."

"My heart bleeds. You drove me to the airport countless times. You met Juan there. There was no reason a 15-year-old girl would notice a friendly conversation between two strangers. It was you who drove me to the airport that day. I told you about the man with the Nancy Drew book. You know I have a terrific memory." And, she thought, he didn't know I had blocked it. Click.

"You have a working knowledge of general aviation aircraft. I saw you several times talking with the mechanics while you waited for me to come in." Click.

"You knew Max and he trusted you. When Max called, he wanted to tell me in person what he suspected because he knew your involvement would devastate me." Click.

"In the beginning, you tried desperately to talk me out of joining the agency and these last few months you've been working to get me pulled from the case." Click.

"Still all circumstantial and could fit several people," said Dan.

"And Max left me a goddamn clue."

"No. He didn't have time."

Skye made a fist, then slowly raised the first finger in the air.

"American Sign Language's finger sign for 'D'--Dan Dickson. You're made and you're mine." Click.

She took her gun out of her pocket. "As much as it pains me, Dan. I'm taking you in."

Dan smiled. "There's a part of me that's proud as hell of you, Nancy."

He saw her cringe. Her eyes were dry and her hand was steady, but he'd known her for her entire life. And he was a master manipulator.

"I'll go with you, Skye. I'm asking now for just a few minutes. I want to tell you personally, before any statements, lawyers, interviews. Just you and me." His voice was gentle, the same kind voice Skye recognized. He had to stall her. He told Juan to give him until morning. He needed to know what she knew and who she told.

Skye nodded, but remained standing. "As long as I can see your hands at all times."

Dan smiled at her. "Make that a very large part of me is proud. I'm going over to the bar and get a drink. No tricks. Darling, you've made me, so I'm toast anyway." She didn't need to know about his escape plan and the bank accounts in the Caymans.

"I'm sure your first question is why and I'm going to have to sound like everyone's version of a traitor here. There's the money, the power, the ability to control events. You see, us administrative drones don't get the same kick as you field people." He tried to keep the resentment out of his voice, but Skye heard it.

"But I thought you were happy in the office."

She was engaged in the conversation. Good, he thought. She was interested. Now he needed to throw out the bait. Hook her. Maybe, if he was lucky, reel her in, although all he was really hoping for was a little more time.

"I was only suited for the office, Skye. It was all I could do. Your father and Jim pretty much carried me in training."

Suddenly Skye's eyes widened in horror.

"Did you have anything to do with my mom and dad's assassination?" she asked in a voice of steel and ice.

"No. No. Perry never knew about me. Believe me Skye. I'm not a natural killer."

"What about the attempts on me?"

"That was Juan."

"And Max?"

"I didn't go there intending to kill him. He called me earlier to ask me about the books. I had to find out why. When I saw he cracked the code, that he suspected my part in it, I had to do something. That was self preservation."

"I'll be sure to tell his family that."

"I'm sorry about that, Skye. And I'll pay the price for that impulsive, horrible act." He wished he could work up some tears, but it wasn't happening. "By the time the investigation got launched in England I was in way too deep."

"The pool is about to get a lot shallower. I remembered, Dan. Alex, Jim, and my team are at the location here in Washington. They'll be serving warrants any minute now."

That did surprise him. She could see it did.

"You thought I would only remember the connection between you two?" asked Skye.

"You knew the address of the warehouse? How?"

"Juan gave the address to the taxi driver and Nancy Drew ace detective wrote it down in her logbook. I retrieved it last night out of the wreckage you caused. And that's another thing you're going to pay for."

Dan's mind flew forward. A great deal of his cash was at the warehouse. Jesus Christ, this was a disaster but at least he wouldn't walk right into it.

"I'm not without feeling, Skye. I didn't want to hurt you. Ever. Just slow you down. Even a selfish, unprincipled man like me can have regret. You're good, Skye. Your operation in England was flawless. We decided to cut our losses. You could have the Blythes. We were about ready to cut them off anyway. They were too blatant and getting to be a liability. I swear if Juan wasn't so infatuated with Lady Emily, we would have cut them out a lot earlier. Then that idiot Phillip introduces you to Juan. He has stayed ahead of this agency for all these years, ahead of you for the last few, and Phillip puts you face-to-face. I figured it was just a matter of time before you would place him and put the two of us together."

Dan continued, "And hell, what kind of bad luck places a woman whose code name is Nancy Drew in charge of a case where the two main players use the books for their cipher. I knew you would break the codes. I just thought I would have years to liquidate and make my exit instead of days. You have an incredible talent, Skye. I'll forever regret that you had to turn it on me."

He took a drink of his Scotch and let his hand tremble a bit. Nice touch.

"Skye. Let me go. I have everything all set up. I know I can't take Bitsy with me, but I can deal with that. I just can't go to jail." There was pleading in his eyes.

"I can't." Her heart was breaking. She saw Dan, her friend and mentor. She saw him in her mind's eye laughing at the zoo, waving to her from the terminal, kissing the end of her nose. "I can't."

"How about a trade?" He played the last and most important card in his deck.

"A trade?"

"Yeah." He looked at her earnestly, turning on the Dan of her memories. "I have known something for fourteen years that I've never been authorized to tell anyone. Even you."

A cold wave of dread washed over her.

"What?" she whispered. "Tell me."

"It's about the assassination. I have information I would be willing to trade." He set the bait and could feel the tide turning in his favor.

The feeling of betrayal was nothing compared to the emotions that rocked her now.

"What do you know?" Her voice was just above a whisper.

"No. I'm not going to tell you. Not until we talk about how I'm going to walk away." He had her hooked, he could see it in the tortured reflection of suffering in her eyes and had to force himself to keep the triumph off his face.

Never in her entire life had she been so conflicted. Every decision she'd ever made paled in comparison. She lowered her gun and walked slowly over to the window and stared out. She was in a daze. He knew something. Mom. Dad. She could see the explosion. Could hear their screams. It was so fresh in her memory now. For her, it happened only yesterday. She'd suppressed it for fourteen goddamn years, now she couldn't get it out of her mind. The fire. The smells. The sounds. Her parents. Burning. Got to get them out. Can't. There was nothing she could do. There was nothing she could do after she buried them and tried so desperately to find out who did it. Who could have done this to two of the most wonderful, alive people on the planet. There was nothing she could do back then, and the guilt mixed with grief overwhelmed her. Could she do something now? All she would have to do is let Dan go. He was ruined now anyway. They would be able to pick up his trail again, wouldn't they? Her head was throbbing. Tears flowed unchecked down her cheeks.

Was knowing worth the price she would have to pay? Shame. Shame. How could she go against everything her mother and father fought for? Died for. Tears blinded her. Mom. Dad. God. What do you want me to do?

Dan watched the play of emotions on her face. He knew her weak spot and that was going to be his ticket out. Her Achilles heel always had been and always would be her desire to uncover the identity of her parent's killers. He had always known that. He just had never been able to test it before.

He could see her play everything out in her mind. He had her. He was about to smile in victory when her tears dried up. Her expression changed.

Shit, he thought. She wasn't going to make this easy. Damn. He reluctantly picked up the poker from beside the fireplace and, while she was still vulnerable, he hit her with it.

"You had to come alone and without back up. You had to make this personal. You're just like your fucking father."

Alex stood outside the warehouse with Skye's team. This was just routine now, but he thought she would be there for the finale. This was going to be a headline-grabbing bonanza for the good guys.

They had discovered from the people they had in custody that Juan had indeed been there. They got a general description, quite different than the one they were using, and had been sending bulletins to local law enforcement agencies all night. It was just a matter of time before he was caught.

Jim came up beside him. "Where's Skye?"

"I don't know," Alex said grimly. There was a bad feeling working in his gut. "She's not answering her cell phone. Is it like her to miss something like this?"

"Actually yes. She trusts her team. If she's on a hunt, she'll keep on the scent and not break off for a routine search and seizure. You said Juan isn't in there, so I imagine she is on that trail. Have you been back to the house?"

"No, but Cynthia said she wasn't there and the bed hadn't been slept in. Her fucking guards swear she was still in the house. She shook them for some reason. Damn her. I thought I would see her here…that she just wanted to go check something out alone. They're out looking for her now."

Jim looked troubled. "Hell. That girl is going to be the reason for my early retirement. She could have just been playing with them…teaching them a lesson. She'd think that eluding her guards was some kind of sport. What was she working on?"

"Specifically?"

"Yes."

"I think she wanted to take some thinking time to put together the evidence on the mole."

The men looked at each other.

"After we're done here, our first priority will be to find her."

"And the second."

"To gently persuade her to please be more considerate and let her team know where she is and what she's doing at all times," said Jim.

Alex laughed, in spite of his worry. "Will you want to handle that conversation, or shall I?"

"I think I'll leave it to you. You have both age and conditioning on your side."

"Right."

They looked back at the warehouse. The men knew that both the mole and Juan were out there and the woman they held dear was on their trail. They knew she was doing her job, but they didn't have to like it.

The Justice team watched as the D.C. police detectives served the warrants by simultaneously kicking in several doors and pouring into the building. They stood in the shadows, waiting their turn.

Jim left to try and track down Skye. He called Dan who told him he hadn't heard from her all night. He tried to reassure Jim, telling him Nancy was just out there pursuing a clue. The rest of the team was concerned, but she often took her own path. She would report in when she had time. And from past experience, her report would be thorough and give them a significant boost in the case.

Alex and the team went in behind the local authorities. Every bit of evidence found would be filed with precision. The District Attorney would have everything neatly packaged with the chain of evidence airtight and secure. Skye was a perfectionist and they would be no less. Skye had trained them and whether she was there or not, she would be leading them.

Skye slowly regained consciousness. Her head throbbed but it was the waves of nausea she found most alarming. Dying in the line of duty she could deal with, but chucking her last night's dinner all over the crime scene would be too humiliating. She decided to move very, very slowly until she could keep the room in one place.

A small moan escaped her lips as she turned her head toward a light. There was a slight movement just out of her range of vision. She sat up and tried to focus on the man standing near the bar. Her hand went to a large gash near her temple and felt the sticky flow of blood. She swallowed back fresh waves of nausea when she shook her head to clear it.

"You just couldn't take the deal, could you?"

It was Dan. He had helped himself to another drink and was casually leaning against the shiny surface of the bar. He had her gun. Shit.

"Damn you, Dan. What the hell did you hit me with? Just look at the blood on the carpet. You're going to have to work hard to cover this up. If you miss just one drop, they'll get my DNA."

"You forget. I know that they don't have your location. Your watchdog is back at the warehouse cleaning up the mess there. I just got another call from Jim. They're concerned about your whereabouts and I'm to call if I hear from you. You can imagine how difficult it was to keep a straight face. I told him with just the right combination of exasperation and worry that I was sure you were just off on another of your personal investigations and that you would show up soon with all the answers." He laughed heartily at his little joke. "I think they'll let a few more hours go by before they get serious and by that time, I'll be long gone. Your reputation as a lone hunter is working in my favor now. You're Perry's daughter all right." The resentment in his voice got through even the clouds still covering Skye's brain.

Skye managed to pull herself up on the chair and sit back into its cushions. She was still dizzy, but she could feel some of the adrenalin putting bones back into her arms and legs. She blinked again to clear her vision.

"Either you cloned yourself, or my brain is swelling. There can't possibly be three of you standing there."

Dan snorted. "Do you have any idea how much trouble you're in? I'm just killing time until Juan gets here. Then I'm going to turn you over to him and take the next flight to Buenos Aires."

She buried her head in her hands and moaned, "God, you're such a cliché. I suppose you have a Swiss bank account and a new identity."

"Actually, the account is in the Caymans."

"Don't you think Jim will figure it out? He and Alex will track you down."

"They won't have any reason to. They'll think I'm dead. I've always had a well-formulated escape plan. Just in case."

She moaned again and made gagging sounds in her throat. "I think I'm going to be sick," she managed to say in a soft, desperate voice.

"Fuck that," said Dan with disgust as he automatically reached for the trashcan behind the bar. He started for her as she continued to gag. "Jesus Christ, Skye, can't you just…"

He didn't get to finish his thought. He never saw the first kick coming. She may have had a concussion, but her legs had their own memory. Springing out of the chair, she delivered a brutal roundhouse kick squarely in his chest. She sent him sailing across the room where he slammed heavily into the edge of the bar. The can he was carrying flew in the opposite direction and knocked a picture off the wall. The gun skittered under the chair, effectively taking it out of play for both of them. That suited Skye just fine. She was filled with the rage of personal betrayal and she wanted to kick some ass.

Skye knew she had surprise on her side, but only for a moment. She had to get in some nasty first punches. Pivoting, she got in another vicious kick to the chest before Dan recovered from the shock of the attack. His ribs were cracked and were screaming with pain. Like a mad dog, he growled and went into a counter attack posture. He kicked out with a brutal blow to her chest. She felt her own ribs cave in. Pain nearly blinded her, but she was in a fight for her life. She gauged her strength and knew she didn't have much in reserve. His next blow merely glazed off her shoulder and she ducked. Spinning, she hooked her foot around his ankle and pulled. He went down with a crash and she went for his face. He tried to evade her, but he was too slow and Skye's fist connected with his nose. Blood gushed out of it as the bones shattered under her wicked counterpunch. He nearly lost consciousness as his head snapped back against the edge of the bar. He slid slowly to the floor, moaning in agony.

Seeing the fight fading out of Dan's eyes, she grinned. Feeling nauseous again, she hoped if she tossed her cookies it would be right in his lap. Her head was pounding, her ribs were cracked for sure, and her field of vision was beginning to narrow. Summoning what reserves she had, she reached for the cell phone in her pocket. It wasn't there. Dan must have taken it. She quickly searched his pockets and grabbed his instead.

She quickly dialed.

Alex heard his cell phone ring just as the team was about to enter another room. The number on the caller ID wasn't Skye, so he nearly ignored it. Later he would break into a cold sweat every time he thought of what would have happened if he had.

"Yeah...what?" he snapped into the phone.

"Alex?" she hissed between clenched teeth. When Dan moved slightly beneath her, she slammed her foot up against his windpipe to keep him restrained.

"Skye? Where the hell are you? Why aren't you here assisting with the cleanup?" He assumed she was on her way and was hoping to share some of the feeling of victory with her. He'd felt cheated when she failed to show up. His annoyance faded fast when he heard her breathing heavily.

"I'm doing a bit of cleaning up on my own." She increased the pressure on Dan's throat. "I just had to beat the shit out of Dan."

She felt herself crashing. Now that the adrenalin had been absorbed and used to full advantage, she was on automatic pilot and flying low. She leaned heavily on the bar. "He's dirty, Alex. I'm calling for some backup. He's currently under foot, but I'm fading fast."

"Skye, are you hurt?" He walked quickly for the front door and motioned to her team to stand ready. He could hear the raspy quality of her voice. He could hear the pain.

"Yeah, you could say I'm kind of a mess here, but..."

Skye never finished her sentence. The slight sideward movement of Dan's glazed eyes saved her life. She spun around just as Juan was just about to thrust a long knife in her back. It caught her in the abdomen, but because she was already backing away, it didn't go in deep enough to be a fatal blow. She chopped at Juan' wrist causing the knife to go skittering under the glass top table in the corner. Reflexively she kicked the side of Dan's head and heard a satisfying snap before she turned to face Juan who pulled another dagger from the top of his boot.

"Holy shit...Alex. It's Juan. Hurry...I need back up...now!" she shouted as she tossed the phone behind the sofa. She knew they could trace it if the line remained open. Feeling blood running freely from the cut in her abdomen, she had more immediate problems to deal with. This was very bad, she thought, as if it were happening to someone else. Very, very bad. Well, she couldn't worry about blood loss now. She still had a man with a knife who had murder in his eye standing in front of her.

Instead of backing away from the knife as Juan expected, she charged him, grabbing for his wrist as they both went crashing into the coffee table. She fell on top of him, but he was fresh and she was near total exhaustion. He rolled her over and she could feel the glass from the broken table slice through her blouse and into the flesh on her back. She brought her knee up into Juan's groin, but he anticipated the move and she only managed to put a deep bruise in his upper thigh.

"Skye...Skye," Alex shouted and took off running, still holding his phone. He could hear the struggle and his imagination painted a fearful picture of a life and death battle. His blood ran cold when he recognized some of the sounds of pain were decidedly female. Hadn't she said she was a mess? She must be fighting injured and that made him nearly lose control. He couldn't panic now, he thought. She needed him to remain cool and professional.

"Lucas, Linda, Barclay...you're with me. Now! Skye is down...she's down!" They didn't even question him, they all raced out of the building and hit the car doors running full out. Alex took the wheel and gave his phone to Linda. "Lucas, get a triangulation on the location of this phone, I think it's Dan's. Linda, keep the line open...report what you hear. I have to keep this car under control!"

His eyes were wild with fear and dread, but his hands were steady on the wheel. Years of rigid training forced the panic back and he was driving with hot, simmering determination.

"Oh God, Alex. Hurry!" said Linda, looking at him with quiet desperation. "There's a hell of a fight going on. I can hear furniture breaking. I just heard Skye swear in Italian. I don't understand Italian, but she sounds like she's being very, very difficult." She figured it was best to keep talking. She knew Alex was reaching the breaking point and that if he snapped it could impede his judgment.

"312 Langdon...down this road 8.3 miles and then a left. It's close, Alex. She's close," Lucas shouted from the back seat. "Ambulances and back up called to the scene. They should be right behind us."

"Oh man, oh man. That one I understood," shouted Linda as she reported what she heard. "Shit, Skye...your language! Oh God. Hurry Alex. Hurry, hurry. Skye's mouth tends to run when her physical energy begins to fade. She taunts and tries to distract. She's in really bad trouble."

"When she called, she said she was a mess. Dan must have hurt her...she's fighting hurt. Shit, shit, shit. Why was she there alone?" Alex took another corner on two wheels. Dangerous, but still in control.

"Dan? Dan Dickson?" asked Barclay incredulously. Then he nodded "You know, that does kind of explain a few things."

"She said he was dirty. She had him subdued then it sounded like someone attacked her. Juan."

"Damn. She has them both. Goddamn. That's our Skye!" shouted Barclay. Then he realized they may just have her and sobered fast.

"She's shouting. Knife, knife. She's telling us there's no gun, just knives," reported Linda, the tension obvious in her voice.

"Turn right on St. Frances. There should be a church on the corner," said Lucas. He was sweating now and shaking badly. He had to get this right.

Then Linda heard what sounded like the crunch of knife on bone. She went deadly pale, but Alex was too intent on the road to see the horror on her face. She knew from the sounds, then the sudden lack of it that someone was down in that room...she hoped to God it wasn't Skye.

Before she could stop them, tears slid down her cheeks. She quickly brushed them away, but not before Alex noticed. He put more pressure on the gas and shut down all of his emotions except the need for vengeance. He felt like a savage, his face set and rigid with suppressed rage. He could tell from Linda's reaction that the fight was over and she thought Skye was dead.

"Linda...report!" he shouted through his clenched teeth.

When she didn't respond, he yelled, "I said report, goddamn it!"

She looked over at him with dread clearly etched on her face. "It's over. There are no sounds coming from inside."

"Right here Alex...turn left." The car careened on two wheels as Alex took the corner at Grand. "Just another half mile...there...the building with the blue glass."

Alex grabbed the phone as he applied the brakes and jumped out of the car. "Skye...report...goddamn it...Skye!" Nothing. No sound.

"What apartment?" he asked as he threw the phone back to Linda.

"I don't have that information, Alex."

Frantically he looked at the names. "Apartment C!" he shouted. "Go in armed. Follow me." The name on the box was N. Nickerson.

He ran up the short flight of stairs, gun in hand and without any of his usual caution, kicked in the door with one vicious blow.

The room was in complete disarray. Dan was in the corner, moaning and struggling to gain his feet. Broken furniture was splashed with blood. Juan was on the floor with a long blade in his chest. He appeared to be breathing but was clearly out of the fight. Skye sat on the floor, her back up against the arm of the sofa. Blood was running out of multiple wounds in her chest and abdomen. Her blood was pouring out of her and pooling on the floor where she sat.

"Suspects captured and subdued," she rasped with her last bit of strength.

"I'm going off duty now." She gave them a weak smile, "Carry on." Closing her eyes, she slid down into Alex's waiting arms. He could hear the ambulance coming down the street as he grabbed the towel Linda handed him and applied pressure on the deepest of the cuts...he had to stop the flow of blood.

"Stay with me, baby. God, stay with me," he whispered urgently. "You don't go off duty until I tell you to go off duty." God, there was so much blood. He felt the panic rise again in his chest. He ruthlessly suppressed it. He had to stay calm. Skye needed him to stay cool. He applied gentle pressure to the wounds and tried to assess the rest of the damage. She was still breathing, but it was shallow. He had never been so afraid in his whole life.

He was so intent on keeping any more blood from leaking out of Skye, he didn't even flinch when he heard the shout from Lucas.

"Dan, no!" He looked up and saw Dan reach under the bar and grab a gun. It was his position in the department and the reluctance of everyone in the room to believe his guilt that had him able to get away from the agent helping him to a chair.

Dan shot Juan through the head, then put the gun in his mouth and fired. All Alex could think of as the room exploded in renewed activity was at least it prevented him from having to do it himself. He could feel Skye's faint heartbeat. If she didn't make it, Dan and Juan would have been dead men anyway.

He turned back to Skye as the competent hands of the paramedics took over. "Don't leave me now, sweetheart. Stay and fight. You have to stay with me, damn it!" he whispered as they lifted her gently to the gurney. She was beyond his reach, but he kept talking to her as the paramedics loaded her into the ambulance.

All the way to the hospital the paramedics worked on multiple fronts. They determined the knife wounds were the most serious and quickly and competently worked to stem the flow of blood. They attached monitors to her and started IV's. When they arrived at Georgetown University Hospital, they hit the doors running. A team of doctors and nurses charged out of the building and surrounded her gurney as they pushed her into the emergency room.

Alex was with her all the way, holding her hand. He knew there was nothing he could do medically, but he just couldn't let go.

"Please stand aside and wait in the hallway, sir," said one of the interns. She was kind, but firm.

"The hell I will. I'm not leaving her." He watched as her chest continued to move up and down in a steady rhythm. Her eyes were closed and her hand was getting colder. He was feeling nothing. He was afraid if he let go now, he would start raving like a lunatic. Fear and dread had completely shut him down.

"Please, sir. You can't be in here," repeated the intern. She started to pry Alex's fingers from Skye's. "Let us have her now. We'll take good care of her. We know what we're doing. You'll only get in the way. You'll only hurt her if you stay."

Alex looked up. The words were getting through to him. He felt strong arms go around his shoulders. "Come on Alex. Let the doctors do their job." He looked up into Jim's worried and grief-stricken face and nodded.

"Okay. Okay. But I'm not leaving her." He reluctantly let go of her hand and backed off into a corner of the room. Panic and blind rage gripped him as the nurses ripped away Skye's shirt to reveal multiple bruises, abrasions, and knife cuts. She was bleeding from a head wound that appeared to be the least of their concerns. A nurse was gently cleaning it out as a team of emergency room doctors began assessing the internal damage. Blood was everywhere. Skye's blood. God! Couldn't they see it was running out of her like life itself? Why weren't they stopping it?

"Pulse thready and getting weaker," said a nurse with a hint of urgency in her voice.

The knife that had cut her flesh was no sharper than the knife that seemed to cut into his heart.

"Let me..." said Alex. He had no idea what he meant to do, but Jim had a tight grip on his arm and was pulling him into a corner.

"No, Alex," he said firmly, hoping to get through the terror he saw in his agent's face. "There's nothing we can do for her now. Let's get out of their way."

"We're losing her...BP is falling fast!"

"No!" his mind screamed. *I'm* losing her. "God!" He ran his bloody fingers through his hair, then looked down at his hands. Blood...her blood.

"Cross match her blood and get some units in here! Stat! Have a crash cart armed and ready. Where the hell is that bleeder?" asked the doctor as she carefully probed the deepest wound.

Alex watched as they skillfully and gently tried to stabilize her. He stood feeling helpless and completely vulnerable. There was nothing more he could do and it was killing him. He was supposed to be her protector and her shield.

Damn him. Where was he when she needed him? He stared at her pale face. Searching for life. Somewhere deep inside he felt strongly that if he took his eyes off her for even a minute, she would slip away. He wasn't going to leave her. He was going to remain in his station. The guardian.

He sensed someone step up beside him.

"Alex?" It was Sloane and she sounded as scared as he felt.

"Sloane? How did you get here so fast?"

"Jim called me on my cell phone. I was in class across the street."

The look on his face frightened her more than the sight of her sister on the table in the center of the room.

"Please, Alex," she begged. "Tell me what's happening."

"I don't know, baby," he managed to say. He gathered her shaking body into his arms. "But I can't take my attention away from her. I have to keep watch. I have to keep watch."

"I know," she said weakly. "I won't ask anything more right now." They held each other as the sights and sounds of the frantic work in the room washed over them. He knew just enough about the language of medicine to be very, very afraid.

Twice more, they almost lost her right there in the emergency room. Both times, Alex stiffened and prepared to do battle. There was nothing he could do, but his body didn't know that. His body needed to protect and defend.

When they got her stabilized, they rushed her to surgery. Alex, Sloane and Jim began their long wait in a private room near the operating theater. The room began to fill with people. Linda, Barclay and Lucas came from Dan's apartment. Everything was wrapped up there. Reports, investigations, research could all wait. Their leader was down and they were there to stand with her. Judy and Maureen arrived from the central office. Connie and Bill were called and Carter was right behind them.

They all talked in low tones as the first level cover story was circulated. Jim's heartrending task was to issue a preliminary report and a plausible story that could be shared with friends and family outside the department. Dan, Skye's long-time friend and her father's former lawyer called her for a meeting. He attacked her and a fight ensued in which she was gravely wounded. Dan then committed suicide, complicating the police investigation. Jim, as Skye's godfather and Dan's close friend was called in first and he was standing by to assist in the communication with the family.

Juan, of course, was never mentioned. It appeared as though Skye somehow secured the knife that Juan had brought with him to the apartment to use on her and she stopped him with it. Her battles with both Dan and Juan left her hovering between life and death. This would never be shared with anyone outside the department.

Jim also called Hazel, and a car was dispatched to retrieve her from Virginia. Pearl met Hazel at the emergency room entrance and led her to the waiting area. Subdued and grief-stricken, Hazel wept in Alex's arms.

"Damn Alex. When this is over, we're going to sit in my kitchen and I'm going to find out how and why this happened. Jim said it was Dan. Why would Dan crack like this? He loved that girl. Maybe it was all those crazy women he married after the idiot divorced Abigail. That Bitsy creature would make anyone mad. But why Skye, Alex? Why our precious, precious Skye?"

"We may never know. The explanation may have died with him." Later they would have to create some kind of plausible story. For now, none of that seemed to matter. "First we get her well, so she can join us at the table."

"We'll have pancakes."

"Yes," whispered Alex, with tears in his eyes. "We'll have a whole table full of pancakes."

Jim talked with Washington and London and the local authorities. His cell phone rang constantly and he was efficiently taking care of all the reports and details. He kept one eye on Alex at all times. He knew his man was on the edge. Periodically a nurse would come in to report that there was nothing to report.

Concern, dread, anger, despair, hope, fear, guilt. Every emotion pounded the room and swept through Alex. By the fourth hour, he was numb and wasn't responding to anyone.

Sloane went over to where Alex was sitting alone looking out the window, seeing nothing.

"Alex?"

He looked at her with haunted eyes. He was exhausted, as much by the emotional drain as by the thirty-six hours of constant motion.

"Don't worry. I'm not going to try to boost food or coffee on you or tell you that you look like shit."

For the first time since he found Skye lying in a pool of her own blood, Alex smiled. It was a weak attempt, but it made Sloane feel better. He opened his arms and she sat on his lap, cradling her as she nestled into his strong embrace.

"You know how Skye always boots up when I'm crazed or flipping out? And how she looks at me and knows when I'm primed or when I'm feeling a bit off?" She swallowed audibly and went on. "Most particularly she knows when I slip on the truth and engage in a terminological inexactitude?"

"You mean tell a fib?"

"Well…ya…like that," she snorted.

"She can read you." He unconsciously stroked her hair…to comfort her…to comfort him.

"Well, would you believe me if I tell you it seems like more than that? Like we're connected and she can't just read me, but she can get into my mind?" Alex nodded automatically. He really did love this young extension of Skye. He understood their connection.

"I know I'm not making much sense here. Sleep deprivation diminishes your capacity to think and communicate effectively…anyway…I digress." She could feel his attention begin to fade. He was sliding back into himself and his own dark thoughts again.

"I want to tell you something important." She took his face in her small hands and looked him in the eye. "We're connected. Always have been. We're connected now. She's on the edge, Alex." Tears started sliding down her pale cheeks. "It makes me so sacred I can hardly breathe, but I can still feel her in my heart, in my mind. She's going to fight for us. She's going to do this for us."

The tears turned into a flood and Alex held her close. He swallowed the lump in his own throat as his eyes misted over. Her gentle words did comfort him. He understood connections. He closed his ravaged eyes and kissed the top of her head.

There was silence in the room as the sixth hour came and went. Everyone gave up even the pretence of conversation. Jim paced, Sloane dozed fitfully in Alex's arms, Hazel prayed, and the people who had come in to join the vigil occupied the other chairs.

Just when Alex felt he couldn't stand the tension any longer, a very weary doctor strode into the room. Alex shook Sloane awake, trying to read the doctor's expression. Dread mingled with hope. As they slowly stood, time seemed to stand still. Even the hands of the doctor as she wiped them over her face seemed to move in slow motion.

"I won't keep you in suspense," she began grimly. "Nor will I give you any shallow platitudes. Skyler is still in very serious jeopardy. We've just finished repairing all the damage done by the knife wounds. She lost a great deal of blood." She looked at Alex. "A few minutes later, and I mean minutes, and we wouldn't have been able to save her. She has three cracked ribs, a broken arm, and a serious concussion, as well as some nasty cuts and abrasions. We're listing her as extremely critical. If she survives the next 24 hours we'll upgrade her to critical."

Alex started to shake inside, but his voice was steady. Years of training took over and he covered his fear with a calm, confident demeanor.

"When can we see her?" Alex tried to keep his eyes from moving down to some of the drops of blood staining the doctor's surgical gown. Skye's blood.

"She's in recovery now. You should be able to see her in the next thirty minutes when we move her to intensive care. I'll have a nurse come and get you. Very short visits. This young woman took quite a beating. She may not regain consciousness for days. Until she's out of intensive care, family only, although we can extend the definition of family a bit." She recognized the connection between Alex and Skye and wasn't about to fight with this man over a technicality.

"I know you're all exhausted." Her eyes were filled with compassion. "I'm sorry, but I would suggest that you not leave the hospital. We lost her twice during surgery. She fought back, but she's still on the edge."

Sloane squeezed Alex's shaking hand driving back some of the terror. The doctor's message was clear. She could still die and the family would want to stay close.

"We'll make arrangements for you to stay in a private family critical care room. I must get back to my patient now."

She left quickly. Hazel began weeping into her hands. Jim went to her. Cell phones came out and calls were made.

"She's going to be hundred proof, now," said Sloane firmly. "Alex will you come with me down to the gift shop? I want to buy her one of those funny cards with someone's ass peeking out of a hospital gown."

Hand in hand they went down the elevator and bought her all the cards they could find that showed someone's ass. They came back with 32 cards.

Alex was expecting a negative reaction and steeled his will when he first went into the room where she lay. The steel melted and he nearly needed medical attention himself when he actually saw her. The shock of seeing her connected to so many machines, her strong, confident body buried under bandages and tubes made him weak and nearly brought him to his knees. She was pale and beautiful and as still as death.

Officially, they were allowed ten-minute visits every hour, but once Alex was in her room, he fought any attempt to get him out. He sent Sloane with

Hazel to the family waiting room. Instinctively, they knew he needed the time alone with her and were willing to give it to him. He was grateful.

On the edge of exhaustion, he sat down and closed his eyes against the onslaught of unshed tears and indescribable fear. He knew he had to get himself under control in case she woke up, but for a few minutes he allowed himself to be human. The woman he loved was broken and battered, hanging on to life by sheer will. His heart was breaking and his chest was tight…and he felt the first of the cleansing tears fall down his cheeks.

"My love, my life," he whispered, holding on to her hand. "I'm begging you to live for me."

He didn't move throughout the night and into the next day as people came and went. No one could convince him to leave her side and after awhile, they gave up trying. Once, they thought she might be coming around and once they thought she might slip away forever, but mostly she just lay there.

Late in the afternoon of the third day, he went back to his townhouse for a quick shower, shave, and a meal. Sloane told him that if Skye woke up to see him looking like he did, it would scare her into a coma. When that didn't move him she told him he smelled like a goat. He found he still had Skye's blood dried on his clothes. Alex changed into a clean shirt and slacks, ate something that tasted like cardboard, gave a tearful Cynthia a brief report, and was back in Skye's room within the hour. She hadn't moved.

He was getting agitated by the evening of the fourth day. He was told she'd passed from a light coma into sleep, but he didn't see much change.

"She's healing," the doctor assured him. "She'll wake up when her body is ready. We're administering morphine through her IV. At least in her unconscious state, she doesn't feel the pain so intensely." She pressed the button that gave Skye a surge of the pain-killing drug.

When she saw his expression of concern and anxiety she asked kindly, "may I prescribe something for you?"

"Hmm?" He knew he looked like he hadn't slept in days. Mostly because he hadn't slept in days. He was haggard and worn out. But he couldn't leave. He had to keep watch. Blinking his tired eyes, he frowned.

"You look like you could use some rest. Would you like a mild sedative?"

Was it wishful thinking or did he see her move slightly.

"No. I'm fine."

No. It wasn't his imagination. Skye's hand moved. It moved! Relief poured through him and he felt like he could take his first deep breath in days. He was by her bedside in three quick strides. Exhaustion drained off of him and new energy surged through his body. She moved! He was sure of it.

"Doctor, I think I saw her hand move." He took it in his as the doctor came over and checked her out. She did a quick examination, then lifted her head and smiled.

"What a remarkable woman. I think she's definitely going to make it. There's unambiguous movement and her pupils look good. I'll go tell the family she's close to consciousness." She turned and smiled at Alex. "I'm sure you would like to stay here in case she opens her eyes."

She'd come to know this man who never left her patient's side. She sighed as she left the room to talk to the family. To be loved like that. And by a man like that. When she was young her friends would have looked at him and said "Hubba Hubba." Now she heard her granddaughters saying something like "wicked." Any way you described him he was a hunk and a hunk with a heart.

Alex grinned as he looked down at Skye. She was trying to open her eyes. He was sure of it. He wanted to be the first face she saw. Skye finally did open her eyes but said nothing. It was only for a few moments, but he was sure she was looking for him and that she knew he was there. She was breathing easier now and was upgraded to critical. Everyone was confident she was on the verge of a full recovery.

Celebration, hope, and happiness were in the air and Hazel took Sloane home for a well-deserved rest. Flowers started arriving the minute Skye was moved from intensive care to a private room. It seemed the whole world wanted to wish her well. Alex called in an order for white gardenias to be delivered twice a day.

It was coming into night again. The sounds of the hospital were more hushed and the activity was less urgent. Alex was in his chair next to Skye's bed. He took her hand. It was cold, but her pulse felt strong and steady. He drew it to his lips and kissed each knuckle, slowly, tenderly. Such strong hands, he thought, capable of controlling an airliner and sending regret into an enemy's gut. Gentle, too. He saw them comb through Sloane's hair and pick up an injured bird.

His heart beat a bit faster when he remembered her hands on him. He knew their touch…could almost feel them now. Electricity and excitement traveled through her fingers as they loved and aroused him. He shook himself when he realized that if he went any further down that road he might be tempted to climb into the bed beside her. Wouldn't that give the night nurses something to talk about.

He kissed her palm and felt a slight tremor. His heart leapt as he looked up into her chocolate-colored eyes. They were full of pain, but they were alert and they were smiling into his.

"Did the doctors tell you that you could kiss it and make it better?" she rasped, the smile reaching her lips before a wave of pain made her wince. Relief poured through him but so did the agony of seeing her hurting. He leaned over and gently kissed her lips.

"Welcome back, darling," he said as he smoothed her hair. His heart was bursting with relief.

"Ah, yes. The kiss. You must be Prince Charming." She winced again and the light in her eyes began to fade under the onslaught of pain. Her whole body felt like it had been hammered. "I think this is one princess who would rather go back to sleep for a hundred years."

He reached over and pressed the button that would give her a shot of the morphine. It would take the edge off of what he knew she was feeling. "While I would love to kiss you all over and make it better, I think modern medicine may be just a bit more effective."

"Mmmm…" She was fading as the drugs hit her system. "Better."

Just before her eyes closed, he took her hand.

"Marry me, princess, and make my life worth living," he whispered and kissed her again.

"Marry me, prince charming, and make my life…" she sighed as she slipped back into unconsciousness. "Make my life," she repeated and was asleep again.

Alex sat back down and continued his vigil, never taking his eyes off the battered face of his princess. He smiled a bit devilishly. She may not remember this little conversation, but he was going to hold her to it. He was determined to make a life with her. She would be his wife. Some of the tension of the last few days drained out of his weary body.

He closed his bloodshot eyes and his thoughts drifted into a dream. The sound of the steady heart monitor comforted him and he let his mind wander to a picture of Skye in a wedding dress, watching for him in a tower, waiting to be rescued. Yeah, right. She would have kicked the door down, then beat the shit out of the evil witch and all of her minions. So much for that fairytale. He shifted into a more comfortable position and fell into a deep, dreamless sleep.

When Skye opened her eyes again three hours later, she found her Prince Charming stretched out and fast asleep in a chair next to her bed with white gardenias on every bare surface. Even disheveled and unkempt, he was gorgeous. Smiling, she sighed before pressing the button for another hit of that wonderful miracle drug. Her last thoughts were of him in a lovely tuxedo.

CHAPTER 26

Skye was completing her fiftieth rep with the weights in her home gym. The physical therapist had just left, ecstatic over her progress. She didn't realize that after their rigorous workout, Skye continued with a grueling one of her own.

Skye had come home to Virginia so Hazel and Sloane could watch over her. They needed to do it as much as Skye needed the tender care. Alex was there as much as he could be, but he had been working long hours on both the case and some major business project.

Hazel was currently on a trip to Nashville with her red hat group. She volunteered to drive the bus, but her legs were too short, so good sense prevailed and they hired the man with the Rhode Island tattoo to drive them. Skye was glad to see her go since she did nothing but nag her about Alex. Sloane wasn't much better, but at least she didn't pop in at midnight with hot chocolate, peanut butter-broccoli couscous and at least six more virtues of Alexander Springfield. On the other hand, Sloane was currently between semesters, so she was applying relentless pressure on Skye to officially tie it up with Alex. Skye could simply not escape the marry Alex campaign.

"I don't know what I was thinking. I must have thought I was dying, or something. I know I was way, way, under the influence of mind-altering drugs. I can't marry him, Sloane."

"Come on, Skye!" exclaimed Sloane. Her idea of an ideal workout was watching one. She swore she could break out into a sweat just watching Skye pump iron. "You're absolutely ape-shit over him."

"Even if I could define that gruesome term, which I can't, what difference does that make? Everyone who knows Alex goes ga-ga over him. It's not an exclusive club." She put her weights down and threw a towel over her shoulders.

"Any woman that pumps that much iron, flies a jet liner and can beat the shit out of a squad of ninjas should never say something like 'ga-ga'. What's wrong with 'ape-shit'?"

"God, where did I go wrong?" Skye just shook her head and started her tae kwon do routine. She'd lost a great deal of weight and most of her strength in the hospital and needed to get it all back if she was to return to active duty. She had to get to work. With Hazel and Sloane hovering and Alex calling her constantly, it was the only way to get her life back.

"You're avoiding the real issue. Alex is torching for you and he wants to do the middle-aisle two step with you. You love him. I know you do. Isn't marriage the next move in a mature relationship? He was with you day and night in the hospital until you were out of danger, then every day and now he calls you all the time. Skye, you didn't see him when you came in all bloody. He almost went off the deep end of insanity. He is so gone over you. I thought he was going to need intensive care. Besides, he isn't going to take 'no' for an answer. What are you so jiggy over? You're never, ever, going to strike someone better. You're going to die an old maid and I'll never get to be an aunt. If you don't marry him, I'll just have to grow some breasts and seduce him myself. I swear I will." She stopped to take a breath and Skye grabbed the opportunity to interrupt.

"Look." Skye stopped her routine and gazed seriously at her sister's earnest face. "I really do care for him, but I need to be a pilot. I fly all over the world and he does his thing with the investments and buildings and international law. How can we make something like that work?"

"Skye, I know he's a cop." Now was the time to show Skye her cards, one at a time. If her sister could do 50 reps, she was ready to take the grand slam.

"What?" Skye asked in utter surprise. She'd always worked very hard to hide her other life from her friends and family. The fact that Sloane knew something was both shocking and dangerous. "Don't be ridiculous. You know he isn't a cop."

"I said I know. I mean he isn't exactly a cop…more like an agent. I'm not a pod, Skye. I hacked into some of the records of the Justice Department. I wanted to know about…well…you know…about what happened to you. I went into Dan's office pc. He was really a grunch in formulating passwords. He wasn't only an evil sleezeball, he was a real solid concrete brain. Not so good for someone in intelligence work. Anyway…I passed the unpaid invoices file and took a peek. He had one in there for a first-class ticket for one Alexander Springfield. Now why would someone from Justice be picking up the tab for a big tycoon? Then I remembered about his family and their cop thing. So I went deeper."

Skye was utterly speechless and completely horrified. "Darling. Dan was mentally ill and emotionally stressed. They found a tumor…"

Sloane just stared at Skye and went deadly serious. "Don't, Skye. I know why you're lying…but don't. Please. I saw all the reports. I know."

"God, honey, you know I can't confirm any of this."

"You don't have to. Let's just say for the record that my biggest and best clue is this…why would you reject someone that you itch for and who is so righteous? It just didn't made sense. Two plus two equals four, Skye."

She shuddered to think what would happen if Sloane ever decided to go over to the other side of the law. What was she saying? By hacking into Dan's records she had already crossed the line. She was just winding up to begin her scold when Sloane held up her hand.

"Before you go ballistic on me, I've confessed and groveled to Uncle Jim. He duly chastised me and already determined my punishment. I'm going to be working with him as an intern to prevent other hackers from doing what I did. I get to work with Barclay." She had known Barclay for years and had always pretended she believed the story about him working for the Department of the Interior. She got her first computer from him and had surpassed his skill within the year.

"When did all this happen? And why wasn't I consulted, or at least informed? You're still a minor. You know…me guardian…you kid." It didn't really disturb her too much. Jim and Barclay would be excellent mentors and they could help her keep an eye on Sloane. She might as well use her talents to help fight the good fight.

"I know, I know…and I don't want to be anything but a kid. But not all the time. Anyway, don't get me off track here." She returned to her original conversation. "I know you said you would never get involved with another cop after Jeffrey. But that was so long ago, Skye."

"It seems like yesterday. The reasons for that are complex and personal. Please don't go there, honey. Alex understands this. If he *is* an agent, and I'm not saying he is, he needs that like I need to be a pilot. I understand that but I can't deal with the potential for loss. I've told him to back off this marriage thing. I was way too vulnerable in the hospital and didn't know what I was saying. I will not marry someone who may be in danger. I don't ever intend to be that exposed again. That's the ultimate point."

"Lilly livered chicken shit."

"God, if one more person calls me a coward because I want to protect my heart, I'm going to…" Skye off trailed remembering Alex had called her a coward too. She began her routine again with renewed vigor. She wasn't a chicken or a coward, she was a woman who knew her mind and was going to play it her way. Sweat was beginning to pour out of her in a satisfying surge of energy.

"I know you're an agent too, Skye," Sloane said abruptly. She knew this was the next card in her hand and was playing it just the way she wanted.

"What?" This time Skye stopped in mid-kick and just stared agape at her little sister.

"It isn't like I've told anyone, or that I would, Skye. But, please. Pilots don't go around with the physical conditioning of a super hero and get knifed and stuff." Her eyed clouded over. "I know. I've known for years, but if it helps, you can pretend I don't."

"Look sweetie, you're not giving me room to breathe here."

"Good." Sloane jumped off the stool and came closer. "I've put this off because of your somewhat diminished capacity, but now I'm going to tell you straight. I know what it's like to be scared when someone you love is always flying into danger. I'm scared every day that you might not come home to me. I've been hacking into your files for years. I know what you've been doing and how much jeopardy you're in. I knew that someday I would see you damaged and…and…lying in a hospital so close to death that I…" She couldn't finish her sentence as the tears clogged her throat. "Oh God, Skye. You're all I have left in the world, except Aunt Hazel." Tears flowed from her big luminous eyes but she swallowed and continued. "Jeepers, Skye, you almost got killed. That was no accident or Dan suffering from some mental illness. That was part of your job. If Alex and I are willing to take that risk and love you anyway and want you permanently in our lives, then why can't you make the commitment too?"

She was crying hard now and it broke Skye's heart. Besides the tears, Sloane hadn't said 'jeepers' since she was six. It made her seem so young. Her little hacker sister with a genius IQ was still just this side of childhood.

Skye went over and held Sloane close. Her chest still hurt from the wounds and cracked ribs, but it was nothing compared to the ache in her heart. Sloane had known for years? And she kept it hidden, along with her anxiety? What was she going to do? Sloane made sense, but how could she make a marriage work? She had to think.

Alex had brought up the proposal once again during her hospital stay and then again when he brought her home. He said he was a patient man and that he would wait until her heart left her no choice but to say yes. To say yes again, he reminded her, since in his delusional mind she'd already said yes.

Well she was thinking more clearly now. One of them had to lead with their head and it had to be her.

Could she live with the danger, not to herself, but to Alex? She'd seen him work. He was careful, but bold. He had a daring, heroic style that scared the hell out of her. What if he didn't come home one day? Sloane continued to cry in her arms and Skye had to swallow hard to get past the lump in her throat.

And what about his feelings for her? Skye was never going to give up her job with Justice. Could he live with that? He had lost a sister in the line of duty, for God's sake. Didn't he know the heartbreak she could bring him? That was a silly question. Of course he did. Hadn't he been through hell and back the last few weeks? And what was his reward for his strength, his loving compassion, and his gentle care? She was reneging on her pledge to marry him. She sighed as Sloane's tears started to dry up. Maybe they were right. She would have to think about it. It was just too exhausting to fight them both.

Alex was returning from London tonight. He'd had a lot of paperwork to take care of and had taken on most of hers as well. Depositions, testimonies, reports, meetings. She knew he would rather take on another drug cartel single handedly than be in an office with all that paper, but it needed to be done in order for their work to be complete. She admired him for his tenacity. God, she admired him for everything he did. She loved him. She sighed again. She was ape-shit about him.

She kissed Sloane's wet cheeks.

"You've given me a lot to think about, baby sister. When did you take on the parent role?"

"I've always had it," Sloane sniffled. "I just let you think you were running things so I didn't have to go out and make a living."

"Let me take a shower and we'll talk some more. You have completely blown my mind with all these revelations. I sometimes forget you're some kind of baby genius." Skye gave Sloane another quick hug and kiss. "Does Jim know about this other hacking?"

"Oh yeah…the confession was complete. Needless to say, my internship is for an indefinite period of time." Sloane smiled. She would tell Skye later that it was exactly what she intended to do with her life. Not the hacking part…the working with Jim and Barclay part. She wanted into the intelligence game and intended to start with the internship gig.

Skye turned and went upstairs to her bedroom. Sloane continued to sniffle until she was out of the room, then ran over to her backpack and took out her cell phone.

"Come in quick and hard," she said slyly. "I got her all softened up and gooey. She even made me cry…but just a little. I admitted I knew all about…well, you know. Can't talk on this phone. See ya later." Hmmm, she thought as she hung up on Alex. I could really get into this secret agent stuff.

Skye took extra time with her appearance. She was still a bit self-conscious about the scars on her chest and abdomen, but she figured Alex could handle it. She brushed her hair until the curls were tamed and splashed on Midnight Seduction, remembering the night in London when Alex decided to give into temptation and seduce her. Or was it the other way around? Didn't matter. She put on a form hugging one-piece jumpsuit of white linen and slim leather sandals. This will be easy to shed later, she thought wickedly. She intended to do the seducing tonight.

They hadn't been intimate since she went into the hospital and just thinking about him and their nights together made her ache with need. She craved his touch. If she knew him, he would be quite randy by now too. Good. That would give her some power when they discussed their future.

Skye began to think of alternatives to marriage…just like contingency planning for the department. They could continue to see each other, enjoy a nice physical relationship with no strings. An image of Alex with someone else flashed into her mind. No, amend that. A nice *exclusive* physical relationship with a few strings. Yes, that would be better. She didn't want to share. And she was sure he wouldn't want to. So they would continue on like they were before.

They would have to commute when they could, or meet at other locations. Then there would be their assignments, which would probably send them in opposite directions. Long periods of absence. She wouldn't know what he was doing. Maybe he wouldn't be able to communicate with her regularly. That wasn't such a great picture, either.

Skye stared out the window and sighed. She was missing him, already. How would it be if she didn't know his location and he was gone for months? Oh, bloody hell. She caught herself sighing like a schoolgirl again. She was going to have a glass of wine, maybe two. All this thinking was giving her a headache.

Skye was standing by the window, sipping her Chianti, thinking about her feelings, and enjoying the late sunset when Alex walked quietly into the room. Sloane had let him in, chattering in a low, conspiratorial voice. He knew it had taken Skye *forever* to dress and he would find her staring out the window and sighing.

"Great," Sloane said as she looked him over. "You went with the kind of casual, studly look. Yum, yum. You smell really good, too. Plus, she hasn't seen you in over a week, so she should be good and horny by now."

"Good God, you're a gas," laughed Alex. He was sure glad this little doll was on his side. There was no way he would have been able to win the war if she'd put her considerable talents to work against him.

"I really, really want to be a Maid of Honor...so don't blow it, cowboy. I did my part. I did the logic thing. You know...kind of appealed to her rational side. That's because it's the only side giving us any grief, here." She looked him up and down again. He had lost that haunted look he wore when Skye was so hurt. Now he was back to robust, healthy, and all male. Whew, he was a hottie.

"You look like you have the irresistible man thing covered. You can appeal to her...well...more animal, physical side." She rubbed her hands and grinned broadly. "I think Skye is toast."

Alex just stood and stared at Skye standing by the window. He wanted this moment to savor the feelings he had for her. God, she was beautiful. He looked at the war of emotions playing on her face. In this unguarded moment, he felt he could see into her soul. She was so used to performing a part, playing a role. Tonight he was seeing her without her mask. It was a real show.

When Skye took a deep breath to sigh yet again, her face reflected a wince of pain. Absent-mindedly she rubbed her sore ribs. She pushed the image of Dan coming at her out of her mind. She was done with that chapter. It wasn't the past that troubled her tonight. It was her future.

What was she going to do with all these feelings she had for Alex? She loved him. But could she open herself up again? God, getting stabbed was a piece of cake compared to the pain of thinking of life without Alex in it. Worse yet was thinking about Alex with anyone else but her.

When Alex saw the look of pain, it broke his reverie. She rarely let anyone see her hurting. In the last few weeks, she weaned herself off all medication and worked very hard to get back in shape. His admiration of her courage, always intense and positive, reached new heights since her release. He hoped to tap into that well of courage when he asked her again to take another huge risk. He intended to have her as his wife. And he was a man who always got what he wanted.

Suddenly, she turned. Her senses felt his presence. She abruptly stopped rubbing her sore ribs, slid her defenses neatly back into place, and rewarded him with a broad smile of welcome.

She walked over to him in long, steady strides not showing any of her nerves. Her knees were weak from the sudden rush of passion she felt when she looked at his handsome face and delicious body, but her hands were steady when she held them out to him.

"Alex! How was your trip," she said in a friendly, but non-committal tone.

Well, that was cold, he thought as he took her hands in his. If he hadn't seen the sudden flash of pleasure in her eyes before she pulled the shade over them, he would have thought she considered him nothing more than a casual friend.

Mimicking her reserved tone, he smiled stiffly and said, "Skye, it's good to see you looking so well." He gave her a quick peck on the cheek. "How are you feeling?"

Because they talked every day and had seen each other naked on numerous occasions, this formal greeting was really a parody and completely ridiculous, and they both knew it. Skye's lips quivered upward first. Her eyes sparkled with humor. It made Alex's heart melt and his mood improve immensely. He actually laughed out loud.

"Well, now that we have that first really proper greeting out of the way, can we get right to the kissing and groping?" he asked looking so hopeful, she laughed too, and threw herself into his waiting arms.

"How about one kiss and we get to the groping a little later?" She planted a big kiss on his smiling lips. "I want a complete report. I've been dying to hear all the details. Did you find the paper trail that...?"

Her kiss only whetted his appetite. It had been a long dry spell and he had a lot of hunger stored up. He cut off her questions with a long, passionate, breath-stealing kiss that left her head spinning and turned her thighs into liquid, barely capable of supporting her weight.

When Alex felt Skye sway slightly in his arms, he pushed her away from him and looked with concern into her flushed face. "You okay?" A slight frown creased his brow. He didn't want to push it if she wasn't physically ready.

"Yeah...completely healed...," she sighed with a look of delight on her face...she was more than halfway to her first orgasm. "More...more," she whispered.

"More information, or more me?" he teased brushing his lips lightly over hers.

"More you." She dove back into his arms and put her whole heart into the kiss. His arms went around her, stroking her back and molding her body to his. He continued to kiss her face, her neck, and the place behind her ear that seemed to be her 'on' button.

"Is that a gun in your pocket, or are you just glad to see me?" she murmured Mae West's famous line as she weaved her fingers through his thick wavy hair and arched her body into his.

He laughed again and pulled back. He didn't want to push and cause her any pain and he wasn't sure she was ready for his hands on her. But when he saw the smoldering look in her eyes, he gave up thinking of her as someone who was convalescing. Maybe he could indulge himself a bit. He moved his palms along the sides of her breasts and was rewarded with a moan of pleasure. That was all the invitation he needed, and his hands began a more complete examination of her superb curves. She was too thin, but she was still a delight to the senses…all of them.

He recognized the scent she wore, but wasn't sure of the message. He remembered the night she wore it very well. So did his libido. Midnight Seduction. He sniffed her neck and decided to put his remarkable detective talents to work.

"Was this intended to drive me right over the edge, or was this a random choice?"

She laughed and started to slowly unbutton his shirt. "I think we have time before dinner to provide you with some clues."

"Are you ready for this?" he asked with concern in his voice. Her hands started to stroke his chest and he was sure his body really didn't care much about the answer. It had already cast its vote.

"Darling, I'm almost entirely sure that the doctor prescribed this therapy to ensure my full recovery. You were just lucky to come along when I needed to fill the prescription."

"Well, then…anything I can do to help your recovery. But let's get into a more secure location." He picked her up and kissed her brainless all the way to her bedroom. As he laid her gently on her bed, his hands moved all over her body as if taking inventory. He was painfully slow and gentle. When he saw her scars he paused for a few minutes to put his remembered fear and rage back behind him. It didn't take long against the onslaught of his love and desire. He peeled away her clothes and kissed each scar and fading bruise.

"Oh my," Skye whispered as her breath caught in her throat, with pleasure. "This is like connect the dots. Too bad they stop just above the bikini line."

Her relaxed manner worked its magic on Alex and the last of his anger and concern dissipated in the face of the overwhelming excitement of feeling her under him again…his physical need for her was all that drove him now. He loved her slowly, gently, and found inside her his own cure...his own recovery from the long frightening weeks since her fight for life.

Later he held her as she slept. They had made love until the sun went down and Skye was completely exhausted. They forgot about dinner. Alex looked down at her sleeping face and pulled the sheet over her bare shoulders.

She may think she's fully recovered, he thought, but the exertion of their wonderful romp tapped most of her strength. His arms tightened around her and he joined her in sleep.

When she awoke the next morning, she was alone in the big bed. She heard the shower running and smiled. She'd slept soundly and dreamlessly for the first time since her release from the hospital. It must have been the feeling of his arms around her in the night. She tested her arms, legs, and torso before she moved to get out of bed. She wanted to be sure everything worked and she was capable of functioning properly. Yup, everything seemed to be in order. A bit stiff, perhaps, but wonderfully used.

Alex was an eyeful when he came out of the bathroom and walked across the room with only a towel wrapped around his lean, trim waist. He looked wonderful. His hair was wet and shiny and his muscles rippled along his back as he dug up his cell phone and started making all of his early morning business calls. She sometimes forgot that he was an extremely wealthy man who bought and sold buildings, companies, maybe even entire towns. Her attention to that part of his life faded fast when she discovered he was a fellow agent. She loved to watch him. If the people on the other end of the call knew he was almost naked...well...it was best to get that picture out of her mind.

After his third call, he said in a soft, sexy voice, "have you taken in enough? Can I get dressed now?"

For a minute, she thought he was talking to someone on the phone. When she raised her eyes to his face, she realized he was talking to her. He was smiling broadly as he lifted a brow.

"Hmmm...I was thinking about taking advantage of the situation and asking for an encore." She stretched and preened like a cat.

"I would be glad to oblige, my love, but I'm going to restrain my incredible lust until I'm sure your beautiful, but still recovering body, can take the stress." He knew she would push it beyond endurance, so he decided to be the mature one and make the supreme sacrifice by withholding his favors until he could be sure she was really all right.

"You were willing enough last night," she pouted prettily, grabbing her robe.

"Last night, my darling, I was controlled by a power stronger than my will to resist." He shot her an appraising look. "Seriously, I want to be sure you're really okay."

"Let me take a shower, and then we can decide." As she got up and walked gingerly toward the bathroom, she realized that perhaps he was right. Pride, however, prevented her from whimpering. She kept her back straight and closed the door before she nearly collapsed against the sink and rubbed some of the soreness out of her chest. When she came back out 20 minutes later, he was completely dressed.

"Ah...ha!" she smiled at him. "So you decided to cover up before I lost my head."

"I decided we don't need to rush things." He came over and ran his thumb along her sharp jaw line. "We have time."

He turned to the small table on the terrace. It was laden with food and a fresh pot of coffee and smelled heavenly. One thing about really great sex...it stimulated the appetite.

"Sloane brought up some breakfast and coffee. I think she wanted a progress report."

"In that case, I'm glad you dressed. That girl is too much in love with you and way too smart for her years. I would hate to have you put her off other men for the rest of her life."

"Let's have some coffee and talk about the rest of *your* life, shall we?" he said pointedly.

He poured her a cup. His hands were steady, but not his nerves. It was time, he thought, to finish the discussion she'd put off since the night in the hospital when she asked him to marry her.

"Goodness," she said as she took the coffee with an equally steady hand. Her nerves were also in knots, but she knew how to keep them in check. "We're going to discuss my whole life before breakfast?"

"No, we're going to discuss your whole life while you eat breakfast." He pulled her chair out and she sat down carefully, pulling her robe closed so he couldn't see some of the bruising around the wounds that hadn't been there the night before.

He frowned at her. She seemed to forget sometimes that he was a highly trained observer. "Before we get to your life, what are you hiding?"

He took her hand away from the front of her robe and opened it. "God, I'm sorry, sweetheart," he whispered, looking up with eyes filled with guilt and self-loathing. "It was too soon." He leaned over and kissed her tenderly. "I guess I just wanted to believe it was over. You should have stopped me."

Skye smiled just as tenderly and took his face in her hands. "Please. I really, really needed you last night. I needed to feel like a woman again. I needed to feel something besides pain again. I needed to feel alive again. These bruises will fade."

When his eyes still held guilt, she decided to take another tack. "No...no. please. Don't pull away from me. You'll make me think the scars turn you off. Are you repelled by them? I've been feeling a bit self conscious about them and..."

It worked. The guilt faded away before the onslaught of love and desire that swept through him for this wonderful, precious woman. He interrupted her by taking her hands and bringing them to his lips. "Nothing about you could turn me off, my darling. Nothing. I love you." The guilt was gone from his magnificent blue eyes. Only love was reflected there.

He waited a beat to see if she would return the words to him, but she only leaned over the table and moved her lips over his in a long, thorough kiss. "Thank you," she whispered.

They talked shop through their breakfast together. Skye obviously wanted to keep the conversation on the professional rather than the personal. He brought her up to date with the case and she gave him all the information she'd uncovered. Part of her convalescence was a reluctant agreement on Jim's part to allow her to search all of Dan's computer disks and files. She had to see if what he told her about her parent's assassination had any merit. She was relentless and thorough but found nothing. When Sloane got a little older, Skye thought, she may ask her to employ her massive talent to see if there was anything she missed, but for now she felt Sloane was still too young. Jim may intern her to keep her out of mischief but she was still only 14. Skye could wait.

There were other interesting tidbits of information in the data, however, that she wanted to share with Alex. Some cryptic references and puzzling records were buried in endless reports and unrelated files. Some of it was coded very cleverly. Dan's relationship with Juan and the Blythes were just some of his enterprises she found. He referred to other things that would have to be researched. Skye told Alex that she would love to be able to participate in the investigations and he agreed that it would be satisfying. He still remembered vividly the marks Dan had put on Skye's body. Dan was dead, but going after some of his other enterprises would somehow give him another satisfying kick.

Skye's mind was going in a different direction. Maybe one of the trails Dan left would lead to the information he said he possessed on the assassination. She wouldn't think of that now. She would take up the issue with Jim when she returned from sick leave at the end of the month.

An hour later, while Skye was in the bathroom dressing and putting on her makeup, Sloane came back for the breakfast cart.

"Well? What do you have to report?" she whispered with anticipation.

"We haven't even discussed the good stuff, yet," said Alex with a smile. He fully intended to as soon as Skye got out of the bathroom. He had an idea that she was hiding in there to avoid "the talk."

"What?" Sloane exclaimed with exasperation. "Jesus, pleasus. What do you need, a script? Come on. I'm not getting any younger, you know."

God, he thought...there were two of them. "Our future is next on the agenda."

"Agenda! What kind of talk is that? This isn't a business merger, you know. You sound like Skye...been around her too much, I guess. Agenda...shit...Do I have to do everything?" She poked her finger in his chest and was very impressed with the rock solid feel of it. She decided to poke it again and nearly lost her train of thought. She may only be 14, but she was female. She got her mind back on track quickly. Nothing was as quick as her mind.

"Get on your knees and beg her to marry you. If she says no again, take her down with one of those Judo moves and make her give up. For crying out loud, you're twice her size. Here she comes." She grabbed the tray of breakfast dishes and beat a hasty retreat, giving him an exaggerated wink as she flew out the door. "Go get her, stud."

Feeling like he was just given a pep talk by his old college football coach, Alex felt revved for battle. Then he saw her, all fresh and ready for the day in a sunny yellow t-shirt and matching shorts and his nerves more than revved, they roared out of the gate. With her hair pulled back, she didn't look much older than Sloane. He was blinded by his love for her. He was also more determined than ever that they were going to get things settled before lunch.

"Do you want to go for a walk with me?" she asked pleasantly. She had the need to get away from the rumpled bed and the very domestic feel of his razor on the sink.

"No, I don't," he said in a calm, low voice. She knew then she would have to run if she were to avoid the issue of her future, or more accurately, their future, once again.

"Okay. Well then I guess I'll see you later." Skye started toward the door.

"Oh no you don't," he said in that same calm voice as he grabbed her arm and gently, but firmly, turned her to look at him.

"Huh?" She looked up at him and performed her quizzical look admirably. He wasn't an appreciative audience however, and didn't feel like applauding her effort to look detached. Judging from the slight quiver he felt in her arm, it was indeed an effort for her to maintain the disconnected demeanor. And not a completely successful effort, either, he thought with some satisfaction.

"You're going to sit down and we're going to talk about our future," he said in the tone of voice he reserved for uncooperative associates and suspected felons.

"You can talk about your future all you want. I'll decide on my own." She was annoyed that her body was betraying her. She must not be 100 percent yet, she thought, and frowned down at the hand he still had firmly wrapped around her arm.

"I have no real problem with that. Just so they go in the same direction." When she continued to frown at him, he decided to face it head on with as much grace as possible. So he smiled and put all of his love into it.

"I want to marry you, Skye. You have made it very clear since the night I proposed and, I might add, the night you proposed back to me, that you don't want to discuss it. I've given you more time. More space. Every time I even hint at making our relationship permanent, you smile, pat my cheek, and tell me life isn't a fairytale. Well sometimes there can be a happily ever after…or at least a 'most of the time' happily ever after. I've been working very hard this last month to make it possible."

She decided that sitting down and getting this all settled was a good idea after all. Her stomach fluttered, her thighs quivered. Her body was obviously a traitorous vessel she would have to deal with firmly. Her mind was in control now and it was a formidable force. She was sure she would be able to keep on track. If he would just let go of her arm.

Skye pulled away and went to sit down on the sofa. Instead of being a gentleman about it and taking the chair opposite her, he sat down right next to her. Her mind severely commanded her body to behave and stop trembling.

Skye sat back on the cushions as far from the smiling Alex as she could get. What was wrong with this man? He was actually grinning at her like some kind of idiot. Her heart joined her body in the mutiny and whispered that there was nothing wrong with this man…absolutely nothing. Her mind knew it was on its own now and knew what it wanted to say. She'd been playing this out for weeks. Deciding to take the offensive position, she open negotiations.

"Alex, listen. I'm a captain for International, you're a real estate investor and all around rich guy. For Justice, you work mostly as a special operative, I work in the international branch. It's going to be impossible for us to go in the same direction." She thought she did quite well delivering this rehearsed part of the program. She was about to open the more dicey subject of how they were going to arrange periodic trysts, when he interrupted. How rude. Now she was frowning in earnest and nearly missed his next revelation.

"That may be, but I have a few ideas on how we can reconcile everything. Jim and I discussed this and worked it out." He winced inwardly when he saw the incredulous look on her face. He probably shouldn't have been so abrupt. This was confirmed by her immediate negative reaction.

"You and Jim?" Skye said icily. "Well I hope you two will be very happy together because neither of you have any right to decide my fate."

She nearly got up and would have pulled it off nicely if she hadn't positioned herself so far back in the cushions to put distance between them. That was his fault too, she thought, as he easily pushed her back. The nails were swiftly piling up and she was the hammer that was going to pound them into his coffin.

Christ, he thought. Think! This isn't going to work like a business deal. He was always someone who put his cards directly on the table; he had a reputation for being frank and straightforward. A bit more finesse here, he thought putting his arm out to stop her from pulling out of the negotiations.

Skye's frown turned into a full-fledged 150-watt glare. One of her best, she thought as she stopped moving forward and stared at his arm as if it was nothing but air. She knew better, of course, and chose not to test its strength quite yet. He was still too set and ready. She was always one to time her moves with exquisite precision.

Alex watched her expressions and knew she was waiting for the right moment to strike and escape. He was actually quite amused by it. Staring at her until she raised her flashing eyes back to his face, he decided it wasn't prudent to remind her at this point that Jim was her boss and he could indeed make some of these decisions for her. Jim was an important player in their future and he was extremely enthusiastic about Alex's ideas. As a matter of fact, the deal was almost done. Alex realized now he should have brought Skye in sooner, but a big part of him was afraid she would have balked early and dug in her heels.

"Darling, don't let your stubborn Italian genes get in the way of a really great plan. It's almost a done deal," he said in a reasonable tone. Big mistake.

"My stubborn Italian genes?" she sputtered heatedly and, energized by temper, stood up quickly, this time slapping his arm aside and nearly cracking his wrist. "Almost a done deal? I'll show you done, you snake-eyed son-of-a-bitch."

She glared down at him with her hands on her hips. She had no idea how adorable she was, he thought. Her ponytail was swinging, and her hips certainly were not wide enough to intimidate anyone. He just couldn't help himself. He stood up until she had to look up at him and laughed out loud. Even bigger mistake.

"Why you arrogant, egomaniacal, self-important ass, you…"

He stopped her in mid-tirade with a thorough, arrogant, egomaniacal, self-important kiss. Her struggle dissolved quickly under the onslaught of her own emotions. Her mutinous body and heart joined forces and overwhelmed the calm, rational thoughts swirling through her brain. He deepened the kiss and his own exploring tongue effortlessly flicked off the words that had formed on the tip of her tongue. Her brain tried one last time to reason with her, then surrendered and joined in the fun. Alex celebrated his victory by keeping his big mouth occupied.

"Ah…," she asked when he came up for air and she was able to think again. "Let's see, where was I?" She couldn't seem to get her brain around a coherent thought.

"You were calmly asking me to tell you more about our future plans," he said as he put his arms around her and sat her back down on the sofa. Still under the spell of his kisses, she let him gather her up in his lap. "First we get married."

Skye laid her head on his shoulder and slowly moved it from side to side. "But I'll be flying around the world and working for Justice and you'll be counting your millions and working on other assignments. We can't be married. It wouldn't work."

Alex knew he was making progress. All the fury was gone and only sadness and regret remained.

"I was thinking of some kind of exclusive relationship and we would make plans to see each other when we could," she went on with a weary tone. "I'm sure there will be times when our paths will cross. Other times, we'll have to capture moments when we can. But then I started to think, how can I ask you to, you know, refrain from, ah…" She kind of ran out of steam and sighed.

Alex almost told her to let him do all the thinking…that her idea really sucked. He was a man who learned quickly, however, and kept this particular opinion to himself.

He held her a bit tighter. Now was the time to present the entire package. She appeared to be as soft as she would ever be. "Remember Kris and Joe Ecrov?"

"Of course. They were trainers at the facility in Colorado." She remembered them fondly. The stories of their exploits in the field were legendary and they were always clearly devoted to each other. She smiled at the memory.

"Well," he almost said "duh" but thought better of it. He had to stop hanging with Sloane. It was doing diabolical things to his vocabulary. He had to remember that Skye was operating within a different frame of reference. She was still back there with the idea of an exclusive relationship and a few hurried trysts between assignments. He took pity on her and went on in a reasonable tone. "They're married and they work for the Justice Department."

"Oh no," she said as it dawned on her where this conversation was heading. Popping up, she gave him a look that reflected renewed defiance. "No way. I'm not leaving the field to teach other people how to do my job."

"I understand that. I feel the same way. But that isn't my point." He was getting around to it, but the feel of her pert little butt on his lap was very distracting.

"Well, you better make one pretty soon. I'm not getting any younger." Alex snorted when he realized that Sloane had used the same words. God, he was going to love being a part of their family. When he felt Skye stiffen, he got back on track. There was a point and he needed to make it now.

"The point is they worked in the field together for over thirty years before they retired to Colorado."

That thought actually intrigued Skye immensely. She allowed herself the small luxury of seeing a light at the end of a long, dark tunnel.

"Go on...," she said noncommittally. Although she thought she knew where he was headed, she wasn't ready to concede anything yet.

"Well, I think it's time there's another husband and wife team in the field to create legends and build common experiences. Think of what we'll be able to share with young agents in forty or fifty years."

"But I go back to my original comment." Her brain was making a comeback and it was with some regret that she yielded to the rational side of her nature...something she felt had been missing in action for a while. " I'm a captain for International and you're a money monger. It doesn't sound like we can conveniently co-habit, much less do the husband and wife team thing."

"I understand that at this time you're a cockpit jockey and I'm an incredibly successful financier, but let's look at this another way." When she snorted, he smiled. "Let me present you with a different scenario. One that's not only possible, it's been studied from every angle and deemed laudable by the strategists at Justice." He folded her back into his arms in preparation for the main event. She would either come out swinging or throw in the towel. "How does this sound…you're a private pilot for a major corporation and I'm its owner and CEO. The cockpit jockey and the money monger." He felt her stiffen…so much for the throw in the towel scenario. "The Captain and the Financier?"

She pulled against the restraint of his arms to get into an eye-to-eye position. He had to see her opposition before he got too in love with the idea. How did he ever get Jim to go for this? Jim knew she would never give up flying jets. "No, no, no, no. I want you to know I mean this…" The conviction in her voice was sharp and unmistakable. "I'm not flying some clunker around with you in charge of the show. I'll not budge on this."

"I don't think the manufacturers of the Gulfstream would appreciate their plane being called a 'clunker,'" he said casually, waiting for the reaction he was assured would come.

"Clunker," she said, then did a double take that was so comic it made Alex smile. Gotcha, he thought. Baited, hooked and ready to reel in. Sloane, the little genius, came through again. She fed him the Gulfstream dream and he took it from there.

A Gulfstream, she thought. Her dream machine…this fact almost completely drained her mind of all arguments…almost. It had always been her heart's desire to fly a Gulfstream. She could feel her palms itch. And a private schedule would make it more convenient for her to be where she needed to be to complete her assignments. Especially if the corporation she flew for was owned by a fellow agent. Little waves of excitement and admiration for the idea joined in the surge toward capitulation.

"And the last time I checked, Captain," he said casually, dealing with her objection that he would be in charge. "You outranked me."

"Do you even have a rank?" She could feel herself budging. It was almost embarrassing how fast she was caving. But a Gulfstream! Hot damn!

"Well, not really. And certainly not in the air." He was celebrating victory, but only on the inside. He still wanted to seriously discuss any problems she might have with the idea so that she could not say later that he dazzled her into a premature agreement. "You'll get to select your own crew."

"Well, I'm not going to leave Sloane. I can't move out on her." She was reaching now, trying to give herself some more time to think. Come on brain, she thought, kick in soon or you're out of the game. My own plane. My own crew. She thought Connie and Bill would jump at the chance. No. No. He was hoping she would think that. Clever bastard.

"Our home and global headquarters will be right here in Virginia. Sloane and Hazel will be living nearby, or with us if they prefer."

"Will this home be some kind of mansion, or what?"

"Yup, a mansion with enough space for a landing strip for the plane I'm sure you'll want to buy to replace the Cessna. I have several properties I'd like you to see."

"You mean I can actually be involved in the decision on where we're going to live?" she said sarcastically. It all sounded wonderful, but she wanted to get in a little attitude before the train completely left the station.

"The choice will be yours, darling. I don't care where I live as long as it's with you," responded Alex.

"I'll have to talk with Sloane. She's still a minor child in my care." Skye knew that was weak since Sloane had always been firmly planted in Alex's corner.

"That'll be easy, she's probably listening outside the door right now."

He heard a distinct "Roger" come from the hallway. Then, "You have the blessing of the family unit."

"Beat it, kid…I need to seal the deal."

Alex chuckled when he heard the soft footsteps of his soon-to-be sister-in-law walking casually away from the gap in the door.

"She's just a child…and she wants to be a Maid of Honor much too badly to exercise good judgment," Skye said in a reasonable tone.

"I don't think anyone who knows her would call her a child." Alex responded, in the same reasonable tone. He waited a few beats, then smiled. "Running low on arguments?"

Just when Alex could smell victory, he was nearly undone as the sparks in her eyes were replaced with tears. It wasn't something he was prepared for. Skye had been about to capitulate when the realization of what she was about to do kicked in and she was swamped with an overwhelming combination of sadness and dread.

"Don't...don't do that, darling. I'm sorry. I shouldn't have pressured you. I'll give you more time." He gathered her into his arms and held her gently to his chest. In none of the scenarios he had run over in his mind did this happen. He could feel her chest hitch with the effort to hold back the tears.

"Please...don't...sweetheart...what do you want me to do?" Then another thought occurred to him. "Do you want me to get you something? Are you in pain?"

"No," she said in a quaking voice, filled with an emotion that sounded like hopelessness. "No pain...not yet, anyway."

When she pulled back and stared at him through brimming eyes, Alex had nothing to say. Nothing. A single tear escaped and slid unheeded down her check. He reached out and touched it with his fingertips. Then he pulled her to him again and just held her.

"I keep seeing Max, Alex. Lying there. He was so alive. Invincible even, then dead in an instant at the hand of a friend. We...we can't get married," she said softly. "If something happens to you...I'll die...I'll die. Oh God, I'm so afraid."

"Darling," he said compassionately. "I know exactly how you feel. I've had to come to terms with my own demons on this exact point. Darling, you terrify me with your fearlessness. Jesus Christ, I saw you lying in a pool of your own blood." Skye felt the tremor go through him, then fade as he ruthlessly shoved that picture aside.

Alex decided to face it head on. He didn't know Max long, but he knew the man's heart. He held her tighter and kissed the top of her head. "Skye, darling. What would Max say...what would he want you to do?"

Skye was silent for a moment, then decided Alex deserved an honest answer.

"Get on with life," she admitted, feeling Max's presence. "And quit being so damn hard on you."

"And what about Jeff and your mom and dad?" Alex wasn't sure this was the way to convince Skye, but he needed to shake her before she started rebuilding the wall. He could tell the question reached something inside her...deep inside her...by the way she stiffened against him. It was a punch and he knew it. Then to his intense relief she relaxed.

"They would have wanted me to live...to love."

"Exactly. I know I can't live without you in my life, without you to love. Tell me you feel the same."

When she only sighed, he gave her one more push. "Sweetheart, think of it this way. If we're married and work together, we can watch each other's back. We can protect each other while we make love all over the world."

Skye placed her head on his shoulder and sighed again. Minutes ticked off, keeping rhythm with her thoughts.

"You know that no one can do a better job of protecting me than you," he prompted.

Finally she smiled through her tears. "So you want me to marry you to provide personal protection."

Alex's heart stopped, then started again as it responded to her words. "That's the idea."

"Then I guess I'd better grow a backbone if we're going to give this marriage idea a try."

"So did I hear a yes?"

"Yes." Her voice was just above a whisper, but her tone was strong. Her eyes, when she raised them to his, were shining. Committed. Determined. Sure.

Alex cupped her chin and gently drew her face to his for a kiss to seal the promise. He would start work on the Skyward Corporation immediately and get a ring on her finger before she could change her mind again. Then his brain emptied and all plans faded as he felt the full impact of her decision wash over him.

Complete surrender, she thought with relief as the steel and ice melted from around her heart. What a wonderful feeling. Her heart sang, her body danced, and even her brain was content. She felt liberated as her soul responded to his need and hers. Love was more powerful than fear, than pain, than loss. Love was more powerful than anything.

Printed in the United States
74254LV00004B/79-150